TONI

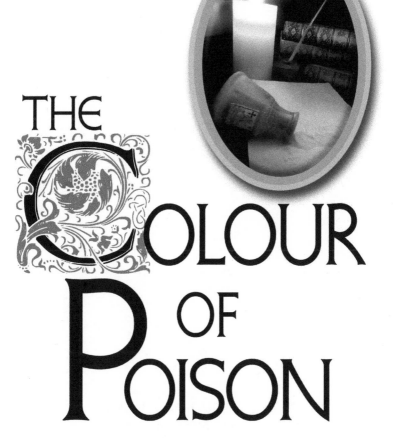

THE

COLOUR
OF
POISON

The Colour of Poison

A Sebastian Foxley Medieval Mystery
Book 1

Copyright © 2016 Toni Mount
ISBN-13: 978-84-944893-3-4

M
MadeGlobal Publishing

For more information on
MadeGlobal Publishing, visit
our website
www.madeglobal.com

Dedication

For Bethan, Owen and Isaac

CHAPTER ONE

May 1475
Tyburn, outside the City of London

THIS WAS the most hellish journey a man could ever make. The only mercy, it would be his last. Dragged on a hurdle, pelted with filth, jeered at by the crowds of Londoners, every stone and pit in the road jarring his teeth in his head. He closed his eyes so as not to see the beautiful summer sky above him, its joyous colour mocking him.

He was not alone in suffering these terrors. Four others were being hauled along in similar, agonising fashion. His fellows in death. He did not know their names – although one face seemed familiar, he couldn't place it – did not want to, any more than he wished them to know who he was. An anonymous death was the best he could hope for. He wondered if his brother would be there, by the scaffold, to witness his end. Or the duke – would he want to view this final insult to life? He doubted it. They'd all disown him now.

The priest continued to intone his prayers without emotion as the ties binding the man to the hurdle at the nag's tail were released. Rough hands pulled him to his feet and shoved him towards the ladder, grabbing at him when he stumbled, as though they feared he might attempt an escape. Not much chance of that when a contingent of pikemen surrounded the scaffold, bristling with steel barbs.

Blood trickled from a gash on his forehead where a stone had caught him, matting his long fair hair, of which he'd been so proud. He could feel the gore, hot and sticky, running down his temple, but it didn't matter now. He looked over the heads of the crowd with some unformed hope that salvation might be at hand. It wasn't. Only a lone crow sat, waiting, on the dead bough of an ancient elm that overlooked the place of execution by the Tybourne stream.

1

The condemned were encouraged up on to the scaffold with pike staves. The man ahead of him, hands now bound behind him, was pushed across the wooden planks of the platform to the foot of a second ladder set against the gallows tree. Here, the fellow was held as a noose was passed over his head. A brazier glowed dully in the sunshine, various metal instruments pushed in to heat among the coals.

• •

A trumpet blast caused the excited crowd to fall silent and one of the two Sheriffs of London stepped forward, a breeze rustling the paper in his hand.

'After due trial by the authority of the lord mayor in this our city of London, the felon, Thomas Witham, has been adjudged guilty of coining. Punishment: death by hanging, disembowelling and quartering. Have you anything to say before sentence is carried out?'

'You're all bastards, all of yer!'

Unmoved, the sheriff replied: 'Is that all? Makes a change from "I'm innocent", at least. May God have mercy on your worthless soul.' He nodded to the hooded executioner who forced the miscreant to climb the second ladder.

The drum began to beat slowly in time with the fellow's hesitant steps. With hands secured behind him it was difficult, but the ladder was propped at a shallow angle. As soon as he reached near the top, one of the executioner's assistants, at a signal from his master, tipped him off the ladder and the drum ceased. The fall was not intended to kill. The fellow's legs thrashed the air, sending a shoe flying into the crowd where it was fought over as a good luck token. His eyes bulged hideously, his tongue stuck out of his mouth, his face turned red, then purple. At a sign from the executioner, the assistant cut him down, so he fell in a gasping heap. A second assistant straightened him out and cut away the man's clothes, revealing an enormous erect cock that brought a murmur of approval from a knowledgeable crowd. More impressive than usual, apparently. Then the executioner took up a butcher's cleaver, stained and rusted with the blood of previous customers.

The fair-haired man could not watch and looked instead at his feet, wondering pointlessly if he had tied his fashionably-piked shoes tightly enough so they should not fly loose. He heard the victim scream but wouldn't look, yet nothing could prevent the stench of searing entrails reaching his nose. Behind him, the third fellow fell to his knees as his legs buckled beneath him, vomiting on the stink. A few folk in the crowd swooned – men among them – as the body was decapitated and quartered, the bloody parts thrown into a straw-filled basket.

Eyeing the crowd, the man still could not see his brother, unsure whether he wanted to or not. No sign of the duke either, though it was hardly to be expected. Nor the miracle of a royal pardon from King Edward. Hands bound, he was taken to the ladder that had been repositioned against the gibbet. The noose was slipped over his head, so he could feel the rough rope chaffing the vulnerable skin of his neck. Not long now, it'll all be over, he promised himself as the trumpet sounded.

Then the world seemed to blur momentarily and he did not hear the sheriff announce his name: 'Guilty of murder. Punishment: death by hanging, disembowelling and quartering. Have you anything to say before sentence is carried out?'

'Why waste my last breath?' he said, speaking too softly for anyone beyond the scaffold to hear.

'Then may God have mercy on your soul.'

The executioner pushed him towards the second ladder.

'Give the buggers a good show, lad. I'll make the end quick for you,' the hooded fellow whispered in his ear, but the man was beyond understanding quite what he meant. The drum began its fearful, rhythmic beat, keeping pace with the blood pounding in his ears as he climbed upwards.

He barely had his foot on the third rung when he heard cries behind him.

'I didn't do nothing, yer honour, honest I didn't. It was me brother Adam what stoled the horse!' The third would-be customer for the executioner's services was on his knees at the sheriff's feet, pleading with him, his snotty, tear-streaked face contorted in desperation.

'Shut your snivelling, you!' the sheriff snarled, kicking him aside.

'But I didn't do nothing 'cept feed the horse fer Adam.' The voice, half breaking, came out shrill and the man, looking down, saw a boy, probably not yet twelve summers old, terrified, pitiful. He realised, after all the horrors he had suffered, he could still feel something like sadness at the lad's plight, surprisingly.

'Take this miserable wretch up next,' the sheriff ordered. 'I want his whinging and whining done with. Gag him if he won't shut up.'

The man was assisted back down from the ladder as the trumpet blared and the sheriff began to read aloud from his paper: 'After due trial, etcetera, etcetera, William Hay-ut, er... Here, you can read, can't you?' he said, turning to the man. 'What does this say?' He held the paper so the man could see it.

'It says: Hauteville. It's French, so the 'h' is silent,' the man explained, forgetting his dire circumstances for a moment.

'Bloody French. I might have known,' the sheriff grumbled, then aloud to the crowd, he continued: 'William Utvil is guilty of horse-stealing. Punishment: death by hanging, disembowelling and quartering. Have you anything to say before sentence is carried out? No? Good. Get on with it, Master Executioner!'

The petrified lad was sent up the ladder in the man's place, the smell of piss strong upon him, his legs buckling so the executioner went up with him, keeping a firm hold as the drum beats began afresh. The boy was whimpering, his sobs affecting the crowd who were muttering about one so young having his life ended so soon. The executioner checked the noose personally before climbing down. At his signal, the drumming ceased and his assistant twisted the ladder away.

The child fell. His body jolted to a halt. There was no "hangman's jig" this time, just a few twitches, the head twisted at an agonising angle. The executioner knew his business and had made the lad's end quick, setting the knot so it broke his neck. The crowd sighed, though whether in relief or disappointment at the loss of an entertaining spectacle was impossible to tell. Though a few jeered the hangman for bungling his work, the man suspected that was not the case. The swift despatch had been intentional. The rest of the sentence was carried out in no hurry. The heated iron in the guts dispensed with, since the victim was beyond suffering now. The lifeless body was decapitated and neatly quartered without undue haste, prolonging the torment of the man still awaiting his fate.

CHAPTER TWO

Friday, the seventh day of April in the year of Our Lord Jesu 1475
The Palace of Westminster

AS SOON as he realised the purpose of his youngest brother's request for an audience, King Edward heaved a sigh and sent the servants scuttling. This would be a private matter. The king slammed the door himself as the last servant departed.

Picking up his wine cup, Edward perched a generous buttock on the edge of the table, watching his brother from beneath lowered lids. The Duke of Gloucester stood before him: slim, wiry, still, sombre in grey velvet doublet, hat in hand. Edward wondered how come he felt ill at ease in his own sumptuous bedchamber, confronted by a subject. But it wasn't just any subject, was it? It was Richard, the most loyal of brothers who served as his wretched conscience, telling him truths he'd rather not hear.

'Well? Get it said, little brother; I don't have all night.' The duke stepped forward, away from the tapestry hanging that screened the door, keeping draughts from royal feet.

'Your grace.' Richard bent his silk-clad knee, never forgetting Edward was king. 'I received a deputation from the Lord Mayor of London this morning. He requested I speak with you, make you aware of the effect your "benevolences" are having upon the citizens. There is discontent and unrest in the city.'

'And since when have you been the lord mayor's messenger-boy?' Edward drank his Burgundy wine in one gulp, poured some more.

'Sire, please don't make light of this. The situation could deteriorate.' Richard's earnest expression was irritating. Everything about him annoyed the king. For one: his lithe, youthful frame, artfully revealed by his close-fitted, fashionable attire when the king was running to flesh these days.

'Ha! You know the Londoners. When are they not discontented? 'Tis their natural way.' Edward loathed his own indebtedness to them. It sat badly with his notions of what monarchy should be. He moved away from the blazing apple logs in the hearth, too warm for the season. He was sweating copiously, felt the wetness soaking into his linen nether-clouts.

'These "benevolences" overstep the mark,' Richard was saying. 'Parliament granted you taxes and trade subsidies. What more do you need? You ask too much.'

'Far from it: it's *not* enough!' The king's face flushed. He would not be told by some subordinate. Even Richard.

• •

Outside the chamber courtiers crowded round the door, listening. Only the king's side of the argument could be heard as he lost his temper, bawling like some common huckster crying his wares. This didn't mean the duke was losing, though. No. Richard rarely raised his voice. Often as not though, when his mouth kept silent, his eyes were eloquent, giving his "silent lectures", as Edward called them.

• •

Within the chamber the argument continued.

'Whatever additional moneys you need, ask Parliament. You could summon them in a week. Most of the nobility are already in London.'

'Damn Parliament! I won't go begging to those tight-fisted buggers again,' Edward screeched, slamming his cup down, denting the silver. 'On the money they allow, I could take six cripples, a spavined nag and a leaking ship halfway across the Narrow Seas. How am I supposed to scare the bloody French witless with that, eh?' The king confronted Richard, standing close, intimidating him with his height and bulk, but his brother did not flinch. It was Edward who moved away. 'How can I terrorise them into suing for peace on *my* terms? I would be the laughing stock of Europe. You hear me, Dickon?'

'I hear you, Ned.' Probably, the entire Palace of Westminster could hear him.

'So, what would you have me do, eh? Benevolences are no bad thing. They're not obligatory. I ask only the wealthiest citizens to make a donation, a gesture of goodwill, earning my favour for the future. What's amiss with that?'

'Nothing. If that's all you do.'

'What are the bastards saying? Tell me!'

'That armed men in royal livery are posted at the doors of citizens not inclined to donate to your cause. Exchequer clerks arrive, unannounced, on the flimsiest pretexts, demanding to see account books. Goods, having passed through the Customs House, revenues paid, are being seized as contraband – '

'How dare you lecture me! Is it my fault my servants are over-zealous?'

Richard said nothing, simply held the king's gaze. As ever, his silence – that look – was worse than any rant. Edward's pale eyes slid away first. He began to pace, betwixt wine flagon and bedside, his gown of blue cloth-of-gold stirring sweet scents from the herb-strewn floor. Still the duke never moved.

'I need money, Dickon. Gold! Plenty of it. How else can I pay for this French enterprise? You expect me to make war with empty coffers?'

'No.'

'Then how, damn it?'

'Pawn your plate and jewels, as I've had to. Borrow the money. Give surety, pay it back when you can.'

'Christ, I'd be drowning in debt 'til bloody Doomsday. No! I'll do this my way. I don't need your advice.' Edward poured more wine. With his back turned, he breathed deeply, sipped the cup, calming himself. 'Anyway, I have other possibilities in hand.'

'Oh?'

'I *shall* have gold, enough for all my needs, whether you approve, or not.'

'How so?' Richard frowned.

'There are ways... men learned in certain arts. Never you mind.' Edward regretted his slip of the tongue. Richard was too quick-witted to be deceived. Years ago, there had been rumours concerning the use of the Black Arts in royal circles. Only Edward, his wife and her mother knew the whole story, but his brother had come too close to the truth.

'Tell me you're not dabbling in – in sorcery again? You swore upon your oath...' Richard held out his hands, palms up, imploring.

'Stop it, Dickon! You think because I make use of a subject's talents – as any monarch would – I'll grow cloven hooves and horns? Anyhow, I don't believe in that nonsense.'

'I beg you...'

Edward was shocked to realise Richard truly feared for him, the fool.

'You're dismissed. Get out of my bloody sight!' The king turned his back again, not wanting to see the concern in his brother's face.

'Please, Ned.'

'Out!'

Edward kept his back turned until he heard the tapestry swish as the duke withdrew, closing the door softly. Then he followed him, wrenching it open again. Richard turned, maybe hoping to be called back.

• •

Instead, the king crooked a finger at Richard's friend, Francis, Lord Lovell, who had been waiting with the other courtiers, listening outside.

Having ushered Lord Lovell in, once again, the king shut the door.

Francis had no idea what this might concern. Strictly, he was in Richard's service, but when the king summoned you, you didn't question his right. Edward turned his charming smile on Francis.

'Lord Lovell. Francis, isn't it?'

'Aye, your grace.'

'Be seated. Take your ease.' The king gestured to a settle, cushioned in green damask, fringed with tassels of Venice gold.

Francis obeyed.

'How are things in my little brother's service, eh? Does he treat you well?'

'Indeed, sire. The Duke of Gloucester is as fair a lord as a man could wish to serve, famed in the north for his honourable dealing and impartial justice.'

A frown creased the king's brow.

'I know that. I asked how he treats *you*, not all the rest, and don't tell me how the northern shires dote upon him.'

Francis blanched, realising his error in praising Richard too highly when his friend was out of favour.

'Forgive me, sire. I can only say he treats me most generously and kindly. We've been friends for many years and...'

'How would you feel about doing a service for me?' the king interrupted. 'It will hardly interfere with your obligations to my brother.'

'Of course, your grace. A man owes allegiance to his king before any other, even the duke.'

'Good, good.' Edward was smiling now. Francis's words pleased him: balm for a bruised pride. 'I've heard that you're a resourceful man,

Francis. One who understands the law sufficiently to make use of it, rather than to adhere to its every word, as some do.'

Francis twitched, wondering where this was going.

'Tell me, do you spend much time at your place of Lovell's Inn?'

'W-well no, sire. I stay at Crosby Place with Lord Richard, should he require me...'

'From now on, you will spend more time at your house. 'Tis in Ivy Lane, is it not? Find an excuse, but on no account is my brother to know what we discuss here. Do you understand?'

'Perfectly, your grace.'

'Excellent. You'll be generously recompensed for your trouble. There may even be a viscountcy in it for you, if you serve me well. You would like that, eh?' Edward watched as a smile stretched the young man's lips. 'Now here's what I would have you do...'

Monday, the twenty-fourth day of April
From Paternoster Row by St Paul's to West Cheap, in the city of London

OUR TROUBLES began upon that Monday. Yet the smoke-grimed city of London was rarely arrayed so fine, barring the king's occasional triumphal entrance or the yearly lord mayor's water pageant. The April downpour had scoured the church spires and streets, washed away the worst of the detritus, leaving the city wet and clean-smelling, gleaming like gold-leaf in the sinking sun. Rain and sunbeams worked their artists' alchemy, transforming the roof-tiles to a palette of rose-madder, vermilion and crimson-lake. A crow, feathers dark and dishevelled as my own hair, watched me from a gable-end, waiting.

I was late. My brother Jude must have been home long since and would worry. I lowered my eyes to the sucking mud of West Cheap to go upon my way, carefully, dragging my leg, leaning on my staff. Yet my soul was singing, uplifted by the moment of magic, and I dropped a penny in a beggar's bowl, receiving his blessing.

The way was slippery, treacherous with water that still dripped from the eaves, forming puddles, grease-slick. Determined to watch where I stepped, I didn't notice the youth, skulking in the doorway. He snatched my staff, sending me sprawling in the mire, then flung it back at me.

He ran off, laughing. Robin Marlow, a neighbour's lad, who so enjoyed taunting me at every chance. I made no sound. Such incidents were commonplace for me then. Besides, who would hear a cry for aid from a cripple? Rather, they would shun the horror. I expected neither kindness nor courtesy in those days.

When I arrived at our rooms in West Cheap, mud-splattered and filthy, I overheard voices within. A stranger, his voice heavy with the accent of the northern shires, was speaking with my brother. I pushed the door open, careful upon the threshold.

Jude was doing his best to give hospitality to a well-dressed man, serving our ale and bread, left from this morn. Hardly suitable fare for one wearing the badge of the Gloucester Boar upon his sleeve. My brother, hands still ink-stained from his day's work as a scribe, offered a cup to our visitor.

The duke's messenger was a strapping fellow with merry eyes and hair the colour of a redbreast's front, so vivid I blinked.

He gave his name as Sir Robert Percy.

Sir Robert unwound himself from the stool to stand as I entered – a courtesy indeed. He stood a head taller than Jude, always the tallest fellow 'til now, and towered above me, though I pulled myself straight as I might.

'Master Sebastian Foxley?' he asked. I nodded, mute with surprise. 'I'm here at the behest of my lord, Richard, Duke of Gloucester.'

'The king's brother?' My query betrayed my bewilderment, but Sir Robert grinned.

'Aye, the same. Lord Richard requests that you both attend him at Crosby Place, by Bishopsgate, at your earliest convenience.'

'W-why? What have we done amiss?' What could Jude or I have done to attract his notice? The duke was Lord High Constable of England, dealing with acts of treason, rebellion and grave miscarriages of justice.

'Fear not, Master Foxley, his grace is interested in your talents as an artist, nought else.'

'Then his grace should speak to our employer, Master Bowen in Paternoster Row. We're his journeymen – '

'Master Bowen is uninterested, says he deals only in books. So his grace would do business with you, directly. He desires a triptych for a chantry chapel.'

'A triptych, sir? I've never painted such a thing.'

'No, but his grace saw the Book of Hours you illuminated for Lord Hastings and – '

'How much would his grace pay?' Jude interrupted.

I gasped at his lack of manners but Sir Robert only shrugged.

'Lord Richard is a generous patron. He will make it worth your while.'

'Tell his lordship my brother will do it.'

'But, Jude, I don't know how. I've never painted on wood.'

'Course you have. You did the sign for the Panyer Inn, didn't you? Will a triptych be more difficult? Just three inn signs hinged together is all. You can do that, little brother.'

'I-I must think on this, sir.' I couldn't have Jude persuading me to undertake such a commission without any thought. Were my talents sufficient?

'Of course, masters. His grace would expect that. I'll leave you to discuss matters. Will it be convenient for you to attend Lord Richard at Crosby Place, by Bishopsgate, come Saturday, to give him your answer? At eight of the clock?'

'Aye, sir, we'll be there,' Jude said. 'Won't we, Seb?'

'Saturday? Aye, sir.' I was not half so certain as my brother and I think Sir Robert knew it, but he smiled at me all the same as Jude opened the door for him.

* *

With Sir Robert departed into a now sunny April eve, Jude stood before me, hands on hips, eyes narrowed in that way I knew to beware.

'You'll be a damned fool not to accept, Seb. Think of the money.'

'But Jude, I...'

A knock at the door distracted us from our disagreement. Dame Ellen, the Widow Langton, bustled in with a hot crock of steaming pottage held in a cloth in her hands.

'Jude, Sebastian,' the elderly woman greeted us. We were her tenants and supper was part of the agreement. A good thing too – I was hungry. 'I hope you'll enjoy this, 'tis cooked to a new receipt I had of Mary Jakes, you know... the draper's wife. And I'll return shortly with your bread and I've made you baked, spiced pears as a treat. Oh, and Emily mended your hose, young Seb.'

Having set down the pot she turned to me, frowning at my muddy state, seeing I was dripping on her floor.

'Lord save us! Look at you,' she complained. 'Jude, whatever are you thinking, leaving your brother like this? Fetch water and wash-cloths this instant. Let's clean him up, poor lad. Seb,' her voice softened. She was always concerned for me. 'Was it another fall?' Her snowy linen wimple brushed my hand as she leaned close to inspect the damage. Once a beauty, so they said, her looks had rounded down the years. She would try to mother me but I had no need of that. My mother had died birthing me, yet I never felt the lack of a woman's gentle touch, but Dame Ellen missed nothing, whether a faint stain on a woman's kerchief or dirt upon my knee.

'Nothing much, Dame Ellen, only a bit of mud. It will brush off when dry.'

'But your knees! That's another pair of hose needing mending and you've grazed yourself, too. Look, blood. Jude, you don't take proper care of your brother.'

Jude grimaced. He hated her scolding him but it didn't do to argue with the landlady.

''Tis nought, please don't fuss,' I said.

'Aye, well I'll go fetch the rest of your supper from next door, since young Emily is running errands. And where's that water, Jude?'

• •

Returning with half a new baked loaf and a dish of spiced pears, all of which gave off tempting aromas that made my mouth water, the widow continued her conversation as though she had only paused for breath.

'And wash-cloths, Jude. If my boy Dick ever got in such a state I'd not let him sit there unwashed, with supper on the table.'

'I doubt your Dick would ever have been in such a case,' I suggested.

'Well, no, he never was, else I'd have boxed his ears.'

I washed my face and hands in the bowl of warm water Jude set before me on the board, being scrupulous, seeing Dame Ellen was watching with eyes keen as a tailor's shears. She inspected me and nodded approval but, instead of going, the good dame settled herself more comfortably on our spare stool and folded her arms, so she wasn't about to leave. It seemed our supper would be cold afore we got to eat it.

• •

'Now, you two, am I right in supposing you had a grand visitor earlier? Not that I'll pry, if it's private business, but I could hardly help noticing such a fine fellow and well-dressed in a velvet cloak – Venice-made, if I'm not mistaken.' As a tailor's widow, Dame Ellen was well-acquainted with the finest textiles and not likely to be in error. 'What did he want? Nothing untoward, I trust? Who was he? I couldn't tell with his hood drawn close. Do I know him?'

'Hush, good dame, and I will tell you.' Jude laughed at her inquisitiveness as he handed me a linen towel, but he too was eyeing the cooling pottage with an air of desperation. 'It was the Duke of Gloucester's messenger, Sir Robert Percy – a likeable fellow.'

He went to the little window, opened the shutter just enough and tipped the muddy water from the basin out into the street.

'Oh!' The widow squealed like a delighted child. 'A royal messenger on *my* property. Just wait 'til I tell Mary Jakes and Nell Warren, they'll be green with envy. Of course my son Dick knows King Edward from years ago. Fought beside him at, er, St Alban's, was it? Can't remember now. Fine lad, a fine lad indeed...' she reminisced, and I wasn't sure who she meant: her son or King Edward. 'What did he want?' she demanded, coming back to the present.

'The duke wants Seb to paint a triptych for his chapel,' Jude told her. Was that a hint of pride I heard, creeping into his voice?

'Well, that's marvellous, Seb. Even royalty must have heard how skilled you are. These high born folk get to hear things, you know. What was he like, this messenger fellow?'

'Well above middle height, broad in the shoulder,' Jude told her.

'His hair was red as furnace coals,' I said, 'With a little v-shaped scar upon his close-shaven chin.'

'But what was he like really?'

'As I told you...' My belly rumbled and I half-hoped she would hear it and recall we were waiting to eat.

'Huh! Men! I despair of you all and I know my Dick's as bad. I mean, was he handsome, charming and courteous or ill-featured, bad mannered and rude, despite his undoubted good breeding?'

'He was courteous enough – and appreciated your ale, dame.'

'Did he now? A man of good taste then,' she declared, deciding she could approve Sir Robert almost entirely. 'But was he handsome?'

Jude sighed.

'Oh, Dame Ellen, men don't notice such matters in other men.' He was becoming exasperated. 'This pottage smells delicious.' He moved to set out two bowls on the board.

'Don't think you'll distract me, Jude Foxley. You must know.' She came between Jude and the pot, which was steaming no longer, so he reconsidered, aware we would have a stone-cold supper if the old woman's curiosity wasn't satisfied.

'Yes, the duke's man was very handsome and charming and chivalrous and well-dressed and well-mannered and perfect in every way! Now may we eat your splendid supper?'

'Don't mock me,' Dame Ellen warned, wagging her needle-scarred finger at him, 'Else I'll tell my Dick how you treat his poor old mother, when next he visits.'

• •

'Poor old mother, indeed,' I laughed when the widow had gone, watching as my brother doled out generous portions into the bowls and divided up the bread.

'How long have we lived here?' Jude mumbled around a spoonful of savoury pottage, 'A year, come St John's Day, and we've never yet set eyes on her wondrous son Dick. I reckon he's just in her imaginings.' He dipped his bread deep into the bowl. 'This is excellent. I approve her new receipt and I suspect the mythical Dick will too, "when next he visits", if ever.'

'Oh, he's real enough, lives down Deptford way, works as a shipwright there and, of course, he's wed to Master Bowen's daughter.' I wiped my bowl clean with the last morsel of bread.

'I didn't know that. Bella Bowen, eh? Small world. But how come you know so much? Your ears must be bigger than a hare's.'

'Not at all. Dame Ellen asked me to write a reply to a letter he had written a few weeks ago, telling her Bella is with child. That's how I know. The good dame receives a letter from him every few months... often asks me to write her reply.' I stared thoughtfully at my now-empty bowl and licked my spoon clean. 'Shall we try the pears?'

'So old Bowen will be a grandfather, then? Can't see that miserable bugger dandling a babe upon his knee, can you?'

Gilbert Eastleigh's apothecary's shop in Ivy Lane

A YELLOW FOG filled the still-room with its sulphurous airs, nosing into every corner. Gilbert Eastleigh suppressed a cough as he poured the mixture from a flask into the bubbling retort. A new cloud of vapour spewed forth, hissing, writhing like a serpent, making the old man's eyes water with its venomous breath. He sipped his wine and cleared his throat, muttering: 'Nearly there. Just a few more days...'

He bent low over his desk. Pushing his spectacles back into place, he took up a quill-pen. As the greenish liquid dripped, droplet by droplet, from the spout of the retort into the glass bottle below, he scrawled his notes, arcane symbols and strange diagrams.

• •

Pleased with his night's work, the apothecary sat back, letting his thoughts wander to the marvellous future he envisaged. Since that night a few weeks ago, when he'd taken up the flask of green-black slime, held it to the candlelight and observed the glint of gold within, everything had changed. The thrill of that moment lived on. Then his private audience with the mighty King Edward... Gilbert embraced the expectation of what was yet to come.

When the liquid ceased to drip, he used a pair of long-handled tongs to remove a smooth, silvery pebble, the colour of the moon, from the noxious brew. He smiled at it, the size of a quail's egg, though more irregularly shaped.

It looked like metal but wasn't one of the seven under the domination of the planets. Not gold nor silver. Neither iron nor copper nor mercury. It wasn't lead or tin either. No, this was something else. According to the ancient texts, it was a metal formed of the quintessence – that ethereal fifth element – created in the furnace of Hermes the Thrice-Times Master, in Egypt at the time of the Wise Ones. In some reactions it brought fire from the air alone. It could enable substances to unite that otherwise refused to commune, yet the stone remained unchanged. This was the fabled Philosopher's Stone.

Except that it was no fable.

His father had kept the stone for years, safe in a little velvet pouch about his neck, claiming that whilst he wore it he would live forever. It had seemed to be true, as William Eastleigh had reached his ninetieth year still in good health until his son became impatient for his inheritance. Gilbert could recall every detail of that moonlit night five years before when, as his father slept, he had removed the stone.

The old man never awakened.

• •

Gilbert washed the stone, wiped it clean. It gleamed, warm on his skin as he hid it away in its pouch, next to his heart, like a lover's keepsake. For the future, he imagined himself overseeing the delivery of the fruits of his labours, under cover of darkness. The king would be eternally grateful, any reward his for the asking.

A knighthood? Aye, *Sir* Gilbert sounded well indeed. He would wear a gown of scarlet brocade, trimmed with sable, a jewel in his hat – a gift from the king himself, perhaps? He could almost smell the new-minted gold. A few more days and he would tell the king's man that he was ready.

The Foxley brothers' rooms

I N BED, listening to the rain on the roof, we discussed the duke's commission. Jude insisted we accept but only I could make that decision.

'I'll help you, Seb. I'll prepare the boards, grind pigments, wash your brush, wipe your arse, if needs be.' He laughed. The thought of more money in our purses cheered him.

'We couldn't go on working for Master Bowen,' I said, talking into the darkness. 'If we let him down, the guild will disown us. Then, when... if... we finish the triptych, no other guild master will employ us.' I pulled at my pillow, trying to get my awkward body comfortable. I had the same trouble every night.

'Someone would take us on.'

'Take *you* on perhaps, but what of me? Half London doesn't dare give me "good day" for fear I'll bewitch them, and the rest would rather bed with Old Scratch than employ the "crookbacked cripple", as though my condition were contagious. I don't want to end my days crouched over a begging bowl by St Paul's Cross.'

'I'd never let that happen to you, little brother, you know that. Besides, it's not as you say. Dame Ellen likes you well enough, as does Emily.' I could hear the smile in his voice as he spoke of our landlady's comely apprentice. Emily was ever kind to me – out of pity, no doubt.

'Aye, but what of others, like Robin Marlow who snatched my staff from under me, causing my fall earlier?'

'Did he? The devil! I'll box his ears on that score.'

'Don't, Jude. It'll only make matters worse.'

'Oh, we'll see. Sleep now, we'll talk on the morrow.' Jude began settling himself, yawning extravagantly. 'I don't want to miss this God-given chance to better ourselves. You have to paint the triptych.'

Jude soon slept soundly but I hardly closed my eyes all night, knowing I must refuse the commission. Yet I found myself sketching designs and images in my head for a work I dare not undertake. I couldn't admit to Jude how I knew my miserable body made it impossible. So many painstaking hours of work would weary me to the bone, render me useless for ought else. Perhaps I wouldn't live to complete the task.

Unless a miracle befell.

CHAPTER THREE

Tuesday, the twenty-fifth day of April
In Paternoster Row

OVER OUR breakfast of bread and ale, I'd told Jude my decision: that I couldn't do the triptych. His look was savage, turning my blood cold. And now, as we made our way to Master Bowen's workshop, my brother argued at every step.

'But Seb, we could be rich!' he yelled, as if I was stone deaf. Goodwife Marlow came out to see what the racket was about, followed by her ne'er-do-well son Robin.

'Good morrow, Master Jude,' she called, 'How's the knee, Master Seb?'

'Healing, goodwife, thank you.'

Jude gave her a grudging touch to his cap, unwilling to cease his tirade.

'You can't refuse the duke,' he said, walking backwards, facing me as I dragged along the street, avoiding the puddles of yesterday, now murky with filth. It would not do to arrive at the workshop begrimed yet again. Besides, I was wearing my last pair of hose.

'What's the point?' I paused to rest, leaning on my staff, shooing away a dog that would use it as a piss-post. I was tired, having hardly slept. 'If I tell him I can do it, it will be a lie, because I can't. Now, let the matter rest. I'll pen a letter to Lord Richard, apologising.'

'No. Let's think about it a little longer. We have until Saturday.'

'Another few days, weeks even, won't make me any more able. You know that.'

'You've never tried!'

Cajoling and irate by turns, Jude continued the argument right to Bowen's door and, although he wrung from me a promise that I'd not inform the duke of my decision until Saturday, I saw my brother's eyes afire with anger, his fashionably-long hair becoming a rat's nest as he kept running his fingers through it.

• •

When we entered the workshop, Master Bowen wasn't there.

'You've missed all the excitement,' Kit Philpot, the apprentice, said, even before we'd crossed the threshold and removed our cloaks. Idle as ever, he was leaning against my desk beneath the window, fiddling with my brushes, spoiling the fine points I'd worked. 'Master and Mistress Meg had the most unholy row,' he went on, 'mistress in tears, master bellowing like a mad bull!'

Jude scowled.

'Be silent! You will not go listening at doors, tittle-tattling about your betters.'

'Listening at doors! They shouted fit to rouse the bones in St Paul's charnel house. I hardly had to listen specially. Then mistress threw pans at master and he slapped her face. Now he's in the parlour, cursing, and mistress is howling in her chamber. I never saw such fun in my life!'

'Keep a civil tongue,' Jude said, clouting him round the head. 'No more of this, you hear me? Get on with your work.'

With a sullen look, Kit obeyed, laying out the pens and brushes I would need for my painting and fetching my leather apron. I saw him poke out his tongue at Jude, but said nothing. I sat at my desk where Bishop Kemp's psalter awaited and took up a silver point pencil to draw a dragonfly in the margin of Psalm 133.

Jude stamped out the back door, across the unevenly-paved courtyard that divided the workshop from the house, chickens squawking and flapping in his wake.

'Mistress Bowen!' he called.

The Foxley brothers' rooms

EMILY APPLEYARD had chores to do before going marketing with Dame Ellen Langton. She went to the Foxley brothers' rooms, next door to the widow's house in West Cheap, to set the place to rights. The mess of crumbs they had left from breaking their fast made her sigh. She picked up a soiled napkin from the hearth, flung there by Jude, no doubt. She'd heard the pair arguing from next door. Probably poor Seb had got the worst of it, as always. She put the napkin in her basket, to be laundered.

In their cramped bedchamber, as usual, Jude's bed looked to have been the site of a battle whilst Sebastian's had been tidied. Firstly, Emily heaped Jude's tattered bedding on top of the large coffer between the narrow beds – that was all the furniture, besides the jordan wedged under Seb's bed for nocturnal emergencies – and pulled the sheets straight before replacing the blanket, tucking it neatly under the straw-stuffed palliasse.

Having repaired Jude's, Emily turned back the blanket on Seb's bed, releasing the smell of him retained in the covers. She closed her eyes and breathed deeply, smiling. She giggled. If only he knew.

Kicking off her shoes, she slipped beneath the sheet, fancying some delicious vestige of warmth from his body lingered there. His pillow bore the dent where his head had lain and her cheek nestled where his had rested. She allowed her skin to soak up the manly scent of him.

I know he's lame, she thought, stroking the blanket, and his back is crooked, but he has such a gentle face. She pictured him, the curve of his cheek and shadows beneath, the straight nose, the sharp angle of his jaw, his lips, his too-rare smiles. A dear face she kissed often in her dreams. She longed for those pewter-hued eyes to look at her, though they never did. Not in that way.

She lay, drinking in the sweet essence of him, hugging his pillow. If only...

'Emily! Where are you, girl? We'll be late!' Dame Ellen called.

The dream shattered.

Bowen's workshop in Paternoster Row

AN HOUR or so later, as I was warming some life back into my numb fingers, holding them to the brazier, Jude strode in from the yard. At least he'd thought of me, shivering over my work.

'This'll warm you,' he said, setting a cup of hot, mulled ale beside me – a peace-offering, perhaps. 'I'm going out.' He took his cloak from the peg by the door.

'Where?' I sipped my ale, thawing my cramped hands round the cup.

'Eastleigh's.'

He left, slamming the door so hard it swung open again, revealing folk hastening about their business, making the most of a spell – however brief – of April sunshine. Kit hurried to close it, fearing the draught would blow the powdered pigments away and disturb the neat piles of collated folios waiting to be sewn.

Without Master Bowen to instruct him, Kit had little to do. He sat upon the collating table, swinging his legs.

'What does Master Jude want with the apothecary-surgeon?' he wondered aloud. 'He looked well enough to me and I went and fetched more binding agents and pigments from ol' Eastleigh, yesterday.'

'Well, we are still short of vermilion,' I told him. 'And you'd best come down from your perch. If Master Bowen catches you soiling his spotless collating table, you'll be for a beating.'

'He's probably at the Panyer Inn by now, won't be back 'til curfew,' Kit assured me, climbing down, nonetheless. 'If my father knew master was such a drunken fellow, he'd never have apprenticed me here. I would tell him, but I'd miss the baked custards I get here if he took me away.'

'Is that all you think of? Your belly and its next meal?' I laughed, elaborating a curving stem to support the dragonfly as it hovered beside Jude's faultless script *Ecce quam bonum:* "Behold how good, how pleasant it is for brothers to dwell together in unity" – if only.

Kit watched over my shoulder. I knew my talent baffled him.

'Now you mention it, master, my belly says it must be dinnertime.'

'And, no doubt, you've done a full morning's work to earn it? What have you done, exactly?' I sketched a delicate leaf on my stem.

'Set out your stuff, put wood in the brazier, gave you good company. What more could you ask?' Kit was idle, incorrigible.

'Go, sweep the storeroom, then grind some verdigris for me, to paint these stems and leaves. Make yourself useful, lad.' I settled to my work and sensed, rather than saw, the obscene gesture he made at me for setting him a task to do. But I ignored it.

Taking a fine brush, I dipped it in the azurite pigment, singing a favourite "Sanctus" I'd heard in St Paul's as I filled in the body of the dragonfly, giving it life upon the page.

Gilbert Eastleigh's apothecary's shop in Ivy Lane

THE APOTHECARY'S still-room in Ivy Lane had been set to rights, the shutters flung wide to welcome in more wholesome airs, the glass vessels washed and restored to their rightful places on the shelves. The bottle with its precious contents was locked away.

Tom Bowen, the apothecary-surgeon's apprentice, found all as it should be when he came to prepare things for the day's work ahead. Only a stray breath of invisible vapour lingered here and there among the pots of herbs and remedies, a faint reminder of obscure nocturnal practices. Tom took down a shapely glass vessel of Venice treacle, dusted and replaced it; then did the same with an earthen bowl of bear's fat. He was bored, resentment chewing at his soul as he took up the broom to sweep the room clean of the debris of yesterday.

Every day the same: dust the pots, sweep the floor, set up the charcoal brazier, heat the water, chop the herbs – finer than that – pound the ingredients, mix and stir. That was the worst thing: hours and hours of stirring pots over the brazier. Winter and summer, the same heat, the same stinks. Tom had never suffered from headaches until he was taken on as Gilbert Eastleigh's apprentice. Now it was an unusual day if he didn't end it with a throbbing headache, sickened by the stenches spewed out of the cauldrons and pots in the airless still-room. He'd lost weight too; never had any appetite.

And Master Eastleigh beat him. For laziness. For stupidity. For being Tom Bowen. Any reason at all. No wonder he had run away – twice.

Then his questing broom found some papers, lying forgotten on the floor beneath the desk. Leafing through them, Tom recognised his master's spidery scrawl but the writing made little sense. Circles and squiggles, meaningless stuff:

> *Pale & black with false citrine,*
> *imperfect white & red,*
> *The Peacocks feathers in colour gay,*
> *the Rainebowe whych shal overgoe...*

False citrine? Peacocks? What was this nonsense? For certain, it was far beyond his comprehension, yet he knew, instinctively, his master hadn't meant for him to see the notes, never mind read them.

He continued to frown over them, intrigued as any man by the scent of forbidden knowledge, until he heard Master Eastleigh's anxious tread hastening down the stairs overhead. The notes must be hidden. Where? A book lay on the desk, its pages loose and the broken leather binding stained by age. Tom opened it at random and tucked the notes out of sight, in between the crackling parchment folios. Time later to think where best to put them, so his master might find them and never suppose someone else had seen them.

• •

Gilbert Eastleigh lowered the shutter at the front of his shop so the early morning light rushed in, flinging aside the gloom like broken shards of darkness. He swung the door wide, as though he expected a rush of customers, eager for his syrups or purgatives, or simply needful of his wisdom on all matters surgical or medical. In benevolent humour this morning, the apothecary even had a smile for his apprentice.

'Good morrow, young Tom. Sleep well?'

Tom was instantly on his guard.

'Aye, master.' He hadn't. He never did these days, wedged in his attic with spiders for bed mates and the wind whistling under the tiles, stirring the cobwebs like dusty curtains. Master was overly-cheerful. It couldn't last.

'Have you swept up? Lit the brazier?'

'I've swept but the brazier is reluctant to light. I fear the charcoal must be damp.'

The hand came out of nowhere, though Tom was half expecting it, catching him a stinging blow that made his ear ring.

'Rubbish. There's nought amiss with the charcoal. It burned well enough last eve. No doubt you didn't bother to empty the ash first, you idle toad.'

'But I did that when we closed up yesterday.'

Another swipe, so both ears were ringing now.

'Well, do it again. I have business elsewhere for an hour. If customers come, you know what to do.'

'Aye, master, sell them a syrup and tell them to come back later, if need be.'

• •

Scowling over his pain, Tom returned to the obstinate brazier in the still-room, but the apothecary was just a step behind him.

'See! Just as I supposed. Arm-deep in ashes. I knew it.'

23

Tom made his apologies but the hand lashed out again, catching his shoulder. It made no sense. He wasn't lying when he'd said the ashes had been emptied last eve but there they were. A grey blanket in the bottom of the iron basket, blocking the holes so the air couldn't get in and the charcoal wouldn't burn.

'And I want the sage and betony finely chopped and the dragon's blood resin pounded to a powder – properly this time, no half measures.'

Then Eastleigh stalked out, huffing, leaving the lad to his chores.

• •

Hurting, suppressing a sob, Tom took the ashes out to the back yard and was about to tip them in the sack where they were stored – nothing was wasted and charcoal ash was useful – when he saw the ruby-eyed glow of heat at the bottom. The brazier must have been used during the night. Strange. Nothing else in the still-room looked out of place. No soiled utensils, dirty bowls. Perhaps master had felt cold, sitting at his desk, writing up those notes.

The notes!

Setting aside the warm ashes, he hurried back to find them. Now was the time to put them where his master would discover them readily, without being too obvious.

But the book was gone. Master had taken it with him.

Bowen's parlour, Paternoster Row

MATTHEW BOWEN, Master Stationer and Bookbinder, seemed to overfill his parlour with his ageing bulk, towering over the apothecary-surgeon like an oak above a sapling. But size had little relevance in their long relationship.

Thoughtfully, Bowen ran a fat thumb down the edge of the worn cover. *The mystery & craft of Limning.*

'It was well bound in its day. Kid skin, nicely tooled, probably done around the turn of the century. London-made, of course.' He leaned heavily against the cushioned settle, pulling at his beard, what there was of it. 'Aye, Gilbert, I can have a fine copy made for you to replace it. Should be ready for collection by St John's Day. Will that suffice?'

Eastleigh sniffed, fingering his furred lapel, as was his habit. He didn't use the book often, but June? The wait would be inconvenient and he was not a patient man.

'Can't it be done sooner?'

'Not if you want similar materials used. Kid skin is harder to come by than pig or cow.'

'No, no. The cover is quite irrelevant.'

Bowen looked offended, as though his old friend had insulted a family member.

'I just want a copy of the contents. Word for word, precisely.'

'My scribes don't make errors. I'll have Jude Foxley pen the copy. You'll find no fault with his workmanship.' Bowen wrote in his order book, totting up figures as he went. 'That will cost you one half penny per ten folios for this size. Then for another half mark, I'll have it illuminated for you.'

'I have no use for pretty initials. Just the text. Unadorned.'

'Sebastian is very skilled.'

'The cripple?'

'Never mind how he looks. He's the best illuminator in London... England, even. I only employ the best.' Bowen preened himself a little, certain his words were true. 'He has worked on books for the king's own daughter and Lord H – '

'I told you, Matthew. Just the text. Nothing more. And you can make it half size with a simple board cover. And I want it by the end of Whitsuntide and I'll pay you a farthing for a dozen folios – not a clipped penny more.' Eastleigh drove a hard bargain, wiping his fingers over his fur, as though trying to banish the stains on them.

'But it could be a work of great beauty.'

'I said no! Either be content with my requirements or I'll take my custom elsewhere.'

'Come, come now,' Bowen breathed noisily. 'There'll be no need for that, Gilbert. It shall be as you say.' He felt exasperated, failing to make good in securing the sale of something more lavish, ever keen to further promote his excellent reputation in the Stationers' Guild. Sizeable orders were harder to come by lately. If old friends wouldn't help you out, who would?

He had reason enough to need help these days, since that wretch, William Caxton, had set up his new-fangled contraption in Bruges.

The printing press.

It was proving popular too. Though it churned out sub-standard goods, there was no denying it was much quicker and cheaper than a scribe, if numerous copies were required. Customers did not seem bothered that the work had to be shipped in and out. There was even a rumour that Caxton was thinking of coming back to England soon, setting up a press in London or Westminster. God help him if the rumour proved true.

As it was, he hoped his customers' interest in printing was a mere passing fancy, but it worried him. At this rate, his profits would be much reduced. Maybe a journeyman would have to go.

Eastleigh was curt, feeling he had wasted enough time on the likes of Matthew Bowen when he had far more important things to do:

'Are we agreed?'

'I suppose so, seeing you're a friend of long standing.' Bowen held out his hand. Eastleigh gave the stationer's great paw a perfunctory shake.

'Done.'

'And how's my boy Tom faring?' asked Bowen. A father was entitled to ask, but the apothecary had already swept out of the workshop in a swirl of expensive cloth and fine fur, leaving behind a faint odour of things long dead and probably best forgotten.

• •

Disgruntled at such bad manners from a man he had always accounted a friend, Bowen lumbered off across the yard to climb the stairway to the private part of the house. On the landing he hesitated for an instant, thinking to confide his troubles to his wife Meg, but no. She was probably still sulking in her chamber, nursing her hurts. Well, she'd deserved them, every one, damned woman. How dare she belittle him like that, even in private? He turned the other way and went to his own room.

It was shabby but comfortable, the way he liked it. The bed hangings were threadbare, the fringes dangling loose here and there, but what did that matter when your eyes were closed in sleep?

Behind a painted screen hung another faded curtain, which he drew aside to reveal his private chapel. It was a very small space with hardly room to move, but it was enough. Within was a tiny altar with a gilded crucifix betwixt two bees-wax candles in silver sconces, though he begrudged his Saviour the expense. Before the altar stood his well-worn prayer desk and above it hung a painting of the Blessed Virgin and the Christ Child in a frame of gilded lead that he had had specially made. The frame was a monstrous thing, so heavy, only he had strength enough to lift the picture down from its peg. Behind it was a niche, set in the thickness of the wall.

Bowen smiled to himself, considering his own ingenuity, such that even when he was seen praying on his knees before the image, it was the stuff concealed behind it that he truly worshipped – gold and silver coin.

In curtained secrecy, he set aside the crucifix, took down the Virgin and removed the leather bags from their hiding place. The prayer desk could be turned over, hinged so it became a cushioned stool, ingeniously crafted.

With a contented sigh he sat, drawing the candles closer and emptying the bags upon the altar. He loved the sight, the glitter of gold. The sound, the soft clink of silver. The feel of it, cool and heavy, cascading through his hands. Aye, and especially he adored the smell of it. That metallic tang that tickled his nostrils and sent shivers of delight down his spine. He counted it, admired it, worshipped it. Lord Mamon was his god and restored his faith daily.

He would forego finery and furs – those things that fade and age – but money never would. So long as he had good food and plenty of decent ale, the rest mattered little. He kept a roof over his wife's pretty head and bought her sugared comfits to content her, and a new gown every Maytime. What more did she need? Perhaps, now he thought on it, a new gown *every* year was a little excessive. He must economise.

Then he heard his wife's voice, shrill along the passageway, ruining his moments of pleasurable peace – blasted woman. But the call of the Panyer Inn was louder and far more enticing.

Bowen's workshop

J UDE RETURNED to the workshop around dinnertime, seemingly empty-handed, though my nose detected a faint whiff of violets, sage and one or two more obscure aromas as my brother swept through the workshop and out again, across the yard with barely a nod.

'If you're going to the kitchen, Master Jude, tell mistress I'm hungry,' Kit called out. Such insolence. 'St Paul's bell struck ten ages ago. It's long past dinnertime.'

Violet oil was good for bruises, I recalled, sage for cuts and grazes. And Master Bowen had slapped his wife that morning, according to Kit. It all made sense now. Little wonder that dinner was late. I prepared my brush to a fine point betwixt my lips and dipped it into the green pigment Kit had made ready in an oyster shell. At a touch, I could tell the paint was gritty.

'This verdigris needs more grinding, Kit,' I instructed him. 'It's nowhere near fine enough. You can't mix lumps like this and expect to get a smooth paste. Grind it some more, 'til you have a fine, even powder, then show it to me again.'

Kit sighed, plainly bored at the thought of more tedious grinding with the pestle and marble slab and all on an empty belly, too.

'When can I start painting, Master Seb?' he asked, more than a hint of whining in his voice.

'When you know how to prepare the pigments properly.' Seeing his disappointed look, I relented. 'Work that verdigris to a fine, even powder and then I'll give you your first drawing lesson after dinner. How would that be?'

He agreed eagerly. Anything to avoid more hard work.

St Paul's Cathedral

ON OUR way home at the end of a long day – for me, at least – I told Jude I wanted to stop by the cathedral to listen to the young choristers from St Paul's School practising, as we did occasionally. My brother used to attend the school, having been a promising scholar. But when our father asked that I should follow him, the authorities came up with endless excuses why this could not be. The truth was, as we well knew, that the school had no place for a cripple, no matter how clever or how wonderful his voice. So I had seemed to shrug off the insult, as I did most others. Even Jude didn't know my true feelings on this.

Yet I couldn't help that I loved the great minster with its soaring spire, stretching up to knock on the very gates of heaven. I liked to come here, to think things through when life cast obstacles in my way. Though Jude could think of far better ways of spending his time, no doubt, he gave in for my sake.

We entered the huge nave quietly, only my staff making a soft tap-tap on the tiled floor. I loved the way the sumptuous draught of incense wrapped itself around me. It made me feel revered, almost, as a saint in a niche. The stained glass shed its bejewelled colours on the floor like fallen leaves – the patterns so rich and complex, I never tired of them, thinking how I might use their gem-stone lights in my work.

We approached the gilded rood screen with its ornately carven saints, half-hidden in a forest of rampant oak leaves like green men. The foliage was painted with verdigris and viridian, so lush it seemed real. I touched a leaf, as I often did, just to make certain.

Then the choir, concealed beyond the screen, began their practising, their scales echoing up into the roof beams far above, higher and higher. I felt my soul rising with them until my feet must surely leave the ground.

I leaned my staff against the screen, unneeded. As the choristers opened the anthem *Te Deum Laudamus* with a glorious top C, I too took a breath and hit the note precisely, holding it steady, on and on, well beyond the moment when most men would have been gasping for air. How I could do this was one of many conundrums posed by my ill-formed frame, as was the fact my speaking voice had broken like any other lad's, yet my singing voice remained the same.

I sang the whole anthem, word perfect, my eyes closed, standing unaided. I managed a near-impossible top note. The choristers had trouble with it and were made to repeat the line, over and over, but I knew I'd sung it perfectly. Now I felt calmer, renewed by the beauty of music, of colour and sanctity.

With a contented sigh, I took up my staff and hobbled off, my brother beside me.

'I wonder sometimes, Seb,' he said. 'Just how much you really need that staff of yours.'

'Of course I need it. I would be tumbled in the mire at every other step without it, you know that as well as I.'

Jude shrugged. He was still somewhat agitated, I could see that. I suppose he hadn't given up the hope of changing my mind about accepting Lord Richard's commission.

• •

As we had missed our dinner, Jude stopped to buy two hot pig's trotters from a huckster in West Cheap, and we found a wall to lean against while we tucked in. At least Jude did. I had trouble keeping a grip on the greasy meat whilst propping myself up betwixt the wall and my staff.

'Here, give me that. I'll hold it, you bite,' Jude said, seeing my difficulty.

We were soon laughing together as grease dripped from Jude's chin. With both hands full he couldn't wipe it away, so used his sleeve instead, resulting in getting grease in his hair and smeared across his cheek.

'You're making it worse,' I said, taking up the hem of my cloak to wipe his face, only to wobble precariously, which set us laughing all the more. 'How are Mistress Bowen's bruises?' I asked. My query stopped Jude's merriment instantly.

'How do you know about them? I never said anything.'

'No, but Kit said she was slapped and then you returned from the apothecary's smelling of violets. I think they were to treat Mistress Meg's injuries.'

'You think too much, little brother, that's your trouble.' He took another bite of his trotter and chewed, considering.

'All the same, I'm right, aren't I?'

He nodded.

'You should see her poor face, Seb. That bastard's knocked her black and blue! If I get my hands on him...'

'He's her husband, Jude, and well within his rights. There's nothing you can do about it. You should be concerned for what he will do to you, if he catches you.'

'Catches me? At what? She asked me to fetch her some soothing ointment for her bruises, so I did. And if I applied it for her, what of that? Her witless maid couldn't have done the task half so gently. It was all perfectly innocent, I assure you.'

I gave him a hard look. He was clever, handsome in a careless sort of way, but utterly reckless. When matters concerned a woman, I sometimes doubted my brother was wholly in his right mind.

'But it isn't always so innocent, is it? You and Mistress Meg, I mean.'

'No,' he admitted after a long pause, shaking his fair head so his hair shone golden, catching the last of the sun's rays. 'No, it isn't.'

'I've seen you return to the workshop with your shirt awry and your points mismatched. And the other day there was a bead of blood upon your lip. Do your kisses have to be so violent? One of these days, Master Bowen will notice.'

'Oh, he's a stupid old fool. And he's drinking heavily these days, Meg tells me, too drunk to notice anything most of the time. Don't concern yourself, little brother.' Jude dismissed the possibility, flinging the trotter bones to a cur snuffling in a nearby midden heap.

'Even so, I wish you'd be more circumspect. Going to her bedchamber in the middle of the day. You think young Kit couldn't fathom what you're about? You're the fool, brother. Please take more care, I beg you.'

CHAPTER FOUR

Wednesday, the twenty-sixth day of April
The Foxley brothers' rooms

'WELL, SAY something, damn you! You *have* to do it!' Jude paced the floor, his lips white. Fearing that any action, any word, would make matters worse, I sat at the table, hardly daring to breathe, my breakfast untouched. I let my hair fall across my face, a concealing curtain. I was so tired of this.

'Give me one bloody good reason why not!' he screeched, thumping his fist on the board, making me jump.

I cowered before my brother when he was like this. He loved me, cared for me, but... I stared, unfocused, at my hands. Why wouldn't Jude let me alone, to wallow in my despair? All last eve we'd argued and still he was not done with me. Now I felt chilled to the bone, despite the cheerful fire in the hearth that glazed our room in a warm glow.

'Why, why, why?' Jude bombarded me with words that flew around my aching head like cannon-shot. The force of his argument was a physical assault. I had no defence except the truth: that I couldn't do the triptych. But my brother refused to hear. 'Why not?' he yelled, hurling his ale cup across the room. He was clenching his fists so tight, the nails must surely cut into his palms. With the question of the duke's commission hanging between us like the Sword of Damocles, my silence angered Jude more than if I'd cursed and shouted, but I couldn't think of anything more to say.

'You're pathetic! You know that? Worse than some snivelling, wet-arsed, puking babe. You have so many excuses for failure and you haven't even made an attempt yet. Whine, whine, whine like a whipped dog. You miserable wretch, you spineless, feeble-witted...' He paused for breath, wanting some response from me. But I sat, staring at nothing, silent.

'For sweet Christ's sake, you stupid fool, you weak-willed idiot, I can't believe you won't even try.'

I let the words wash over me. Everything he said was true – even the name-calling. But I didn't want to try, knowing I would make a mess of the triptych that meant so much to Lord Richard, the money we would have to repay. My eyes burned with hot tears I dared not let fall. If Jude despised me then I had nothing left, not love, not respect. Nothing.

How could Jude ever think I could do it? My wretched body wouldn't allow it and that I resented most of all. No, it was more than that. I *loathed* my body. God – or the Devil – had created a mockery for others' amusement and *I* had to live with it – if such an existence could be called 'living'. Jude was still shouting, throwing things, but I was overwhelmed by my own misery. A single, scalding tear spilled down my cheek.

I glanced up. My brother towered over me, eyes ablaze with fury, like the flash of a thunderbolt cleaving the air between us.

'Are you listening to me?' he snarled. His strong, capable hands locked around my neck and began to squeeze. The stool overturned. Thumbs pressed harder on my windpipe; my eyes bulged. I struggled in vain. Just as my vision began to cloud, Jude flung me aside with a curse, dropping me like a discarded rag. I fell, gasping, whimpering with shock. He kicked the stool away and slammed out the door. I lay sprawled on the floor, hurting, gulping air that raked my mangled throat, my world a desolation.

Bowen's workshop in Paternoster Row

JUDE IMMERSED himself in his work. He was good at it, as fine a craftsman as any and far better than most. He set the apothecary's old book on the stand – *The mystery & craft of Limning* – open at the first folio, ready for copying, and laid out a ready-ruled parchment on his desk.

The air was damp in Bowen's workshop that Wednesday morning and the fine parchment was inclined to curl, so he pinned it down beneath a three-sided frame he had invented himself to keep it flat, smoothing it gently. He loved the feel of the supple skin, soft as a woman's breast, the quill stroking against it, leaving a tracery of darkening ink, proof of their liaison; the caress of a lover. He thought of Meg in her chamber across the way, how much he wanted her, how much he needed her to work off the last of his foul temper, his guilt from earlier.

Cheapside

MAKING MY way to Paternoster Row, I hobbled along, stopping frequently. I kept my collar pulled high to conceal the worst of the angry weals as I paused again, struggling to maintain my balance.

'Good day, Master Seb!' Emily Appleyard called out, a hint of laughter in her voice. At my expense, no doubt. She was at the conduit, filling her ewer with fresh water. I looked up, lost my precarious footing and fell against her, spilling water over us both, soaking her skirts.

'F-forgive me,' I stuttered. My voice was rasping, unsteady as the rest of me. 'I-I didn't see you there, Mistress Emily.'

'No matter, the ewer's easily refilled.'

'But your gown is soaking wet. I'm so sorry.'

'It will dry and no harm done. But what's amiss with you?' Emily set down her ewer and took my arm to steady me.

'Nothing. I'm not so good this morning, clumsy, worse than usual. Sorry.'

'You look pale, tired. Are you unwell, Seb? Come, rest for a while in the house. Dame Ellen won't mind.'

'No, I can't. I'm late.' I turned to walk on but sagged against the conduit, hardly aware the water was pouring over my shoes.

'No arguments. You're coming back home with me.'

Bowen's workshop

ALMOST TWO hours later I finally reached the workshop. I'd had my fill of Emily's coddling and petting me like some grand lady's lap-dog. She'd fussed over my wet feet and my mud-stained hose, bathed my face and plied me with what she called 'a benevolent remedy'. It was as well I kept my shirt close-fastened else the undoubted marks on my neck would have roused her to pity me all the more.

I entered Bowen's courtyard through the side gate and crossed to the workshop, fully expecting the wrath of God, or of Matthew Bowen at least, to rain down upon me. Instead, I was met by a stony silence. Jude was alone, working at his desk, copying from an old book, propped on the stand beside him. His work was perfect – a faultless hand. I watched, fascinated by the ease of movement, the certainty. They were strong hands indeed. I swallowed with difficulty, wincing more at the memory than the hurt.

Without removing my cloak, for the workshop was so cold my breath formed little clouds in the chill air, I took my seat. Twice I picked up a brush to lift a gossamer-fine sheet of gold leaf and put it down again, unused. Too weary for such painstaking work, I set the parchment aside, put my elbows on the board and rested my head in my hands, eyes closed.

'Where have you been?' Jude asked at last. It was hard to determine his tone.

'Nowhere.'

'You took your time about it, all the same.'

'Sorry, Jude.'

'No, it's me that should be sorry.' He pushed back his stool and came over to me though he did not touch me. 'I shouldn't have done it. Are you quite recovered, Seb?' So he did care then.

'I'm here, aren't I?'

'You look cold.' Jude returned to his work, taking up his pen. 'Why don't you sit by the brazier? Warm yourself.'

'I should get on with this gilding...'

＊ ＊

Our stilted conversation was interrupted by the arrival of a customer. Alderman John Barker stood just within the shop door off the street, hesitating.

'Master Bowen!' he called. 'Service here, if you please.'

'My apologies, sir,' Jude said, leaving his desk, 'But Master Bowen is from home at present. I am Jude Foxley, his journeyman scribe. How may I assist you, sir?' Alderman Barker grunted, clearly not expecting to conduct business with an underling. 'Perhaps you would partake of some ale, sir, if you wish to await Master Bowen's return?' Jude called out for Kit, the errant apprentice.

The lad sauntered in from the yard after Jude had shouted a third time.

'Fetch a stool and a cup of ale, you.'

Kit scowled but did as he was told – slowly.

I tried to concentrate on my work. I was supposed to be putting gold leaf on the large capital D of *Domine refugium*, Psalm 89, though the draughts from doors and windows bedevilled my efforts, unless I took care. I dared not cough or sneeze, else the weightless gold would scatter like leaves in an autumn gale. It was delicate work indeed.

Kit served the ale then leaned against the wall, cleaning his nails with Jude's fox-headed penknife, idle as usual.

The alderman sat by the brazier, taking all the warmth, sipping his ale and tapping his foot. He had waited barely long enough to say a Paternoster or two when he drained his cup and slammed it down on the collating table, spilling the last few droplets on the pristine surface. Master would be livid. The alderman stood.

'My time is too precious to waste sitting here. When will Bowen be back?'

'I do not know, sir,' Jude said. I saw him force a smile but there was an ominous edge to my brother's voice. 'Perhaps I may help?'

'You? What would you know of producing fine Books of Hours?' Alderman Barker straightened his hat and pulled his cloak about him, preparing to depart. I saw there was a darn in the woollen cloth. Someone had used red thread on the russet cloth – it was neatly done but did not look well.

'I know more than you may think, sir,' Jude told him. 'I wrote the text for Lord Hastings's Book of Hours and my brother Sebastian illuminated it, doing the decorated initials, marginalia and miniatures...'

'What? That!' The alderman turned, finally taking notice of me, hunched silently over my work. 'You mean to say, that creature?' He pointed an accusing finger at me. 'That thing passes for an illuminator?'

I saw Jude's eyes flare, the colour fade from his cheek.

'My brother is the finest...'

'I don't care. I'll not have one of Satan's minions desecrating my sacred texts with his filthy hands. How dare you even suggest – '

My brother's fists were balled, every sinew drawn taut as vellum on a drying frame, straining the skin.

'Sebastian's work is good enough for royalty,' he growled, 'So it ought to be bloody good enough for the likes of you, you pompous, bigoted...'

'Jude! No.' I hastened to intervene, standing beside my brother, for fear he was about to strike the alderman. But the man backed away. I couldn't say which of us two he most feared: Jude in a temper or me, the Devil's helpmate.

'Don't you speak to me in that manner. I'm an alderman of the city. I shall be taking my commission elsewhere.'

'And good riddance, you despicable old scoundrel. We can do without your custom!' Alderman Barker scurried out, cloak flapping, and Jude slammed the door after.

• •

Hardly a moment had passed for us to catch our breath when Master Bowen returned with a stationer's lad a pace or two behind him, loaded down with fresh reams of paper.

'You're late!' our master snarled at me. 'Bloody late! If you want a day's pay you can either work through the dinner hour, or stay after, if there's light enough to see by. And you...' He turned to the lad with the reams of paper, 'Put that in the storeroom and bugger off.'

It was a busy morning and another customer came in. Bowen went off to the storeroom to show him his near-finished volume that required only the decoration on the binding.

'You've put him in an evil mood, being late,' Jude said to me in an undertone, so Kit would not hear. 'And I didn't like the look he gave me, either.'

I glanced up warily at him.

'I pray he didn't overhear your exchange with Alderman Barker.'

Kit, seemingly fully employed for once, matching up folios by their catch-phrases, left his work to join us, a glint in his eye that boded well for no man.

'Don't worry, Jude,' Kit said, pointedly omitting the correct form of address, 'Ol' Bowen has no idea that you've been tupping his wife, unless I decide to tell him, of course... Or I could tell him what you said to Barker.'

'You little ferret.'

'A mark might buy my silence, for a while.'

'You're not getting a bent farthing out of me!'

Man and boy glowered at one another until Kit turned away and went back to collating folios. Jude took a deep breath, his muscles slackened, and he went to the ale jug to pour himself a cup, only to find it empty. He cursed. Things were going from bad to worse. I thought they could but get better. But it was not to be.

• •

Our next customer was a wealthy grocer, the lord mayor's cousin. Master Bowen's expression warmed instantly as he spread his hands in unctuous welcome.

'Good sir, how may I assist you? Will you take wine? Kit! Set a chair here for Master Rowley.' Wine was served this time, cushions were plumped. Master Rowley sat, balanced on the chair's edge, poised to flee. He took a gulp of wine.

'I would cancel my order.'

Bowen froze. Everything ceased. The workshop held its breath.

'Cancel?' The word dropped like a corpse into a silent pool, the deathly ripples spreading outward, wrapping everyone in their awful embrace. 'Cancel? But you cannot. I have already...'

'I can and I have. Master Caxton in Bruges can do the job in three days that will take you three weeks. Even with the time required to cross the Narrow Seas, I get it quicker and it works out cheaper. Time is money in my business. I'm sorry.' He didn't sound it. 'Thank you for the wine.'

The grocer rose from his seat, a picture of wounded innocence, as though it was *his* livelihood in jeopardy. Matthew Bowen escorted him to the door. The man left without looking back.

• •

The stationer remained facing the empty doorway. Even at that distance I could tell he was breathing heavily, his fingers twitching. When he turned, livid with rage, his face would have given Satan pause for thought.

'That does it then!' He kicked a stool across the workshop. 'Another bloody order lost to that bastard Caxton across the water.'

'Pardon me, master, but did you speak with Alderman Barker earlier, after he left here?' Kit's sycophantic tone made my flesh crawl. I glanced at Jude. He'd turned pale.

'No, I bloody didn't. Why?' Bowen helped himself to the grocer's discarded wine.

'He was going to place a sizeable order, master. Wanted a luxury edition of *The Game and Play of Chess*...'

'You lying little goat!' Jude leaped at Kit but Bowen dragged my brother back, grabbing a handful of his jerkin and keeping hold.

'So. Did you take the order?' He shook Jude like a dog with a rag.

'No, master, he didn't,' Kit answered instead. 'He told the alderman he was a pompous, bigoted, disreputable old scoundrel. That's what he called him.' The apprentice's glee was writ plain upon his features as Bowen wrenched Jude around to face him. My brother was tall but the stationer was built like the Tower of London and his monstrous fist caught Jude full in the chest. He fell down, winded.

'So, that's bloody it! You're out of a job, you bastard. Get out, Foxley, you're finished here.'

'B-but you can't,' Jude wheezed. 'I'm halfway through the apothecary's text and working towards my masterpiece... you can't do without me. I'm the best scrivener in London.'

'I can do without someone who insults the bloody customers and loses me commissions! Kit's not half bad these days and your brother's as fair a scribe as any and can do the illumination – which you can't. You're just a bloody luxury I can't afford.' Bowen was a little calmer now, but still white around the mouth.

'You can't do this to me!' Jude yelled, clambering to his feet, overturning the desk, ink pots, pounce pots and sand going everywhere, pens flying.

'Oh, but I can! Now get out.' Bowen strode to the open door. 'Out!'

Unsteadily, I pushed myself up from my stool. Leaves of gold foil wafted to the floor in the draught. I was shaking, weak at the knees. But I stood, somehow.

'If my brother goes, I go too,' I said. My knuckles showed bone as I gripped the edge of the desk, determined not to fall. Not now.

'No, no, there's no need for that.' Bowen changed his tone suddenly, laying a hand on my uneven shoulder. 'Caxton can't do illumination – there's still plenty of work for you. You can stay. I still need an illuminator.'

'No, Master Bowen, I won't work for you unless you employ my brother also.' Bowen's face suffused with anger again, his eyes narrowed.

'I'll report you to the guild if you walk out on me now. I'll see neither of you works again. No one will ever employ either of you miserable dogs!'

'Jude, take me home, please...' I was having increasing difficulty in remaining upright. 'Now.' My voice was almost gone but I hoped my brother recognised the desperation in it. He grabbed his cloak. I hadn't removed mine in any case. Jude handed me my staff and took my free arm to guide me to the door.

'I'll be back for our money and our tools,' he told Matthew Bowen as we left the workshop.

• •

'By Christ, you shouldn't have done that, little brother.' Jude was struggling to keep me on my feet in the street outside. 'The rent's due next week. What are we supposed to live on, for God's sake? Tell me that.' But I could give him no answer, slipping to the ground as he lost the battle to keep me upright.

The Foxley brothers' rooms

JUDE CARRIED Seb home. It wasn't far and his brother was mostly skin and bone, so it was no great task. He propped Seb on his stool so he could lean back against the wall, and fetched the blankets from their beds, for he was chilled and shivering as he sat, eyes closed, white as new milk. Jude got the fire going and set some ale to warm, but he had seen his brother like this before and knew blankets and mulled ale weren't going to be enough to restore him. Seb was sick, his feeble body so prone to chills and fevers. That he'd lived to the age of two-and-twenty was little short of a miracle.

The one thing Jude would not own was that it might be *his* fault Seb was ill. As his younger brother dozed fitfully in the chair, his head lolled to one side, showing a perfect thumb-print bruise, a disfiguring ink blot on the parchment-pale skin. Testament to an uncontrolled temper, it seemed to screech at Jude accusingly, until he pulled Seb's shirt higher and tucked a blanket about his neck. No need to invite enquiry from the likes of Dame Ellen or Emily. True, Seb was always bruised from so many falls but that mark – a mark of Cain, almost – and its partner on the other side of Seb's throat, would be hard to explain, indeed.

Jude pulled out the large coffer in their bedchamber and threw back the lid. He rummaged beneath their spare linen, moving aside some precious folios, sewn but not yet bound – his masterpiece, if he ever finished it – and pulled out a small leather pouch. He tipped its contents into his hand. Coins, pitifully few but enough for the month's rent due next week, but after that... He counted the remainder: a groat, four pennies, one half penny and five farthings: hardly enough to feed two men for more than a week and Seb needed medicine... and wood for the fire... and their parish church of St Michael le Querne would be enquiring about their Easter tithes soon, which were still unpaid. Perhaps Dame Ellen would give them a week's grace on the rent.

Then what? He'd have to take work, labouring may be. Anything. Coming to a decision, he took up his cloak again, put the spare coins in his purse and went out.

Eastleigh's apothecary's shop

GILBERT EASTLEIGH'S place was in Ivy Lane, between Paternoster Row and the Shambles. Despite the proximity of the Shambles and its stench of rotting offal, Ivy Lane was a desirable address. Just as Jude arrived at the apothecary-surgeon's, he saw a group of horsemen swing into the gateway of the grand house opposite. He remembered the place was called Lovell's Inn. He watched a young lord, laughing with his peers, all smiles and good humour. Lovell – if it was he – even glanced at Jude, but looked straight through him.

Inside, the apothecary's shop was redolent with such a mixture of odours, some easily discerned, like aniseed and musk, others unidentifiable. There were flowery perfumes combined with animal stinks and earthy smells overlaid by metallic tangs, all emanating from the darkened still-room behind the curtain, since Master Eastleigh knew daylight and fresh air could reduce the potency of his preparations. The jar of dried frogs on the counter and the dusty serpent's skin suspended from the rafters, among the herbs hung there to dry, made the place seem more a witch's den than an apothecary's shop. Empty-eyed animal skulls glared at him, accusingly, from the shelves. Jude could detect oil of violets, such as he had purchased for poor Meg. Should he get some for Seb's throat? No. The women would know the smell and ask questions. Besides, better that Seb suffer a little for his obstinacy, serve him right.

Thinking about it now Jude realised his actions, committed in the heat of the moment, had been, in truth, both rational and justified. Aye. Seb had to be made to see reason. Hopefully, he would now understand he had no choice but to accept the duke's commission. After all *he*, Jude, was the elder brother and Seb needed reminding of the fact that he should damned well do as he was told. And that would be the end of the matter.

At Jude's call, the apothecary himself peered around the curtain, emerging from his lair like some reluctant creature of the night, narrowed eyes blinking behind his spectacles at the unaccustomed brightness. Nervous fingers were wiped hurriedly upon a soiled cloth, grey hair plastered his forehead from toiling over the still in his fiery cavern.

'Master Foxley.' He greeted Jude, his lipless mouth curving in a rictus smile for a frequent customer. 'What is it you require today? Lapis lazuli? I have a fine batch just in from Venice – the most superb blue you could ask for. More oil of violets?'

'No!'

'Good. So how is Mistress Bowen?' It took Jude a moment to register the connection.

'In truth, Master Eastleigh, I haven't set eyes on Mistress Bowen, nor am I likely to. What I need is...'

'You haven't seen Mistress Bowen?' the apothecary interrupted, 'She hasn't taken a turn for the worse, has she?'

'No, no, not so far as I know. It's just that, well, I suppose I can tell you, it won't remain a secret for long. I'm not in Master Bowen's employ now, neither is my brother. In fact, Seb is the reason I'm...'

'You've left the stationer's? Why? I thought you and your brother were doing so well there. You're supposed to be copying a book for me and your brother's a marvel at illumination, so I've heard. I can't believe that boy, Kit Whatsisname, is by any means good enough to replace you. Why have you left?'

Jude was surprised to think the man had taken that much interest in what the Foxley brothers did.

'A difference of opinion, I suppose,' Jude told him, not wanting to tell the whole story.

'What about my book? Who's making the copy now?'

Jude shrugged. It didn't matter to him. It wasn't his business any longer. Why should he care?

'But my brother...'

'What of him? Is he going to make my copy?'

'No. He has a chill, I believe, like last time.'

'What? You left Master Bowen's employ for a chill? I don't understand. So who will copy my book? 'Tis most important. Urgent.'

'I only came here because my brother has a chill, not to discuss what Bowen is going to do about your book. Sorry.' The apology was added as a half-hearted afterthought.

'I see.' The apothecary sounded annoyed, wringing his capable hands in agitation.

41

Jude had a sudden flash of inspiration.

'Look, if you don't think either Bowen or the apprentice will make a good enough job of it, get the book back and I'll do it for you as a private commission, just between ourselves.'

'You will?' Somewhat relieved but still uncertain, Eastleigh was hesitating. 'B-but Mistress Bowen... I mean *Master* Bowen... he will lose money?'

Jude could not see any problem in that. If Bowen's workshop couldn't produce goods of the standard required by the customer, that was too bad. The customer had every right to go elsewhere. He could only suppose Eastleigh was considering the effect this might have on his long friendship with Bowen, but friendship and business were never happy bed-fellows, in Jude's opinion. Best to keep them separate. Whatever was decided, there were more immediate requirements.

'About my brother, he needs some of that medication you made up for him last time. It worked well then.' Jude was running low on patience. He had not planned to leave Seb alone so long.

'I'll look it up in my book. I make a note of every customer's prescriptions for just such an eventuality as this.' The apothecary disappeared, back into the darkness of his still-room, reappearing with a well-used volume. Setting it down with a thud on the counter, he leafed through its pages, stained with the ingredients of past medications. 'Ah! Here we are: "Sebastian Foxley... a compress, a mustard and camphor poultice, a liquorice and henbane electuary. Aye, that's the one. 'Tis a fact, your brother is a good customer of mine.'

'Nothing against you, master, but we both wish it were not the case,' Jude said with sincerity.

'I dare say.' The apothecary was measuring out ingredients carefully. 'Normally, my wretched apprentice would be doing this, if he wasn't taking forever on an errand for me. There.' Master Eastleigh held out a small earthenware bottle, stoppered with a greased linen plug. 'A spoonful every three hours, as St Martin's bells chime the offices. If he's no better by the morrow, send for me and I'll conjure his horoscope, bleed him, if necessary. That'll be a groat.'

'How much? But that's far more than I paid before,' Jude queried, horrified to think he would be parting with such a large proportion of his limited resources of coin. The apothecary shrugged.

'Piracy on the high seas has put up the price of so many of my ingredients that come from far-off lands. Liquorice alone has trebled in value over the winter and this cold April, with no hint of spring, has brought on coughs and chest complaints in so many folk, half my customers require the stuff and I only buy in the best quality liquorice, of course.'

'Of course,' Jude echoed dubiously, handing over the money and taking his purchase.

'Call again soon,' the apothecary sang out as Jude left the shop.

'I bloody hope not. We can't afford it.'

The Foxley brothers' rooms

THAT EVENING, as Seb slept, swathed in blankets, Jude sat by the dying embers of the fire, wondering how he could make money. He was about to put another log on the fire but stopped, realising fuel was now a luxury he couldn't waste.

Again, he tipped their savings onto the board but, no matter how many times he counted the coins, they didn't increase in either value or number. He sighed heavily. In a week they'd be destitute, once the rent was paid. Sooner if Seb required Master Eastleigh's continuing services. The more he thought about it, the more certain he became that they had to accept Lord Richard's commission. Seb *must* agree to paint the triptych. But Seb said he had no idea how to adapt his skills to achieve such a piece.

And then their terrible argument... the dreadful names he'd called his little brother, the fearful things he'd said, aye, and done... All that... but his vicious temper had solved nothing. Why was he burdened with such a useless brother, weighing him down, overloaded like a jagger's horse? It wasn't fair. And now this. This was Seb's fault. He could still have been working for Bowen, but no. He'd walked out. He was an imbecile – a bloody costly one, too.

Jude moved the coins around the table. This pile for rent, that for food, this for fuel, that for tithes... this for more medicine, if Seb had need. The rent wasn't due until the end of next week, and if he went without dinner for a day or two... Aye, perhaps there was just enough money for him to carry out his plan.

CHAPTER FIVE

Thursday, the twenty-seventh day of April
The apothecary's shop

NEXT MORNING, having fended off Dame Ellen Langton's questions as to why he looked to have been from his bed all night, and why he hadn't gone to work, Jude fed Seb some warm bread sops in milk, gave him his medication as St Martin's chimed for the office of Terce, and told him he had to go out. Seb nodded vaguely and went back to sleep, exhausted with the effort of breaking his fast.

Jude returned to Ivy Lane, hoping to catch Gilbert Eastleigh at his shop before he left to visit his wealthier patients, those who could afford to have him attend them at home. He was in luck. Both the apothecary-surgeon and his apprentice were still there.

'Master Foxley, good day to you. Is your brother in further need of my attentions?' the apothecary asked. Jude shook his head, wondering if the man asked such a question so merrily because the affirmative would mean more money in his coffers, or was he just insensitive? Perhaps he was simply a very happy fellow who could not be other than joyful in his work, but he doubted it.

'No, my brother is improving, I believe... thank you for asking. I came about that other matter. Your book. The one concerning the limner's art. I wondered if you might have decided whether... if... you still want me to copy it for you?' Jude's words spilled out in a nervous rush. 'Unless you prefer to let Bowen's workshop do as best they may...'

When he first suggested it yesterday, it had been on the spur of the moment. Since then, Jude had realised the book might serve a double purpose. Firstly, if he did the copy, he would earn money, enough to keep them fed for another week or two, at least. Secondly – the idea had come to him in the middle of the night – Seb could learn from the book how to paint the triptych. Then he would have no excuse and could take on Lord Richard's commission after all. But Jude was also aware, now he'd thought it through, of the trouble it might cause with the guild, stealing his former employer's commission.

Just then, a fat woman came in with a squalling brat in tow and a toddler in her arms. Gilbert Eastleigh greeted her, waving Jude aside since he hadn't come as a customer to spend money.

'I'll think about it,' he said. Jude left the shop, sighing.

• •

He hurried home, anxious for Seb, left untended so long, passing a cook shop from which emanated enticing smells that made his mouth water and his belly rumble. But no, today he would have to fast at dinnertime. At work, Meg Bowen always fed them – when she wasn't hiding away with her bruises – dinner was part of their wages. Dame Ellen supplied breakfast and supper to her tenants, for a consideration, naturally. 'Nowt for nowt' was ever the way of things.

The Tower of London

FRANCIS LOVELL stood, stewing, in the ante-chamber, waiting upon the king's pleasure. And everyone knew King Edward's pleasure was to rise late. Having spent the night cavorting with one mistress or another, the monarch needed his rest. So then, Francis wondered, why had he been summoned from his bed in Ivy Lane before daybreak by a mounted messenger who hid his royal livery beneath a plain frieze cloak, only to be kept on tenterhooks for hours? No one had offered wine or even a seat. He pulled at his clothes – miniver-trimmed damask in a tawny colour that showed off his olive skin and jet-black hair and eyes: the looks of an Italian ancestor overriding the English – wondering if he had done right in wearing his finest. He feared sweat stains would ruin it in this stifling, windowless room.

But he wasn't alone. Lawyers, priests and petitioners cluttered up the space between the outer door and the inner, where guards stood ready to turf undesirables from the king's bedchamber. A fellow strummed a lute whilst he waited – no musician he. Such discordant caterwauling put Francis in a worse humour yet. Perhaps there had been some mistake, the messenger in error as to whom he should summon to the Tower.

A distant cacophony of roaring announced feeding time for the lions in the royal menagerie. Aye, it must be close to dinnertime by now, Francis's belly reminded him. There had been no time to break his fast earlier.

The bedchamber door opened and a liveried servant announced in ringing tones: 'Francis, Lord Lovell of Tichmarsh, Deincourt, Holland and Grey, step forward, please!' At last. Francis pushed through the crowd, straightening his doublet and plumed hat as he went.

• •

Once in the bedchamber, he bent the knee, removed his hat and bowed his head, watching the king from under heavy brows, awaiting the order to arise. King Edward, resplendent in a voluminous crimson silk gown that fell to his knees, disguising the increasing royal girth, was choosing the rings he would wear from an entire treasury of gemstones, sliding on a hefty sapphire and a broad gold band over white kid gloves.

'Move your skinny backside, Will,' King Edward said, ignoring Francis still on his knees. 'Things to do, things to do, my good fellow. Now come along. Our friend is waiting.' The king turned, accepting his tasselled baldrick from a squire and slipping it over his head. Having settled it in place, he allowed the squire to hang his sword and scabbard from it. 'Get up, Francis. Stop crouching there like a whipped hound, won't you.'

'Aye, y-your grace.'

'Ready, Will?'

William, Lord Hastings, was Edward's closest friend and Lord Chamberlain. He must be all of twenty years older than the king, his unfashionable short hair and neat beard striped like a badger's. A veteran of many battles and conqueror of even more ladies' bedchambers, if rumour ran true. Francis doubted it. What woman in her right mind would want to share her bed with a man so far past his prime, who stank of liniment and liquorice linctus?

Wherever they were bound, the monarch led the way, Francis and Will Hastings having to skip along to keep up with the king's massive strides. Will was soon puffing and coughing, trying to hurry. Francis, young and fit as he was, soon had a stitch in his side as they hastened across Tower Green, the king's thinning red-gold hair fluttering in the breeze off the Thames like pennons of war.

On the green sward, dust-covered masons were chiselling away at lumps of sandstone, but these were not intended for any construction.

46

The misshapen stones were being fashioned into perfect spheres: gun-stones, harbingers of destruction when fired from the Tower's arsenal of new cannon.

'How much are these things costing me, Will?' the king asked.

'The masons earn sixpence a day, my lord, and make two gun-stones in that time, plus the cost of the stone itself. I would reckon about threepence ha'penny each.'

'Just to blow the bloody French to pieces? Are they – the French, I mean – worth the cost?' he asked, laughing. Francis and Hastings made out to laugh also, as etiquette required.

They passed by some rickety sheds where the sound of clanking and thudding beat a regular rhythm: the Royal Mint. Francis recalled that Hastings was Master of the Mint, but it was merely a sinecure. The man would not be required to sully his hands with such hot, dirty labours as those sweating over the coin-stamping hammers and silver working. But he did carry a ring of sizeable, ancient-looking keys. There were guards posted at the door to the Devereaux Tower, a stout, stone construction with a heavy oaken door that looked to have been reinforced with iron straps quite recently.

Hastings, still wheezing, inserted a rusty key into a lock the size of a man's hand. It turned easily, well-greased. The chamberlain stood aside so the king could enter. Francis followed. Against the stone walls were piled great heaps of dull grey metal. Some of it was in ingots, neatly stacked. But much of it looked to have been used before, twisted into odd shapes and dumped there.

'You know what this is?' the king demanded, waving his hand at the gloomy heaps.

'Metal, my lord?' Francis suggested.

'It's lead. And why would I need so much of it, eh?'

'I-I don't know, sire.' Francis felt a fool. 'For the roof?'

'You think I'm a bloody plumber?' Edward's face was grim. Oh, Christ, this was going badly. Hastings was tut-tutting under his breath, by the door.

'No, sire. Of course not. I thought...'

Edward came close, scowling down at Francis.

'Lead is not what I need, is it? What I bloody need is that blasted apothecary to transmute this pile of scrap into gold. Gold! You hear me?' Francis nodded, mute. 'And when is that going to happen, eh? Tell me.'

'I don't know, your grace. Eastleigh said the moon was in the wrong aspect and he had to wait.'

'The moon? What's that got to do with it? Well?'

'I don't know,' Francis repeated. This was awful. Sweat was trickling down inside his shirt. He swallowed down his rising nausea.

'Then go and bloody find out! What am I paying you for? Tell that devil-damned apothecary to get on with it. I've got men to indenture for the war with France and what am I supposed to pay them with, eh? Tell him I'm tired of waiting. I want results, not excuses.'

• •

Francis tried to be dignified but it was all he could do not to flee from the king's presence. He was trembling as he collected his horse from the gatehouse stable and made for the nearest inn for a cup of best Burgundy wine to settle his stomach and his nerves.

The Foxley brothers' rooms

I WAS CURLED in bed when Jude's noisy arrival roused me.

'Jude? I was wondering where you were,' I called, rubbing sleep from my eyes.

'Missed me, did you? I doubt it, unless you needed the piss-pot?'

'Well, now you mention it,' I struggled to sit up. I felt weak but better than before. My throat still pained me but I wouldn't mention it.

'That's all I'm good for, I suppose.'

'Where have you been?'

Jude went to the window, pushing the shutter wide to empty the piss-pot in the street.

'Gardy loo!' he shouted, up-ending the pot. 'Eastleigh's... to see if I could get some work to do.'

'With the apothecary? He has an apprentice already.'

'Don't be stupid. He wants that book of his copied – you recall, the one I was working on yesterday, about the limner's art, before everything went amiss – but he fears it won't be done accurately if left to that idle lout Kit Philpot, and he's right, it won't be. So I offered to do it privately for him; earn some money to tide us over.'

'Has he agreed?' Jude ignored my question.

'Here, 'tis almost Sext, time for your next medication.' He poured the liquorice-tasting medicine into a spoon and I swallowed it, obediently. 'Now go back to sleep; I have to go out again.'

'But Jude...' My protest went unheard. Jude was gone already.

• •

I felt cold, thirsty too, and eased out of bed. The ale jug was drunk dry and the fire in the room we grandly called the parlour was hardly a glimmer. Bare-foot, swathed in blankets, using the door jamb as a prop, I eased myself down onto hands and knees – never a simple matter for me. In church I always prayed standing up, leaning on my staff. I lifted the last log from the basket, one-handed as I held onto a stool with the other, and went to put it on the fire, but it was heavy and slipped from my grasp. It fell into the fire, sending up a cloud of wood ash afore it rolled down, out of the hearth, towards my knees, bringing with it a hot ember that immediately set the floor rushes smouldering. I cursed but didn't panic. I couldn't reach the water bucket by the door, so I spat into the palm of my hand and beat out the tiny flickers of flame, gritting my teeth and wincing as they burned me. Thank God, I had the good sense to use my left hand, but it would take two good hands to pull myself up, so now I would have to crawl, crouched like an ageing dog before the hearth.

I hadn't even managed to get the log on the fire. It had rolled away, under the board, out of reach and down here, on the floor, the draught from under the door stirred the charred rushes around me with its chilling breath. I pulled the tangle of blankets close and huddled into them as best I could with only one hand. The other was burned and painful but, even so, the medication Jude had administered was strong enough to make me sleep and there I lay, until I should be found.

• •

It was Emily who discovered me.

'Master Seb!' she cried, setting down a pile of clean linen and a platter of oatcakes on the table before rushing to my side. 'Did you fall?' I stirred at her touch.

'No, not really. Could you help me up, please?' Emily was strong, her work-roughened hands firm but gentle. She looked shocked at the state of me as she eased me onto a stool and tucked the blankets around me.

'The fire's gone out. Where's your brother? I thought he stayed away from work today to care for you. A fine piece of caring this is, leaving you lying on the floor! I'll give that Master Jude a few choice words when he gets back!'

'It wasn't his fault.' I defended my brother. 'He has other concerns that weigh on his mind, apart from me.'

'Such as wondering which cook shop to go to, to get his dinner, I suppose, or which pretty wench to make eyes at next?' Emily was on her knees, rekindling the fire. 'Is there no wood?'

'A log has rolled under the table but that's the last one.'

'So he hasn't bothered to buy more fuel either. Have you had any dinner today, Seb?' I thought before giving any answer, not wanting her to find yet another reason to think badly of Jude but, truthfully, I was hungry.

'Not yet, but I'm certain Jude has gone out to buy us something.'

'But it's near three of the clock. The time for dinner was five hours since!'

'So late as that?' I hadn't realised.

'No matter,' Emily said, brightening. 'Dame Ellen and I baked you some oatcakes. Here, have one.' She gave me an oatcake from the platter and took one herself. They were excellent.

Realising I was in my nether clouts beneath the blankets – hardly fitting dress to keep company with a respectable maid – I attempted to pull the blankets closer about me. I forgot my blisters and yelped as the rough wool broke the damaged skin.

'Poor Seb. Are you hurt? What's amiss with your hand?'

'Don't!' I spoke sharply. I didn't want her pity or sympathy. She took my hand in hers but I snatched it away. 'Leave it. Just let me be, can't you?' But she had seen my palm.

'Those burns need tending, else they'll fester.'

'It'll be well enough.'

'Don't you care if you lose your hand? I can do it for you. Let me bathe the blisters, put some salve on them.'

'I said no. And there's an end to it.'

A strand of hair had escaped her kerchief, golden and amber and russet. Lustrous hues. I would remember them in my work. She tucked it back out of sight with a quick gesture.

I allowed my gaze to linger upon her but she glanced away. Of course she did. What right-minded wench would want the likes of me looking at her? So I took another oatcake, studied that instead. But I had seen her eyes were the colour of sun-washed sapphires with flecks of dancing light. I swallowed down the tightness in my throat that had nought to do with yesterday's bruises, and bit into the cake.

'Oh, I'm in such a tizzy, Master Seb,' Emily said, turning to face me suddenly, dancing about, swinging her skirts. 'You recall Monday next is Mayday?'

'Mm.' I swallowed. The oatcakes were very good.

'You must know, I told you, they chose me as May Queen and my new gown is near finished. Dame Ellen chose the cloth herself and 'tis such a fine hue – I won't tell you what it is, so it will be a surprise when you see it. You'll love the colour. And I have a new girdle too, and...' She stood still for a moment. 'You will come to the revels, won't you, master? You will see me?'

'What would I be doing at such frivolities?' Her bleating on about new gowns and girdles was wearisome indeed.

'But you will come, please? Oh, please, Master Seb, say you will.'

● ●

Fortunately that errant brother of mine saved me from such matters, returning in a whirlwind of raindrops that ushered him through the door. He came in, cursing the sudden change in the weather that had soaked him in his dash from the cook shop, where he'd wheedled a stale pie from the serving wench with his smile and sweet words.

'Mutton and onion pie!' Jude announced, dripping on the threshold. 'Ah, so you're up and about, little brother! I'm pleased to see it and oatcakes too. We'll have a feast, the three of us,' he declared, sidling meaningfully up to Emily, who edged around him to stand on my other side. He gave her a look of puzzlement. Wenches rarely drew away from him, but his clothes were wet, so that no doubt explained it. He shrugged it off, along with his sodden cloak, seating himself on a stool and taking up an old knife to divide the pie. 'Here, Seb, get your teeth into that.' He set a generous portion before me. 'You must be half-starved by now.'

'Thank you,' I said, though I wasn't so hungry any longer. I leaned towards him: 'There's blood on your lip,' I whispered. Jude, startled, took the hint and wiped his mouth surreptitiously on his sleeve.

When the pie was devoured, mostly by Jude, we set about the remaining oatcakes. But Emily took her leave.

'I have errands to run for Dame Ellen and supper to cook,' she said. 'And as for you, Master Jude, you should be ashamed of yourself, leaving your brother, helpless, trying to fend for himself.' Then she darted out.

He threw a napkin at her parting back, calling out:

'My brother is a man grown, not a babe!' He turned his attention to another oatcake. 'Interfering wench! Why can't she keep her long nose out of things that don't concern her, eh?'

'I believe she was trying to be helpful, but I hate the way she pities me.' I decided I wouldn't tell Jude about the mishap from which Emily had rescued me, though my blistered palm would prevent me forgetting it for a while. 'I take it Mistress Bowen is recovered from her bruises then,' I said, changing the subject.

'What?' Jude spluttered crumbs of the oatcake he was scoffing and frowned.

'She bit your lip again, didn't she?'

He grinned, sheepishly.

'Love of God, Jude, you don't even work there any more. What excuse could you give for being there, if Master Bowen caught you?'

'He didn't but if he had, I had good reason to being there, to claim our pay that's owed and collect our tools and stuff.'

'And did you?'

'Did I what?'

'Collect our money and equipment.'

'No. The workshop was locked. I couldn't get in, and there was no sign of ol' Bowen. I expect he was in the Panyer Inn, drowning his sorrows at losing you.'

'So you thought you'd visit Meg Bowen one last time, just to say a proper farewell, and she bit you, giving you another scar to remember her by.'

'There's no need to take that tone with me, *little* brother.' Jude emphasised the word. 'Just because you can't...' He stopped himself but already he'd said too much. He must have seen the anger and hurt flash in my eyes, sharp as a sword's edge. 'Forgive me. I didn't mean that.' He reached out a hand and covered mine, resting on the board. I didn't pull away. 'Sorry.'

'Forget it,' I said with forced cheerfulness, deciding I would eat the last oatcake.

· ·

It was dark but we lit only a single cheap tallow candle. It gave off a rancid smell with its smoky yellow light. With the logs all gone, we sat at the board, wrapped in every item of clothing and all the blankets we possessed, lingering over the bacon pottage Emily had brought us for supper.

'We have no choice now, you know that.' Jude pushed his empty bowl aside since not a single morsel more could be scraped from it. 'I know you can do it, Seb. Everyone says you're a genius with pen and brush. How different can it be, painting on wood? By the time 'tis primed and prepared, it'll be like working on parchment.'

'But bigger. Much bigger.'

'Oh, for pity's sake, Seb. Don't be so pathetic. You must have faith in yourself, as I have, as Lord Richard has... Our livelihoods depend on *you* now.' Jude's wheedling tone changed suddenly, his anger welling up. 'You bloody owe me that much!'

I shivered. It was true. Jude now had to depend on *me*. It was a dreadful responsibility, one I did not feel I could take on. Yet I didn't dare let him down. All my life Jude had watched out for me. Now it was my turn to repay the debt. I would have to try, though my blood ran chill at the prospect. But the remembrance of his fingers closing like a vice around my throat was equally terrifying, so I nodded, my hands straying to the bruises on my neck.

'Very well, Jude,' I said quietly. 'I don't know how, but I'll do it.'

CHAPTER SIX

Friday the twenty-eighth of April
The Foxley brothers' rooms

L AST EVE, my brother and I had sat at the table as the remaining log burned down to nothing, making notes, listing the things we would need to make Lord Richard's triptych, until Jude's fingers were too numbed with cold to write any more.

Now it was morning, chilly and damp as ever in our tiny parlour. We had no fire, only a cold, grey hearth. It was dispiriting indeed. But Jude had his list of items required. We broke our fast on the remainder of Dame Ellen's bread from yesterday's supper and drank the last of the ale.

'Now or never, little brother,' Jude said, flinging his still-damp cloak around his shoulders. 'Are you in agreement with me on this?'

I nodded. What alternative did I have?

'Aye, that I am. Take the money... do what you can for the best.' I handed the coin bag to Jude. It was appalling lightweight now, so few coins left. 'At least I have no need of any more of Gilbert Eastleigh's potions now,' I said, forcing a smile. Jude smiled back and then, on an impulse, embraced me.

Cheapside

O UT IN West Cheap, a gang of children were playing games, jumping the puddles from another night of rain, laughing, seeming not to notice the keen wind that tugged at shawls and caps, turning their bare feet blue with cold. Jude called out to them. Two were Goodwife Marlow's youngest girls – better natured than their idle lout of a brother. The lads came from all along the street and further afield, grubby-faced urchins all.

'Where's yer tame cripple, today?' one shouted, doing a wicked imitation of Seb's shuffling gait and bent back. 'Where's yer three-legged man, eh? Done away wi' him, have yer?'

Jude crossed the road in two strides, grabbed the youngster viciously by the ear and, without a word, dragged him into St Michael le Querne's church close by. They were met, just inside the door, by old Father Thomas, who wheezed a greeting.

'Good father,' Jude said without preamble. 'I have a sinner here for you, ready to confess!' He shoved the urchin forward so he fell to the floor. 'Go on, you little turd, tell Father Thomas what you did!'

'I didn't do nuffin.' The lad cowered at the priest's feet.

'You want I should beat a confession out of you?' Jude responded savagely, raising a threatening hand. The priest gestured to hold him back from any act of violence.

'What did you do this time, young Jack Tabor?' Father Thomas asked, helping the lad up. 'Thieving again, was it?'

'No, I never. On'y asked how his bruvver was, is all. The cripple,' he added maliciously. Before the priest could prevent it, Jude's hand caught the youngster a vicious swipe across the side of his nit-infested head.

'You need a bloody good hiding, not shriving!' Jude told him, calmer now that he had vented his anger a little with that blow. 'I'll have words with your father on this matter!'

'Ain't got one!'

'Your mother, then.'

'Ain't got one o' them, neever.'

'He's orphaned,' Father Thomas explained. 'Lives with his uncle, the cooper at the sign of the Lamb, and precious little love and care he gets there, I'm afraid.'

'I see,' said Jude, relenting just a little. 'Well, you give him a good talking-to, father, about not making mock of the afflicted, else next time I'll take the birch to him myself.'

Bowen's workshop

STILL NOT in the best of humours, Jude went to Paternoster Row, intending to collect the wages he was owed and the equipment that belonged to him and Seb. The door was not locked this time, so he simply walked in, bold as you please, despite not knowing what to expect.

Kit Philpot was lounging, idle as usual, at *his* old desk, ink pots and pens strewn about, all untidy. It didn't look as though any work was being done. Gilbert Eastleigh's precious book was closed upon its stand, the folio on the desk unmarked except for two misruled lines, sloping at an angle.

'You call that a morning's work, you lazy devil?' Jude said, disgustedly, looking over the apprentice's shoulder.

'What do you care, Foxley? You're not my master,' came the careless reply.

'True,' Jude conceded, 'And I thank God for it. Where's Master Bowen?

'Around somewhere, maybe he's shafting his wife, seeing she's short a prick or two these days,' Kit said, instinctively avoiding the blow he knew was coming.

Just then Nessie, Meg's maid servant, came in with a jug of ale, intended for Kit and his master.

'Master Jude!' she cried, setting down the jug in the midst of Kit's "work" so she could run to Jude and fling her arms around him. 'I knew you'd come back, didn't I, Master Jude? I'm so happy!' Jude tried to disentangle himself from her arms, but she clung with the tenacity of a limpet.

'Hold off, Nessie.' He pulled on one arm that had a vice-like grip around his neck, before she could choke him. 'Let me go, you silly wench.'

'Nessie!' It was Mistress Meg Bowen herself, standing in the doorway from the yard, stern and implacable as the Grim Reaper himself. 'Get back to work, girl. There are onions to chop and worts to wash for dinner, so see to it.'

Reluctantly, Nessie released Jude and slunk away like a whipped cur, only to turn in the doorway to give him a wave and her gap-toothed, fatuous smile, before skipping back to the kitchen. Mistress Bowen turned to Kit.

'As for you, master needs charcoal. Here.' She gave him a coin from her purse, 'Go and get it.'

'What for?' Kit demanded.

'You heard your mistress, you insolent bugger!' Jude shouted but Kit didn't move.

'What's the charcoal for?' he repeated, feigning weariness with the whole matter, as though he'd asked a dozen times. 'For the brazier or for drawing with? Makes a difference what I buy.'

Seeing her error, Meg told him tersely:

'For the brazier, you fool, what else would it be?'

Kit glared at her, then collected his cloak. Money in hand, he made towards the street door, pausing a moment to mouth at Jude:

'Don't do anything I wouldn't do to the panting bitch!' Then he was gone, leaving Jude alone with Meg.

• •

Suddenly, soft as butter on a summer day, Meg melted into her lover's arms.

'I've missed you, Jude.'

In answer, he pulled her closer, running his free hand over her breasts, firm and thrusting beneath the constraints of her tight-laced bodice.

'God knows, I need you, woman,' he whispered, nuzzling into the silky white softness of her neck.

'So I see.' Her hands worked lower. She leaned against the wall and looked up at the roof. A monstrous cobweb hung from the rafter above. That would have to go. Meanwhile, Jude groaned, pushing hard against her, fumbling his way through heavy skirts and linen shift. If he dares rip my new linen, she thought. 'No... not here,' she said aloud.

'Where then?' His hand found hot moist flesh at last and he gasped with the pleasure of it, searching fingers clumsy in their eagerness. 'I want you, Meg.'

'My bedchamber.'

'Kit and Nessie?' He whimpered with need.

'I don't care, Jude.'

'Then neither do I.' He swept her up in his arms, running across the yard and up the stairs to her chamber. He saw Nessie watching from the kitchen door, but, as he said, he didn't care.

• •

A short while later, satisfied and in a better humour, Jude came back down to the kitchen. Nessie was still there, snivelling over the onions.

'Your mistress swooned,' he lied, knowing the girl was stupid enough to believe him, 'I had to loosen her clothes but she's quite recovered now. Go up and help her dress, there's a good lass.'

'Aye, Master Jude. I s'pose 'tis 'cos mistress is in the family way then?'

Jude looked aghast.

'Whatever makes you think that, Nessie?'

'Don't know.' Nessie shrugged her skinny shoulders. 'Mistress's friend, Mary, said t'other day: "Mistress felt poorly 'cos she's in the family way", though which way that is, she didn't say, master.'

Jude laughed, realising Nessie had no idea what the words meant, thank God, though she'd given him a nasty moment there. The possibility had never so much as crossed his reckless mind, until now. It made him uneasy. Suppose Meg did get with child? She had been wed for four years with nothing to show for it, yet Bowen had two children by his first wife. Could it happen? Oh well, no use worrying.

Thoughtful, he went back to the workshop to await Matthew Bowen's return. In the meantime, he searched around for his and Seb's tools, which they had had to leave behind two days before. His temper began to rise again when he could find no sign of them. However, he found Gilbert Eastleigh's book and, on a whim, decided he would make the apothecary's decision for him. He tucked it inside his jerkin. He would chance it, make a perfect copy of it then present it as a finished piece. If the apothecary paid him for it, well and good. If not, well only his time and labour had been wasted. Besides, *The mystery and craft of limning* could be useful for Seb – with this instructive book his little brother would have no excuse for not getting on with the duke's commission.

'Looking for something?' Matthew Bowen snarled, catching Jude on his knees, about to start rummaging through a storage chest.

'Only for what's rightfully mine and my brother's.' Jude was shocked at the man's unheralded arrival.

'I didn't hear you ask my permission to go through the chest.' Bowen slammed the coffer lid shut, barely missing the younger man's fingers. Jude's eyes narrowed dangerously as he stood up, glaring at his recent employer.

'I want what's ours and our wages owing.'

'I don't have them, so you'd best leave now, before I summon the sergeant of the watch.' Bowen showed Jude the door, just as Kit returned to view the spectacle of master and journeyman sizing up to each other.

'You must have them. My penknife with the fox's head... We need our tools...' Jude protested as Bowen tried to push him out into the street.

'No you don't! I've seen to that. Your names are to be struck from the list of stationers and limners at the guild meeting next week. You're finished, Foxley. You and your crouchback rat.'

Stunned by such venomous words, Jude was shoved over the threshold, so he stumbled and fell on his backside in the muddy street beyond, Bowen's scathing litany following on behind. 'You and that wretched crippled brother of yours, you're both finished! Finished! You hear me?'

'You can't do that. I demand you hand over our belongings, you bastard!'

'I've sold your stuff and got a fair price for it too, so don't come back... ever!' The door slammed shut in Jude's face.

'I'll kill you for this, Bowen!' Jude was shaking his fist in frustration. 'When I get my hands on that fat neck of yours, God help me, I swear, I'll choke every last filthy living breath out of you.' He got up, awkward in his anger, backing away from the door. 'You'll regret it. I'll get my own back – I promise you that!'

• •

Rescuing his sodden cloak from a puddle and brushing down his mud-soaked hose, Jude tried to compose himself, to rein in his temper. He breathed deeply and finally took the time to look about him, realising the whole neighbourhood had witnessed his humiliation, Kit Philpot among them, a sneer of triumph disfiguring his youthful face.

'What are you all gawping at?' Jude demanded ferociously of the crowd gathered around, kicking out at a mangy dog that dared to come close enough to sniff his boot. 'Bugger off, all of you, idle bastards and lazy bitches.' He was no longer shouting. His curses were all for his ears alone now. 'Bastard. Bastard,' he muttered as the crowd dispersed now the spectacle was over, until only one remained: Jack Tabor, the filthy urchin.

'Got yer cap, master,' the lad said, warily holding out Jude's bedraggled headgear. Jude took it.

'What do you want?'

'Nuffin.'

'The likes of you always wants something. If it's coin, you can bugger off – I haven't got enough to buy dinner, never mind give to bloody charity cases.'

'I don't take charity,' the lad said with a pride at odds with his wretched appearance. 'I works fer me keep.'

'Doing what, exactly?'

'Anyfin', whatever needs doing. An... and I'm sorry.'

'Sorry? What about?'

'Earlier. Calling yer bruvver a cripple. Farver Thomas said I was t'say sorry to yer. I didn't mean nuffin by it... honest I didn't, master.'

'The day you're honest, Jack Tabor, I'll eat my hat,' Jude told him, his humour somewhat restored by the lad's apology, 'But then again, perhaps not.' He looked sadly at the cap the lad held out to him. It had once been of blue woollen felt with a proud feather. Now it was a muddy, shapeless rag, the feather broken. 'Come on, lad. I'm in need of a decent dinner.'

The Foxley brothers' rooms

'HERE! WILL these do?' Jude asked me, laying three boards of timber on the table. I ran my hand along them, feeling the wood's fine grain, its excellent quality.

'Perfect. Where did you get them? There wasn't money enough for this stuff in our purse.'

My brother did not answer but took from his scrip a quire of good paper, a collection of little pots, pumice stone, a bundle of quills and brushes and a selection of silver points for drawing.

'But these aren't mine... the ones I left at Bowen's workshop,' I said.

Lastly, Jude took out a large pasty, wrapped in a cloth.

'Dinner!' he declared with a flourish.

'But Jude, we can't afford all this!'

'Just eat your dinner, Seb, then we can get on with preparing the wood for painting. We've only got until tomorrow to learn how it's done, afore we have to tell Lord Richard we'll do his triptych for him.' I looked at him doubtfully. 'Come on. Eat up,' Jude chivvied me.

'But where's my stuff?'

'Bowen sold it, the bastard. But I've got you everything you need, new.'

'How? You haven't run us over the ears in debt, have you?' I wondered whether the beautiful, steaming pasty before me had been got on tick.

'Not a debt in sight, little brother. The brushes and chalk and gum arabic, all that I purchased at Eastleigh's place. No pigments, unfortunately, he'd sold out, but we can buy those later, when we're ready to use them.'

'And these pieces of fine oak? You never bought those from Gilbert Eastleigh nor the paper, nor our dinner, come to that.'

'Well, no,' Jude grinned, 'I admit, I had a little assistance in acquiring them.' He went to the door and called to someone outside. 'Seb, I want you to meet our new apprentice... unpaid, of course. This is Jack Tabor.' He ushered in a dirty, bare-foot urchin to stand before me. 'By the way, Jack owes you a grovelling apology. Go on,' he told the lad sternly, 'Apologise to my brother, as you promised you would.'

Jack took a deep breath.

'Master Seb, I'm truly very sorry for what I called yer and it won't never 'appen again, not ever. There! I said it.'

'Mm. Not very convincing but I suppose it'll have to suffice,' Jude said.

'What is he sorry for, exactly?' I was mystified.

'Doesn't matter.'

'He's a thief. You do know that, don't you, Jude?' I said, eyeing the boy suspiciously, 'I've seen him filching stuff from the cook shop across the way. Oh, no, Jude! That's how you got this pasty, isn't it? And the timber! Where did that come from?'

'Stephen Appleyard can spare it, he has a backyard full of fine timber, seasoning away there. He won't miss a few boards.'

'Is this how you mean for us to live? By stealing? If Lord Richard comes to learn of this, he'll withdraw his commission immediately. You'll be arrested, Jude!'

'Don't worry, nobody saw us. Jack is a master of his art,' Jude laughed. 'I was watching for it and I still didn't see him take the pasty. And the way he went over Appleyard's back fence... like an eel he was.'

'Stop it!' I flung my stolen dinner into the fire. 'I won't be a party to this – this thievery!'

'And while we're on the subject of theft, I've brought this home for you to read and study.' Jude pulled the apothecary's book from inside his jerkin and shoved it on the board, under my nose. 'That should instruct you as to how to paint that bloody triptych.'

'Did you steal this too? Jude, I can't go on this way!'

'Then you best hurry along and accept the duke's offer and get us some money to live on, hadn't you?' Jude was plainly annoyed by my ingratitude over the filched pasty and bitter about everything. 'It's your fault we're penniless. You shouldn't have walked out on Bowen. He dismissed *me*, not you. You could have stayed. All you've done is get us struck off by the guild!'

'Struck off? I-I thought he would want to keep me on,' I said miserably, 'I thought, if I threatened to leave as well, he wouldn't dismiss you. I thought...'

'As I'm forever telling you, Seb. You think too bloody much! Just get the damned book read. Come on, Jack, we've got more work to do. Wood for the fire.' With that parting remark and a large wedge of pasty in his grip, he strode out the door, leaving me in a state of fear, dreading what he might be up to next.

Gilbert Eastleigh's apothecary's shop

'YOU DID what?' Gilbert Eastleigh's voice was a high pitched shriek of disbelief and horror. 'You stupid fool! How could you do this to me, Thomas Bowen?'

'I-I'm so sorry, master.' The apprentice cowered on the floor of the still-room before his master's wrath as the birch rod came down yet again, stinging across the back of his bare neck. 'I thought the notes'd be safe inside the book,' Tom whimpered as the next stroke cut his shoulders. 'Please, no more, master, no more. Please don't hit me again. I'll get them back, I swear.'

'Indeed you will. I've a mind to terminate your indentures right now, you useless worm. What good are you to me? Giving away my precious notes. I should flay your worthless hide for that, skin you alive.' The rod came down one last time, cracking across the lad's skull so he sprawled out, his arms clutched defensively over his head. 'See if that knocks some sense into that empty pate of yours!' The little apothecary threw the birch aside. 'Get up. Clean yourself up then go to your father's workshop and get my book back. And make damned sure my notes are in it. If they're not...' he growled, leaving the sentence unfinished as words could not describe the consequences if the notes weren't there.

So much work... years of patient labour. Surely it couldn't all be lost by a single moment of unthinking action by that careless young fool? Surely not. Gilbert Eastleigh felt faint at the possibility and sunk wearily onto the seat at his desk. Beatings always tired his small frame.

Tom returned, his face freshly washed. A red weal glowered on his cheek, another on his neck. The rest did not show. He was a good looking lad otherwise, but now his expression would curdle milk.

'Wipe that surly look off your face and pour me some wine before you go.' The lad obeyed but his resentment could be smelled in the closed room, the stink of rebellion clung to his dark hair and blotched his shirt darkly, like a newly-acquired stain.

Bowen's workshop

IT WAS getting dark in Paternoster Row. Outside Bowen's workshop, Tom sat on the cold doorstep in the fading light, fighting his own silent battle. Sick with terror and despair, he didn't know whom he should fear most now. He had always been scared of his father's mighty fists. How could he march in and demand Master Eastleigh's book be returned? His father wouldn't stand for that, probably knock him senseless before he could explain. But he couldn't go back without the book and, if he lingered here much longer, the watch would get curious. Was there a more misused and miserable fifteen-year-old in the whole of London? He doubted it.

The door opened so suddenly Tom toppled backwards into the workshop.

'What the hell do you want?'

Taken unawares, Tom was slow to answer but he breathed a deep sigh of relief, seeing it was one of his own kind – the apprentice, Kit Philpot, not his father with those fists like sides of beef. He clambered to his feet, wincing as his shoulder hurt him, sending pain like a blunt blade sawing at his back. Looking round the workshop, he felt wistful, comparing its spaciousness to the hot, smelly dark hole in which he spent most of his days.

'N-nothing. I need to speak t-to my father.'

'Run away again, have you? He'll knock you into next week, if you have.'

Kit, his elder by a year, had no sympathy for him, that was plain. Tom wondered whether he should tell Kit what he wanted. It would save having to ask his father.

'Your father's down at the Panyer, drinking himself witless as usual,' Kit continued. 'If I were you, I'd get back to your master before he knows you're gone.'

'Master sent me. He knows where I am.'

Kit stood scowling at him, hands on hips, doubtful.

'He does... honestly. I'm not lying to you.'

'So? Why have you come at this time of night?'

'My master needs his book returned. Now.'

'What book?'

'The one he brought in for copying the other day. He needs to read up something urgently, unexpectedly.' Tom cast his eyes about, couldn't see the book. 'Where is it?

'How should I know? Your father puts things anywhere these days... can't find stuff half the time. The other day I found his shoe in the sand bin. God alone knows how it got there.' Kit laughed but quickly put his stern face back on – he was the senior apprentice of the two and it didn't do to make jests with those of lesser rank, even if he was, by right of birth, a son of the house.

To cover his error, Kit went over to the board where the stationer had left a flagon of ale. It was still near full, so he helped himself, carelessly sloshing the golden liquid into a cup. He turned back to Tom who watched, licking parched lips.

'Want some?'

Tom considered his reply, thinking the elder boy was most likely teasing him and would refuse him if he said "yes". He nodded.

Kit shrugged. 'Pour your own.'

• •

After his trials earlier, the ale slipped down Tom's dry throat like liquid amber. He emptied the cup in one draught and set it down, grinning like a lack-wit. It was strong stuff and went straight to his head. He poured another cupful and Kit joined him.

'Where's my master's book?'

'No idea.'

'Better look for it then.' Tom giggled to himself as he began searching about the workshop in haphazard fashion. 'Not in there.' He up-ended a bag of chalk powder that was used for whitening parchment, tipping it all over the floor, all over his shoes. 'Nope. Definitely not there.' He began flinging aside a ream of paper, sheet by sheet, laughing.

'What are we looking for?' Kit was into his third cup by now.

'Er, um, my master's book.'

'What's its title?'

'Don't know. Can't remember.'

'So how'll we know when we find it, eh, Tom?' Kit leaned heavily on Tom's injured shoulder so the younger lad jerked away with a cry. 'Wass up?'

'Master beat me,' Tom said, wiping tears from his eyes.

'Yeah? Bastard. I got beaten this morning – wanna see?' The two apprentices began comparing their bruises.

'Hey, Kit, that one on yer arse looks like a bleedin' goat.'

'Does it?' Kit did contortions in an effort to see this wonder on his own backside, but lost his balance and fell into the pile of chalk dust, knocking over a bottle of ink ready prepared for the morrow. Both lads burst out laughing. Tom pulled Kit to his feet, out of the mess. He watched the chalk turning from white to grey to black as it soaked up the ink, like the Devil gaining grip on a sinner's soul.

'Le's have mor'ale, eh?' Disappointment followed when the flagon proved empty.

'I know where ish kept,' Kit said.

'Wass in'ere?' Tom wasn't willing to give up the search for the precious book, even if he couldn't remember which one it was. The coffer contained pens and brushes, ruling sticks and pins and a penknife with a fox head carved into its bone handle. He also found jars and pots of pigment, familiar to him from Master Eastleigh's stock. Lapis lazuli... he threw the pot aside, heard it shatter behind him. Madder lake met the same fate. Kit came to join him, rummaging through the precious contents of the coffer. Yellow ochre. Azurite. Malachite. Tom sobered momentarily when he found the orpiment, remembering his master's dire warnings of its venomous nature.

'Wha's thish, Tom?'

'Orpiment.'

'Pretty, loo's like gold, sparkly.'

'It's deadly stuff, master says.'

Kit sprinkled a little on the floor amongst the rainbow of spilled pigments. It really did look like gold dust, glittering in the candlelight.

'Bes' put it back, Kit, don' wanna poison usselves, do we?'

'Nah, though there's some I wouldn' mind gettin' rid of.' They sniggered together.

'Who? My master?' Tom suggested hopefully.

'Nah, mine.'

'My father, yer mean?'

'Mm. Don' mind, do yer?'

Tom shook his head.

'Be glad to see the last o' him, the ol' braggart.'

● ●

A while later, with the workshop looking like a demon wind had ripped through it, the apprentices gave up their fruitless search. Kit fell asleep on the floor, propped against the coffer, hiccupping softly between snores, his mouth open.

Tom, was not so drunk now, his terror at having failed to retrieve his master's notes was enough to sober a cup-shotten Dutch mariner from the docks. There was nowhere left to look except for his father's private chamber or that of his whoring stepmother, and he had not the courage to search either. Besides, she was probably bedded down with one of her pox-ridden lovers and he dared not disturb them.

Instead, Tom crept back to Ivy Lane, fearing his father might be returning from the Panyer Inn at any moment, fearing the watch might catch him and think him a thief in the night, but more than anything, fearing what Master Eastleigh would do to him in the morning when he couldn't produce the notes.

Meg Bowen's chamber

H E SHINNED up the ivy-covered wall at the back of the house and climbed through the open window, but he was there to give as much as to steal. The musky scent of her perfume hung heavy in the air, a cloying cloud but one he relished as the source of all his clandestine delights. Meg sat on a stool by the curtained bed, combing her flaxen tresses.

'You shouldn't have come, Jude.' From her tone, he knew she had been expecting him all the same.

He wrapped his arms around her, tight as bindweed stems, and crushed her willing lips with his own, so hard in his eagerness that he tasted blood.

'I had to. I can't be without you, Meg. I need you.'

'My husband could come at any moment.'

'He won't. I saw him go into the Panyer. You know he'll be there until they throw him out. By then, he'll be too much in his cups to bother you.'

'But Kit is still here. If he sees you, the little sneak will tell.'

'He won't because I'll kill him if he does and he knows it. Besides, Kit has company too.'

'A wench? Surely not.'

'Well, I don't see why not. But no. Your stepson is with him, getting drunk in the workshop, from what I overheard.'

'Tom? What is that wretched creature doing here? Has he run away from Gilbert, yet again?'

'What does it matter? Everyone is too busy about their own affairs to bother us.' Jude moved to the bed, unlacing his hose and pulling back the curtains. The sheets were already rumpled and tossed about. 'Come, Meg, come to bed, please...'

'Oh, Jude...'

• •

Satiated for the moment, Jude was snoring on his stomach, mouth half open, one arm flung across Meg's breast, pinning her down. She stared up at the bed canopy. The candlelight showed it needed dusting. She would have Nessie do it tomorrow, first thing. Oh, aye, and they needed onions from the market, but not those mouldy things like last time. Jude snuffled, stirred, his fingers twitching her nipple. Even in sleep he had little else in mind, so it seemed. You've had your share, Meg thought, now I get what I want out of this affair.

She had planted the first seeds long ago when she found Jude a more than willing slave. Then it had seemed to be all to no purpose, when her wretched husband had dismissed him, but she never realised how deeply she'd ensnared the handsome fool. Now here he lay, oblivious. It was time.

Meg crept down to the kitchen, careful not to waken Nessie. Little fear of that. Nessie was snoring loudly from the palliasse that served as her bed in the alcove beside the chimney. Meg took two pewter cups from the shelf and poured a generous measure of good Gascon wine into each. The glass vial Gilbert had supplied provided an added ingredient for one cup – a sleeping potion. A single drop was all it took to ensure a lover didn't over-tax her, a trick she'd learned – among others – whilst married to her first husband. He had been like Jude in many ways – too many, poor devil. She'd been fond of Giles but no need to think on him now. Things to be done.

About to return upstairs with the tray, Meg drew back, hearing the voices of Kit and her no-good stepson, Tom. They were at the workshop door, across the yard and would see her if she left the kitchen to climb the stair.

'Don't touch tha' stuff!' she heard Tom saying, slurring his words. There was a deal of larking around in the yard, drunken sniggering and crashing about, knocking over a storage barrel. Meg feared it would waken the neighbours. Even Nessie mightn't sleep through that racket.

'Be glad to see the last o' him, the ol' braggart,' one of the lads giggled as they went back inside the workshop. Meg smiled thoughtfully and took the chance to return to her lover.

Having drained his wine, Jude would sleep soundly for an hour or so, giving her time.

* *

'Jude. Jude. That's Matthew. He's home.' Meg shook her drowsy lover awake. He yawned and dragged himself back to wakefulness, stretching 'til his joints creaked. He rubbed bleary eyes. Noises rose from the courtyard. Someone was very much in his cups, stumbling about, cursing. Then a door opened and closed. Male voices were heard below, in the kitchen: one slurring his words, the other cajoling. A jug chinked against a cup. Another curse. Then all was silent.

'I must leave, my sweet.' Jude flung the sheets aside but Meg clung to him.

'No, my hero. Don't go yet. 'Tis hours before dawn. You cannot leave me now.' She smothered his lips with hot kisses, her tongue questing deep. And no, he couldn't leave her, not yet. He responded in kind, eagerly. 'Jude! Oh, Jude...' Only her teeth nipping his lip caused him to draw back sufficient to let her take a breath.

* *

Later, much later, they were roused in the greyness of pre-dawn by the sounds of someone down in the courtyard being horribly ill, groaning in their plight.

'The old miser, serves him right,' Meg murmured half asleep. Jude turned over, nuzzling her neck.

By the time the first fingers of daylight were reaching into the courtyard, all was quiet as Jude, reluctantly, went back down his ivy stairway, out into the alleyway behind Paternoster Row, making good his escape along Ivy Lane.

Bowen's courtyard

HIS EVERY tortured breath hung suspended in the still air of the cold yard. He vomited again. It hurt. He tasted blood. All his life he'd been told that the righteous go to Heaven, but Heaven would not want him, not in this state, unshriven. All those prayers to Mamon served no purpose now.

Death sat silent in the corner of the yard, patient, watching, waiting until he was done. The sleep of Death, they called it. Sleep? That was wrong, made it sound peaceful, easy. It wasn't. Every breath was a fight against oblivion hovering darkly behind the shutter of his eye. Death was waiting for him to falter, his first hesitation would be his last, so he gulped down another breath to fuel the fires in his poor belly, which was cramped like screwed parchment. His heart was fluttering, a helpless bird caged within his ribs. Icy sweat drenched him. He fell down and could not rise. His flaccid great body lay immoveable. The crow flapped away on heavy wings, up on to the chimney top.

Matthew Bowen was cold, dead as stone when his wife found him. A fox-headed knife protruded from his chest like an obscene phallic symbol.

CHAPTER SEVEN

Saturday the twenty-ninth day of April
Gilbert Eastleigh's apothecary's shop

THE MORNING had gone badly for Tom Bowen but, he thought, perhaps not so badly as he deserved, nor expected. Last eve he'd managed to get back without being picked up by the watch and he'd succeeded in tiptoeing past master's chamber without waking him, before climbing up to his attic in the dark.

He had awakened with a blacksmith pounding an anvil inside his head and the merest whiff of breakfast had made his belly recoil in horror. But he'd managed not to vomit until after Mistress Meg arrived, all of a panic, screaming for Master Gilbert to come in haste. Master was not yet up and dressed – it always took him an age to decide which gown to wear – and, naturally, Tom had asked her what was amiss that she should be all of a lather so early in the day.

'I think he's dead... your father... slumped in the yard like the drunken sot he is.' For a moment Tom was sure he must have misheard, but it seemed his stomach had heard well enough. He'd barely managed to reach the door and rush out into Ivy Lane in time. Dead? Not his father, surely? Tom wiped his mouth on his sleeve, his tongue tasted foul as a dog's arse. The old man must have come home drunk, fallen, struck his head so bad. Aye, that must be it, he fell. It couldn't be anything else, could it? Oh God, no. Tom retched in the gutter in the middle of the lane. He couldn't really remember what he and Kit had actually done last night, they'd been so drunk, but he recalled something of what they'd talked about, vaguely, and it had better not be...

• •

When Gilbert Eastleigh returned from Paternoster Row, he'd been surprisingly gentle with Tom, took him into the parlour – where he was never allowed otherwise – sat him down by the fire and told him of his father's death. Never mentioned the notes. Didn't beat him, either.

'How did my father... how did it...?' Tom's voice trembled. He could hardly force the words out, he so dreaded the answer but he had to know. His master understood this as grief and took the lad's hand in his own skinny claw, patting it reassuringly.

'A knife, Tom, straight into the heart. It would have been a quick end, mercifully.'

'A knife? But that's – that's w-w-terrible.' He'd almost said "wonderful". He wasn't to blame. It wasn't his fault. Elation swept through his veins like an elixir until he felt almost as drunk as last eve, hard pressed to keep the smile off his face. His father, the old bully was dead, but it wasn't his fault. He was safe! Innocent!

But someone else was guilty.

The Foxley brothers' rooms

I HARDLY SAW Jude again until Saturday morning. I had eaten Friday's bread and salt herring supper alone, not that I had much stomach for food anyway. Since Jude had got his way, convincing me I was entirely to blame for our parlous state, I had agreed to accept Lord Richard's commission. It was utterly against my better judgement. I knew I would fail but, even so, I spent all day yesterday reading up about priming the wood for the triptych. I'd done it as best I could, according to the book, treating the wood with a white ground of chalk and size before leaving it to dry. Then an hour rubbing it down, scouring it smooth with pumice. Many more layers would be required to produce the perfect white surface on which I would draw the figures for the triptych, but I had already made some sketches for the duke's approval. There was little more to be done until the wood was prepared and that would take a week or two. For now, I was fairly satisfied with the finish I had achieved with the first layer.

I was examining the surface for imperfections, holding the wood angled against the early morning light that glanced through the window, when Jude returned, full of the joys of spring. I noted a speck of blood on his lip but said nothing.

'Ah, dressed already, little brother. You must be eager for our audience with Lord Richard.'

'I never undressed, did I? I worked most of the night, preparing the wood, as you told me I must.' I was tired indeed and in an ill humour.

'Oh, come on, Seb. Let me help you wash, then we'll break our fast together.'

'I'm not hungry.'

'Of course you are. Christ's sake, Seb, here's last night's herrings barely touched.' Jude took up the loaf, still unbroken. 'Did you eat anything? No wonder you're just a bag of bones.'

He put our water pot onto the fire to warm – new logs had been delivered mysteriously yesterday, in the afternoon. I knew not from whence they'd come, or how, and dared not ask. Seating himself on a stool at the board, Jude poured ale for us both and handed me some bread to go with it, but I put it down again. Food did not interest me.

'I can't do it, Jude.'

'What? Eating? Just take a bite, Seb, chew and swallow... easy.'

'I can't face the duke!' I thumped the board. I wouldn't have him make a jest of my fears.

'Yes, you can.' He munched his bread and the left-over herring.

'I don't even know if I can walk so far in time, all the way to Bishopsgate.'

'I've already overcome that problem for you. Young Jack will be here at eight of the clock with his uncle's hand cart – the one he uses to deliver his barrels. We can fill it with straw and cushions and take you there in fine style. How will that be?'

'Are you trying to make me look a fool?'

'Would you rather I carried you on my back like a sack of cabbages? No, I thought not, so the cart it is then, unless you walk.'

'Then so be it. I *will* walk.'

'Well enough. And I'll take the hand cart for when we are in danger of being late.'

'Don't mock me, Jude!' I cried, 'Not today of all days.'

'Mock you, little brother? I'll never do that, you know,' he said quietly. 'Now, let's get you clean and tidy for the duke, eh?'

I nodded, reluctantly allowing him to help me out of my shirt – a difficult task when my left arm couldn't be raised over shoulder height.

As usual – unless he was in a foul humour – he helped me get washed down and dried off. He hunted in the coffer for our most respectable attire and there I stood, before the fire, clothed in my best linen shirt and drawers with hose and doublet of dark green wool. The hose had been mended at the knees after a fall and the doublet was rather faded, but this was my finest. Jude was most particular this morning. The fuzz on my chin was shaven, my unruly dark hair combed and the ensemble set off with a plain grey hat – modesty had to be my watchword. Of course, Jude looked splendid, whatever he wore, his bright tawny doublet and red hose – a vanity I could only dream of daring to wear – vivid in the pale sunlight of the morning beneath the bright blue hat that set off to perfection his golden hair and blue eyes.

• •

As we travelled along Cheapside and Poultry, every wench in London gave Jude the eye, including Dame Ellen and Goodwife Marlow, who should have known better. Beside him, I was seated in the handcart, struggling to maintain some vestige of dignity with my staff, scrip and portfolio tucked in beside me, pushed along by Jack Tabor. Jack's filthy ragged appearance only made Jude look all the more splendid – a fact of which the man was, no doubt, fully aware, even if the urchin didn't care.

As I rode in the barrow down Poultry, I saw the squawking chickens squashed into crates and baskets. I watched their necks being wrung, one by one, their gizzards slit and the innards thrown to the ground, steaming in the chill morning air. My throat constricted, my own gizzards twisting in fear of meeting Lord Richard. Lucky hens, I thought, all unaware of what fate awaits them.

Crosby Place by Bishopsgate

IN BISHOPSGATE, by St Helen's church, we stopped at the gatehouse of Crosby Place, the Duke of Gloucester's London residence. The gates were open, folk coming and going, on foot or on horseback, gaily clad bucks, liveried servants and sombre churchmen, all intent upon their own... or someone else's business. The fellow at the gatehouse looked like Hercules stuffed into a suit of livery far too small for him. But he seemed friendly when Jude stated our business, calling to a servant to show us the way to the great hall. Jack was to wait at the gate with the handcart whilst we were otherwise engaged, and Jude told him to behave himself. Meanwhile "Hercules" had lifted me from the cart as though I weighed no more than a coney and set me down. The fellow was kind enough to hold me steady until I'd balanced myself with my staff.

'There you are, masters. Now Hal will show you where to go, but take care on them steps,' "Hercules" warned.

'Thank you, Master...?' Jude replied.

'Thwaites. Peter Thwaites of Yoredale.' The man smiled, adding: 'That's in Yorkshire, mind.' Jude returned the smile.

'I could have guessed you weren't of London, Master Thwaites, that's for certain.' The gatekeeper laughed.

• •

Crosby Place was impressive, indeed. The flight of stone steps with its ornamental balustrade was like nothing I had seen before.

'Grand enough for a king,' Jude remarked to the servant, Hal, as they assisted me on the tortuous climb. At the top, they paused so I could catch my breath.

'My Lord of Gloucester *is* the king's brother,' Hal pointed out.

'Don't remind me,' I muttered, nervous enough without thinking how high born and powerful was the man we were about to meet. I was becoming more apprehensive by the minute. Jude, standing so close, must surely have felt my trembling as we waited by the door into the great hall, whilst the servant went to announce us.

'Not worried, are you?' he whispered, admiring a fine tapestry hanging, feeling the quality, rubbing it between his fingers. 'Mm, silk, I believe.'

'No, scared witless is all.'

'Why? He's a man like any other. Farts and fornicates like the rest of us. You think he shits pearls and rubies?' I grinned, despite the writhing serpents in my belly.

'No, but he may want to see my work.' I glanced at the portfolio my brother carried under his arm.

'But your work is a wonder, so why does that bother you?' He bent to rub a smudge of mud from his boot. 'Sir Robert told us he's seen the Book of Hours you did for Lord Hastings, he must have approved that, else why offer you this commission in the first place? Don't worry, little brother, all will be well, I assure you.' I gave him a doubtful look. 'Honestly!'

'If you say so, Jude. I just pray his grace is in a good mood. I've heard he has the Devil's own temper, like the king.'

'I'm sure that's only a rumour. Come on, Seb, smile! This is a great day for us, so look the part: confident, eager and able.'

I closed my eyes and leaned heavily against the wall as we waited. I should never have sat up all night, working on the wood. Now I was too tired for this.

'I wish we hadn't come.'

'Remember, the alternative is starvation,' Jude said in my ear as the servant bade us follow him into the great hall.

The hall was something quite beyond my imagination. St Paul's was bigger but nothing like this, with its gilded hammer-beam roof and luxurious hangings. Jude looked around, stunned by such magnificence but I had eyes only for the knot of finely dressed men gathered by the table near the window. I recognised Sir Robert Percy and wondered which of the other gaudy peacocks was the duke. A young broad-set man with black hair and olive skin outshone the rest in blue velvet, but I prayed God he wasn't the duke for his face was hard, the eyes pit-dark when they saw us. He would forgive nothing.

Sir Robert was chuckling at some comment made by a man garbed in a sunset of yellow velvet and red silk. I caught Sir Robert's eye and he winked at me, grinning, showing his white teeth. Two priests stood by, deep in their own conversation, and a slim, dark-haired man in grey stood, leaning over, studying some papers. At a word from Sir Robert, the man in grey turned and came forward, his thin lips stretched in a smile, his hand held out in welcome. Jude removed his hat and bent the knee. I took off my cap and bowed as low as I dared.

'Master Foxley, Master Sebastian, welcome to Crosby Place.' I was surprised to see a duke so modestly attired and he spoke quietly for a man who must be always giving orders. 'I'm most glad to meet you, having so admired your work. I apologise for being late in greeting you, but the king summoned me to Westminster first thing and there's no gain-saying a king, is there?' he laughed.

'Certainly not, your grace,' Jude laughed with the duke, but I hardly managed to force a slight smile. This man was my nemesis but I had to concede, his eyes held a glint of humour.

'Will you take wine, masters, or maybe you prefer ale, as I do myself so early in the day?'

'Ale, my lord, please,' Jude replied, 'And for my brother also.'

Looking at Lord Richard, so inconspicuous in a gown of light grey wool, my brother seemed over-dressed in his tawny, blue and red. In fact,

I realised, looking at the duke – we were both of us dark of hair, soberly clad and much of an age – there wasn't a deal to choose betwixt us, if you ignored my darned hose and badly worn cuffs and my lameness and crooked back, of course, and my empty purse. But perhaps this meeting wouldn't be quite the ordeal by fire I'd dreaded.

• •

'Come to the table, masters, and we can get down to business directly,' Lord Richard instructed, signing to a servant to pour ale into four cups set upon the board. 'Lords Lovell, Scrope, you may withdraw if this matter holds little interest for you. My lord bishop, my lord abbot, I pray you stay or go, as you wish.' All four men bowed and departed, leaving only the duke, Sir Robert and a few servants. 'Be seated. Master Sebastian, take my chair – it will be more comfortable for you.'

The order came as a surprise and I feared my dusty old clothes might soil the fine silk cushions, but it seemed prudent to obey. Jude looked at me with eyebrows raised, grinning. The duke made do with a wooden bench to sit on. Everyone sampled their ale, except me. I was so nervous still, I was certain to spill it.

'Now, masters, the triptych.' The duke laced his fingers, elbows on the board, and rested his chin on his thumbs. 'Will you accept my commission?' Jude gave a slow nod.

'Aye, my lord. My brother and I have discussed it at length. We will accept.'

'Good. I'm glad,' the duke smiled broadly, his eyes seeming to light up with pleasure. 'But we must first discuss terms. These must be acceptable to you also. Martin!' He called over one of the servants. 'Go find Master Metcalfe. Ask him to attend me with the documents we drew up yesterday.'

The servant scurried off.

'Miles Metcalfe is my lawyer,' Lord Richard explained, 'I took the liberty of having the contracts for this commission drawn up in the hope you would oblige me.' The duke played with a ring on his finger, then straightened the sheaf of papers on the board, though they could be no straighter. Might he be nervous too, I wondered. 'But whilst we await Master Metcalfe,' he said, 'Perhaps I could describe to you the elements I wish to be included in the triptych. Is that agreeable to you both?'

'Aye, my lord, please do so,' I said, finding my voice now that we were finally arrived at the point where my expertise was required. 'Would you object, sir, if Jude makes notes and I sketch as you describe?'

'That sounds eminently sensible.'

Jude opened the scrip and took out his wax tablets and stilus, paper and silver point for me. The duke took another mouthful of ale and seemed to brace himself.

'In the central panel of the triptych, I would have Our Lord Jesu Christ in glory, seated on high, upon a rainbow. Beneath Him, I would have the Blessed Virgin, Our Lady, and St Joseph and Christ's earthly brother, Saint James.' Jude wrote it down, I sketched a few lines.

'I know this is unusual,' the duke continued. 'But 'tis the Holy Family, you understand. That's what I want this triptych to embody, the thought of "family". The background can be however you think best – that is not important, so long as it does not detract from the subject. Family, aye,' he mused, passing a be-ringed hand over his eyes. I saw a brief gesture of assurance from Sir Robert, seated at the duke's side.

'Then, on the right-hand panel, I would have the image of my lord father, Richard, Duke of York, in armour, kneeling in prayer.' Lord Richard paused. Though Jude continued to write, I stopped drawing, aware of the rising tide of emotion in my new patron. 'And the left-hand panel – it will have the image of my brother, Edmund...' The duke faltered slightly. 'Earl of Rutland, likewise in armour and also in an attitude of prayer.'

'Might your grace describe your lord father?' I asked hesitantly, taking a fresh sheet of paper – obtained at such expense but, hopefully now, our empty purse would be replenished.

'I anticipated such a need,' the duke said, his voice still a touch unsteady. 'I have drawn my lord father and brother Edmund as best I can. Poor attempts indeed, but I can hardly describe in words the shape of a nose or eye so well as they can be drawn.' He took up one of the sheets of paper that had been lying on the table all the while, seemingly blank. He turned it over and showed me. It was the face of a young man, perhaps of sixteen or seventeen years, not unlike the duke himself, with the same fine, angular face. But there had clearly been difficulties with the chin, which showed evidence of having been redrawn numerous times. Even so, it betrayed a certain talent for depiction.

''Tis a good likeness of the young Earl Edmund,' Sir Robert said, speaking for the first time. 'I'll tell you that, for my lord is too modest to say so.'

'Nonsense, Rob. A blind man could have got a better line for the chin. You can see that, Master Sebastian, can't you?'

'With a little practice, my lord, you could make a fair living as a limner,' Jude said casually. The duke laughed out loud.

'I doubt that, Master Foxley, but I'll bear the thought in mind when next I find myself penniless.'

'Ah, this is my lord father.' He turned over a second sheet with the sketch of an older man, in his fifties perhaps. It was a strong face with a straight, narrow nose that seemed to be a family trait. One eyebrow was quirked severely by a scar that continued down the cheek. I examined the charcoal drawing closely, noting it was well executed for one untrained in the art.

'Do you want the scar to remain?' I asked. 'Most patrons would probably prefer such imperfections to be left out, my lord.'

'No. The scar should stay. I cannot remember a time when my father did not bear it. He came by it in France, long before I was born. His hair was once dark, like mine, but greying by the time...' The duke left the sentence unfinished. He fiddled with the single heavy ring on his right hand, looking down at it as though noticing it anew. 'My father's ring is all I have left of him now. It bears an 'R' upon it... see? No use to my brothers then, which is why I have it. He wore it always, so it should be included in the image.' I looked over at the ring then returned to my sketching.

'Your lord father's eyes, what colour were they?' I asked.

'Grey.'

'Like your own, my lord?'

The duke considered for a moment before turning to Sir Robert.

'What would you say, Rob?'

'Your lord father's eyes were lighter than yours, I reckon. But Edmund's were darker grey, more like yours, as I remember, though 'tis a long time ago now, nigh fifteen years since Wakefield... hard to recall precisely. Yet your lady mother used to say you and Edmund were as alike as two peas in a pod, did she not?'

The duke smiled at this.

'Aye, she did, indeed. Does that help you, masters?' I nodded, and after a few more lines, turned the paper so the duke could see my drawing. What if he did not approve? My stomach churned at the possibility.

• •

Seeing Lord Richard's expression, I feared he was displeased, the more so when he put the drawing down on the board and turned away without comment. My nervousness returned, bad as ever. Sir Robert picked up my sketch and took it to the window to examine it in the light.

'This is excellent. The Duke of York to the life. In a few well-considered lines, you have caught the likeness of the man precisely. Here he is, looking out at me, his eyes alight with vital spirit. I can see there must be some alchemist's secret to capturing the image, aye, and the very soul of a man, in a few marks made on the page. How do you do it?'

'Practice, sir,' I answered. Sir Robert shook his head.

'No, I could practice from now 'til Judgement Day and never achieve anything like this. 'Tis a wonder, Master Sebastian, it truly is. You have a God-given gift.'

Not knowing how to receive such high praise, I finally took up my ale cup and drank, hiding my face behind it, still concerned that the duke had failed to respond. I glanced at Jude for reassurance. My brother was keenly observing the duke, who seemed to be staring out of the window at the busy courtyard below, still playing abstractedly with his ring. Suddenly he turned, striding purposefully to the door.

'I must see what keeps Master Metcalfe,' he said, leaving the hall. It seemed an odd thing for the duke to do in person when there were servants standing idle who could have been sent to find the tardy lawyer.

• •

Sir Robert resumed his seat and poured more ale for us all.

'Tell me how you plan to go about this work,' he invited, but I was looking anxiously at the door, fearful that I'd angered the duke somehow. 'Don't mind my lord, he'll return shortly.'

'I fear I've upset him,' I said.

'Lord Richard has just seen his father's ghost raised up before his eyes and his grief is as raw as it ever was. You must forgive him.'

'Is my drawing too lifelike? Should I make it less so? I never intended to distress the duke.'

'No, don't change anything – it is exactly what Lord Richard wants. God knows, it put a lump in my throat too and the man wasn't *my* father. He wants all who see the triptych to think of their "family", the love and loyalty that "family" inspires in *him*. He wants others to feel that too. If it makes a soul weep, then so much the better. Leave it exactly as it is. Now, what of his brother Edmund?'

I added a little shading to the second image to denote the fall of hair and passed the drawing to Sir Robert for his opinion.

'Aye, you've caught him too. How did you succeed in drawing so accurately the chin of a man you've never seen when Lord Richard couldn't get it right himself?'

'"As alike as two peas" you said, so I drew the duke's jaw line, chin and mouth, 'tis not so hard.'

'Not hard for *you*, may be,' Sir Robert said wryly, 'Damned impossible for the rest of us.'

• •

By the time the Angelus bell rang at midday in St Helen's convent, the contracts had been signed and sealed and Jude's purse weighed heavy with an advance payment of the Duke of Gloucester's coin.

'I think we deserve a belated but well-earned dinner, Seb!' Jude declared enthusiastically as I was trundled in the handcart back down Bishopsgate. 'You too, young Jack. What takes your fancy? Mutton pies? A roasted capon? Come on, Jack, push faster and we can get there before the market is sold out.'

'Too late for that, master,' Jack said knowledgeably. 'If I wants to nick a decent capon, I has to go right early, afore six, before the regrators get there. By now, it'll only be the left-overs – nuffin good.'

'Damn!'

'I could get us a pasty from the cook shop,' Jack offered.

'Steal it, you mean.'

'Aye, well then I can keep the coin,' said Jack brightly. Jude nodded, laughing.

'And I have a better idea. *I* shall buy the pasties and *you*, young Jack Tabor, shall have a groat for yourself, so long as you *don't* go thieving. That way we both stay on the right side of the law.'

'But yesterday we...'

'That was a case of "needs must", lad,' Jude interrupted, 'And will never be repeated. I'm no criminal, even if you have a mind to dance the hangman's jig one day. No thieving! Not whilst you're in my employ. Understand me?' Jack nodded seriously. 'Good. Now push Master Seb home, then take your groat and go buy some soap. I'm going to get you cleaned up and...'

'Soap!' Jack shrieked, 'But soap kills ya... rips all yer skin off! I ain't gonna...'

'You want to work for me? Then clean you'll be, like it or not, if you are to bide with us. I'll be back before the hour with our dinner, so get my brother home.'

• •

Jude went off, leaving Jack to push me home in the hand cart. All the way down Cornhill, into Poultry, then back along Cheapside. I could hear the lad snivelling behind me.

'What's amiss, Jack? Is a good wash so fearful as all that? Or is it the thought of not going thieving any more that disappoints you?' The lad paused in his pushing to wipe his nose on his sleeve, sniffing loudly.

'Master Jude said I was to bide wiv yer? Did he mean it, Master Seb?'

'Perhaps. We'll have to ask Dame Ellen Langton's permission and I can't believe she'll grant it unless you're clean and law-abiding. What do you think?'

'S'pose so,' Jack admitted. 'Would I have a blanket to sleep in? I ain't never had a blanket afore.'

'No blanket?'

'Just a pile of rags me uncle gave me. I sleep wiv his dogs to keep warm when 'tis cold.' He couldn't see my shocked expression from behind – little wonder the lad stank like a kennel.

'I dare say we'll get you something better than that.'

The Foxley brothers' rooms

I WAS RESTING but working over in my mind how I would compose the triptych, particularly the central panel, the need to balance the figures – four was an awkward number, three or five being more usual for a good composition, and the proportions had to be correct. The armour for the duke and the earl – I would need to see a suit of armour, how it fitted together, how the pieces moved. Perhaps Lord Richard would oblige me, send an esquire to show me. And what of the background?

Jack was seated on a stool by the board.

'I could get us somefing,' he said. 'If yer give us coin, I won't pinch it, honest, master, and I'll bring yer back the change.'

'What?' My thoughts had been miles away, imagining the hills of the Holy Land with the city of Jerusalem for the backdrop of the panels or the green fields of England... the duke might prefer that.

'I could fetch us dinner.' There was more than a hint of frustration in Jack's whine.

'No, no. Master Jude will return soon, just as he said. Why don't you set out the platters and spoons? They're up on the shelf there.'

He obeyed me, which came as a shock. The task was done in a few moments.

'The bells went ages ago, master.' Now he was fiddling with a horn spoon.

'Did they?' Clearly, the lad was going to be more trouble than I needed. How could I think with his constant interruptions?

'I could've had three dinners by now, if I was on me own! Ain't yer hungry, Master Seb?'

'And had three birchings for stealing too, I don't doubt.'

'Don't care. Least I wouldn't be goin' hungry.' There was a brief silence. 'I'm taking the cart back,' he announced.

'Well don't be long, else you'll miss dinner.'

'Fat chance,' I heard him mutter as he hurried off, the ungrateful little wretch.

• •

I was still alone when Jude finally came home, carrying a huge chicken and oyster pie in a basket, apple dumplings in a cloth and a box of marchpane sweetmeats.

'Food fit for the king himself!' he announced triumphantly, 'Sorry it took so long. Where's the lad?'

'Took the cart back. Smells good, Jude.'

'Aye, and I've got such news to go with it, will make your hair stand on end.' He cut the pie into three generous portions and spooned the gravy onto the platters, licking it off his fingers. 'That's why I'm late. I had to learn the whole story.' We both made a start on the food. It was as delicious as it smelled, the pie filling succulent and well-spiced.

'Perhaps we should wait for young Jack?' I suggested, suddenly feeling a little guilty, my spoon poised in mid air. Jude shook his head.

'Not likely – I'm starved. Anyway, you want to hear my news or not?' I nodded, my mouth full of oyster gravy.

'Well, there's been murder committed and you'll never guess who...'

'Who?'

'Matthew Bowen!'

I nearly choked on the food.

'By all that's holy! I know he has a terrible temper but murder? Who did he kill? Not Kit, surely, though the insolent young beggar probably deserved it.'

'No, no...'

'Not Mistress Meg? Dear God, he hasn't found out about the pair of you, has he?'

'No! Don't be a half-wit. Bowen himself was murdered. Meg found him dead in the yard this morning, cold as charity, he was. She was terrified, ran to Gilbert Eastleigh for help but, of course, he was far beyond helping... nothing Eastleigh could do.' My brother took another large mouthful of pie – apparently, the thought of death did nothing to temper his appetite.

'How did he die?'

'Stabbed, so she told me, a knife in his chest.'

'She? Oh no, Jude, you've been with Mistress Meg, haven't you? No wonder it took you hours to get this food.'

'I had to pay my respects, didn't I? I only went to Paternoster Row after I'd heard, to console the bereaved widow.'

'Oh, I'm sure you were precisely the consolation she needed! You're a fool, Jude. How do you think that will look, eh?' I shoved my platter aside, anger quelled my appetite utterly.

'I don't understand what you mean.'

'Jude! Somebody killed Matthew Bowen and there you are, drawn like a wasp to a ripe plum, warming his wife's bed afore 'tis even gone cold. Who more likely to have murdered him than his wife's lover? Tell me that!' He looked at me, appalled.

'Is that what *you* believe?'

'Of course not, but just think with your head, for once, instead of your prick. Stay away from Paternoster Row!'

After that, even he didn't seem to feel much like eating. The pie on his plate went cold.

• •

When Jack returned, he finished off the pie, the apple dumplings and started on the sweetmeats.

'Why ain't yer talking, masters? What've I done wrong now?' he asked, having taken the edge off his hunger sufficiently to think of other things, finally realising neither of us had said a word the whole time he'd been eating.

'Nothing,' I told him, 'And leave off scoffing the marchpane – you'll make yourself sick.' He looked at the half-eaten sweetmeat that he held and seemed about to put it back in the box but then, seeing it with a bite missing, he ate it anyway.

'I never had marchpane afore, 'tis very good.'

'I'm going out,' Jude said suddenly, leaping from his stool as if stung by a bee.

'No! You're going nowhere, Jude Foxley,' I told him. 'Now sit down. You're staying here, where I can see you, so I know you're not going anywhere near *that woman*.' I scowled at my brother. He sank back on his stool, burying his head in his hands.

'What woman?' Jack asked, his curiosity roused by this unexpected turn of events, looking from one to the other of us. I suppose Jude had always seemed to be in command – he was the elder, after all – yet now *he* obeyed *my* order.

'Never you mind, what woman, Jack,' I said, then sighed, shaking my head in disbelief and exasperation at Jude's folly.

• •

That evening, after Emily Appleyard had brought us a supper that only Jack had any interest in, I sat at the table, working on the drawings for the central panel of the triptych, but I wasn't happy with it. Somehow, St Joseph had the features of the recently-departed Matthew Bowen and, no matter how I tried to do the face otherwise, it always came out the same. Bowen's sparse beard, his sharply receding hairline greying at the temples, and the dark, deep-set eyes stared out from the paper, forlorn, beseeching, tormenting me until I threw down the silver point in despair.

'I can't do this! I told you I couldn't.'

Jude looked up from his own work, polishing another layer of white ground on the wood to a perfect finish, on top of what I'd done already.

'He's haunting my thoughts.'

Jude inspected my drawing.

'Mm, I see what you mean. 'Tis Bowen, isn't it? Rip it up, start afresh, now we can afford the paper.'

Angrily, I did as he suggested, flinging the pieces into the fire where they flared up and were soon reduced to a few blackened flakes. Jack's eyes were wide with horror at such waste but he had sense enough to hold his tongue on that score. Instead, he asked: 'Master Seb? What was the duke like? Was he big and terrible, like you was afeared he would be?'

'I was not afraid. And, no, he was neither big nor terrible.' I sipped my ale.

'But kings and dukes have t' be big. Like King Edward is. I seed him once.'

'Well, Duke Richard is quite unlike his brother.' In truth, the difference had surprised me – Richard was much younger than I'd expected, bearing in mind his reputation as a captain of men and hero of Barnet and Tewkesbury, those blood-red stains on the folios of England's recent history.

'Was he little, then?'

'No. He's tall enough – but gracile indeed for a warrior.'

'Graysy what?'

'Fine-boned, graceful almost.'

'Like a wench, then?'

'Good grief. No, of course not.'

'What does it matter how he looked,' Jude interrupted, 'He's rich and he paid up handsomely, in advance, for three bits of wood and a lick of paint. That's what's important.'

I glared at him. Was that all he thought the triptych would require, a lick of paint? 'Sorry, little brother, only jesting. I forgot about the hinges.' He and Jack laughed. I didn't.

• •

Later that eve, we retired to our bedchamber, leaving the young lad already sleeping, curled upon my second mattress beneath my second blanket – as promised – snoring softly before the glowing embers of the fading fire. Jude assisted me out of my clothes and into my night smock. He, of course, slept naked as God made him, like most folk, but I kept clothed for both warmth and concealment of my crookedness, even from my brother to whom it was neither a secret nor a source of disgust. But it had always been that way.

Once in bed, I had more trouble than usual getting comfortable on a single mattress with only the one blanket to warm me now. I fidgeted about, keeping Jude awake in the darkness. In the quiet, my teeth beat a faint but rapid tapping noise, chattering with cold. I heard Jude get up, groping about. He fetched our cloaks from the pegs by the front door and spread them on my bed.

'Thanks, Jude. God keep you,' I whispered and settled to sleep, hearing the old house creaking as it, too, settled for the night.

• •

'Seb? Are you awake?' Jude asked softly. I didn't answer, allowing a lengthy silence to stretch out, hoping he would think I was asleep. 'Seb,' he repeated, more loudly.

'What is it?'

'I've got a confession to make.'

'Save it for Father Thomas.' I didn't want to hear it, whatever it was. My imagination was bad enough without Jude confirming my worst fears.

'It's about Meg Bowen, I was with her last night.'

'I know.'

'You know! How?' He propped himself up on one elbow so I could just make out the darker shape of him by the little moonlight that managed to ooze around the warped wooden shutters.

'Shh, you'll wake the lad. You had blood on your lip this morning, again. You may as well announce the fact with a herald's trumpet.'

'Oh, God, I never realised. You think anyone else noticed?'

'How would I know?' This subject for discussion would make a saint peevish in the middle of the night.

'He was alive last eve, Bowen I mean. We heard them come back from the Panyer Inn, late it was.'

'Them?'

'A friend of his, I suppose. Then it went silent for a while 'til we heard him crashing about in the yard, throwing up his bellyful of ale.'

'And where were you all this while?' I was now fully awake and alert.

'In Meg's bed, of course. Where else would I be?'

'Where else, indeed. What did you do after that?'

'Me and Meg. We...'

'Spare me the details. I don't want to know.'

'I was about to say we went back to sleep 'til first light. Then I dressed and climbed out of her window – like I usually do. I lowered myself down into the narrow alleyway at the back of the house. It's not much more than a gutter really and floods when it rains. It runs along the back of the houses in Paternoster Row, then turns sharply and comes out in Ivy Lane, opposite Eastleigh's apothecary shop, beside Lovell's Inn.'

'Did anyone see you?'

'Not really.'

86

'What does that mean? They did or they didn't?' I pulled my blanket closer. The night was becoming colder at such an hour, as was the blood in my veins.

'Well, I saw that fellow, Lord Lovell, and his escort riding out. I suppose he had to leave so early to attend the duke at Crosby Place. But it was still dark in the shadows and anyway, you know his kind, had his nose so damned high in the air, he'd never notice a common sort like me, even if he rode over me.'

'I pray you're right, Jude, I truly do. Supposing he recognised you later? Did we encounter him at Crosby Place?'

'Aye, he was the sour-faced one in blue velvet.'

I sighed, remembering the man with the unforgiving eyes. I did not sleep well after that.

CHAPTER EIGHT

Rogationtide Sunday, the thirtieth day of April
The Foxley brothers' rooms

THEY CAME for Jude at dawn on Sunday morning, hammering on the door as if to rouse the dead.

'Foxley! Open up or we'll break the door down!' It was as well that we were already up and dressed, for the watch didn't seem to be willing to wait. Jude opened the door.

'What's so damned important at this early hour?' he demanded, but the three heavy-set men on the threshold didn't bother to reply.

'You Jude Foxley?'

'Aye, what of it? Who are you?'

'William Stockman, Sergeant o' the Watch – not that it makes no odds to you. You're under arrest.' The man stepped aside so the other two could grab my brother. Jude resisted.

'Leave go of me! You have no right to...'

Stockman smacked him across the mouth. I moved forward, blocking the doorway with my staff.

'Of what crime does my brother stand accused?' I demanded, as if I couldn't hazard a guess. My voice sounded reasonable enough but my blood was draining into my shoes. I knew the answer already.

'Bloody murder,' the man said, seeming to relish the words in his mouth like morsels of tender meat, 'The murder of Matthew Bowen, stationer of Paternoster Row. The inquest's been heard last eve with the coroner Master Fyssher and the sheriff deciding Jude Foxley is the most likely felon.'

I looked the man in the eye.

'He is innocent; you know that.' Stockman couldn't withstand such a direct stare and glanced away. 'My brother didn't do it. You have the wrong man.'

'I don't take the word of no stinking, idiot cripple.' The man spat copiously on my foot. 'Take this murdering bastard away!'

'Where are you taking him?'

'The Whit, where bastards like him belong!'

Oh, God! Whittington's Palace. That's what they called Newgate, since old Dick Whittington's bequests had paid for the new gaol fifty years since. These days it was a filthy cavern of iniquity and degradation.

It took all three men to drag Jude outside, as he writhed and cursed them all to hell and back. They bound his arms and beat him into silence before carting him away.

. .

Devastated, I stood on our doorstep, helpless, watching. I couldn't even run after him to shout encouragement, to urge him to take heart. How could I, when despair engulfed me in its suffocating black embrace? How would I manage without my brother? Since our father's death two years since, Jude had done everything for me. What was I going to do? It was pitifully selfish, I know, worrying about myself instead of him. But I was a lost soul without his aid.

'Master? Master?' A childish voice broke in upon my misery. 'What we going t'do now?'

I had no answer to that. I looked at Jack's grubby face, those huge beseeching eyes, his skinny elbows and arms like twigs that extended far beyond the ragged sleeves of someone else's cast-off clouts.

'Master?' Jack edged towards the board.

A log settled in the hearth, sending up a shower of sparks, startling me.

'Can I have me breakfast now, master? I'm hungry'

'Aye, Jack, eat if you wish.' Even the lad was reliant upon me now. How was I to cope with that? I watched as he wolfed down the bread – Jude's share and mine as well as his own. I would have to manage somehow.

. .

All the platters were empty bar a morsel of bread – that he'd left for me, I suppose – and Jack sat on the stool, scuffing his bare feet in the rushes and crumbs on the floor.

'When's Master Jude coming back then?' he asked.

'I don't know, lad. I wish I did.'

'Did he really kill somebody?'

'Of course not.'

'Well who did it then?'

'I don't know that either.'

It was then that I realised, all the while Jude was incarcerated, assumed guilty, the real murderer would still roam at large. This fact at least dragged me from my self-pity. I felt sick with fear on my brother's behalf. God alone knew how he would suffer in that Devil's den. Now it was down to me to prove his innocence. But how? And how long did I have to accomplish the task?

'Finish your ale, Jack, we have to go out.'

Draining his cup in one go, the youngster snatched the last wedge of bread and tucked it inside his stained jerkin for later.

'I'm ready,' he announced. 'Where we going?'

'Church.'

'Church? But it's too early. They're not beatin' the bounds 'til after nine o' the clock.'

'Church is where the dead are taken.'

'We payin' our respects to ol' Bowen, then?'

'You could say that.'

Crosby Place

'FRANCIS, MAY God give you peace this Sabbath day. I have missed you of late.' Duke Richard rose from his seat, smiling at his friend. Lord Lovell nodded. The closest he ever came to making an obeisance before anyone but the king, even the king's brother. But he and Dickon had grown up together, the duke's rank an irrelevance between them – almost. 'Wine? 'Tis never too early in the day for you, is it?'

Francis frowned. Was his friend implying that he drank too much?

Here, in his privy chamber at Crosby Place, Richard thought nothing of pouring his friend's wine himself, rather than troubling a servant. Francis was of the opinion that he demeaned his rank by doing so and had said as much, many times, but it was just wasted breath. Dickon wasn't concerned with trifling matters.

'What brings you here? By your look, this is no social call to discuss the weather.' Richard resumed his seat by the fire, awaiting some response as Francis sipped the wine. A chessboard, the game half-played out, sat at Richard's elbow, awaiting an opponent. Not Francis, for certain. He was a bad loser and it took more skill than he possessed and too much patience to defeat the duke.

The wine was good stuff and Francis needed it to fortify his courage. Dickon wasn't going to like what he had to say. He took the chair on the other side of the hearth, fidgeted with his fine damask gown across his knees, gulped more wine.

'The Foxley brothers... those fellows you commissioned only yesterday to make this triptych thing you're so obsessed about...' Francis watched the duke's eyes darken from steely blue to thundercloud grey. He should be more tactful. 'One of them has been arrested as a felon, for killing his employer. I advise you to withdraw from your contract with them. It doesn't look well to be associated with their sort, as I warned you at the time.'

'Which brother has been arrested?'

Francis shrugged. It hardly mattered which.

'The straight-backed one, I suppose. I doubt the other would be capable.'

'Jude. Jude Foxley has been arrested?'

'Mm, this wine is excellent, Dickon.'

'Is there no question of his guilt?' The duke was playing with the ring on his finger, twisting it around, pulling it on and off, on and off. It drove Francis mad to watch. He knew the signs only too well but ploughed on, regardless.

'Guilty as bloody Lucifer, if you ask me. I saw him myself, creeping out of the alley beside my place in Ivy Lane, yester morn, ere they found the corpse. I suppose you realise that very passage backs onto Paternoster Row? I never liked the look of either of the Foxleys. I wish you wouldn't consort with the common rabble, as you do. But will you listen to me? No, of course not, not you. You always know best. Now look how matters have turned out. You've a filthy murderer in your pay. The king is going to be mightily impressed when he learns of it.'

'What has my brother to do with this?' Richard's voice was soft but his eyes were hard and dangerous as lance tips.

'Nothing, nothing at all. Forget I mentioned him.' Francis drained his cup, wishing there was more wine in it, regretting that his tongue had got the better of him – again.

'You've been at the Tower and Westminster a good deal of late,' Richard said, still twisting that blasted ring. 'I warrant the king has seen far more of you than I have.'

Was that an accusation, or a simple observation? Francis couldn't tell from the tone. Of course, what Dickon said was true, though Francis had tried to be discreet about it, it was to be expected that someone would inform the duke of his activities. So long as Dickon remained ignorant of the substance of those activities, it wasn't important. All the same, the king's coin in his purse seemed to weigh more heavy of a sudden, pulling his belt lop-sided. He prayed Dickon hadn't noticed and resisted the impulse to hitch it up, fearing to draw attention to the bulging leather.

'His grace summoned me,' Francis admitted. 'Just as he occasionally summons you. He is concerned with preparations for his French campaign this summer. What of it?'

Richard stayed silent, looking his friend straight in the eye. Francis lowered his gaze, staring at the empty cup in his hand with no servant present to relieve him of it or replenish it.

'Do I ask you what you discuss with the king?' Francis blurted out, suddenly on the defensive. 'No, I never do.'

'Did I ask?'

No, Francis realised, Dickon hadn't asked... not in so many words. Not at all, in fact. It was his own guilty conscience, slipping unasked questions into his ear. He realised he wasn't very skilled at this cloak-and-dagger business, but he would learn. He had to.

'It's betwixt the king and myself, no concern of anyone else.' He'd said more than enough already but the words slid off his tongue, unbidden. 'Even you.'

Richard sat there unmoving, a stone effigy. A fingertip tapped against his ring, that movement alone proving life was still present. Francis had been unpardonably rude. The silence dragged out, measured in the dissonant heart beats of both men until, finally, the duke recovered his powers of speech.

'I am grateful to you for the information concerning Jude Foxley. I shall consider the matter. Now, my lord, if you will forgive me, I should have been at mass some little time ago.' The duke's tone was courteous and even enough, as though he hadn't noticed the offence, yet he had addressed Francis as "my lord" – something he never did when they were alone. The formality was unnerving.

Francis set his cup down on the hearthstone, made a hurried but proper obeisance this time and withdrew as swiftly as dignity allowed, having escaped retribution, hopefully.

The Church of St Michael le Querne, West Cheap

I T WAS a slow drag for me to St Michael le Querne, even with Jack's assistance, the lad shooing away dogs that liked to sniff at my staff and hens that fancied my shoes might be edible. I near fell in the gutter as I hurried out of the path of an uncaring horseman determined to reach his destination afore ever he left home. We were both mud-splattered as we reached the church – not that it noticed on the lad's filthy clothes. He held the door open whilst I climbed awkwardly over the threshold, into the incense-laden gloom of the nave. We were greeted by Father Thomas.

'You're early for the office, Master Sebastian. Oh, back again, young Tabor? We don't usually see you so often as this – twice in one week. What crime have you committed this time, eh?' The old priest's voice held a trace of amusement.

'Nuffin', Farver, honest. You ask Master Seb. I've been behaving meself, ain't I?'

'So far as I know, he's led a blameless life for two whole days, at least, Father Thomas,' I assured the priest, who nodded approvingly, though his expression was one of mild surprise. 'That's not why we've come. I want to see Matthew Bowen, his body. He is here, isn't he?'

'Aye, he is. Stephen Appleyard brought him here in the common coffin, but the women are laying him out at present. Best you wait 'til he's decent, laid out in his own box. Truth to tell, he doesn't fit in any coffin ready prepared. I've had to grant Master Appleyard a dispensation to work of a Sunday, making a new one specially.'

'No, I can't wait for that, Father. The sooner I see him the better.'

'Why the hurry, Master Sebastian? He's not going anywhere, not 'til after vespers this evening, at least.' The priest pulled at his worn cassock, scratching at a flea under his neck band.

'Please. I have good reason, Father Thomas.'

The priest shrugged.

'Oh, well, if you insist. He's down in the crypt. Can you manage the stairs?'

'Aye, needs must.'

It took fully the time to say ten Paternosters for me to get down to the crypt with Jack's aid. Matthew Bowen's body was laid out on a trestle. Two women were struggling to remove the clothes from the huge corpse, which was stiff in parts where *rigor mortis* had set in.

'Lordy, what a stink! State of this 'un, eh?' one woman said to the other.

'I couldn't see Mistress Bowen doing this for her "dear departed", could you, Aggie?' said the other, whom I recognised as the local midwife.

'Mistress Lucas?' I said. 'Are these Matthew Bowen's clouts?' I pointed to a pile of clothes discarded on the stone floor. My breath puffed in the chill air.

'Ah, Master Sebastian, come to pay your respects to your employer, have you?' The midwife looked up from her work, attempting to get the corpse's hose unlaced behind. 'Not a pretty sight, I warn you!'

'Never was,' I replied, realising I was quite without emotion for the man who had so recently been paying my wages. Was I so unfeeling?

'I wouldn't touch his stuff, if I was you. Messed himself something fearful in his death throes, I reckon. Death takes some folks that way, you know,' Mistress Lucas explained. 'But this one's the worst I've seen. What about you, Aggie?'

'Never seen one so bad as this,' the other woman replied, moving a candle to better illuminate her work.

Despite the warning, I picked up Matthew Bowen's doublet and shirt. The once-fine doublet was stiff and stinking with dried vomit but, surprisingly, neither it nor the shirt showed any trace of blood, not even around the rent in the cloth obviously made by a small, sharp blade. This was most odd, I thought.

'May I see the body?'

'We ain't washed him off yet, master,' the woman Aggie told me.

'That's just as well.'

• •

I looked into the face of my one-time employer. The pasty features looked strangely drawn and haggard, like those of a man who had been sick for many weeks, yet I knew Bowen had been fit and well on Friday at least, when Jude had rowed with him about our wages and belongings. The teeth of the corpse were bared in rigor's deathly grin – stained and yellow.

'Hold the candle close will you, Jack?'

'Not me, master. I don't go near no dead 'un.'

I saw the lad hadn't moved from the bottom step into the crypt. Mistress Lucas took up the candle.

'What was you hoping to see, master?' she asked, leaning close. I could smell onions on her breath, more powerful than the sickly-sweet stink of death that was beginning to develop around the body.

'His teeth are bright yellow. And here, inside his lips... and yellow bits between his teeth...'

'Vomit,' Mistress Lucas explained succinctly.

'But that wouldn't have stained his whole mouth. Look, you can just see enough of his tongue. That's yellow too.'

'Jaundice. That'll do it every time.'

I shook my head.

'But he didn't have jaundice, not the last time I saw him on Wednesday. Can jaundice develop so swiftly as that?'

The midwife shrugged.

'Jaundice ain't my concern, usually. Birthing 'em, and shrouding 'em, that's what I does, master. If they're poorly between times, I leave that to Master Eastleigh. You best ask him. I was fined for malpractice last time I brewed a potion for somebody – even though it fixed 'em up proper. Now, will you let us get on with washing him?'

'Not yet, mistress. What about the knife wound? I couldn't see any blood on his clothes.'

'Weren't none nor on the ground where he died, neither, so Stephen Appleyard said.' She bustled around, finding the soiled clothing to show me what I'd already noted – the absence of gore. 'Now why d'you suppose that'd be, eh?'

I made no comment but inspected the body, examining the small wound to the chest. Bracing myself, I fingered the lips of the wound. Although the corpse was, as yet, unwashed, the injury itself looked clean and was quite shallow, hardly enough to prove mortal, I thought.

'What sort of knife did this?' I asked myself, but Mistress Lucas had sharp ears.

'This!' she said, holding out a horn-handled penknife. 'Nobody else cared to remove it. Not even Master Eastleigh, and you'd think he would've.'

In the gloom of the crypt I felt myself blanch, though none could see that, fortunately. The penknife was Jude's own, the one he used for preparing his quills at work, left behind with the rest of our belongings and sold, according to the now-deceased Master Bowen. Since his initials, JF, were carved boldly on the handle that ended in a fox's head, little wonder they had arrested him for the murder.

Hesitantly, I took the knife and examined it in the light of the candle. There were dark, inky finger-marks plain to see on the pale horn handle. Whose were those? Jude's? I peered closer but realised I needed to see the knife in daylight, to be sure of what I saw.

'May I take this?'

Mistress Lucas shrugged.

'Don't seem nobody wants it, master.'

I turned to Jack. 'Would you ask Father Thomas to come down here, lad?'

Jack darted up the steps, two at a time. I felt a twinge of envy at those healthy young limbs, bounding up the stairs.

• •

'What is it? Is the body ready for my attentions?' the priest asked, coming down to join us.

'No, Father. I'm afraid I've kept these good women from their work. Rather I want you to observe this knife closely. Don't touch the handle, if you can help it. See here... finger-marks.'

The priest squinted but shook his head.

'I can't see anything. 'Tis too dark down here for my old eyes to make it out.'

'Then would you carry it upstairs, please, good father?'

'Aye, if I must. What's this all about?'

'I'll explain to you, up in the daylight,' I told him breathlessly as I struggled on the stairs behind him, leaving the women to their unsavoury task.

Once at the church door, I pointed out the finger-marks on the knife handle so Father Thomas might view them as I had.

'You see? They are quite fresh and you, Father, and the good women are my witnesses that these marks were there before ever I touched it?'

'Aye, it appears so.' The priest sounded bewildered as to the purpose of this discussion.

'Now, observe this mark closely.' I pointed out a smudge of ink. 'A thumb-mark, judging by its position. Yes?'

The priest nodded.

'And see here, Father. A straight line where the ink is missing. Why do you think that might be?'

'I've no idea. Why on earth does it matter? Matthew Bowen died of it and there's an end to it.'

'No, Father. That's not the end to it. This is my brother's knife and he has been arrested for the crime.'

The old man looked alarmed, crossed himself repeatedly.

'I did not know...'

'Well, I dare say the whole of London will know soon enough, but I swear to you, Father Thomas, upon my soul, upon the Gospels, upon any holy relic you name, that Jude never killed Matthew Bowen. But I believe this thumb-mark may be a clue to the real culprit. It *is* a thumb-mark, you agree?'

The priest twiddled his fingers about, deciding how the knife must have been held in order to make the mark.

'Aye... it seems to be where the thumb would go.'

'Good. And this mark overlays all others, so must have been made by the last inky hand to hold the knife. Now see this white line that goes across the mark?'

'Mm, I see it now. What is it?'

'I think the thumb that made the mark bears the scar of an old cut. Here...' I held out my index finger, 'I have a similar mark here, where I cut myself years ago, trying to break a linen thread I had tangled, fearing a beating if it was found so.'

'And does your brother have a similar mark on his thumb?' the priest asked, realising the significance now.

I shook my head.

'I don't believe so, but I think it's most important that I find out who does.'

'Aye, young master, I think you may be right,' Father Thomas acknowledged. 'And may the Lord God guide you in your search.

'Thank you, Father. And would you keep the knife safe for me, meanwhile, please?'

'Aye, I'll put it in the tithes' coffer as only I have the key. Thinking of which, I believe you still owe your tithes?'

'We do and shall pay them very soon, I promise you.'

Newgate Gaol

T HEY DRAGGED Jude all the way to Newgate, cursing and kicking him when he stumbled, never giving him time to regain his feet properly. He fell again in the filth of Bladder Street, into a reeking pile of yesterday's offal. The watchmen laughed, which they did often as they shoved him along. They were enjoying this, the buggers. The few folk out early enough to see stared and muttered among themselves. At least no one shouted aloud, broadcasting the news that Jude Foxley was taken as a felon, but they would do so soon enough. He could hardly believe this was happening to him, this nightmare.

At the gatehouse of the Whit, he was pushed into the eager grasp of the turnkey. Stockman and his men stamped off for a late breakfast, still laughing. The heavy door slammed shut behind them.

The turnkey's face was yellowed as old parchment, tooth stumps like black misshapen letters, badly inscribed. They seemed to spell "HELL". With his damned teeth tormenting him more than usual this morning, he was of a mind to share the torture – Jude had chosen a bad day to impose upon his hospitality. He barred his thin lips in an ugly grimace of pain... or it may have been a smile of welcome. As a spider might greet the hapless fly.

'Come to my place, then? We've always got us a bit o' room fer one more... if yer can find it, any road.' He coughed and spat a gobbet of dark phlegm at a passing rat. Well practiced, he hit it even as it scurried off behind a pile of broken wood. Something oozed from behind the wood stack, a stinking greenish trail.

Jude tried to cover his nose and mouth with his tied hands, heaving on the stench.

The turnkey smiled nastily. 'Yer ain't smelled nowt as yet. Jus' wait 'til I get yer down stairs, to me best 'commodation.'

• •

In the darkness, Jude fell down the last flight of unseen stairs, onto the few wisps of wet straw that covered the stone floor. The fall knocked the wind out of him and he gulped at the foetid air that lurked in the blackness, a waiting malevolence that would get the better of him, if he wasn't careful. His arm throbbed. He'd landed badly. His knee was no better. But then something moved, something more solid than the heavy air. He sensed movement, closing in from the darkest corners.

'Fine shoes,' said a cracked voice. 'They'd fit me a treat.'

Jude felt something slither against his foot. A serpent. A rat, perhaps. But rats don't speak.

'And red hose... I always wanted red hose,' a second voice said.

How in hell's name could they tell, he thought. It was too bloody dark to see his own hands in front of his face.

'Nice hair too,' said the first.

Jude shrieked as something, the Devil alone knew what, touched his head, pulling his hair.

'Get back! Don't touch me!' He went to shove it away, whatever it was, but there was nothing there. 'Leave me be.'

'Feisty young beggar, ain't he? I likes 'em with a bit of spirit though. Come, my pretty one... come to yer Mam, my wee one.'

Jude screamed as a hand brushed his cheek.

'Get off me, you old bitch!'

The voice cackled and the hand grabbed his hair, dragging him away from the stairs. With his wrists still bound, it was a double fist that lashed out, crunching against bone in the darkness. He had no idea what he'd hit but the hand released him directly and went whimpering back to its corner.

• •

As his eyes became accustomed to the faintest glimmers of light, Jude could make out the slimed walls, the nauseating pools on the floor and the heaped-up straw in the corners where his fellow miscreants hid from the biting cold and the ravenous rats. He curled himself into a foetal ball at the corner of the last step, shivering. He'd pissed himself – something he'd not done since he was three. The utter shame of it. And he wept, sobbing salt tears of stomach-wrenching misery.

Lovell's Inn, Ivy Lane

'COME!' BACK on his own turf at Lovell's Inn, Francis felt more at ease, though it would be a while before he could erase the memory of Dickon's face, a graven image with eyes of frozen obsidian that could pierce a man to the soul. He stood at the window in the parlour that overlooked the lane, observing the comings and goings below. He turned as the door opened.

'Sir Robert Percy, my lord!' his chamberlain announced grandly, absurd little man that he was. Francis only continued to employ him because his obsequious attitude was soothing to a delicate ego.

'Rob.' Francis greeted his friend with a forced smile even as his stomach churned. Dickon's guard-dog. He could guess why he'd come.

Robert bent the knee and bowed his head, as courtesy required of a knight before a baron. *This* baron in particular, even though they had been friends for years, fellow henchmen at one time, along with Lord Richard, to the mighty Earl of Warwick, God rest his soul.

'What may I do for you, Rob?' Francis asked, turning back to his interrupted observations at the window.

The knight looked about the sumptuous parlour before answering. He knew Francis was one of the wealthiest lords in England but rich enough to fling priceless Turkey rugs on the floor and walk all over them? Francis was standing on a veritable sea of azure, his feet sinking into the luxurious pile. And he must stand there often for the pile was trodden down in two foot prints, like corn flattened by a storm.

'About Dickon,' the knight said at last. 'You've upset him, Francis. You shouldn't have done that.'

'It's none of your business.'

'Someone upsets him, I make it *my* business. You know that.'

'Dickon can fight his own battles. He doesn't need you to do it. Go and fight the blasted Scots instead, it's what you're good at. And take precious bloody Dickon with you. He's better off dealing with the Scots than meddling in politics in London, which he knows nothing about.'

'If you weren't a friend of longstanding, Francis Lovell, I'd knock you through that window for those words.' Robert's voice was taut with rage, his face flushed more than normal. This was no empty threat, but Francis chose to ignore it. He would calm down, he always did.

Robert came to stand behind him at the window. He was still breathing hard but Francis could hear it easing as the tall man's temper cooled, and he wouldn't let himself be intimidated by sheer brute strength and size. Besides, Dickon's silences were far more frightening.

• •

Looking over Francis's shoulder, Robert could see Ivy Lane below, folk coming and going, many in their Sunday best, hastening to church. What was it, he wondered, that so intrigued Francis that he stood here, hour upon hour, as he must have done to wear holes in the rug? Across the way was a fine house, a servant shooing a stray pig from the doorstep as his master was about to leave. Next door was an apothecary's shop, the tall, narrow building leaning away unsociably from the glover's place next door to that. The shop sign hung outside, an image of a pestle and mortar, squeaking on its hinge as it swung in the wind.

The apothecary's apprentice came out to close up the shutter before they too went off to beat the bounds for Rogationtide. The youngster, a good-looking lad, had a stick in his hand, ready to strike at every wall, fence-post and tree that marked the parish perimeter – a pagan activity, Robert reckoned, if ever there was one. Then the apothecary followed him. A wizened little man, over-dressed in fine blue wool with white fur linings – illegal for a humble artisan, of course, but nobody bothered about such things these days.

Of a sudden, with the departure of the apothecary, Francis seemed to lose interest in the view and left the window, jostling the knight aside.

'Now then, what was amiss with our Dickon?'

The Church of St Michael le Querne

AS I planned, Jack and I went to church that morning for Rogationtide Sunday. St Michael's was crowded, for we would be beating the parish bounds later. I knew it wasn't because folk were eager to hear one of Father Thomas's mumbled sermons. It seemed the new Widow Bowen was a considerable attraction, basking in her new-found freedom, resplendent in a furred cloak far above the station of a mere artisan's wife. Escorted by Nessie – gap-toothed and giggling – on the one hand, and Kit Philpot – brimming with self-importance – on the other, Meg was reaping attention from every quarter for all the wrong reasons.

'Will you look at her, Maudie,' I heard Dame Ellen mutter to Goodwife Marlow. 'Such airs she gives herself, hardly appropriate for one so recently bereaved.'

Maudie Marlow snorted with laughter.

'Bereaved? Relieved, more like it, that one... her morals a damned sight looser than that gown of hers. Do you reckon she could be... you know my meaning?' She nudged Dame Ellen who considered the possibility, gauging Meg Bowen's waistline with a practised eye.

'Nothing would surprise me, willing as a butcher's bitch, from what I've heard.'

'Aye, but I wouldn't mind having that cloak of hers, would you, Ellen? How can she afford it? I thought her man was broke, too poor to pay young Jude Foxley his wages. They say that's why he stabbed him.'

'Hush, Maudie! Jude Foxley is my tenant and there's nothing proven against him,' Dame Ellen said curtly, anger simmering. 'Just as likely it was that nasty apprentice of his,' she whispered.

Glancing about, I saw folk staring at me – the murderer's crookbacked brother – and suddenly wished we hadn't come. I could hear snatches of talk. Jude's name seemed to be on everyone's lips, near as often as Meg Bowen's. None of it sounded in the least charitable, words of condemnation repeated all around the crowded nave.

When the bell rang for the elevation of the Host beyond the rood screen, at least the congregation had manners enough to be silent for a few moments, crossing themselves before resuming the threads of interrupted conversations.

As soon as the office ended, I made for the door, hoping to leave first, but I was too slow. Jostled by everyone with the same idea, my staff was knocked aside in the press and I would have fallen had not Emily Appleyard and Jack come to my aid.

● ●

Beyond the crush in the porch, they helped me around the side of the little building to where a buttress made an angle with the church wall and I could prop myself whilst I recovered.

Jack went back inside to search for my staff, leaving Emily to keep me company.

'Are you hurt, Master Seb?' she asked, holding my arm gently. 'Oh, pity me, there's yet another rent in your hose and a tear in the sleeve of your jerkin.'

'There's no harm done, Em, just my pride in tatters, as always.' I gave her the best smile I could, trying to disguise my distress after some of the awful things I'd heard said in church. If truth were told, I felt more like weeping than smiling. I wanted to shout aloud, tell everyone Jude was innocent, but they wouldn't believe me, which simply made me all the more determined to prove it.

• •

Whilst we were there, awaiting Jack's return, Kit Philpot came sauntering round the corner of the church, whistling tunelessly. Seeing me and Emily together, he leered at us.

'Give her one, crookback, if you know how. Oh, no, can't, can you... lost your crutch...' He sniggered. 'What a bloody shame. Always losing things, you Foxleys... brother lost his job and his penknife, you lose your prop... careless buggers, ain't you?' He moved on a step or two to the other side of the buttress where he relieved himself copiously – obviously his original reason for passing that way.

'What an ignorant oaf!' Emily said loudly enough that Kit should hear. 'Given the chance, I'd see he lost his crutch too... and make sure it hurt!'

'Shh!' I hushed her, afraid of what the spiteful apprentice might do. But Emily only laughed, telling me she had no fear of loud-mouths like young Philpot.

• •

Jack reappeared with a staff in his hand.

'Sorry, master, yer crutch is broked so I borrowed this one fer yer, off ol' Father Thomas. He keeps a spare in his vestry.'

Kit could be heard snorting uncontrollably with mirth beyond the buttress, having given Jack's innocent words every double meaning possible. When he returned, still chortling, he stopped to look at me, sneering.

'How's that brother of yours, eh? He'll hang for certain, when I tell what I know.'

'And what *do* you know?' I felt panic rising like bile in my throat.

'I'll tell when I'm good and ready,' he declared dismissively, as though it was suddenly unimportant. Pleased to have so obviously alarmed me, he grinned maliciously before continuing on his way.

Still discomforted, I turned to Jack.

'Well, I'm grateful for this staff, but does the priest know you've taken it?' I was thinking that "borrowing" might be just another word for stealing, in Jack's vocabulary.

'Course. I asked him fer it!' Jack exclaimed, all affronted. 'I told yer I wouldn't nick nuffin' and I ain't, not fer days, leastwise.'

'Then I thank you, Jack, for your ingenuity.'

'Me what?'

'Your good idea.'

'I wish you wouldn't use them daft words, master. Shall we get yer ready to beat the bounds? Yer don't want t'go home, now, not afore we...'

'No, lad. Now I've come this far, I don't want to waste the effort. I'm going to see Gilbert Eastleigh in Ivy Lane. I have one or two questions to ask him.'

Just then, Dame Ellen came bustling over. Dear Lord, help me, I prayed under my breath. My landlady folded her arms across her ample bosom, her look implacable. John Appleyard, the dame's apprentice as a tailor, stood half a pace behind her, as usual. As Emily's brother, younger by a year, he was skilled with his hands – not only with needle and shears but with a bow as well, his father being warden archer for the parish – and Dame Ellen had high hopes for him in his craft.

'Well, Sebastian,' the good dame began. 'I heard all the shouting and commotion this morn, rousing me from my bed betimes. I think you might have had the courtesy to come and explain matters to me after, instead of my hearing of it from the gossips.'

'Forgive me, Dame Ellen. I apologise. I wasn't thinking clearly. Sorry.' My grovelling litany seemed to soften her features, just a degree.

'Aye. Indeed. Well, tell me this, Sebastian. Is your brother guilty or innocent? A truthful answer now.' She looked me straight.

I returned her stare, hardly flinching.

'Jude is innocent, I swear upon my soul before this church and all who hear me. My brother is no murderer.' I saw then that quite a crowd were become my witnesses and they muttered and nodded among themselves.

'Very well. That's good enough for me,' Dame Ellen concluded. 'I'll expect you and that urchin at dinner then. Mind he's scrubbed clean afore he comes to my table. And John, here, will fashion you a new staff. Won't you, John?'

'Aye, I will. I'll get some suitable wood from my father's yard.'

Guilt swamped me. That wouldn't be the only piece of "suitable wood" I had acquired in recent days from Stephen Appleyard's timber store. I should have to pay him for it all, when I could think of a way to broach the subject of the stolen boards for the triptych.

'I'm obliged to you all,' I said.

The dame nodded once and departed.

'And thank you for your assistance, Emily. I'll see you at dinner, no doubt.' I touched my cap courteously. But she remained beside me, still clutching my arm.

● ●

Though I had intended to go to the apothecary's shop, as it happened we didn't have to trudge to Ivy Lane, for Gilbert Eastleigh was standing alone and idle by the old cross, looking very bored.

'Good morning, Master Eastleigh,' I greeted him. He seemed to consider a moment before replying in like fashion, smiling even.

'How do you fare, Master Foxley? Well, I trust? Mistress Emily.' The apothecary touched his hat to her but ignored Jack, not surprisingly. Who notices the likes of a street urchin?

'Aye, I'm well, thank you, master. May I ask you a question?'

'If you're quick about it. I have business elsewhere.'

'This won't take long. You see, some years back, when I was first apprenticed to Richard Collop, he told me that some pigments we used were very dangerous, poisonous, he said.'

The apothecary frowned.

'Master Collop,' I continued, 'told me vermilion was fearful stuff and Emily's dog got so sick the other day, I wondered if it could have been at my pigments. Would vermilion cause such terrible vomiting and the flux, do you think?'

Eastleigh smiled, looking relieved.

'No, no, not vermilion.'Tis slow to have an effect, causes trembling and loss of hair.'

'Verdigris, perhaps?' I suggested.

Eastleigh shook his head.

'Orpiment, then? Would orpiment make the dog ill in that way?' I hoped my enquiry sounded innocently enough.

'No, definitely not. Orpiment causes, er, severe headaches, nosebleeds, nothing like the dog's symptoms you describe,' Eastleigh said with certainty.

'Oh, well, must have been something he filched from the shambles then, poor creature. Emily will have to keep him chained up in future,' I said with a dismissive shrug. 'Thank you, Gilbert, and farewell.'

● ●

'What dog?' Emily demanded. 'I don't have a dog, Seb.'

'No, of course you don't, I had to...'

'Hey! See that?' Jack butted in, 'See who he was waiting fer? Widow Bowen, that's who!'

I looked back. Jack was right. Gilbert Eastleigh was escorting Meg Bowen home from church. A considerate neighbour? A friend and colleague of her late husband? Or was there more to their relationship than that?

'Mm, what a strange pairing they make,' I said.

Emily giggled.

'Mistress Meg must be the taller by two hand spans at least. But I must hasten. Dame Ellen will be expecting dinner served on time. You will be there?'

'For your fine cooking? We'll be there, but we have an errand to accomplish first.' I watched as Emily hurried off, kilting her skirts so she wouldn't trip upon the hem, showing her stockings muddied to the calf.

'She's got good legs, ain't she master?'

'I wouldn't know, would I? I don't look at such things and neither should you.'

Jack chortled.

'Course not. Where we going now, master? I want to go with th'uvvers.' He meant that he wanted to march around with the rest of the congregation, following Father Thomas in beating the bounds. But whacking every pillar and post with a stick was not what I had in mind and seemed a pitiful waste of effort when there were far more important matters in hand, like getting Jude released.

'The Panyer Inn.'

'Thank Christ fer that! I'm starving,' Jack sounded gleeful at the prospect of dinner, though it was far too early in the day. Perhaps he hoped it would make up for missing the fun around the parish. St Michael's was a very small parish anyway. No doubt, for Jack, getting fed was more important.

'That's not my reason for going there.' His face fell. 'I need to ask a few questions; that's all.'

'Not more questions,' my young companion moaned, looking woeful, but I ignored his complaint.

The Panyer Inn

THE PANYER Inn in Paternoster Row was busy as ever, patronised particularly by the local tanners – one of whom hadn't even bothered of a Sunday to discard his reeking apron afore purchasing his ale, thus adding to the general stink of soot, ale, grease and unwashed bodies.

Rarely frequenting such places, I wrinkled my nose at the stench but Jack seemed immune to it. The innkeeper gave us a cursory glance, raising a furry eyebrow as he noted me, the local cripple – very bad for trade – and decided to ignore us, hoping we would leave, yelling to someone that three more bowls of rabbit pottage were required. The very words had Jack drooling in anticipation, looking up at me, longingly.

'Good Master Innkeeper!' I called out, not knowing the fellow's name and wanting to attract his attention. We were ignored. As my eyes became used to the gloom, I saw an empty space on a bench over by the fire and pointed it out to Jack who elbowed his way through the crowd, making a pathway for me to follow. Once seated in the warmth, I was disheartened to see folk melting away, withdrawing to other tables and benches to avoid me, as though I carried the pestilence.

'Least we gets the best seat,' Jack said.

The innkeeper came over, scowling, pushing up his sleeves over his brawny arms, as if ready to make a fight of it.

'Well? You've half-emptied the place. This better be a sizeable order to make up fer it!'

'Two pots of ale, please,' I said. The man's expression darkened.

'Yer best... and two bowls o' stew and bread and cheese!' Jack added hastily, grinning like a gargoyle.

'I'll see yer coin first.'

Reluctantly, I took a penny from my purse. The man didn't move, so I added another penny. This time the man nodded, took the money and ambled off like the great bear he was. I flicked the lad's shoulder.

'I said it was too early for dinner, you greedy little wretch. We're dining with Dame Ellen later, after we've cleaned you up.'

Jack winced.

'Aye, but I think the innkeeper would have throwed us out, otherwise... besides, yer can afford it now the duke's paid yer, master.' The lad was irrepressible.

'But I haven't earned it yet and may never do so at this rate. I'll thank you not to spend it for me, Jack.'

'Sorry, master. Just think o' it as a bribe.'

'Bribe? Why should I bribe you?'

'Not me, the innkeeper. If yer wants him t'answer yer questions, it's as well to have spent some money in his tavern,' the worldly-wise Jack explained.

'Oh, I see what you mean. Aye. Could be you're right, lad. I hadn't thought of it quite like that.'

Jack might be a useful ally yet, knowing how best to wheedle information from the unwilling, as I did not.

• •

However, when the ale and food were brought to the board, it was a serving man who carried the tray, dumping it before us with ill-concealed contempt for a cripple and his urchin.

'A groat,' he demanded, holding out a greasy palm.

'That's outrageous! I've paid already and this mess isn't worth a penny, never mind four.'

'A groat, or I takes it back to the kitchen!' the fellow insisted loudly, drawing the attention of the other customers, as he intended, I don't doubt.

'This is daylight robbery.'

'Please yerself, yer can starve fer all I cares.' The fellow began to put the bowls of stew back on the tray.

'Serve this good man properly, you oaf!' A stern but powerful voice came from the doorway. 'He is in the Duke of Gloucester's employ.'

Turning awkwardly to look towards the door, I saw Sir Robert Percy, a real ray of sunlight in that dingy place. He came striding over to join us on the bench by the fire, adjusting his sword – a badge of his rank rather than a weapon for use, as the city ordinances allowed – so he might sit in comfort.

The servant, suddenly showing far more respect, set a bowl of steaming stew before me. Seeing it held the bigger helping, I pushed it towards Jack, accepting the smaller portion for myself. I held out another two pence to pay for it but the innkeeper came hurrying over, shaking his head and muttering about there being some mistake as there should be no charge for the Duke of Gloucester's man.

Sir Robert peered at the stew and said he'd have the same and, of course, there would, likewise, be no charge, since he was also the duke's man. The innkeeper looked reluctant to comply, frowning at the White Boar pendant on the chain around the knight's wide shoulders. The knight was even more well-muscled than himself.

• •

'Good day to you, Master Sebastian,' Sir Robert greeted me courteously, helping himself to a morsel of cheese.

'Sir Robert, thank you for what you just said. I'm obliged to you.'

'You're more than welcome. I confess, I'm surprised to find you in this thieves' den.'

'Find me? Were you looking for me then? Does the duke wish me to attend upon him?'

Sir Robert shook his head.

'We have heard a rumour, an unfounded lie, no doubt, but...'

'Concerning my brother Jude, I suppose?' So this was it. The duke required his money be returned and the contract was null and void.

The knight nodded and I felt the earth shift beneath me.

'I'm sorry, sir, I fear ill-news travels so swiftly. 'Tis true, Jude has been arrested, accused of murder. That's why I'm here, to ask questions. I must unravel this matter, prove my brother's innocence.'

Sir Robert's meal arrived and he took up the horn spoon provided, wiping it on his sleeve before sampling the stew. Meanwhile, Jack's bowl had been emptied and scoured dry with a piece of bread, so he now sat quietly by, watching my untouched food go cold. I pushed the second bowlful before the lad. Eating was the last thing on my mind.

'My brother *is* innocent. Foolish, perhaps, but innocent. And I have to find a way of proving it before...' Before what exactly, I dared not say.

'Perhaps I may assist you, Master Sebastian, that is, if you need my aid?' Sir Robert offered. 'This stew is surprisingly good.' He stirred the meat in his bowl, a thoughtful expression on his freckled features.

'Would the duke be able to spare your services, sir?'

He laughed.

'I dare say our Dickon will manage without me for a day or so. Probably glad to be rid of me, if truth be told. After all, I do little but get under his feet these days, since there be no Scotch reivers to put to flight this far south and the king will be a while yet, raising the money for his French enterprise. He'll probably have to pawn his shirt eventually, as our Dickon has already.'

'Is the duke so poor as that?'

'Fear not. You'll be paid for the triptych. That money is set aside.'

'I wasn't concerned for that,' I protested. 'I simply wondered...'

'Well, you should be. No man ought to work for nowt, unless he be a slave.' Sir Robert chewed a while on a less than tender piece of meat.

'That's right, master, he shouldn't,' Jack added his pennyworth.

'Eat your dinner,' I told him. 'Keep silent when your elders are conversing.

'I've finished. What's connervarsin'?'

I ignored his ignorant query. But I was curious.

'Why is the triptych so important to his grace that he would pauper himself?'

'It will be his legacy to his family, if...' Sir Robert sighed. 'If the worst should befall him in France, God forbid.'

'Is it likely to be so dangerous?'

'It's war, my friend. Wars are always dangerous and, knowing our Dickon, he'll be in the thick of it, as will I.' Sir Robert gave a wry grin. 'In the meanwhile, it'll be a change to have something meaningful to do, saving your brother from the hangman's rope.'

'I'd welcome your aid, sir.'

'Good. Then perhaps you'd better tell me what has come to pass. And call me Rob, if you will.'

CHAPTER NINE

Later on Sunday
The Panyer Inn

THE HOUR for dinner with Dame Ellen came and went – I would be in deep trouble for that later – whilst I told Sir Rob everything I knew about the murder, all that I supposed, even a few vague possibilities. I also revealed my fears for Jude, thrown into Newgate gaol to await trial, whenever that might be.

'I can't imagine how Jude will be faring, locked in that terrible place with cutthroats and thieves for company. I've never known him to spend a day within doors, if he could be outside. Poor Jude. Will they feed him decent, sir, do you think?' I was twisting my hands in agitation, envisaging my brother's plight.

'We could visit him, if you want, take him some food and bribe the gaoler to treat him well,' Sir Rob suggested. 'And find out when he's due in court.'

'For the trial?' I knew nothing about how such things were conducted.

'His first appearance in court could be tomorrow – but that's May Day – so more likely Tuesday. That will just be for the pleading, whether he'll plead guilty or not guilty. If he pleads not guilty, as no doubt he will, then a date will be set for the assize trial by jury.'

'And they will let us see him before then?'

'Certainly. Have you finished your food? We could go now, seeing the gaol is but a stone's throw from here. We can take him his dinner.'

'The pigeon pie looks good,' Jack piped up enthusiastically, seeing one being served at a nearby table.

'Oh, aye. Sir Robert, this is Jack Tabor.' I thought I'd better introduce the lad, rather belatedly. Jack hopped off the bench and bowed to the knight, grinning idiotically, showing food caught between his teeth, his uncombed hair flopping across his face.

'Your servant, is he?' Sir Rob queried dubiously, eyeing the scruffy, bare-foot creature before him.

'Not exactly. I'm not sure what he is really. He eats enough for an army, I know that much. My brother seems to have adopted him recently, though I can't think why.

'But, before we leave this place, I have questions to ask, concerning Matthew Bowen's activities on the night he died.' Returning to the matter in hand, I attracted the attention of the innkeeper, who was reluctant to oblige, fearing it would mean serving the duke's men with another free round of ale, so I began chinking coin in my purse, implying payment this time. 'Master Innkeeper, if you permit, I would ask you, concerning Matthew Bowen last Friday eve, what time did he arrive here?'

The man's eyes darkened and narrowed 'til they were mere slits in his large face.

'The dead un, yer mean? What makes yer think he came here at all, eh?'

'Well, he did most evenings, so I'm told, usually not returning home 'til long after curfew when you threw him out. Was it any different last Friday?'

'Yer 'spect me to recall every damned customer that crosses me threshold? How would I know?' He wiped up a puddle of grease from the board with a grimy cloth.

'Perhaps a coin or two would aid your memory?' I fingered my purse meaningfully. 'Was Matthew Bowen alone? Did he leave with a friend perhaps?'

'Get out! I don't care if yer duke's men or King bleedin' Solomon's. I run a respectable place here. I don't remember seeing 'im that night nor any other. So clear off, or I'll summon the watch, the sheriffs an' all! Bugger off an' don't come back!'

Newgate Gaol

THE WHIT was a terrible place, its very stones ingrained with the hopelessness and depravity of past inmates, the stench of decades of filth and desperate existence. Sir Robert gained us instant respect and attention by showing the Duke of Gloucester's badge, but we were all reluctant to enter the grim gateway. The courtyard was a morass of mud, such that both Sir Rob and Jack, unbidden, took me by the arm so I shouldn't slip.

'This way,' the gap-toothed moth-eaten gaoler encouraged us, jangling his keys. 'Mind these steps in the wet.' The dark stairs seemed greasy rather than damp, the slime on the walls glistening in the uncertain light of the guttering torch the gaoler carried. At the bottom, the man unlocked a heavy oaken door, the hinges creaking as he opened it, releasing a gust of foetid air, like a stinking breath from the bowels of Hell itself. Sir Rob covered his nose with his cloak, Jack appeared unaffected but, requiring both hands to steady myself, I gagged on the stench and had to pause to recover. This was even worse than I'd imagined, and poor Jude had been here all morning, breathing in those putrid vapours.

• •

There were more stairs down into Hades pit, the moans and cries of the damned rising upon the vile airs to assault our ears. A hideous shriek from below died to a pathetic wailing sound and then to maniacal laughter.

'Going t' Bedlam later, that one, any road, afore she turns us all mad,' the turnkey explained. 'Shut yer racket, you!' he bellowed into the darkness, but the laughter only grew louder in defiance. 'I'll set them bleeding rats on yer, so I will,' he threatened, and the laughter ceased abruptly to become a wailing 'no, no, no!' 'Well shut up, then, else I will!' The wailing stopped. 'Afeared of rats, she is,' he cackled. 'Seeing the place is alive with the buggers, she'll have rats fer company, like it or not.' He chuckled to himself as he led us along a narrow passage. 'Here he is, in here.' He sorted through the heavy keys on his belt, unlocked the door and pushed it open. 'Ye've got ten minutes, any road.'

'Leave the torch with us,' Sir Rob ordered.

'And how will I find me way then?' the gaoler demanded, hawking and spitting into the blackness.

'I think you know your way around this midden as well as the rats do,' the knight replied, taking the torch and holding it to light the doorway.

• •

It was fortunate that he did, else we'd not have realised there were yet more steps leading down into the cell until we fell down them.

'Jude! Jude, it's me: Seb. We've brought you food and drink.'

My brother was sitting on the bottom stair, hugging himself for warmth in the icy cell. He turned to look up at us, blinking in the torchlight.

'Seb!' he cried. 'Am I free then? Can I get out of this freezing pest hole?'

I faltered, realising his mistake.

'Oh God, Jude. I'm so sorry. No, you're not free. Not yet. But you will be soon, I promise you.' I felt tears welling up, threatening to choke me. 'I'm sorry, Jude, so sorry.'

'What! I-I can't leave? Christ, Seb, I thought at least you'd...'

'Here.' Sir Rob came forward, taking the pigeon pie and the ale jug from Jack's grasp. 'Get that down you. You'll feel better for it,' he said in a business-like tone. 'Your brother's doing all he can to set this matter to rights, never fear.'

Jude snatched the food and began to eat the pie, but there were stirrings in the darkness below and shapes moved forward. Rats I thought at first, but then realised they were Jude's fellow inmates, hoping to share his dinner. Jude climbed higher up the steps, away from them.

'Get back, all of you. You're not getting your stinking hands on my dinner!'

'Share 'n share alike in 'ere,' snarled a threatening voice from the gloom. Sir Rob partially unsheathed his sword. The swish of steel was enough to deter them, for now.

'We'll stay whilst you eat,' he said. 'When do you plead?'

'Tuesday morning, they told me, at the Bailey.' Jude spoke with his mouth full. 'But what are you doing here, anyway, Sir Robert?'

'Helping a good cause.'

'Lost cause, more like – that's Saint Jude for you. Patron of lost causes.' Jude laughed humourlessly. 'Does the duke know about me?'

Sir Rob considered his answer before replying:

'Not exactly. He heard the rumour, but I haven't told him yet that it's true.'

'Who told you the rumour?'

'A friend.'

'One you can trust?'

'It seems he reported true, as far as it went. He didn't know that much for certain, but he did assume, wrongly, that you must be guilty.'

'Well, you can tell him that I'm not.'

• •

'Time's up!' the gaoler shouted from down the passage. Jude handed the empty ale jug to Jack.

'For pity's sake get me out of this cesspit, Seb.'

I nodded, too choked up to speak, seeing the look in my brother's eyes, full of anguish and suffering.

Outside, the clean air cut like a knife. I had to lean against the wall in the courtyard, feeling quite ill, but I rallied and set off with my borrowed staff at as fast a pace as I could manage.

The Hart's Horn Tavern, Giltspur Street

WE LEFT the stench of Newgate with relief, Sir Rob guiding us up Giltspur Street, behind the hospital of St Bartholomew, to a more welcoming tavern, the Hart's Horn, where the goodwife who ran it knew him well.

Seeing us, she hastened to greet us, wiping her hands on her clean apron and tidying her kerchief.

'Ah, Sir Rob! Come in, come in and good day to yer, sir, and where's Lord Lovell, then? He ain't graced my place fer a week or more.'

'Goodwife Fletcher, good day to you.' The knight greeted the hostess courteously, planting a smacking kiss on her offered cheek. 'Lord Lovell sends his apologies,' he laughed. 'But I have brought along two new friends to make your acquaintance in his stead. May I present Master Sebastian Foxley and his servant, Jack Tabor.'

Young Jack leapt forward, eager to kiss her as Sir Rob had done, to be greeted in return by the smiling, homely woman. I was less inclined to force even such slight attention on anyone, well aware how reluctant most folk were to make my acquaintance, but Goodwife Fletcher greeted me merrily and kissed me, as she had Sir Rob and Jack. I caught my breath, taken aback at such an open demonstration of courtesy. I gave her what I hoped was the semblance of a smile and sat on a stool opposite Sir Rob, at a board by the window.

• •

The knight hadn't ordered anything, but Goodwife Fletcher reappeared with a platter of oatcakes, still warm from the griddle, a dish of honey and some soft cheese. The tapster brought a brimming jug of frothy ale and three cups. The ale was excellent – no wonder Sir Rob was a frequent customer – as was the food.

'Feeling better?' Sir Rob queried after watching me devour an oatcake with relish.

'Aye, much.'

''Tis a pity the questions you asked in the Panyer fell on deaf ears.'

'Mm, we are none the wiser as to Matthew Bowen's activities Friday last,' I said, wiping my mouth on my napkin. A bell chimed the hour of nones across the way in St Bartholomew's, and other bells followed its lead across the city. Three of the clock.

'Yeh, w'are,' Jack mumbled, his mouth crammed with food. 'I asked the tapboy at the Panyer. He's a mate. We go... used to go,' he corrected himself, 'thieving togever. He said ol' Bowen was in as usual, guzzling ale and soon was worse fer wear, staggering out to the yard fer a piss, swearing and cursing like a mariner down Queenhithe. And he weren't alone all eve, neever. He was talking with another fella what Mark – me mate – didn't know, but they was getting loud, Mark said, or Bowen was, leastwise.'

'Your friend Mark told you all this?' I asked, surprised.

'Aye.'

'Can we trust what he says, do you suppose?' Sir Rob wondered.

'Course! Mark wouldn't lie to me. Why should he? We're mates – I told you. I'd trust him wi' me life. Well, maybe. But he told me true, I know.'

'Well, I'm grateful for the information, Jack, but did your friend give any more description that might identify this other man?' I enquired. I finished my cup of Mistress Fletcher's excellent brew and poured another. It was refreshing.

'Eh? What's "idify" mean?'

'I mean, did Mark say if Bowen's companion was tall or short, fat or thin, dark or fair or anything else?'

'Nah, master. He said it was too dark to see proper – it's always dark in that place – couldn't tell nuffin about him, 'cept fer his smell.'

'Smell? Was he a stinking beggar? I'm surprised one such should be allowed in a tavern, even the Panyer.'

'Nah, not a beggar. Mark said he smelled like something gone bad, sort of old and rotten, as if he had a dead rat in his purse, or an egg gone over.'

'Oh, I see. A rat-catcher, perhaps. That may be of great help to us, Jack. Well done, lad.'

Jack beamed with pleasure. I suppose no one had commended him before.

• •

'So Bowen was with a rat-catcher, or some such, possibly arguing, the eve before he died,' Sir Rob summed up. 'But did the same man accompany him home? I suggest your next task, Seb, should be to follow up this information, assuming it to be correct.'

'Aye. I fear an interview with Widow Bowen is going to be necessary... a task I don't much fancy, not with *my* brother accused of *her* husband's murder,' I said, sipping my ale, careful not to spill a drop.

'You think she'll be grieving too deeply to want to answer your enquiries?'

'If she is, I'll know it for a mummer's play. Meg Bowen is Jude's mistress – 'tis him she should be weeping for.'

Sir Rob looked doubtful.

'Oh, I'm not so sure. She wouldn't be the first widow to change her opinion of her husband once he's dead. I know a washerwoman at Middleham Castle, never had a good word to say about her man whilst he breathed, but dead? It was another matter entirely. You'd have thought he was a veritable saint, to hear her praising his virtues night and day and she meant it.'

'Well, let's find out, shall we?' I set down my empty cup.

Sir Rob tossed the appropriate coins on the board to settle our account and, with a wave and a smile for Goodwife Fletcher, he led us out into the street.

Bowen's house, Paternoster Row

FORTUNATELY, IT wasn't too far to walk from the Hart's Horn Tavern back to the Bowen house because I was weary with all this walking – and probably a surfeit of good ale too, if I'm honest, but we did have to pass Newgate Gaol again. I gave my fullest attention to side-stepping around a pile of steaming horse dung rather than spare even a cursory glance for that fearful gateway to Hell, but I knew it was there, looming over this corner of London.

Rather than enter the Bowen place through the side door to the yard and workshop, as in the past, I knocked on the front door that opened into the private parlour. After a lengthy wait it was opened warily, just an inch or two, by Nessie. But when she recognised me, she shoved the door wide and dragged me over the threshold so precipitously, I would have overbalanced if Sir Rob hadn't grabbed me.

'Steady, Nessie, for heaven's sake!'

'Master Seb! Master Seb, you're back. I've missed you so much!' Nessie shrieked in delight, dancing around me. Sir Rob must have wondered what was going on as the lass hung onto my arm, almost upsetting my balance a second time. 'Come see the mistress, she'll be so pleased.'

'I doubt that,' I muttered, pulling myself free of her tenacious grip. 'Is Mistress Meg receiving visitors then?'

'Ooh, no. She said I should tell visitors to go away but you're Master Seb; not "visitors". Who's this?' she asked rather rudely, noticing my companions for the first time. 'Are they "visitors"?'

'Er, no, Nessie, these are my friends. Sir Robert Percy and Jack Tabor.'

'That's alright then. Where's Master Jude?'

'He won't be coming today.'

'Ooh, mistress'll be sooo disappointed.'

'Aye, no doubt. Can you remember my friends' names to announce us, Nessie?'

'Yes, master: Sir Rowland...'

'Robert,' the knight corrected her.

'Oh, aye, sir, begging your pardon, sir. Robert, what was it now?'

'Percy.'

'Aye, Sir Percy Rowland and...'

'Robert!'

Yes, sir, I know that. Sir Percy Rowland and Robert.'

'May the saints preserve us!' Sir Rob rolled his eyes heavenwards in desperation. 'Aye, go and announce us then, you addle-brained wench. Good Lord, Seb, have you had to put up with her all your working life here?'

'I'm afraid so. But after a while you get used to Nessie. She's harmless enough.'

'Mistress'll see you now!' Nessie yelled down the stairs to us most improperly. 'You can come up, all of you!'

• •

Widow Margaret Bowen was seated in her chamber upon a cushioned chair, regal as the Queen of England herself, wreathed in a cloud of heavy, musky scent. Her new widow's weeds, worn like coronation robes, were spread around her, displayed to best advantage to show off the expensive marten fur lining. I wondered at such finery, knowing Master Bowen had been forever complaining about his lack of funds, cutting down on our ale allowance and bemoaning the cost of inks and pigments, parchment and paper, as a matter of course.

Meg Bowen, plump and still on the right side of thirty, was the perfect image of a wealthy artisan's widow, but a grieving one? It seemed not, as she smiled graciously at me and my disparate companions.

• •

'Good day to you, Master Sebastian,' she said formally. 'Pray, introduce me to your friend.' At this, she turned to Sir Robert, smiling demurely and glancing up at him from beneath her eyelashes, darkened with kohl. I sighed, knowing she was playing the coquette with the handsome knight – how could she resist – despite her so-recent widowhood. The formal manners, the coy looks were all for his benefit. Meg Bowen couldn't help herself when a good-looking man was present.

'Sir Robert Percy, at your service, dearest lady.' The knight made his own introduction before I could oblige, sweeping off his hat and bowing over her hand as though she truly was some fine "lady". He fawned, she simpered. Clearly there was going to be little sensible conversation achieved that afternoon.

'Nessie. Nessie, dear,' Meg Bowen called to her maid, but there was no reply. 'Nessie! Come here!' she raised her voice a little, but still no response. Annoyed, she rose from her chair, excused herself to Sir Rob, and bustled to the head of the stairs. 'Nessie!' she shrieked, fit to rouse the abbot from his post-prandial nap in Westminster.

Finally, the maid must have heard and came thundering up the stairs.

'What's amiss, mistress? Is there fire?' Nessie gulped breathlessly, arriving at the door and bobbing a hasty courtesy, seeing there were visitors watching.

'Don't be impertinent! Fetch wine and wafers for my guest... guests,' Meg ordered, returning to her chair and arranging her skirts as before, turning her most endearing smile on Sir Rob once again. 'Excuse my stupid maid. She was born rather deaf,' she explained. I saw Sir Rob raise an eyebrow, thinking "daft more like" after his earlier experience with Nessie, but I knew it was probably wilful disobedience that had made Nessie so slow to answer the summons.

'It matters not,' Sir Rob said dismissively. 'When there is a feast set before us already in your beauty alone, Mistress Bowen. My eyes could drink in your loveliness for hours. What need is there for mere food and wine?'

Meg twittered prettily, basking in his flowery compliments, fluttering her eyelashes and pouting her generously rouged lips shamelessly.

I groaned, thinking what a bawd she was and wondering how my friend could stoop so low as to flirt with the hussy. But Sir Rob was clearly enjoying himself, chatting up this silly woman as only a courtier knew how. As for Jack, he was covering his mouth with both hands, hard pressed not to laugh out loud at this mountebanks' show. Better than any you'd see at St Bart's fair.

Wine, very cheap, was served. Wafers, mostly broken, were offered. Etiquette was strained to the limit. Eventually, I could bear to watch no longer and asked if Jack and I might be permitted to withdraw and go down to the workshop, for old time's sake. Meg, no doubt delighted to have time alone with her new acquaintance, agreed, though the knight's momentary glare revealed to me how much of an act this was on his part. I felt relieved at that.

• •

With Jack's aid, I went down the narrow stair, through the kitchen and out into the courtyard. The air was fresh after the cloying cloud of Meg's perfume upstairs.

'Christ alive, she's a right slut, ain't she?' Jack observed – a man-of-the-world, even so young as he was. 'Pretty though, nice big tits!'

'Mind your mouth and your manners,' I ordered, but Jack just laughed.

'What a whore, an' her just widowed an' all. Gawd 'elp us!'

'Be silent, damn it. Try using your eyes and wits, instead of your mouth.' I spoke rather angrily but wasn't sure why.

'What d' yer want me to do?'

'This is where the body was found, so Jude said. Look around the yard here and see what we find.'

'Like what?'

'I don't know. Anything that shouldn't be here, I suppose.'

Jack wandered about aimlessly. I searched with deliberation, though what I hoped to find, I couldn't say. The yard was generally well-kept and fairly tidy, showing signs of having been washed down recently, though the corners seemed to have been overlooked for in one, behind a bucket, I found a pile of leaves and wisps of straw. Stirring the heap with my staff, I noticed a piece of paper, screwed up amongst the detritus. I picked it up and put it safely in my purse.

'There's a load o' puke behind this barrel,' Jack called out. 'S'pose that should have been cleared up.'

I hobbled over to peer behind the barrel.

'Is it not a strange colour, do you think?'

'What? Blue? Nah. It's puke colour, o' course.' But it was in deep shadow there.

'Can you shift this barrel for me, Jack?'

The lad shrugged but obliged, finding the barrel was empty and easy to nudge aside a few feet.

'What colour does it seem now?'

'Bit yeller.'

'A bit? It looks to me as though whoever was ill here had been eating saffron by the pound.'

'Saffron's pricy, ain't it?'

I ignored the irrelevant comment.

'I'm certain vomit shouldn't be this vivid yellow colour,' I explained but Jack wasn't bothered. Puke was puke, so what?

• •

We found nothing else even vaguely interesting in the courtyard, so went into the workshop. It was deserted. No one had bothered to tidy up at all since Matthew Bowen's death. The place was in chaos, things flung everywhere. Costly pigments scattered across the flagstones – a pitiful waste. Broken pots and sheets of paper strewn about. The place had been ransacked or else there had been a terrible fight. More vomit was splattered on the floor, unwashed cups on the collating table with an unstoppered flagon, the storage coffer left open. Nothing had been put away.

'Kit! Kit Philpot!' I called out, wondering if the apprentice was anywhere about, but it seemed he wasn't. So I felt free to poke around in the place where once I'd worked. I sniffed the flagon. Just ale. So I put my finger in the top and tilted it, then licked it tentatively. 'Master's best ale.' Jack tried it too.

'Good stuff,' he agreed, 'Me an' Mark used to nick the good stuff from, well, don't matter where from, but it's best fer getting pissed with. Don't give yer such a 'angover as wine.'

'I wouldn't know. What a good thing I have you to advise me on such matters, Jack.'

'Yeah, 'tis, ain't it.'

• •

Looking through the contents of the coffer I found some things I hadn't expected: Jude's scrip full of pens, rulers, pins and thread for marking up the pages; his pounce for whitening erasures and sand for drying the ink; and my own bag of brushes, oyster shells for mixing pigments, willow charcoal sticks and silver points for drawing. So Bowen hadn't sold them as he'd said. I wondered whether it would be right to take our possessions now, but decided that might be unwise in the circumstances.

Besides our belongings were other surprises: small earthenware pigment pots, each covered with waxed linen. Perhaps not such a strange discovery in a limner's workshop, but for weeks before I had been telling Master Bowen we were short of pigments, only to be informed there was no money to spare to buy any but the cheapest ochres, red lead and weld. Now here before me were pots of the finest powdered ultramarine, bluer than a summer sky; ground vermilion, red as blood; clothlets of iris green and the rarest terra rosa from Naples. Such pigments – and each little pot was full – were worth a ransom. I gazed longingly at such perfections of colour, my fingers twitched with eagerness to pick up a brush and put these glorious pigments to use. But why were they here, now that no one in Bowen's workshop was even capable of making use of such beauty as could be produced from the contents of these little pots? It made no sense.

Searching among the clean linen rags in the coffer I found other pots, little pouches and tiny boxes – verdigris, orpiment, realgar, azurite, saffron – Bowen must have bought up all the expensive pigments in London, but none looked to have been used, except the orpiment perhaps, since that pot was half empty, as was a box of white lead. If some ignorant fool used those two together, he'll have ruined his work, as I knew these particular pigments reacted badly with each other. But why was Bowen hoarding colours? It must be a recent thing, for I was certain they hadn't been in the coffer on Monday last, when I'd searched for clean rags to wipe my brushes. How had Bowen, forever bewailing the penurious state of his purse, afforded them all? He certainly hadn't made any profit from selling our scrips, since they still lay in the coffer.

• •

'Look here, master.' Jack interrupted my train of thinking. 'See these cups? They've still got dregs in 'em, yeller dregs. Ale, I s'pose, but they ain't the same.'

I limped over and inspected the cups on the collating table – surely Bowen hadn't permitted the pouring of ale on his precious, spotless table.

'Fetch a clean linen clout, Jack. There are plenty in that coffer. Now fold it so we have fair white linen uppermost, aye, that is right, and tip the dregs from this cup onto it. Good. Now from the other cup beside it... and a few drops from the flagon.' It didn't take a genius to discern that the dregs from one cup were of similar colour to the ale in the flagon – a little more concentrated due to evaporation, yet much the same, but those from the second cup were quite different. I took the cloth to the doorway, to observe it in a better light.

'Jus' like the puke?' Jack suggested. The lad might be ignorant but he certainly wasn't slow-witted.

'Mm, I believe so.'

'Saffron p'raps, like you said?' I shook my head.

'No, not saffron, no hint of red here,' I said definitely, colour being my field of expertise. 'See there?' I held the cloth so a shaft of pale sunlight from across the yard sparkled and glittered on the smudge of pure yellow colour.

'It's gold,' Jack said, his eyes wide.

'No, not gold. These sparkles are minute grains of mica that catch the light. In the past, this stuff has been used to imitate gold, but this is orpiment. Don't!' I cried in alarm, seeing Jack put his hands to his mouth in amazement. ''Tis poison!'

'Poison? But it don't look like the colour o' poison.'

'No, but looks can be deceiving, Jack, beauty can be deadly. Go, wash your hands at once and thoroughly.'

The lad obeyed, hurrying to the water stoop by the door. Having folded the cloth and stowed it in my purse, I did the same.

When we were done, Jack looked at me earnestly.

'What d' yer reckon, master?'

I considered.

'Same as you, I shouldn't wonder. I think Matthew Bowen was poisoned by his own supply of orpiment. The questions now are: by whom and can we prove it?'

'And why?' Jack added.

'I don't care why, just so long as Jude goes free.'

• •

As we made our way back to West Cheap, Sir Rob asked if we had found anything of significance in the workshop. I shrugged and said there had been nothing much to find, except two cups, suggesting that Bowen had indeed come home with someone on Friday night. Fortunately, Jack had sense enough not to contradict my version of events. After that, the rest of the walk was completed with much mirth and merriment, mostly at Meg Bowen's expense, as Sir Rob told hilarious tales of the widow's conduct that afternoon and her unsubtle attempts to seduce him.

The Foxley brothers' rooms

AFTER SIR Rob had left to go and retrieve his horse from a stable by the Panyer Inn and we were back home with a good fire going, Jack couldn't resist asking me the obvious question.

'Why didn't yer tell him about the orpi... stuff?'

'Orpiment. Because he's the Duke of Gloucester's man and we have no proper evidence.'

'Don't yer trust him then?'

'Aye, I think I do, but telling him would make it, I don't know... official, somehow and, for now it's only a possibility, an idea. I'll tell him when we know something more certainly.'

• •

I sat quietly, gazing into the flames that leapt around the logs in the hearth, grateful for the warmth seeping into my aching bones and weary muscles – I'd done far too much walking today.

Emily Appleyard came in, bringing our supper from Dame Ellen's kitchen next door. Jude had given the widow a little extra rent the day before, after the duke had paid us, asking if Jack might be considered to lodge with us now. It had been agreed so, despite poor Jude's enforced absence, Emily still brought supper, bread and ale enough for two.

'Good eve, to you,' Emily sang out as she set the food on the board. 'Don't forget, Master Seb, 'tis May Day on the morrow. You will be there, won't you? Oh, and you, Jack. 'Tis Jack, isn't it?'

'Aye. That's me,' Jack responded, already dipping his spoon deep into a bowl of steaming, savoury pottage.

'What of you, Seb?' Emily rested her work-worn hand on my sleeve.

'I doubt it. You think I have a mind for such pointless frivolities whilst my brother languishes in the Whit? I have more important things to do.'

'I'll come, mistress.'

'You'll do as you're told,' I snapped at Jack, wiping that idiot grin from his dirty face.

'Well, I'm sorry you won't be there to see me.' Emily turned to leave but hesitated. 'Oh, and Dame Ellen is most displeased with you about missing dinner. Such a fearful waste, she said, and threatened to give your food to the pigs. I thought I best warn you, as you'll probably get it served up cold for supper tomorrow.' She seemed about to say something more but shook her head instead.

Meanwhile, Jack devoured his supper, even cast greedy eyes on my bowl. Having lived a hand-to-mouth existence for ten years – he'd said it must be about that many – I suppose it was difficult for him to realise it might not be needful any longer to grab every mouthful that came his way. So he started on the cherry tart without considering that I had eaten nought, as yet. I had no desire for food, but resumed my contemplation, staring blankly into the fire.

'You want your pottage? It's near cold now,' Jack said.

'No.'

'Can I have it, then?'

I didn't reply, unable to think of a civil answer.

• •

It was dark, the candle lit. Bowen was buried by now, I realised, in St Paul's churchyard, since the one by St Michael's was hardly "God's acre". The patch, smaller than the backyard behind Dame Ellen's house, had long been filled with the earthly remains of past parishioners. A token four mourners and two torch-bearers the Stationers' Guild was sending, Father Thomas had said – so Bowen had few friends and little standing with the guild. Not much to show for fifty-odd years, poor devil, I thought. Yet how had he afforded those expensive pigments and left his widow clad in fine fur? That was a mystery indeed.

Jack was yawning, ready for sleep in his blanket by the hearth, but I had no intention of going to bed, too many thoughts rushing round in my head. Besides, I couldn't waste time. No. I would sit up all night, work on the drawings for Lord Richard's triptych.

• •

Whilst Jack snored softly in the chimney corner, I set out my new drawing equipment on the board and looked over the sketches I'd made yesterday. Yesterday – was it truly such a short time since our visit to Crosby Place? It seemed more like weeks ago, so much had happened since, most of it bad. Putting aside the drawings of Lord Richard's father and brother, I decided to work on the central panel of Christ in glory with his family around him. Taking up a silver point, I began to sketch the face of Christ with all the love and gratitude I felt for my Saviour flowing from the drawing tool onto the page. My usual way was to base an image on a face I knew, but that seemed irreverent in the case of Christ. Even so, as the drawing formed, I recognised Lord Richard's fine, straight nose, hoped the duke wouldn't recognise it. The firm jawline might have belonged to Emily's father, Stephen Appleyard. The mouth was definitely Sir Rob's, in his more solemn moments, yet with a hint of compassion.

It was late and the night quiet, nothing disturbed my concentration as I worked, outlining a face at once benevolent but filled with sadness for the short-comings of so many sinners. I decided it was a good face as I shaded the eye sockets to give them more depth – eyes that knew how it felt to suffer in place of the truly guilty. May God forgive me, I prayed, for what I'd drawn were not the eyes of Christ at all, but Jude's as he had sat on those steps at the Whit, wrongly accused, hurting. All the same, the drawing was undeniably fine. I would keep it.

I then began working on St James, Christ's brother, but the features weren't right at all. Too much of Kit Philpot – the most unsaintly wretch on God's good earth – around the nose and mouth. That image would have to wait until the spiteful apprentice was less in my immediate thoughts, so I set the sketch aside.

• •

I poured myself a little ale, spilling a few drips on the board and wiping them away with my frayed sleeve. Sitting back with my cup, I remembered the scrap of paper I'd found among the rubbish in Bowen's courtyard and rummaged in my purse for it, discovering also the ale-stained linen. This last I set aside for safe-keeping, but the paper I smoothed out on the board.

Moving the candle closer, I read the writing clear enough. In Bowen's own hand – one I knew so well – was a list of names: grocers, apothecaries, limners, all of London. The top half of the list, though still legible, had most names struck through. William Philpot, Kit's father, a wealthy grocer by trade, headed the list and was ticked as well as crossed out. Richard Collop, my old master, who had taught me all he knew, was second, his name crossed through but not ticked. Gilbert Eastleigh was third on the list, again ticked and crossed out. Next was Alan Dale, another apothecary in Lombard Street, his name neither ticked nor struck through. I recognised other familiar names: Master Rowley, Nicholas and Hugh Kent, all grocers in East Cheap; Harry Morton and his nephew Edmund Lacy, limners from Cheapside; and Widow Bess Chambers, who ran her apothecary shop in Bishopsgate. Seeing them listed, I wondered what they had in common and what the ticks and crossings-out might mean. But I was too tired for such puzzles tonight and fell asleep at the table, surrounded by my drawings.

Gilbert Eastleigh's apothecary's shop

IT WAS late and the liquid stillness of the night wrapped around him, clouds hiding the moon's face, but that was for the best. The fewer witnesses the better as Francis, Lord Lovell, made his way down the narrow alley beside the apothecary's shop, opposite his fine house in Ivy Lane. He entered the tiny yard at the back of the shop and knocked smartly on the door. He wasn't used to using back entrances for any purpose but he was learning.

'Hush, not so loud.' The apothecary's rasping voice came from within, the sound of the door being unbarred. Lovell pushed his way in, urgency being of greater import than good manners. 'God give you good eve, my lord,' Gilbert Eastleigh said, making a hasty gesture of obsequiousness. He was very nervous, Lovell could smell it, even above the stench of rotten eggs and other nauseating stinks that assaulted his nose in the confines of that horrible little still-room. 'Will you take wine, my lord? I have some upstairs in my parlour, a good Burgundy.'

'You know why I've come, Eastleigh. I don't have time for social niceties. The king is becoming impatient for his gold. Where is it?'

'These things take time, my lord, they cannot be rushed.'

'You said that last week, and the week before. You told me May Day! That is tomorrow. Now where is it?'

'Keep your voice down, I pray you, sir. My apprentice will hear you.'

'The gold! The king needs it now, not next year sometime. He has ships and men to equip in readiness for his French campaign and his patience is wearing thin, as is mine!'

The apothecary retreated behind his table, keeping his bubbling still between himself and Lord Lovell.

'I-I-I don't have it, yet, b-but soon, I swear.'

Lovell thumped his fist hard on the table. Eastleigh jumped. So did the apparatus, giving off a sudden spurt of noxious vapours that made the dark-visaged baron step back. A vial fell and shattered on the floor, leaving a pool of yellow ooze and glass fragments.

'Oh, God! That's the last of my refined elixir, you clumsy fool!'

Nobody insulted Lovell like that, ever. He snorted like a mad bull and came round the table to grab the little apothecary by the shoulders, shaking him so hard the man's teeth seemed to rattle loose in his jaw.

'You have until tomorrow night.'

'No-no, I need more time. I can't have it ready so soon.'

'Why not? The king has been waiting nigh on a month already. Are you wasting the coin he gave you? I'll wring your wretched skinny neck if you are. I've spent days, weeks watching over you and your pathetic little shop, seeing you come to no harm. Making certain no one hinders this accursed enterprise. Now it's time you kept your side of this wretched bargain.'

'I can't, not yet.'

'Why not?' Lovell was not particularly tall but he loomed above the little apothecary like a great black cloud of doom, his eyes dark with menace.

'Be-because I don't have the receipt,' Eastleigh blurted out the words. Full of terror, he cowered, expecting dire consequences, but it seemed his words had shocked the disbelieving lord.

'But you told the king himself you had it, you dirty, lying little spider.'

'I did, b-but it's gone.' Eastleigh licked his dry lips, but his mouth was like old parchment. No spittle left.

'Gone where?' Lovell was shaking him again, his fingers digging deep into the apothecary's scrawny shoulders.

'We think...' He did not elaborate on the "we". 'We think Jude Foxley took my notes. They were inside a book on the limner's art. We think he took it, stole it, when he murdered Matthew Bowen.'

'Foxley, eh? That bloody felon.'

'The same, my lord.'

'Then you'd best retrieve it, hadn't you?'

'I can't, sir. I'm but a weak old man, not made for contesting the likes of Foxley.'

'He's in the Whit. Have you forgotten? Even *you* could get the better of his miserable crippled brother.'

'No, my lord. The king requires me to make his gold *when* the receipt is recovered.' Eastleigh had regained his composure now. '*You*, my lord, are paid to ensure nothing prevents that occurrence. *You* must find the receipt at the Foxleys' place for me, else how may I obey the king's command?'

Lovell snarled. Keeping a watch on Eastleigh was one thing. Committing acts of thievery on his behalf was quite another. Not to mention how demeaning to a man of his high status. He hadn't bargained on such activities being required of him when he accepted the king's commission, but the lure of yet more coin in his bulging coffers and the promise of a viscountcy had been too tempting to refuse. But now, since he was sworn to secrecy in the matter, he could hardly employ another to break into the Foxleys' hovel without telling them what they sought. Money would have to be paid over, questions asked. It seemed the lord had little choice.

CHAPTER TEN

Monday, the first day of May – May Day
Smithfield, outside the city walls

WEST SMITHFIELD, beyond St Bartholomew's Hospital, was
where the good citizens of London came with their longbows
to set up the butts and the ale stalls every Sunday. I rarely went to the
Sunday afternoon archery practice decreed by law for men aged between
twelve and sixty – excused, for obvious reasons – and watching those
lissom able bodies only ever made me more painfully aware of my short-
comings than usual.

But today was May Day, a special celebration. Jack was eager to
attend and he had persuaded me along, much against my inclinations.
With Jude suffering the torments of the Whit, it seemed wrong to
participate in any kind of joyous occasion. Jack and Sir Rob, who was
interested to observe the standards of the London archers compared to
those back home, had bullied me into coming along with them. It was
early as yet.

'Anyone you might be thinking to investigate or question will be at
the revels, so you may as well be there also,' Sir Rob was saying. 'Besides,
Lord Richard is attending later. It would be wise to be seen with him, if
only to assure folk you are still in his good graces, despite everything.'

'Mm, "despite *everything*". I see. You may be correct, sir. Folk do
appear to be exercising their right of avoidance of my person even more
than usual.'

'Their right of what, master?'

'Keeping well away, Jack.'

'Oh, aye. And there I was thinking it was Sir Rob's great hulk
putting 'em off,' Jack said, nimbly ducking under the knight's intended
cuff across the ear and racing off over the field to join other youngsters

picking swathes of May blossom from the hedgerows, in preparation for the revels, singing as they went. The sun was a blurred pearl behind a thinning gauze of mist.

Elsewhere on Smithfield I saw a thousand details of colour and form, wet grass rustled like silk beneath our feet as Sir Rob strolled and I limped beside him. Fire pits had been dug and two great oxen were already roasting, had been since before dawn, to ensure they were cooked in time for dinner. Pigs and sheep were also being spitted, ready for the fire, the latter a civic gift from the mayor and aldermen. Someone said they thought King Edward himself had sent the oxen, to recompense the Londoners for the fact he preferred to conduct his own merry-making at Westminster.

A peddler played his hurdy-gurdy in the shade of a lime tree, drowning out a blackbird's piping – which I would rather hear. His barrow was gay with ribbons and trinkets and other worthless nonsense, though a ribbon in a particular shade of blue caught my notice. For one foolish instant, I imagined it tied in a braid of golden, amber and russet hair, complimenting a pair of sapphire eyes. I was more insane than a Bedlam inmate.

The men of Farringdon Within and Cheap Wards were gathered around Master Stephen Appleyard as the warden archer organised them for early practice. The archery contests would be in the afternoon, after the crowning of the May Queen and the Mummers' Plays with St George and Robin Hood and all the other heroes.

I felt a pang of regret. Jude was supposed to be playing the part of Robin this year. I wondered who would replace him, else Maid Marian would be lonely. Perhaps I would pluck up courage enough to visit my brother. Later, much later.

A fanfare from the Civic Trumpeters in their red and gold tabards called attention to the corner of the field by Duck Lane, where a garlanded archway had been constructed for the grand entrance. Led by a corps of drummers and the official sword-bearer, Lord Mayor Robert Drope, rotund and smiling, his lady on his arm, processed beneath the arch, followed by the sheriffs and aldermen in their livery. They made a fine sight, I thought, as the bright colours and gold thread glinted in the watery sunlight, a patchwork of reds, blues and purples that moved like a many-hued serpent across the grass to the dais, set beneath a fringed canopy. Just this once during his year in office, the mayor sat in a comfortable chair to the right, leaving vacant the old gilded throne, wreathed in May blossoms.

Another fanfare returned our eyes to the archway as the sound of the pipes and flutes and tabors of the City Waits grew louder, shimmering in the misty air. Sir Rob lifted young Jack onto his shoulders so he could see over the heads of the crowd. I could see nothing as I was shoved aside. Having taken one jab in the ribs too many and an elbow to the ear, I retired to the back of the mob. I didn't care anyhow. What was there to see but my fellow Londoners, done up in ridiculous costumes, pretending to be something they were not – royalty, heroes, fairy-folk and monsters for a day? It was probably going to rain, anyway.

But loath as I was to admit it, even to myself, I wanted to see Emily. Lord knows, I'd heard so much about the new gown, the girdle of silk roses Dame Ellen had helped her make and the fine blue leather shoes with gilded buckles. She would make a stunning May Queen and, I conceded grudgingly, I wanted to see her hair hanging loose. It was always pinned back under a kerchief but sometimes an errant strand escaped and I knew it to be fair. Today, as a virgin queen, she would have it combed out, in all its glory. That it would be glorious I had no doubt. I could almost feel it, slipping through my fingers like gold leaf, sparkling in the light like a cascade of rain drops, a silken waterfall shimmering down her back. But I still had to see for myself, this one and only time.

The crowd was laughing. That would be Jack-in-the-Green and his cavorting wodwoses, henchmen of the Green Man, passing by. Then a cheer for the Green Man in person, anonymous behind his leafy mask. And finally, the oohs and ahhs, and cries of "God bless the Queen of the May!"

I saw nothing of the crowning ceremony, my view blocked by the broad back of Goodman Marlow and a gaggle of women neighbours when the lord mayor put the circlet of wild flowers on Emily's head. Only when the coronation was done and Marlow, Dame Ellen and the rest of the crowd drew back behind the maypole, could I see her on her throne, surrounded by garlands.

The waits drew breath, piping for all their worth, and the dancing began. Children dressed as wodwoses and sprites skipped around the maypole, twining coloured ribbons in an intricate pattern, weaving the rainbow like a magic spell to the music.

But I watched only Emily, doing her best to appear regal and dignified when it was plain she could hardly wait to be up and dancing with the rest – never one for sitting still. Beside her throne stood the Green Man, his face masked, but he kept leaning down, talking to her and she was smiling, laughing at his words. Who was he? I couldn't recall who had drawn the lot for that part, wouldn't have given it a thought if Em wasn't the May Queen. But I was soon reminded as I overheard Dame Ellen and her friends talking close at hand.

'Oh, Bennett looks very fine in that costume I made him. Don't you agree, Maudie?' Dame Ellen asked Goodwife Marlow.

'Aye, well enough, I'd say, Ellen. Make a good pairing, him and young Emily,' the goodwife replied, flapping her apron to cool a hot flush – the bane of her life at present.

'I hadn't thought of that, but you're right, Maudie. They do make a good pair. His father is quite wealthy, isn't he? I'll have to look into the possibilities of a match betwixt them.'

And Dame Ellen and Maudie Marlow went off happily, considering their schemes to unite Bennett Hepton, the fishmonger's son, with Emily Appleyard in holy wedlock while my heart plummeted into the depths of desolation.

• •

There was Emily, stepping down from her throne, being escorted into the circle by the Green Man to begin a stately measure. They skipped lightly across the grass, toes pointed, twirling to the sound of pipe and sackbut. Her hair shone like sunlit marigolds, lustrous as I knew it would be. My fingers ached with longing to touch. But it was the Green Man whose hand brushed against it as he led her around. I shuddered; my case was hopeless.

That oaf. That fishmonger's lad. The lanky fellow with the spotty nose and chin. Better if he kept the mask on permanently. I leaned against a tree, watching them through narrowed eyes, unable to drag my gaze away.

They passed close by in the dance, arms entwined, laughing. She never cast a glance at me.

'Good ain't it, master?' Jack came bounding over.

'If you like this sort of foolery.'

He frowned at me, poked me with a finger.

'Master's got the grumps. Why's that?'

'Leave off. I haven't. Why don't you go away and annoy someone else?'

'Master's got the grumps,' Jack told Sir Rob as the knight came over, bearing a platter of hot honeyed apple rings. They were last autumn's crop, wrinkled and soft but enjoyable nonetheless. Jack helped himself to more than his share, as usual, so I slapped his hand away. Sir Rob looked at Jack and shook his head.

The next distraction was *Saint George and the Dragon*, a comical mummers' play, and Jack insisted we moved closer for a better view.

'In cooms I, breve Sent George!' The supposed knight made an elaborate obeisance before Emily, now seated once more upon her throne. But he tripped on his lance, which was twice as long as it should be, setting the audience laughing, before he capered off on his wooden hobby horse, yelling for the cowardly dragon to show itself.

The dragon, in its gaudy suit of green and gold leather scales, huffed and puffed its way through from the back of the crowd, blowing out gusts of chalk dust through a pair of bellows between its cumbersome jaws – I suppose it looked a little like smoke. It was probably because the unwieldy headdress blinkered him so that the dragon barged into me, since I wasn't nimble enough to move aside. He knocked me flat, but neither of us was hurt and the dragon continued on his way. Only my pride was lacerated, my patience falling victim to the monster.

'Enough of this! I'm going home,' I told them as Sir Rob and Jack helped me up and brushed me down. And I would not be persuaded otherwise.

'I'll see you home,' the knight offered.

'No. I'm better on my own.' I grimaced as I limped away on my borrowed staff in the direction of Duck Lane, mortified and angry at everything and everyone, especially myself. But I didn't get very far.

• •

A cavalcade was riding up Duck Lane, the out-riders wearing the Duke of Gloucester's livery of murrey and blue with his White Boar cognisance snarling on their chests. They completely blocked the way and I had to stand aside as Lord Richard, handsome in pearl-grey silk velvet, rode up. I bowed my head low but, even so, much to my dismay, the duke recognised me and addressed me by name. Such an honour, but one I would rather have done without at present.

'Master Sebastian Foxley. On your way to enjoy the revels? I'll see you there, join us at dinner, won't you?' It sounded like a polite invitation but, from the lips of a royal duke, it had to be treated as a command.

'Your grace, I shall be hon...' I said, but the duke was already gone, urging his white stallion beneath the flowered archway onto the field.

All I could do was turn back the way I'd come, swallowing my temper and hoping no one noticed my return.

• •

The crowds parted like the Red Sea for Moses to make way for the duke, the men uncovering their heads and, all that were able, bending the knee. By the time I had followed his path through the crowd, Saint George was making an elaborate flourish, sweeping off his feathered cap. The dragon was excused. Lord Richard slid from the saddle, handing his horse's reins to a gathering of youngsters, all vying for the privilege – Jack to the fore among them. His cheeky face was a picture of joy when the duke gave him a handful of pennies, bidding him take good care of the animal and to share the coins with his fellows.

With long easy strides, Lord Richard went to the dais where Emily sat enthroned in floral splendour, blushing like a wild rose. Bejewelled hat in hand, the duke went down on one knee in the muddy grass before her, as if she truly was the queen.

'Arise, my-my lord, quick, afore your hose are spoiled beyond saving,' she said.

He rose, laughing.

'Your highness, my hose are much indebted to you for your consideration although, before such gracious beauty as yours, any man should be honoured to remain upon his knees. But, since you have commanded otherwise, may I be so bold as to claim a seat upon the dais beside you?'

Miraculously, a chair appeared, as did velvet cushions, and the duke took his seat on Emily's left hand, smiling, enjoying himself immensely. Emily looked nervous at first, but I watched as Lord Richard worked his own sort of magic, putting her at ease, and they were soon chatting like old friends, including the lord mayor in their laughing conversation.

• •

With the crowd in good humour, Saint George began his absurd contest with the unruly dragon all over again. He must surely be the most inept knight since chivalry was first thought of, the dragon repeatedly getting the better of him. Was this how the play was scripted, I wondered, or was that wretched beast being particularly perverse? There were moments when even George himself, a journeyman carpenter by trade, looked as though he was beginning to doubt the outcome of the match, which was going on too long.

Eventually, as the audience began to tire of the jest – a monster that refused to die – the dragon at last admitted defeat and lay on its back, golden-scaled feet waggling in the air. Both contestants were panting hard as the saint raised his blunt wooden sword in victory, the beast belched out one final cloud of chalk dust and fell still. The crowd applauded and cheered as Saint George took his bow, at which point the dragon usually removed his headdress and also received his due. But not this time.

The dragon struggled to his feet and stamped off, leaving the space clear for Robin Hood and his merry band to do their piece. Folk found this new ending with the dragon, evidently such a poor loser, quite gratifying and his unusual departure was cheered and promptly forgotten.

• •

The sun was hot now, burning in a cloudless sky. I found myself a seat on an upturned half-barrel in the shade, out of the way. I didn't want to watch some other fellow usurping Jude's role as Robin, and Emily was safe from the attentions of the Green Man, welcome or otherwise, with Lord Richard so close at hand.

Instead, I wanted to consider the implications of that list I'd read last eve, now, while my mind was fresh. I realised all the folk named there were the very ones who would know that orpiment was a poison and may have killed Matthew Bowen. I had to find out who. But how? They weren't likely to admit to such a deed.

But my peaceful solitude was short-lived as I was suddenly shoved from behind and sent sprawling on my face. The dragon took my seat, arranging its tail, the painted eyes malevolent, the open mouth showing pointed wooden teeth.

'What was that for?' I struggled to regain my feet after the awkward fall. 'You can cease playing your part now, whoever you are.'

Muffled laughter issued from the ferocious mouth.

As I got to my knees and retrieved my staff, the dragon pushed me again, snatched away my support, sending me over on my back this time. I knew now that my first rough encounter with the beast had been no accident.

'Why are you doing this to me? What have I ever done to you?'

The dragon now stood over me, having no intention of allowing me to get up. Every attempt I made, he knocked me down again. The creature had one boot, decorated with gold scales, planted in the middle of my chest, hurting my ribs, making it hard to breathe. And he was laughing behind that hideous mask as he pressed down harder. I felt my ribs creaking.

'Please!' I had no breath left to say more but felt my borrowed staff beneath my hand as I lay on the grass. I got a good grip on it, raised it and shoved it into the dragon's gaping maw.

'Ow! Ow! You bastard!' the dragon shrieked in an all-too-human voice, staggering back as it wrestled with its head. Free of it, throwing the head aside, Kit Philpot stood there, blood streaming from his nose. 'You bastard, Foxley. It was only a jest, a bit of fun, you blasted cripple. Can't you take a joke?'

'Not when it's nearly killing me, I can't.'

'I'll pay you back for breaking my nose – you and that damned brother of yours...' His words were muffled as he tried to staunch the bleeding. 'Just see if I don't. Besides, I know things...'

With that, the "dragon" retrieved its head and went off to lick its wounds, complaining loudly, leaving me sprawled on the grass, trying to recover my breath and wondering what the apprentice knew that he wasn't telling.

. .

A man in the duke's livery lifted me to my feet – "Hercules", the duke's gate-keeper, I recalled.

'My lord saw what happened,' the man said. 'Are you injured?'

'Lord Richard saw?' I hoped the grass would swallow me whole, that the duke should have seen me flat on my back.

'Aye, sorry I wasn't quicker, else our dragon would have more than a bloody nose. You want I should go after the stupid oaf?'

'No. I'm grateful for your assistance but a broken nose will suffice, I hope.' I straightened my muddied clothes, ran a hand through my hair, which was bedraggled and damp, for the grass in the shade was wet still. My ribs felt sore indeed.

'My lord asks that you join him for dinner, when you're ready.'

'Dressed like this?' No amount of brushing down and pulling straight was going to repair the state of my doublet and breeches. "Hercules" shook his great head.

'Fear not, the duke's near as muddy as you are. Besides, he sees through to the man beneath, has no time for finery, frippery and gee-gaws. You'll do well enough.'

I thought about that silk velvet the duke was wearing, the bejewelled hat. No time for finery, eh? Aye, and there was I, looking like I'd been dragged at a cart's tail.

● ●

On the dais, having requested Emily's permission, which she granted with a laugh, Lord Richard stood to address the crowd.

'My lords, ladies, gentlemen and good citizens of this fair city.' He did not raise his voice and yet it rang clear to folk at the back. 'I am grateful to you all for your warm invitation to join you in your revels and, to demonstrate my thanks in an appropriate manner, I ask that you will join me at meat. My men have been encamped over yonder half the night, to ensure the oxen are well cooked in time, so I trust you, one and all, to do justice to their labours and enjoy the feast. Help yourselves!'

'Three cheers for his grace!' someone shouted, and the crowd erupted in joyous commotion at the prospect of free food.

● ●

'Seb? Are you certain you're alright?' Emily asked as we shared a platter of hot sliced meat, perched on the edge of the dais. 'We saw what happened, that dreadful dragon.'

'We?'

'Lord Richard and me. We saw...'

'You like him, don't you?'

'The duke? Of course I like him. He's kind and courteous... and handsome. Really made it seem I was the queen when he went on his knee before me.' She shook out her long tresses, picked at the silk roses on her girdle, forgetting the food.

I wrapped some slices of beef and mutton in my kerchief for Jude later.

'He was only playing his part. No different to the Green Man or Robin Hood.' I don't know why but I wanted to make Lord Richard less of a hero to her, somehow. It was mean of me, small-minded, but I couldn't help myself.

'I know, but he need not have. He could have just marched in and turned me off my seat and sat there himself. But he didn't.'

'No. How gracious of him.'

Emily frowned at me.

'You don't have to be jealous of the duke, Seb.' She put her hand on mine but I pulled away.

'Jealous? Me? Why should I envy him with his good looks, fine clothes and bottomless coffers? God knows, I'm the fortunate one, assured my place in heaven by my suffering in this world, as Father Thomas insists on reminding me. I have nought but pity for Lord Richard, poor blighted soul that he is.'

'Seb, don't. Don't talk like this.'

'You're right. I shouldn't spoil your day with nasty truths.'

'If you can't speak well of Lord Richard, then I don't want to hear it,' she said, dropping her knife on the platter and walking away. I let her go.

• •

When dinner was done, the meat carcases thrown aside for the red kites and crows to pick clean, it was time for the afternoon's sports. Those who possessed a horse, or even a donkey, were preparing their mounts for the races at the north end of the field, where a course was roped off around the horse pool and back again. Skittles and bowls were being played behind the dais by Duck Lane, with a farrow of piglets to share amongst the winners.

But the rest of the field was given over to the archers – the older men at the butts competing for a yard of ale in a contest of accuracy. Best of five. Others demonstrating their speed of shooting. How many shafts loosed in the time taken to say five Paternoster prayers. The more able apprentices and young men, London's hopes for the future, were under Master Stephen Appleyard's personal supervision, whilst the younger lads were instructed by a swarthy veteran of many battles, known as "Nosey" for the simple reason that he lacked one, having had a close encounter with an enemy blade at St Albans years ago. Despite his fearsome looks, Nosey had endless patience with lads new to the art of toxophily.

There were even some women competing amongst themselves, sleeves rolled up, skirts kilted, veils removed so you couldn't tell a respectable wife from a Winchester goose. They seemed to be enjoying themselves. Sir Rob drew my attention to a tall lass with lustrous hair who even seemed to know what she was doing – ah, yes, it was the May Queen herself, still wearing her wilting diadem of flowers.

• •

Still not in the best of humours, my ribs aching, I paid little attention to the knots of activity across the muddy grass, concentrating rather on the music drifting from St Bartholomew's Priory on a westerly breeze that stirred my hair.

Jude should have been here, shooting with the best, famed particularly for his speed, if less-so for his accuracy. He often ended the day with a yard of ale or two for his trouble.

'Lord Dickon will be dismayed at the poor standard of marksmanship, what with the king's forthcoming "enterprise" with the French.' Sir Rob disturbed my train of thought. 'He'd have them practising dawn 'til dusk, week in, week out, 'til they got it right. Look at that fellow there, standing too square to the target, elbow held too high. He'll miss by a country mile. So much for London longbowmen.' As Sir Rob's prophesy proved correct, the shaft sailing off to the right of the butt in a leisurely arc that fell short by yards, someone tapped the knight on the shoulder.

'By your speech you're a Northman, ain't you? One o' Gloucester's men?'

'I am and proud to be so.' Sir Robert drew himself up to his full and impressive height. The man looked him up and down, appraisingly, raising his eyebrows but not intimidated.

'Breed 'em big in the North Country then, I see, good for wrestling, no doubt, but any good with a longbow, eh, Northman?'

'Try me, Londoner.' Sir Rob was grinning.

The man laughed.

'That wouldn't be a fair match. I'm Stephen Appleyard, warden archer, but I'll wager you can't out-shoot my apprentices.'

It was Sir Rob's turn to laugh as he watched a couple of them missing their targets.

'Agreed. What's the wager?'

'Honour and the customary yard of ale.' The knight and Master Appleyard shook hands and the warden archer went off to set up the contest and select his apprentices.

'This may not be a wise thing,' I warned Sir Rob. 'He has some fine marksmen.'

'We'll see. We'll see.'

• •

I saw Tom Bowen and Kit Philpot, no longer in his hateful costume, laughing together at one of the ale stalls, making eyes at a saucy wench in a low-cut yellow gown. "Making eyes" was as far as they were likely to get with her kind. They didn't look much like a grieving son and an apprentice whose master was but lately deceased, but seemed to have entirely forgotten their loss, or didn't care.

Kit was sporting a very fetching swollen nose and the beginnings of a black eye, for which I felt a tingle of satisfaction and wondered what explanation he gave for his war wounds. Not the truth, that was certain. He was downing ale like one rescued from the parched lands of Araby, his prominent Adam's apple bobbing in time with each swallow as he drained a second cup.

Tom caught me watching them and returned me a furtive glance. What had I done to earn that? Or was I the one seeing more than I should? Were those two up to some new devilment? I could believe it of Kit, but Tom always seemed a better-disposed lad, if somewhat timid. Yet, there again, he was looking at me over the rim of his ale cup.

• •

Jack, who had been busy chancing his arm with Nosey, despite his lack of years, came racing over to us.

'Yer going to beat the warden archer, sir? I heard yer was,' he shouted, childish glee spilling over at the prospect.

'Calmly now, young Jack. Wait and see,' Sir Rob told him. 'As yet, I don't even have a bow.'

'I'll find yer one... the finest.' And Jack was off, scampering like a hare across the field. I saw him run, leaping for the sheer joy of being young and able. I averted my eyes.

'Isn't he supposed to be tending the duke's horse?' I asked.

Sir Rob grinned.

'No. It's just Lord Dickon's excuse to give a few pence to the lads. His horse is over there.' The knight indicated with his head. 'Being readied for the racing by his groom.'

• •

I found another shady spot beneath an elm tree beside the horse pool whilst Sir Rob went off to hunt up some ale. The rookery in the branches above was noisy and raucous as Billingsgate market on a Friday morn, the birds quarrelling and flapping like fishwives. But the quiet water looked cool, hardly a ripple to disrupt the green reflections. Sunlight sparkled on the tiniest imperfections of the surface, lights dancing, dazzling the eye. The verdant spears of water irises pierced upwards, the unfolding tripartite flowers just showing as tips of gold. Next week I would gather some of the blooms, use them in the triptych to symbolise the Holy Trinity, as I had used purple ones in Lord Hastings's Book of Hours. Red kites, distant specks in the sky, wheeled in lazy circles on their never-ceasing quest for carrion.

Sir Rob returned with a jug of ale, which we shared, seeing the swallows dart, arrow-swift, over the pool. Jack appeared with a bow stave in one hand and the string in the other, grinning like a cat that had found the cream pot unguarded.

'Best bow in London,' he announced proudly.

Sir Rob looked first at the stout stave and then at the lad who, surprisingly, returned his gaze.

'I didn't steal it or nuffin'. I asked if yer could lend it.'

'Borrow it,' I corrected out of habit.

'Aye, borrowed it then, from ol' Nosey. This bow was his father's, at Azincor, so he says. But the string's new an' untried.'

Sir Rob took the stave of fine English yew, bent it against his instep and strung it with the ease of a man of great strength and much practice. He tested the string, plucking it like a lute string and, hearing the note, shortened it a little in the notch, until it sounded as he required. Satisfied, he strode off to where Stephen Appleyard was in discussion with his youthful archers.

● ●

Everything was ready.

'I need a brace!' Sir Rob called out. Half a dozen were offered and he chose one. The warden archer laced it on his wrist for him. He was then given a quiver of ten shafts so he might get the feel of his new bow and get his eye in.

Sir Rob was good. Even his first shot was on target and the last six were all centred on the red inner. He would be hard to beat, I could see that.

'Now, Master Northerner will shoot against young John, here, in a trial of speed,' the warden archer announced, calling forward Dame Ellen's apprentice tailor. 'He's more used to a needle than a clothyard shaft but the lad will do his best, won't you, John?'

John nodded.

'Right. So it's how many arrows shot in the time it takes to say five Paternosters, the first Paternoster will begin when I say "loose". Make ready, masters.'

Sir Rob had set two dozen arrows, point down most, in the earth at his feet. John had done the same. Each man had his own butt to shoot at.

'Nock your shafts... brace... draw... loose!'

As shafts whistled away from the bowstrings, the crowd began to chant the first Paternoster rapidly, slurring the words. Two, three, four and five Paternosters: "Amen!"

'Cease!' the warden archer yelled.

Sir Rob still had an arrow ready nocked that he hadn't released. I glanced across at the apprentice's remaining arrows. There were just two shafts standing upright as sentinels on guard and the lad's hands were empty. Sir Rob had three left in the ground, one in his hand.

'Check the butts, only shafts that prick the target and stay put count.'

It seemed to me the knight had lost but then the Londoners groaned as one of John's shafts drooped tiredly in the butt and fell out. It wouldn't count. But their dismay turned to laughter as a little dog trotted over and fetched it back, dropping it at the lad's feet.

'Master Northerner, nineteen shafts to count. Master John...' The pause seemed endless. 'Twenty shafts!'

The crowd cheered good-naturedly. Sir Rob was commiserated, thumped on the back and given a cup to refresh himself. He went to the victorious apprentice to congratulate him but the lad only smiled self-consciously and turned away.

'That was fine shooting, sir,' I said, hobbling forward.

'Not fine enough, apparently. Young John is quite a wonder for a slip of a lad.'

'Jude will be sorry to have missed this. He's quite an archer, too.'

'Aye, but it's not done yet. We still have the contest for accuracy. Who will my opponent be this time? Another poor, wee apprentice that shoots like a demon, I suppose, or the dog, maybe?'

I didn't answer. I thought I probably knew.

• •

When Sir Rob was rested, the contestants were called forward for the next round. Emily was chatting with the warden archer. I said nothing to Sir Rob.

'Master Northerner, this is Mistress Emily, your opponent,' Stephen Appleyard said.

Sir Rob looked shocked.

'You don't mind taking on a lass, do you? Only I fear our decent archers are few.'

'No, I have no objection, except that it seems less than fair to challenge a woman, and one so young, at that.'

'She's willing to take her chance, if you are. Aren't you, Em?'

Emily smiled at Sir Rob.

'It will be a pleasure, sir,' she said, restringing her weapon with the ease of a master bowman. I thought she might be more difficult to beat than Sir Rob had bargained for. Was a yard of ale worth the risk of his being bested by a wench, I wondered? Well, the honour of the North was also at stake here so I supposed he couldn't back down now. He seemed calm enough as he stripped off his doublet and rolled up the sleeves of his fine lawn shirt.

They were to shoot at the one target, taking turns, five shafts each. Sir Rob's borrowed arrows were fletched red, Emily's green. Normally contestants drew straws but Sir Rob insisted that the "queen" should go first.

Her first arrow hit dead centre. He matched it, his shaft nudging hers a little crooked in close companionship. This was fine marksmanship, nothing to choose betwixt them. The crowd was growing, folk drawn in from all quarters, the skittles and bowls abandoned.

Her third shot knocked Sir Rob's first arrow out of the target, though it had been there long enough to count.

Rob licked his lips, wiped his sweaty hands on his shirt, which clung damply to his body, revealing well-honed muscles as he nocked the next arrow. It landed a good inch above centre.

I saw him wince at his own failure as Emily levelled her bow for her fourth shot, her arm steady, her grip clean and sure. Her arrow pricked dead centre, splitting the shaft of her first right down to the head buried in the target.

She stepped back, her face impassive.

He sighed. How could he better that? Even so, his shaft tucked itself neatly in the centred cluster – it was good.

The crowd held its breath as Emily took up her position for the last time. She bent the bow, exhaled halfway and loosed the shaft, crying:

'This one's for you, Seb!' as it sliced Sir Rob's previous effort in two.

The knight's final shaft landed two inches to the right. The worst shot of all.

Would he ever live it down, I wondered? What of the honour of the North?

As Sir Rob turned away, he must have been dismayed to find Lord Richard standing there. He'd seen it all, the disgrace of it. Sir Rob, a man so rarely out of humour, was scowling now, but his lord and friend said not a word. The knight shoved the bow at him.

'You do it, then, Dickon. Northern honour and all,' he muttered, as though the duke had criticised his efforts. The crowd took up the cry.

'Duke Richard to shoot!' It seemed fair enough and Lord Richard agreed with a show of reluctance that appeared genuine. To judge from his practice shots, of which two hardly pricked the outer and one fell wide, his reluctance was understandable.

I looked at Sir Rob standing beside me and was surprised to see him grinning broadly; his good nature returned.

'Now you'll see some *real* archery,' he whispered.

Lord Richard removed his fur-trimmed gown and made much of folding it and smoothing the velvet before dropping it on the muddy ground.

'What a way to treat such fine cloth! Did you ever see such a thing, Mary?' Dame Ellen said to her friend, the draper's wife, as she and her cronies looked on behind me.

'Shush, Ellen! He's concentrating.'

'He's got a fine stance, I'll give him that,' said Stephen Appleyard beside them.

'And a finer arse in those tight hose,' giggled Maudie Marlow.

'Hush now. Give him a fair chance,' Mary scolded them. 'He's not a Londoner, poor fellow. We can't expect too much of him.'

After delays to quaff a mouthful of ale, re-roll his sleeves, have someone re-tie his brace and tightening his tooled leather belt more than once – tactics that confirmed to the crowd that this northern lord was all wind and no substance whilst, at the same time, increasing their expectations – Lord Richard was ready.

Requiring no fanfare, he took up position, nocked his first arrow with two more in the dirt in front of him, and let fly: once, twice and thrice. It was done.

No one had sight sharp enough to see anything but a blurring of goose feathers, but all three arrows quivered there, in the centre of the target, each slotted through the flights of the one before, splitting the shafts perfectly in half.

After a moment of stunned silence, those who had blinked having missed it, the crowd applauded with restraint.

Lord Richard bowed slightly, looking a little disconcerted by his own skill.

'My lord,' the warden archer spoke stiffly. 'It is the tradition that you win a yard of ale for such a display of, er, marksmanship.'

'So much, Master Appleyard? A cupful will do for me. Share the rest among your bowmen, although there is one reward I should savour more.'

Stephen Appleyard looked doubtful, fearing what his lordship might ask.

'A kiss from the queen?'

The warden archer, relieved, pushed his daughter forward.

'Go along, Em. Give his grace his reward.'

Emily hesitated for less than a heartbeat. I watched her press her lips against Lord Richard's cheek, still damp from his exertions on a day that had turned quite hot. She let her lips linger for just a little longer than was proper. A look passed between them.

His eyes, which had been closed whilst she kissed him, now regarded her, bright and mischievous. He smiled, his mouth curving in pleasure, before he bowed gracefully.

'Thank you, your highness, my lady.' He backed away, as from the presence of royalty, still smiling.

A royal duke, I thought, but a man all the same, and a mountebank, besides.

● ●

'It was all a trick, you know that,' I told Sir Rob afterwards. 'John and Emily are the warden archer's children, born with a bow in their hands. It was hardly a fair contest for you.'

'Fair?' Sir Rob shrugged. 'Life is rarely fair. Besides, I think we ended "honours even" betwixt the North and London. Lord Dickon saw to that. Did you see the warden's face? I swear his jaw was hanging to his knees after Dickon's last shot.' He chortled at the memory as we walked up the field. 'Come on, they'll be lining up the horses for the first race and I'm expecting as much of Dickon's stallion as I did of his master.'

'No, I have to see Jude.'

'You want me to come?'

I looked at him, knowing he preferred to stay for the races but felt obliged to offer.

'No. I'm grateful to you but Jack will assist me. We'll manage, won't we, Jack?'

The lad's ferocious scowl said it all. He wanted to watch the horses too, not accompany me in visiting that filthy gaol.

'Won't *we*, Jack?'

'S'pose so.'

On the way to Newgate

RENNER STREET was living up to its popular name of Giltspur Street as knights rode their fine coursers and destriers towards the fields in time for the races.

We had to draw back into the doorway of the Hart's Horn Tavern to allow a particularly mettlesome beast to go by, tossing its head and pawing at the air. The rider was none other than Lord Lovell, whom we'd seen briefly at Crosby Place on Saturday last, looking as ill-tempered and frustrated as his mount, his violet coat streaming out behind him.

'I'm thirsty, master. Can't we have us some ale here first?' Jack whined. Anything to avoid the Whit.

'No.' I felt equally reluctant but the best thing was to get it over, not put it off.

Jack trailed along beside me, dragging his feet almost as much as I did my lame leg. Our pace was slowing, what with the lad's disinclination and my weariness. My ribs hurt and I was no longer sure that one wasn't broken when I had to breathe so shallow, else it felt like a knife in my side. Waves of nausea kept flooding over me, hot and cold together.

Newgate Gaol

THE PORTAL at Newgate was as intimidating as ever but the turnkey remembered us.

'Come t' see the murderer, 'ave yer? Well 'e ain't gone nowhere, any road.'

I nodded, gave the fellow a penny for his trouble as he escorted us into Hell's bowels as before. The stench got no better.

Jude was hunched on the bottom step, as he had been yesterday. Perhaps he hadn't moved.

'I brought you some meat,' I said, sending Jack down the steps with the greasy kerchief-wrapped slices of beef and mutton. I remained leaning against the mildewed wall by the door; didn't dare risk the stairs.

Jude didn't reply but snatched the bundle greedily.

'Are you well?' I called down. What was there to be said at such a time and place?

Jude looked up at me, meat juices dribbling down his chin.

'Don't ask. But you look like Death's handmaid! Who's been knocking you about?'

'Nobody.'

'Liar. You think I don't know the signs by now?'

'I was clumsy, fell. It was nought.'

'It was Kit Philpot what beat him,' Jack said. 'Dressed as a dragon.'

'Dragon?' Jude spoke round a mouthful of half-chewed mutton.

'Aye, Saint George's... at the revels it was,' Jack added.

'I'll give him "Saint George". I'll bloody slay the bastard myself, when I get my hands on him. He's gone too far this time, soon as my back's turned.'

'It doesn't matter, Jude. Forget it. You can't do anything about it in here.' I was feeling bad, what with the stench of the gaol and the pain in my ribs. I couldn't keep standing much longer.

'It matters to me. How sorely are you hurt?'

I made no answer.

'Kicked his ribs in, I reckon. Right poorly he was, on the way 'ere, groaning an' swooning and throwed up, he did.'

'Jack, stop exaggerating.'

'Exer what? I ain't telling lies.'

'Ignore him, Jude. I'll do well enough...' I was about to say 'when I leave this place' but thought that would be like pouring vinegar in an open wound for my poor brother.

• •

'Time's up,' the turnkey said, waving his torchlight dangerously.

'Don't you feed folk in here?' I demanded of him, seeing how ravenous Jude was.

'Folk get fed. Bloody murderers don't, not if it's down t' me, any road.'

'I paid you good money yesterday to see my brother got food and drink.'

In answer, the man spat.

'Oh, 'e'll get wots comin', rely on it.'

'I'll see you in the morning, Jude. I'll be at the hearing. I promise.' I didn't know what else I might say to cheer Jude and left, before the stink and the black misery got the better of me.

• ●

As soon as the door banged shut, Jude was leapt upon by the other inmates. They tore the rest of the food from his grasp, yanked his hair, clawed his face, screeching and cursing. He tried to fight them off but there were five, maybe more. He kicked and lashed out but a fist caught him on the jaw and the darkness slammed down, bursting with stars.

• ●

By the time his senses settled, the food was gone, even the last tantalising whiff of roasted meat overpowered by the stench of other people's shit and unwashed bodies. He grieved for his lost dinner. He'd thought he had no tears left, but he did.

When Seb got him out of here, proved his innocence. Aye, what innocence would be left by then? He would kill these filthy animals who shared this sewer, all of them... and the bloody turnkey-gaoler. Especially the gaoler, that perverted bastard.

Jude loved women, that was natural. But what had been done to him because he was a "pretty lad". That wasn't. There were no words to describe what the gaoler did last night.

Jude shuddered. He'd tried to make out it was some other poor bugger who suffered at the hands of that whore's son, refusing to feel the pain and humiliation inflicted on his own body, sending his spirit away to hide in some dark corner, untouched, 'til it was over. The pretence had worked. Almost. Whatever the future held, it couldn't be worse than that. But he still had to survive tonight, God have mercy.

And another thing. That wretch Kit Philpot was going to regret his bullying, come what may, if it was the last thing Jude did.

CHAPTER ELEVEN

Monday eve
The Foxley brothers' rooms

I T TOOK a long time for me to struggle home from Newgate after visiting my poor brother. At times I was almost on my knees and Jack, though a strong lad, wasn't tall enough to support me for, if I'd been able ever to stand straight, Jude reckoned I would have been nigh six feet, like him. As we turned along West Cheap, by the conduit, and came within sight of the front door, we saw Sir Rob standing there, waiting. He sprinted towards us and took my weight, propping me against the lych gate of St Michael's church.

'I've been waiting for you,' he said. 'Where have you been?'

'The Whit. Jude's not faring so well. He hasn't...' But Sir Rob wasn't listening.

'I have to tell you, my friend, I'm sorry, but your place has been wrecked.'

'What? What's amiss with it?'

'It looks as though thieves got in, whilst the whole neighbourhood was at the revels. They've turned it upside down, I'm afraid.'

'What did they take?' I asked, realisation dawning slowly. Sir Rob shook his head.

'In all the mess, I can't tell. You need to see for yourself.'

• •

A madman had torn our rooms apart. There wasn't a stick of furniture undamaged. Our stools had been smashed to kindling. Every cup, bowl and platter was broken. Every item of linen, bed sheets and undergarments, was ripped. My nascent triptych lay beneath a broken stool in pieces, beyond repair. But what brought tears to my eyes were the drawings of Christ that I'd spent hours working at last eve, now strewn in a spillage of ale, gum arabic and splintered wood, the Saviour's face obliterated. It was sacrilege, an act of blasphemy.

'Why?' I cried, expecting no answer. None came. Sir Rob, Jack and the little knot of neighbours beginning to gather by the door remained silent, shaking their heads, 'til one muttered:

'Because yer brother's a damned murderer, no doubt.' The words came as a shock, like cold water thrown over me. Was that it?

'Is anything missing, Seb?' Sir Rob asked, re-calling my attention. 'Money? Valuables?'

'The duke's coin, the money should be in the linen coffer by the beds but that was probably what they were after. Oh, God, what will the duke say?'

'This it?' Sir Rob came from the cramped bed chamber, holding aloft the little leather bag in which we kept our savings.

'Aye.'

Sir Rob tipped coins into his hand.

'Still here.'

I sighed with relief.

'So what were they after?' Sir Rob asked as he replaced the gold angels and nobles and gave me the bag.

'We don't have anything else of value, unless they were after the old book. But no one even knows Jude borrowed it.'

'Where do you keep it?'

'Jude put it in his hidey-hole. I can't reach it, which is why he didn't put the money there. There's a loose brick up high, on the side of the chimney.' I pointed. 'I don't know why he hid it there, it's not worth much. That brick... to the right.'

Sir Rob lifted out a loose brick, revealing a space within the thickness of the chimney.

'If it was the book they wanted, they didn't get it.' He handed me the tattered little volume. 'Come on! All of you by the door! Stop gawping and help us set this place to rights. Can anyone lend a stool or board or bed linen?'

● ●

Later, with the rooms restored as best they could be, with borrowed furniture and treenware, Jack and I were left alone, contemplating a belated supper from the cook shop across the way. But I felt distracted, unable to settle. A piece of violet cloth was snagged on the splintered end of the table and I worked it free. It was fine quality and I recalled seeing the colour recently but not where. Jack, having demolished more than his share of plum tart, was bored, perched on a neighbour's spindly stool, drumming his fingers on the mended board.

'Love of God! Will you stop that afore it drives me insane! Go out, see your friend Mark, or something... and for pity's sake, stay out of trouble.'

But Jack was gone already, like a hound let off the leash, the door banging behind him.

I had enough to worry about, without him. I took up the once-beautiful drawings of Christ, but they were soul-destroying to look at now.

• •

Needful of something less dismal to think about than beginning my work over again, I lifted Gilbert Eastleigh's old book down from the shelf and turned the pages. It was fragile, puffs of paper dust rising at my touch. But nothing caught my interest. That was until I came to a stark heading in red ink: "Care Reqd", it announced. It was a list of ingredients used by limners down the ages, indicating those that were unhealthful to use, the precautions to be taken in each case and the likely symptoms if that care proved insufficient. In a few instances, the treatment and antidote, if there was one, were given also. I ran my finger down the list. "Vermilion". Aye, the symptoms were much as Gilbert had described them to me. "Orpiment". Vomiting, the flux... now, that wasn't at all as Gilbert had said. The hairs rose on the back of my neck. I swallowed hard as the words spelled out, in far too lurid detail, Matthew Bowen's last moments.

He had been poisoned with orpiment. I was now convinced of that: a lethal dose served in ale to disguise the colour and, perhaps, the taste too. But what of Jude's knife? The weapon that *hadn't* caused Bowen's death?

And Gilbert Eastleigh? Why didn't he tell me the true symptoms of orpiment poisoning? Was he mistaken? Or was he purposefully attempting to mislead? Don't leap to conclusions, I warned myself out loud. It may have been a fearful accident, nothing more, the knife a distraction to draw attention from the mishap. Aye, that must have been the way of it. Gilbert simply misremembered the symptoms. Even so, I took up pen and paper and copied out the entry under "Orpiment", before closing the book with a thud of finality, like the fall of a dead man.

A page fluttered loose, or rather a few. Not parchment but paper, folded in two. I retrieved them from beneath my borrowed stool. It was a poor hand indeed, not much better than a scrawl, but it was legible, just...

Pale & black with false citrine, imperfect white & red,
The Peacocks feathers in colour gay, the Rainebowe whych shal overgoe,
The spotted panther, the lyon green, the crowes bil blue as lead,
These shal apeare before thee perfect white, and manie other moe...

I skipped to the next page, ignoring the strange symbols.

Take thou ambergris & derive it smalle & ore of Jupiter in the fire
With Venus in her grene gowne & Mars armyd red as blode.
Aftyr the Moon ascendeth in the scorpyon bynd therewith the dragon's sede,
And thou shalt have for alle thy payns that whych thou shalt most desyre,
From nakyd povertie be delyvered when Sol shal overwhelm thy nede.
Grete shal be thy powere, domynant in alle thynges of this Erthe
When Sol shal bryne fierce & men do falle that of Eve had byrthe.
The Stone of Antient Hermes Thrice Magister forgyd in Erthes fire set free
Shal graunt thre thynges to thee of richys & knowlige & perfect bodyly.

My eye was drawn to those last words: "perfect bodily". Was I reading this correctly? I held the paper to the candlelight and re-read every line with care. The stone that could grant riches, knowledge and a perfect body. I didn't understand much of what I read but I reached out an unsteady hand for the ale jug. There was only one stone that could do all those things. The famed Philosopher's Stone. Could this be the receipt for making it, or using it?

I thought back to the wreckage of Bowen's workshop. Could the old man's killer have been searching for this? Had it been in Eastleigh's book all along or had it been hidden there later, whilst it was in the workshop? Riches and knowledge... there were men who would kill for those. And a perfect body? I knew the answer to that.

Despite this new-found intelligence, after all that had happened, I wanted nothing more than to lie down and sleep on my borrowed palliasse, between borrowed sheets and beneath a borrowed blanket, but it seemed Emily wouldn't let me escape the anguish of the day so easily.

She bustled in, smiling, carrying more clean linen.

'Look, Seb, I've got one of my brother's old shirts for you. Yours is filthy and torn. Take it off. I'll wash and mend it for you. You can wear John's for now.'

'No, Em, this will suffice me.'

'And tomorrow? What will you wear when you attend the Bailey, since this is now the only shirt you have that's not rent to rags?' I shrugged, too tired to care what I would wear tomorrow. 'Come now. Let me help you with it.'

Women! I objected in vain as Emily grabbed the points that laced my mud-stained jerkin down the front and had them loose afore I could fend her off. My shirt followed. In moments she had the linen up over my head and peeled the cloth from my awkward arm last of all. I was left naked from the waist up before her eyes, reduced to tears of rage and humiliation that she should see me thus, my hateful body revealed in all its frightfulness. I tried to cover myself but she did not recoil in horror. Instead, what I saw in her eyes wasn't revulsion but hot anger.

'Who did that to you, Seb? Who dared hurt you so?' I couldn't think what she meant. My body had always been like this and she knew full well that Kit Philpot had bruised my ribs. But she reached out and touched my neck with gentle fingers and I remembered there were older bruises there as well. Too late to hide the evidence, I put my hands to my throat where the marks made by Jude's powerful fingers still blotched the skin, like stains on cloth.

'It's nothing, nothing at all. I hurt myself, weeks ago it was.' The look Emily gave me said clearly that she knew I was lying.

'Who did it?'

I closed my eyes, prayed she would go, leave me in peace. But she didn't. Instead she slipped her brother's old shirt over my head, helping me to get my left arm into the sleeve.

'It was Jude, wasn't it?'

'No!' My response was too quick, too vehement. I could tell by her eyes that she knew she was right.

The attic room above the apothecary's shop

YOUNG TOM Bowen struggled to wakefulness through the cobwebs of nightmare, wondering how he'd managed to sleep at all. He lay on the straw, hag-ridden and sweating as the terrors ebbed away. The cobwebs were real enough but they were the weavings of the homely spiders who shared his room, not the Devil's constructions, as he'd feared. Thoughts of the Devil, Old Scratch, whatever name you gave the Evil One, terrified everyone, but Tom knew the Devil was real and took human form. He knew because he had met him, face to face that day, seen what he could do.

Tom had been instructed by his master to attend the May revels – a rare treat, indeed – but there had to be some stipulation, of course, though it didn't sound too onerous a task. He was told to keep a watch on Seb Foxley. He'd had no notion why but, when Foxley seemed engrossed in some activity or other, Tom was to report this to Lord Lovell at the Hart's Horn Tavern.

In truth, Tom had forgotten his orders half the time, drinking ale with Kit Philpot and jesting with some likely wenches – without success. He never won his bet to earn a kiss from the buxom lass he had a fancy for. No matter. Belatedly, he'd remembered to keep an eye on Foxley and, seeing his quarry engrossed in the archery competitions, had run to the Hart's Horn.

Lord Lovell had been sitting in a dark corner, devouring a roasted chicken, washing it down with copious amounts of red wine. The lord complained about Tom's tardiness and then moaned about him arriving before the meal was done. There was no pleasing some folk. Tom watched him eat, hoping to be dismissed, back to Smithfield, but no. Lovell had more work for him.

The dour-featured lord had ordered him to follow as they hurried to West Cheap. Tom was shocked that they walked. His lordship's beautiful boots would be ruined in the reeking mire of the Shambles.

'This Foxley's hovel?' Lovell had demanded. It was. Lovell lifted the latch and went in, wrinkling his nose at the poverty of the place, not the smell, for it was clean enough. 'Search it!'

'What me, my lord?'

'Who else? Get on with it, you imbecile.' Lovell closed the door and leaned against it, folding his arms, a sneer on his fulsome lips.

'W-what am I looking for?'

'You should know better than I bloody do. You lost the damn book.'

Tom began carefully lifting blankets and bed sheets and smoothing them back in place, fearing Seb Foxley might know the place had been gone through. Tentative as a mouse and in silence, he raised the coffer lid and sorted through some linen, releasing the smell of lavender. It made him sneeze.

'I'm sorry, it's not here, my lord.' Tom was sweating with apprehension. There were so few places to look.

Lovell left his post by the door and in three strides had Tom by the scruff of the neck.

'The fucking thing's here! Now find it.' He flung Tom to the floor and whipped a gleaming blade from his belt. Tom felt a dribble of urine, hot in his hose, his eyes riveted to the knife. But Lovell lifted the palliasse from one of the beds and slit it, like gutting a pig, so the musty straw spilled out, then did the same with the other bed. Having failed to discover the missing book, he ripped the sheets and blankets with the knife.

Tom didn't understand. How could a volume – even a small one – be hidden in the thickness of the linen? But Lovell didn't seem to care. He emptied the coffer, though it was too heavy for him to overturn, but every threadbare shirt and darned hose was rent to ribbons.

In the other room an axe stood against the chimney, ready to chop kindling. Lovell wielded it as a man used to weapons of war. Tom cowered in the corner while the lord smashed everything to splinters: stools, tables, wooden bowls and cups, grunting with each thud of the axe. The shelves were swept clear of jugs and lamps and quills and ink pots. Sheets of paper were torn asunder and trampled.

When there was nothing more to destroy, Lovell leaned against the chimney to recover his breath, throwing the axe aside. Tom squealed as it smacked the floor just an inch or so from his leg, but it seemed the lord hadn't done it on purpose to scare him. More likely he didn't even see Tom cringing by the hearth, for there was madness in Lovell's eyes. The flames of Hell itself burned within those black orbs, his face contorted with rage.

Blinded by anger, the lord stormed out, snagging his sleeve on the splintered table, cursing. Tom was forgotten.

• •

Only when he was sure Lord Lovell was gone, did Tom scurry off home, to hide in his attic, knowing he had seen the Devil for certain. He prayed he would never see the like again.

Tuesday the second day of May
The Bailey

JUDE WAS to appear at the Bailey soon after nine of the clock but, by eight, we were ready. I wore the same darned hose and frayed jerkin but at least Emily had freshly laundered my shirt beneath.

But Jack was another case altogether: Dame Ellen and Emily had cut down some of the widow's son's clothes – Dick: he that had been long away – and remade them for the lad. Now Jack looked so clean and kempt as to be hardly recognised, especially since Emily had insisted on cutting and delousing his hair that very morning. Jack had hated every moment of that and Dame Ellen had clouted him for the foul language he used to Emily, the ungrateful little toad.

It took me a while to make my way along West Cheap, Bladder Street and the Shambles. Robin Marlow caught sight of me by the cook shop and took the opportunity to lob a handful of mud, knocking my cap off and smearing my face and hair. Jack was enraged and charged after Robin who was twice his size, at least.

Jack came back a few moments later, dusting off his hands, grinning in triumph.

'What did you do to him?' I was wiping my face with the back of my hand. Jack fetched my hat.

'Horse trough. See 'ow 'e likes it!'

· ·

Sir Robert was waiting outside the Bailey and gave us a cheerful greeting. I made some suitable response, I believe, but felt overawed by the grave and brooding portal before us. I'd seen the place many times but never had cause to go inside. I couldn't have been more nervous if I was the accused. I wouldn't admit it but I felt queasy, my heart thumping; never had I been more eager to run in my life – if only I could. A crow squawked from the turret above the entrance, its wicked eye regarding our every move. I hated their kind, the Devil's acolytes all.

An hour or more we must have stood in the crush of spectators, squeezed into the open court of the Bailey to watch the proceedings – a murderer always drew the crowds. Jack was restive, fidgeting with impatience, uncomfortable, no doubt, at the proximity of various officers of the law, some of whom knew him rather too well – not that they'd recognise him now, washed, shorn and in his new clothes.

My back ached, having to stand for so long, yet this was outweighed by my mental agony on Jude's behalf. Only Sir Rob seemed at ease. Perhaps his time spent as a courtier meant he was used to standing around, waiting on events.

• •

At last the bailiff thumped his staff of office three times and demanded that all should rise for the entry of the judges and their clerks. As usual, elbowed to the back of the court, I couldn't see what was going on. The first man brought out was apparently accused of coining, a crime regarded as treason against the crown and, therefore, reckoned even more serious than murder, but far less interesting to the crowd. I heard the fellow plead 'not bloody guilty, you buggers!' but wasn't able to see what made Sir Rob and others laugh. The judges called for order and the bailiff shouted and thumped his staff 'til the merriment subsided.

'What did he do?' Jack whispered to Sir Rob, since he also was lacking sufficient height to have seen for himself.

'Pulled down his hose and showed the judges his bare arse,' the knight whispered back, grinning.

Jack smothered his mirth, just about.

'I wish I'd seen 'im.'

• •

Jude was up next, his name announced in ringing tones, his alleged crime of murder read out loud. The crowd murmured angrily at this crime against one of their own, even if not a particularly popular one, craning their necks for a better view of Jude.

'This one 'ere's 'is crookback'd bruvver,' someone said close at my left hand and a small circle suddenly opened up around me. Folk stared.

'What him? The filfy 'unchback?'

'Yeah! Stinking bloody cripple.'

'What's he doing 'ere wiv decent folk, eh? Get the ugly devil out o' 'ere!'

'Kick 'im out!'

'Get the 'unchback bastard!'

• •

Suddenly, I was surrounded, set upon by the crowd. It happened so swiftly. An angry mob separated me from Sir Rob and Jack. I fell to the floor. Shoving his way through the crowd, Sir Rob succeeded in reaching me, picked me up bodily and shouldered his way to the door. The mob cheered, mistakenly believing he was throwing out the wretched hunchback, not realising this was a mission of succour.

The court was in uproar. The judges' and the bailiff's shouts for order went unheeded. Arrests were made, a dozen or more charged with contempt before the court was cleared, proceedings abandoned for the day.

• •

There was a commotion of some kind out in the open court, towards the gate. At first Jude took no notice, feeling wretched after what Fate had flung at him over the past couple of days. He couldn't get the filthy image of the turnkey's face out of his head: that leering, black-toothed cavern of a mouth coming at him, a demon spewed from Hell. And worse, the defilement, the perversions forced upon his body. He'd never reckoned himself an innocent, but even in his worst nightmares he couldn't have imagined being subjected to such vileness. Despite the heat of the court, he shivered convulsively at the memory, swallowing down bile.

But the commotion was increasing, sounding more like a riot, shouting, yelling, crashing bodies. A scream alerted him to the present. His guards were distracted, more interested in the sudden excitement of a fight than their prisoner. Jude seized the opportunity, whilst one guard was craning his neck for a better view and was jostled off-balance, to elbow the other in the eye, vault the bar that separated the accused from the public and sprint for the door behind the judges' bench.

It was done in a moment with no thought for the consequences nor for his next course of action. He was out, free, and that was all that mattered. He made his way along the backs of the buildings of the Bailey. The waste ground there was overgrown with nettles and brambles overhanging the ditch that ran along the bottom of the city wall. In places, the wall was in disrepair, making it climbable – except that his hands were still tied. He crawled between the collapsed masonry of an old bastion tower and a gnarled willow tree that grew in the foetid ditch. He knew this bastion was next to Warwick's Inn on the other side of the wall, where the extensive gardens stretched all the way to Amen Lane.

In the shallow, stinking mud at the bottom of the ditch, amongst the rubbish, Jude found what he needed – a bit of rusted metal that had once been a tool or a boot-scraper, perhaps – and went to work, wearing through the rope that tied his wrists. At first it seemed the ropes would defeat the iron, rubbing away chunks of rust and cutting into his flesh. But finally the cords began to fray.

The sounds of the hue and cry were coming closer. Men shouting and, worse, the baying of hounds. They would find him for sure. In desperation, with his hands not yet loose, he crouched in the mud, praying its stench would hide his scent from the dogs, though the smell made him retch as he disturbed the black slime sucking at his shoes.

• •

The dogs were coming nearer, having followed his trail to where he had crossed the ditch further up the Bailey. He could hear them snuffling, questing for his scent, their handlers cursing at the prospect of getting covered in filth. With renewed urgency, he worked at the ropes, straining at them 'til his wrists were bleeding. Suddenly, the last threads broke but there was no time for relief. He scrambled up the uneven ivy-clad stonework of the bastion, the makeshift repairs of centuries giving him handholds enough to climb the city wall and tumble over into the garden of Warwick's Inn on the other side.

It was a longer drop than Jude had expected, knocked the wind out of him. He lay there, trying to pant silently as a dog howled in frustration below the wall on the other side. It had found his scent just a moment too late. How long would it take them to go around to Newgate or Ludgate and enter the city? Then they would have to gain entry into Warwick's Inn. He had a little time, or so he thought.

He heard voices, the sound of boots scrabbling on stone and realised his pursuers were following his trail literally. Too close and too soon. Jude was up, running through a rose garden, the thorns tearing at his clothes, into a little orchard of ancient fruit trees – apple, pear and cherry. But they would follow him there. Somehow they'd got the damned dog over the wall as well.

• •

In the orchard, a little old fellow was struggling with an unwieldy pruning hook to cut off a branch of an apple tree that was white with mildew after all the rain. He looked more a danger to himself than the diseased leaves. Without thinking, being so accustomed to assisting his brother in difficulties, Jude grabbed the tool and had the tree trimmed in a moment, tipping his cap to the old man who grinned after him.

'Gawd bless yer!' he called out.

Jude shook his head at his own stupidity. As if he had time to waste when his freedom depended on haste. The dog was gaining upon him.

'Up the tree, lad!' the man shouted.

Jude saw a ladder, propped against a great pear tree and, having no better idea, took the old fellow's advice – at least dogs couldn't climb trees. The man trudged over to the ladder, whistling a tune to himself, and removed it to another tree.

Jude, climbing high as he dared, to where the leaves and white blossoms were thickest, cursed himself for a fool again. Now he was trapped, at the fellow's mercy.

He watched from his high vantage point as his pursuers reached the orchard, their dog nosing the long grass eagerly. He tried to shrink into the leafy canopy, holding his breath, wedged in the fork of a gnarled bough.

'You lookin' fer the tall lad wi' fairish hair?' he heard the old man ask. Oh Lord, no! That was it, now.

'Aye. Have yer seen him, the bastard? 'Scaped the bloody Bailey, him.'

The old man sucked his teeth and nodded, pointing.

'That way, over the roof o' the gatehouse. Never seen the like. Climbed like a squirrel, he did.'

The men thought this over, one eyeing the dog dubiously since the animal seemed determined upon going further into the orchard in its quest for the miscreant.

'Come on, yer stupid bugger.' The man hauled on the dog's leash, dragging it in the direction of the gatehouse at the north end of the garden. 'Get it wrong one more bloody time and I'll drown yer meself, yer useless mutt. What do I bloody feed yer for, eh?'

• •

With the men and dog gone to search elsewhere, the old man settled down beneath the pear tree, pulled his cap over his eyes and dozed off in the dappled sun and shadow of the quiet orchard. He did not move for an hour or more, by which time the pursuers were long departed, to try their luck elsewhere.

'You can come down now, they're gawn.' At last, the old man set the ladder in place for Jude to climb down. 'Don't know what you did to have the likes o' them comin' after you. Don't want to know, but you're safe fer the time bein'.'

Jude was grinning as he descended the ladder.

'My thanks for this, goodman.'

The old fellow shrugged.

'One good turn an' all that. An' the name's Bartholomew. The best way out o' this garden is through my place down there, house with the cat-slide roof. See it? It's not locked and looks out on Amen Lane, if'n you're goin' that way.' He winked at Jude, patted him on the arm. 'You best be more careful the company you keep in future, lad.' Then he took up his long-handled tool and went back to his pruning, still whistling.

Chuckling, Jude jogged down the row of fruit trees, towards the long, steeply-sloping roof of Bartholomew's house. As the old man had said, the back door wasn't locked and Jude went in, the lintel so low he had to stoop.

The single room was dark, lit only by a slant of sunshine that sneaked through a gap in the window shutter. Two stools, a lop-sided trestle board and a small coffer was all the furniture. More sparse than home, Jude thought. The hearth was cold but a solitary wooden cup and trencher sat upon the board. No sign of food nor drink. Jude crossed to the window and looked through the gap between the shutter boards.

Amen Lane was thronged with folk going about their afternoon business: goodwives with baskets, apprentices shouting their masters' wares and services, fine folk mincing around the worst of the mire, a drayman yelling at his horse, which had its own ideas about which way to go. Jude sat on a stool, thinking. Was it best to leave now, lose himself in the crowd? Or wait until dark, when the streets would be empty?

And where could he go? Not home. First place they'd look. Sanctuary? Perhaps, but few religious houses could guarantee safety these days. Look what happened four years ago, in Tewkesbury Abbey. That had been a scandalous affair, the talk of England, when King Edward had marched into the abbey after his victory over Queen Margaret's Lancastrians, and dragged his cowering enemies out of sanctuary, declaring the abbey had no such rights.

As Jude looked out through the shutter again he saw a cavalcade of liveried riders, coming out of Warwick Lane and trotting down Ave Maria Alley opposite, escort for some man of rank, no doubt. There was a handsome litter, bearing the arms of the Duke of Clarence: the king's middle brother. Of course, he was the current owner of Warwick's Inn, Jude remembered. A crowd pressed close, hopeful of largesse from the occupant of the litter. This was his chance to join them whilst attention was drawn to the procession.

He latched on to a group of entertainers, musicians piping and drumming as they went skipping along. Others were turning somersaults in the street, leaping and jumping. He skipped too, dancing and cavorting like an idiot, plastering a stupid grin on his face. Someone even threw him a coin, which he caught neatly.

As the cavalcade continued on down Spurrier Row – probably to the Duchess of York's riverside place at Baynard's Castle – Jude detached himself from the entertainers and turned into the precincts of St Paul's, strolling along as though there was naught of concern to him in the world.

The Hart's Horn Tavern

GOODWIFE FLETCHER stepped back to survey her handiwork. 'There, Master Seb, I've done my best for you, but you'll need to see a surgeon about that eye, I think.'

'I'm grateful to you, mistress,' I said quietly, leaning back against the warm chimney wall in the kitchen of the Hart's Horn.

'She's right, Seb. It's a nasty gash you have there. It'll probably need a few stitches,' Sir Rob said, handing me a wet cloth to wipe away a renewed trickle of blood. 'Does this sort of thing happen to you often?'

'No. I tend to avoid folk who don't know me too well and, if that's not possible, Jude's always there to look out for me. No one crosses him, if they know what's good for them.'

Jack nodded agreement. I held the cool, damp cloth to my eye. It was swelling rapidly, so I could barely squint between the lids. My hands still shook. Carefully, I touched my jaw, my cheek. My face must be a mass of bruises, my hands cut and my ribs hurt from yet another pounding. Maybe bones were broken this time but, for the moment, I was too weary to do anything but rest where I was.

'You ought to be abed,' I heard Sir Rob say.

• •

The bed upstairs at the Hart's Horn was warm and comfortable. The surgeon, Master Dagville – I had been sufficiently aware to insist I didn't want the services of Gilbert Eastleigh – had attended me, stitched the gash above my left eyebrow and another on my right arm, smeared an evil-smelling ointment on my face and ribs to bring out the bruises and administered a potion of willow bark so bitter it made me shudder. And he had charged six pence for the tortures inflicted.

I must have slept fitfully for a while, I had no idea how long. It was dark in the room with the window shutters closed, so it could be day or night. I seemed to be alone, for I sensed no one else with me, only the sounds of the busy tavern downstairs and the smell of food cooking in the kitchen below. I lay, dozing for a while until raised voices broke in on my half-conscious mind.

'You can't tell him now. He's in no fit state,' I heard Goodwife Fletcher say.

'He must be questioned,' said an angry male voice I didn't recognise.

'You go in that room, you'll answer to the duke for the consequences.' Sir Robert sounded threatening.

'He don't know nuffin anyhow!' Jack shouted. 'How can he? He's been abed since dinnertime.'

There was no doubt they were talking about me. Questioned about what, I wondered, but I must have drifted off to sleep again.

• •

'I don't believe you! It can't be true.'

Sir Rob sat on the bed, looking at me with a sorrowful expression.

'I'm sorry, Seb, but it is. Jude has escaped from the Bailey. He's on the run. He took advantage of the commotion when everyone had their attention on the riot around you and gave his gaolers the slip. Gave one of them a black eye even worse than yours, apparently. Now the damned fools want to question you.'

'But why? I don't know anything.'

'That's what I told 'em,' Jack put in.

'They seem to think the mob's attack on you was all part of a plan to give Jude the chance to get away.' Sir Rob was doing his best to explain but I couldn't make black nor white out of what he was telling me.

'No. No! That's absurd!' I thumped my fists on the coverlet. 'God knows, there was no plan. You think I pay folk to near beat my brains out, to break my bones?'

'Damn it, Seb, I never thought anything of the kind,' Sir Rob protested, striding across to the window and flinging the shutters open, letting in the fading light of dusk.

'Well, perhaps I should have done. I know Jude would have done as much to get me free.'

'That's just foolish talk. The law must take its course and...'

'And get my innocent brother hanged!' My voice broke into a shuddering sob on the last word. 'Oh, God help us! Help us, please,' I prayed, rocking back and forth on the bed. Sir Rob put a comforting arm about me, but I shrugged him off. So he took the hint and went downstairs. Jack left too, but Goodwife Fletcher sat quietly with me, stroking my forehead and hushing me like a babe until I slept again.

St Paul's Cathedral

JUDE ENTERED the little church of St Gregory on the south side of the cathedral, blessed himself with holy water from the stoop by the door and crossed the nave. A priest was chanting prayers on his knees before the altar, oblivious to Jude as he kept to the silent shadows. The latch of the door into St Paul's clunked loudly, so it seemed, but the priest did not interrupt his prayers to look.

Once in the west end of the cathedral, Jude went straight to the steps that led down to the crypt. He knew the place well, had often come here as an apprentice, to Matthew Bowen's paper store, to collect fresh supplies.

The crypt smelled musty, of old incense, candle wax and parchment. Piles of elderly vellum were stacked around, liberally adorned with dust and cobwebs. Reams of paper were stored at the east end of the crypt, by St Faith's, but here, at the west end, the stationers' stocks were largely forgotten, the owners probably in the charnel house by now. Jude knew of a dark corner, where he'd taken a wench or two in his younger days, hidden away behind timber and scaffold poles that looked to have been there since St Paul's was built. The timber leaned idly against the wall but behind it was a little alcove, which seemed to serve no purpose but to be a hidey hole for lovers, or sinners of some other kind.

It was still there. More cobwebs than ever, the dust of decades on the stone floor – all undisturbed, just as he'd hoped. This would be his sanctuary for a while, until matters were set to rights. But, for tonight, he had a matter to settle elsewhere that shouldn't take long.

By the Saracen's Head, off Carter's Lane

JUDE HAD found his quarry, coming out of Bowen's shop, much as expected, and followed him, keeping to the shadows of dusk. Kit Philpot, thinking to flaunt his black eye and swollen nose as badges of heroism where they'd be best appreciated, made for the Saracen's Head tavern in Carter's

Lane, south of the cathedral. The tavern wenches there were more friendly than most, and obliging. He'd dipped his wick with brown-eyed Jane over a year since – hoping she never realised she was his first. Jane had continued his instruction in the art ever since, for a halfpenny a time.

Jude waited outside. He knew Kit Philpot, despite his youth, had an old man's bladder and would be coming out to the alley for a piss before long. The narrow alley behind the tavern was in darkness, despite the efforts of the moon as clouds skittered across its half-face, its light flaring and dying like a candle in a draught. Cats yowled.

The alley reeked, with a pig-pen at one end, completely blocking the narrow passage, and the other end, opening into Carter's Lane, being used as a house of easement by the patrons of the Saracen's Head. He knew of better places to wait, but this was the most likely. Too bad about the stink. It took his breath away.

Men came and went, relieving themselves against the walls, jesting, seeing who could aim highest, making derogatory comments. One even unlaced his breeches and squatted to do his business, adding to the foul airs.

Jude drew back as far as he could without disturbing the sow, rootling merrily in her pen. He thought about what he should say, how best to put the fear of God into the wretch.

Footsteps and a woman's giggling warned Jude in time for him to withdraw into the shadows. Though slurred with drink, there was no mistaking Kit's voice with its habitual sneering tones, even whilst he tried to seduce a wench.

'Come on, Janey, you promised me a quick grope at least.'

'I said a kiss. Nothing more.' There was a long pause. Jude could hear the rustle of clothing, a few grunts. It may have been the pig.

'You know you want me. Let me get...'

'I said no!'

'I'll pay you...'

'No. Not tonight. I've got my monthly courses.'

'So, it slips in easier. You took the napkins off for me last month. You didn't mind then.'

'Well, I'm not of a mind now, so leave me be.'

'You're a bloody cock-teaser, Jane. Bring me out here, get me all het up and then... nothing. Come here, you bitch. I'll teach you...'

There came the sound of a slap, like wood on wet cloth, then a male-mouthed curse. Jude wondered who'd done the slapping. There was a brief scuffle and the hurried steps of a wench, fleeing.

'Shit and bugger it! You're a whoring cow, Janey!' Kit yelled after her, but his words sounded muffled, as if he held his hands to his mouth. Jude grinned. Serve the devil right.

Jude stepped out of the darkness, into a sudden shaft of moonlight. Kit was dabbing at his lips with his cuff.

'Well, now. She certainly caught you a hefty swipe. I'll give the lass credit for that.' Jude took pleasure in the mess that was Kit Philpot's face.

'What! How come? What are you doing here, Foxley?' Kit took a step back until the wall prevented further retreat. Kit's good eye glanced to left and right. To the right was the pigpen – no escape there. To the left stood Jude. 'What d'you want?'

'To give you some advice about my brother.' Jude stepped closer.

'What about him?' Kit held his arms close to his chest, hugging his fear to himself. 'Don't know why you trouble over that worm-ridden carcase. He's useless as a pile of turds...'

Jude lashed out, catching the apprentice a clip across the shoulder.

'You lay a hand on my brother ever again, you'll regret it 'til the day you die. I swear you will.'

The youth barked a laugh.

'And how will that be? You'll have danced the hangman's jig by week's end. I'll see to it: I'll call the watch now.' He made a move to get passed Jude but Jude grabbed him. Kit tried to shout for help as Jude's hands closed around his neck, thumbs pressing hard on his Adam's apple. The whites of Kit's eyes grew huge, his tongue protruding in a parody of insolence. Jude gnashed his teeth with the effort of it, smelled the hot stink of another man's piss. There was a soft sound, like the breaking of an over-ripe pear. Kit gargled, choked once, then fell limp.

Jude let go. The body slumped in an untidy heap – pulseless.

• •

He'd never meant for this to happen. Staring at his hands, colourless in the moonlight, Jude wondered at what those hands had done. The hands of a pen-pusher. How come they had such strength? They were now a killer's hands, though he was no killer. They were someone else's hands that had done this deed. They had acted of their own volition, as things quite separate from himself. God's instruments, perhaps? Or the Devil's?'

A cloud covered the moon. Those hands hung slack now, unseen in the darkness.

CHAPTER TWELVE

Wednesday the third day of May
West Cheap

NEXT MORNING, Jack borrowed his uncle's handcart again in order to get me home from the Hart's Horn. Sir Rob walked alongside, leading his horse – a superb animal of at least sixteen hands that Jack kept a wary eye upon. I didn't trust those evil-looking teeth either. As we neared the conduit by St Michael's, the women seemed to have forgotten their pails and pitchers, all flapping and clucking like hens with a fox in the coop.

'What's amiss, good dames?' Sir Rob asked, steadying his horse and letting it drink from the cistern. He then helped himself to a draught of cool water from the stoop before passing some to me.

'Murder, sir! That's what!' an old crone cackled. I knew her to live in Foster Lane, by St Vedast's.

'But that news is grown cold for a week,' Sir Rob said.

'Oh, no. 'Tis another murder,' added a middle-aged matron, rubbing her chaffed hands gleefully. 'That's two, sir, in a se'enight.'

'Christ preserve us! Who this time?' he asked. Hearing the dreaded word "murder", Jack pushed the handcart closer so we could both hear.

'What has come to pass?' I asked, straining forward, the better to hear above the play of water, gurgling and gushing.

'Slip of a lad, sir. Strangled, he was,' said the crone, 'And I reckon it's that 'scaped criminal, that wicked devil, Jude Foxley, that's done it again, too!'

With that, Jack forced the women to make way, using the cart like a battering ram, determined to get me home swiftly, before worse things were said, I suppose.

The Foxley brothers' rooms

BACK AT home, Sir Rob sat with me at the board while Emily brought ale from next door. My bruises and black eye alarmed her but I waved aside her concerns. She departed with a sigh, looking worried, but I wanted none of her sympathy.

'Jude's a damned fool to have run. Better that he should have stayed in Newgate!' I ignored the ale Jack poured for me.

'What? In that filfy place? Yer can't mean it, master.' Jack sounded horrified.

'Well, I do. At least there he would have had an unassailable alibi.'

'A what?'

'I'd have known where the idiot was. And where in Hell's name is he? Where was he when this latest murder occurred? Who's dead now, do we know?'

'I can find out,' Jack volunteered.

'Aye, Jack, see what intelligence you can extract from your fellow denizens of the back-streets.' But then, seeing the lad's expression of doubt, I said: 'Find out all you can.'

'If I hadn't gone to the Bailey and been set upon, Jude would have had no opportunity to escape. Now he can be accused of two murders instead of just one.'

'Oh, this second incident probably has nothing to do with Bowen's death,' the knight assured me. 'Some young cut-purse fell foul of his last victim, maybe, something like that. Do you suppose Dame Ellen Langton might have something to eat? I'm ravenous. Shall I enquire next door?'

I shrugged indifference. My friend's appetite was the least of my worries.

• •

'May I tell you what I believe came to pass during the night of Friday last?' I said when Sir Rob had returned, laden with a platter of a dozen oatcakes or more.

He helped himself to the ale.

'If it helps you get things straight in your mind.'

'It will.' I leaned my elbow on the board – lately mended by good Master Appleyard – picking at the stitches on my arm. There were three, crusted with dark scabs, like untidy cross-hatching. 'I'm now convinced that Matthew Bowen was poisoned, using the yellow pigment orpiment, that he was given a lethal dose in a cup of ale.' I showed Sir Rob the ale-stained linen that I'd kept safe. 'I believe he was stabbed later with Jude's knife, simply to mislead us. The other day, at the revels, Kit Philpot claimed to know something about the murder of Matthew Bowen, though it's possible he was just bragging, but he may know more about the penknife.'

'Why do you think that?' Sir Robert slapped at my hand. 'And stop that, you'll open the wound again.' I tucked my offending hand under my arm.

'Because Matthew Bowen's body seems to have been found in the yard next morning, after young Kit should have begun work for the day. I think Kit had already discovered it earlier and, because he loathes my brother Jude, he took Jude's knife, which I now know was still in the workshop, and stabbed Matthew Bowen, hoping Jude would be accused. And he got his wish.'

'Why should the apprentice hate your brother enough to want him accused of so foul a deed?' Sir Rob looked thoughtfully at the now empty platter, wetted a finger and picked up the last wafer crumbs to transfer to his mouth.

'I'm not certain, but I have my suspicions.'

'Such as?'

'I have little evidence but Kit made no secret of knowing Jude was Meg Bowen's lover and, young as he is, I think he has a liking, no, more than a liking for her himself.'

'Jealousy, then? Though I can't say I admire his taste in women and she would be a good deal older than him, I suppose.'

'Not that much. He's sixteen and Meg is what... about Jude's age? Four- or five-and-twenty. So eight years, but some men prefer older women, do they not?'

'Aye, the king himself for one.' Sir Rob laughed briefly and then became serious once more. 'But, if Kit did as you say, he wouldn't be the first to dispose of a rival by having him falsely accused. That makes sense. Anything else?'

'Yes. I may as well tell you everything. There's Gilbert Eastleigh.'

'You mean the apothecary-surgeon whom Meg Bowen summoned to attend her dead husband that morning?'

'The same. I asked him about the symptoms of orpiment poisoning, not directly, of course, and he told me they were headaches and nosebleeds. But the book I have says otherwise. He had told me so much nonsense, but only concerning orpiment. Perhaps he recalled it wrongly but I made a copy of what the book says.' I showed the knight the notes I had made.

Sir Rob nodded approval as he read my page of careful script.

'Mm, horrible indeed. And these symptoms tally with what you know of Matthew Bowen's death?'

'Aye, they do. But there's a further mystery surrounding Gilbert Eastleigh, though it may be nothing, but after church on Sunday, he escorted Widow Bowen home. They seemed...' I paused to consider, 'very close, closer than I should have expected perhaps. And Eastleigh's quite well-off. Has he bought her fine clothes for her, I wonder? Could they have been friends for a long time and...'

'And?'

'Dame Ellen suspects Meg Bowen may be with child. That could complicate things, couldn't it?'

'If she's correct.'

'From what I've heard, Dame Ellen is rarely mistaken in such matters.'

'I think we need to question this Philpot fellow and the daft maid Nessie... always supposing she's got sense enough to answer. Maids usually know about their mistress's, er, indispositions.'

'Nessie has more wit than she makes out, I can assure you. Playing daft is a fair way to avoid responsibility.'

'I admit, I never thought of that,' Sir Rob said with an amused grin. 'Perhaps I'll try it myself, when Lord Dickon has enthusiasm for one scheme too many, as he does all too often.'

● ●

The knight was rising to leave just as Jack burst through the door, breathless.

'It was the 'prentice...' he gasped, leaning on the board to catch his breath, holding the stitch in his side. 'Kit Philpot... was strangled, they say.'

'Damn!' Sir Rob cursed. 'That's one less witness who can shed light on Bowen's death... one less that we can question.'

'And another victim Jude can be accused of wanting put away,' I said, despairingly. 'We just clear up one murder, almost, and now this? What am I going to do? God spare me. Why didn't you stay in gaol, Jude, you fool?' I paused to steady myself before asking Jack: 'And my brother... any news of him?'

'Nah, master, nuffin, not a word.'

'Then we can but pray he has made good his escape, taken a boat for France or Spain. I hope he's a hundred miles away by now. I shall pray to St Christopher, patron of travellers, and to St Jude, his own saint and patron of lost causes, to keep him safe.'

Sir Rob put his hand on my shoulder in a gesture of comfort.

'I'm certain things will turn out for the best, Seb,' he said, but what could I say? He turned to Jack, telling him to take care of me, then left quietly.

• •

As soon as the knight was gone, Jack grabbed my injured arm, causing me to wince.

'It ain't true what I telled yer! I knows where Master Jude is but I didn't want to say in Sir Rob's hearing 'cos, like yer telled me, 'e's the duke's man.'

'What's that? My brother? Tell me, for pity's sake. Where is he?'

'In Saint Paul's.'

'In sanctuary? Jude has claimed the right of sanctuary! That's wonderful news.'

'Nah, master, not really. Master Jude's hidden down in the crypt, in a place me and Mark use sometimes, fer stowing, er... stuff. They calls it "the Shrouds" down there, and it's dark and 'orrible. Mark seed 'im there when... don't matter when.'

'Take me to him, Jack, I must talk some sense into him.'

'Can't do that, master, yer'd never get in the place where 'e's hid. It's behind a load of scaffold poles an' timber what's been left fer years. It's better if yer don't know where ezackerly.'

I nodded. Perhaps Jack was correct to be so cautious.

'Can you get to him, without being observed, er, seen?'

'Course I can. Me and Mark get in and out easy. Don't fret. I'll see 'e gets fed and watered. Me and Mark'll do it, turn and turn about. He'll be safe 'nough.'

'Are you sure of this?'

Jack nodded.

'Aye.'

'Then take some coin, buy food and ale for him and take a blanket – it's cold of a night still – he'll need it. Tell him to stay hidden 'til I send him word, though God alone knows when that will be.'

'Don't worry, master, 'e'll be safe. Me and Mark'll see to it, I swear,' Jack tried to reassure me but two wayward urchins responsible for my brother's life? Dare I trust them? Did I have a choice? As ever, my wretched body denied me the possibility of aiding Jude myself and I thought again about the strange writings in Eastleigh's book – particularly the line which referred to being *perfect bodyly*.

If only...

Thursday, the fourth day of May
The Foxley brothers' rooms

JACK WENT about his duties, seeing my brother had meat and drink with such keenness, I thought the lad must be missing the nefarious life he used to lead and was happy to be back with his old compatriot Mark, sneaking around dark alleyways after curfew and well before dawn. He certainly looked happy, a permanent grin on his once-again dirty face.

• •

With young Jack off on other business so much, I was alone on the Thursday morning. It had taken me a while to dress myself, what with my bruised ribs afire and the stitches on my arm pulling with every movement. At least my eye felt less swollen this morning.

Emily came to see how I was faring and immediately became annoyed with Jack for deserting me. She set a platter with a mess of eggs before me. Parsley and thyme were sprinkled on top and the delicious smell made me realise how hungry I was. My condition must be improving.

'No, no, Em, I've sent Jack off on a far more important task,' I assured her. 'He'll be back for breakfast soon enough.'

'The young rascal, I don't know why you trust him, Seb. He's probably up to no good.'

The thought had crossed my mind.

'I dare say, but what choice do I have? Besides, I think he's a good hearted lad.'

• •

'What's this?' Em asked, picking up the scrap of cloth I'd left lying there, the piece I'd found snagged on a splinter after our rooms were ransacked.

173

'Well, Em, working for Dame Ellen, you must have an eye for cloth.'

'I dare say I do. Why?'

I explained about finding the cloth caught up on a splinter yester eve. 'So it might belong to the thief,' I suggested.

'I doubt it. The violet dye is very costly.' She rubbed the scrap between her fingers, then held it to the light. 'This is of the finest quality with so many threads to the inch. It's a mixed tabby weave, teasled on both sides with the nap sheared four, maybe even five times, to get such a smooth finish. See?' She showed me.

I nodded, as if I understood.

'This is no ruffian's dress, Seb. Only a lord should be wearing such fine cloth.'

'Maybe he'd stolen that too, from a rich man's house.'

'I could show it to Dame Ellen. She might know who made it, if it was woven in London, or the mercer who sold it, even the tailor who sewed it – can you see the broken thread here? Dame Ellen can tell by the stitching.'

'Does it matter who made it? How will that help?'

She shrugged. 'It was you who asked me, Seb.'

So I changed the subject.

'Emily, tell me truly. How's my eye looking? Am I presentable enough to go out?'

She glanced up briefly from spooning out more egg but failed to answer. Her expression said more than words – I was still like to frighten children and cause an apoplexy in the elderly. 'Oh, well, that's too bad. My errand can't wait until tomorrow, folk usually look the other way when they see me coming in any case.'

'Where are you thinking of going?'

'St Paul's. I have a body to inspect, if they'll allow. By tomorrow, it will have been coffined and interred. I have to go now.'

'But St Paul's is too far for you, Seb! With broken ribs? you can't!'

I ignored her protest. She put down the spoon, stood hands on hips. I noted a splatter of egg on her otherwise spotless linen apron.

'Why do you need to see a dead body, anyway?' she demanded.

'Because mistakes can be made. Folk said Matthew Bowen was killed with my brother's knife, yet I know he was poisoned.'

'What! Poisoned? Are you sure?'

'Aye, sure as I can be. So you see, they say Kit was strangled. Supposing he wasn't? What if he drowned or cut himself and bled to death? I have to see for myself. And there are other things I need to know too.'

'Such as?' Emily looked intrigued and took a seat on the stool across the board from me.

'I have to see his right hand. His thumb, to be precise.' I told her about the inky thumb mark I'd found on the handle of Jude's penknife, with the scar across it. 'So I need to know if it was Kit who made that mark.'

'I see.' She sounded cautious. 'But, Seb, if he's shrouded, they won't let you unwrap him to look at his hands.'

'I know. That could be a difficulty.'

'I have an idea! Will you trust me?'

I considered. The Lord knew, I trusted every other, from northern knights of briefest acquaintance to thieving urchins foisted upon me at a moment's notice. Why not Emily? At least we'd known each other for some years, been close neighbours for two. And she'd seen my body as no other woman ever had.

'Of course. I trust you to unfasten my shirt for me, do I not? How can a man be any more trusting than that?' I felt my lips struggling into a smile for the first time in an age.

'You tell me what else you want me to look for on the body and promise me you'll stay at home today. Leave it to me. Will you do that, Seb?'

• •

Left alone I ate my breakfast, thinking, mulling over a problem, a matter of conscience. If Gilbert Eastleigh had murdered Matthew Bowen – because the stationer found his notes on the Philosopher's Stone – and if Eastleigh then killed Kit – because either the apprentice also knew about the stone or knew who had poisoned Bowen – then the apothecary must be made to pay the price. I ought to tell the authorities, then Eastleigh would be arrested and my brother proven innocent. That was how it *should* be.

However, I couldn't help wondering whether that precious Philosopher's Stone might be a remedy for me. If only it could make me stand tall and straight as other men. But Eastleigh couldn't use his knowledge if he was imprisoned or hanged. So I had to decide.

Emily brought me a large bowl of mutton stew for dinner, with ale and a fresh baked loaf. I saw she was bubbling with anticipation, eager to tell me all about her morning's activities, but Sir Robert had arrived to enquire after my injuries, whether they were improving. I could see Emily was uncertain whether to make known her discoveries in front of him, so I asked her outright.

'Well, Em, did they permit you to see Kit's body?' I enquired, as I offered Sir Rob a helping of bread and stew.

'Of course they did,' she announced, perching on the edge of a wooden crate we were using as an extra stool. 'After all, I was the tearful, grieving, loving cousin, wasn't I, with a last gift for the dear departed?' She brushed invisible dust from her blue linen gown.

I was suddenly aware that it showed off certain of her curves to perfection and reflected deeply in her sapphire eyes. I felt a surge of blood flushing hot in my loins, but swiftly shook off my pointless visions.

'Em! You never told lies, surely?'

'What of it?' she shrugged, tossing her head so her kerchief went a little askew, allowing the escape of a russet curl by her left ear, a bronze curlicue I wanted to tuck back for her.

'I got the information you needed,' she was saying. 'Kit Philpot was definitely strangled. I saw the finger marks clearly on his neck when they folded back the head cloth, so I might kiss my favourite cousin one last time. Horrible!' She glanced deliberately at me, at my throat, where I'd fastened my shirt high to conceal the yellowing bruises.

I prayed Sir Rob didn't notice her look.

'And yes, you were right, he does have a scar on his right thumb, just as you described to me.'

'How did you manage to see his hand since he was, obviously, already shrouded?' Sir Rob asked. He pushed aside his empty bowl with a satisfied sigh and took up a last piece of bread.

'Oh, that was easy. I showed the priest my St Christopher pilgrim badge, left me by my mother.' Em took a small pewter badge from her purse and passed it to Sir Rob for his inspection. 'I told the priest I wanted to put it in my dearest cousin's hand, so it could see him safe on his final journey, St Christopher being his patron saint, and all. At first the priest said no, but the tears gushed like a conduit in a thunderstorm and, eventually, he allowed it, for I nearly had him weeping with me, I was so convincing. Of course, I only made out that I put my precious badge in the corpse's hand. I wouldn't part with it, in truth, certainly not to the likes of him!'

'You're very resourceful, Em. Well done,' I congratulated her, but couldn't help adding: 'You best make your confession to Father Thomas on the morrow.'

'Were you intending to go to the funeral after vespers this evening?' Sir Rob asked me. I shook my head.

'No, I doubt it. Why? Do you think I should?'

'It might be informative to see who turns up,' the knight suggested, refilling his ale cup. 'By the way, any news of Jude?'

● ●

As though in answer to his question, there came a fierce rapping on the street door.

'Open up in there, you bastard!' bellowed a powerful voice from without. 'I know yer in there. Open up or I break the door down!'

Sir Rob was on his feet in an instant to wrench the door open. The surly watchman and his fellows almost fell into the room.

'What do you mean by this offensive behaviour?' the tall knight demanded imperiously, displaying the Duke of Gloucester's badge on his sleeve. 'How dare you come here, causing an affray and disturbing the peace, harassing respectable citizens. I'll report you to Sheriff Thomas Hill myself. Your name?'

'Er, I've come lookin' fer the 'scaped felon. Foxley,' the man stammered.

'Your name?' Sir Rob repeated, ignoring the explanation.

'William, William Stockman,' the watchman said reluctantly.

'Well, Stockman, I shall be reporting your actions to Master Hill this evening and you'll count yourself fortunate if you're not dismissed from your post forthwith. Now get out of my sight.'

'But I've orders t' search the place, sir,' Stockman added the courtesy grudgingly.

'He isn't here, so I'll spare you all the trouble of looking.' With that, Sir Rob slammed the door in the watchman's face. 'Insolent devil,' he muttered, resuming his seat. 'At least we know they haven't found your brother yet.' He turned to Emily, touching her hand. 'No need to concern yourself, mistress. I'll deal with his kind.'

In truth, Emily didn't look especially concerned, but I was.

'No, but I dare say they'll be back when you're not here, sir. They won't take "no" for an answer, I know that.'

• •

With Sir Rob returned to Crosby Place to report to Lord Richard, I took up my drawings to work on the triptych. For now I hadn't the heart to redraw the figure of Christ but that of Our Lady was my next challenge and, as usual, it would be easier to breathe life into the image if I based the likeness on someone I knew. Most women of my acquaintance were too old – Dame Ellen and Goodwife Marlow. Though Emily was young enough, she was no soft-featured beauty, her face too sharply delineated. I pictured her in my mind. Her lovely eyes – the windows of the soul – and her hair... the thought thrilled me in ways it should not and I cast it aside.

So, who else was there? Ah, yes, Widow Bowen. Comely enough to use as the basic figure but hardly suitable otherwise, what with her airs and graces and the morals of an alley-cat. Looks could be so deceiving. As an artist, I knew that all too well. Had I not offered to paint Lord Richard's father without his ugly scar, all for the sake of improving his looks? How correct the duke had been to insist the scar remain, how honest of him.

I took up my silver point and began to sketch the figure of Our Lady upon her knees, arms out-stretched in love and supplication towards the son she had borne, now elevated to the highest realms of Heaven. The proportions were good and I was well pleased with it thus far, though I hesitated over the face. Meg Bowen was attractive enough in a bold, brassy way – more of a Mary Magdalene, than a Blessed Virgin. I wondered how to adapt Meg's features to look more, well, holy! I wasn't sure I could.

My way of working was always instinctive so, when in doubt, I would set a subject aside, turn my attention to something else for a while, knowing inspiration would return when least expected. Instead, I took out the sketches for St James, which before had looked too much like Kit Philpot for comfort. Somehow they had been spared the destructive attentions of whoever had broken in, as my sketches of Christ had not. Now, St James' features appeared more anonymous and, with the addition of a few judicious lines and shading, the image became that of a saintly young man, a spiteful and devious apprentice no longer – this was how my work often took shape.

I was pleased with St James, the image now ready to be transferred to the central panel of the triptych itself – though that required mending. This was the first figure to acquire the necessary detail before the preliminary stage of gilding could begin, the laying down of areas of bole, like little cushions, ready for the gold leaf of the halos and the underlying areas of the sky and robes.

These latter I would eventually paint over before using a sgraffito method to give the impression of gold-thread patterned cloth. I'd seen sgraffito done once, by an Italian limner who visited my old master, Richard Collop, some years before. It was a painstaking procedure that required a steady hand and endless patience. But I was determined Lord Richard's confidence in me would be repaid in full, that the triptych would be an object of beauty.

• •

It was difficult to keep working on Lord Richard's commission when I had so much else to worry about, so many thoughts to distract me. Was Jude safe, hidden in St Paul's crypt? Was Jack delivering the food and drink that I paid him to buy and smuggle in to Jude? Or were he and Mark – whom I'd never even met – squandering the coins on enjoying themselves, leaving Jude to starve? No, my brother would not starve. He would leave his hiding place and risk discovery, rather than die of hunger.

Again I cursed myself for the disabilities that forced me to forever rely on others to do those things I was desperate to do myself – like helping Jude and proving his innocence. But my searching had produced little reward so far, except that Gilbert Eastleigh was now a possible suspect. As to his motive, that was little more than conjecture, based upon a single fact, that Eastleigh had escorted Widow Bowen home from church last Sunday. That was hardly sufficient grounds to accuse a man of murder, even if he was remiss in remembering the symptoms of orpiment poisoning.

Thinking it over, I realised that everyone I needed to question, or simply keep an eye on, would probably be at Kit Philpot's funeral later that evening, after vespers, and I ought to be there too, if I could.

St Paul's Cathedral

WITH EMILY'S strong arm and a new staff fashioned by her brother, I walked to St Paul's in time for the funeral, arriving breathless, with a sharp stitch in my side. The mass for the dead was already in progress. A chill hung about the great minster, colder than death, seeking out every dark and intricate corner of the nave. I shivered.

The scent of incense barely disguised the stench of the charnel house.

The cathedral was a den of iniquity. Money-lenders and whores walked among the honest folk in the nave and plied their trade secretively behind the pillars, thinking God could not espy them there.

Meanwhile, the body of young Christopher Philpot was being prepared for burial and, in this case, though he was only a second son, there would be nothing cheap or penny-pinching about the funeral – unlike Matthew Bowen's – since the lad's father was a wealthy grocer and master of his guild. William Philpot would see that standards were maintained and the deceased lay in a side chapel at Saint Paul's with three priests saying masses continually and a dozen torches burning to light his soul on its last journey.

The service was taking place in St Michael's Chapel – the archangel being the grocers' own saint – but the crowd spilled out into the nave, so many folk wished to impress the powerful Grocers' Guildsman, William Philpot, by attending his son's requiem. I wondered if any had come out of love or respect for the deceased himself. Close family alone filled the little chapel, so those folk in whom I had an interest were, like me, left in the nave.

Emily was by my side to assist but I'd expected her to be the only female present, yet Widow Bowen was there, Alderman Collins was accompanied by his wife, even old Richard Collop, to whom I bowed as my one-time master, had his new young wife hanging on his arm. And there was Widow Chambers from Bishopsgate too, so it seemed a Philpot funeral was quite a social occasion.

Meg Bowen was, again, the centre of attention, flaunting her furs, continually adjusting the neckline of her gown.

'Such jewels!' I heard Emily say with a sigh.

'What of them?' I whispered.

'Nothing. I was just thinking how can Widow Bowen afford that wondrous pearl collar she keeps drawing our attention to?'

'Does she? I hadn't noticed.' It was true. There was only one woman who could catch my eye.

'Typical man!' Emily jested in a whisper. 'Look now. See how the pearls gleam in the candlelight. Are they not worth a king's ransom at least?'

It was a few minutes before the widow turned in such a way that I had a clear view of the collar. It was beautiful indeed and hardly fitting for an artisan's widow – more appropriate for a king's mistress, maybe.

'Someone's paying highly for her services,' said a familiar voice from behind. Sir Robert had returned. 'Interesting company we have here,' he observed, looking around the nave. 'Aldermen and sergeants, a judge and one of the sheriffs, Thomas Hill, I recognise. Mm, I didn't realise our dead apprentice was a lad of such importance.'

I gave Sir Rob a welcoming smile, glad of my protector's return.

'He is not, but his father is. William Philpot is expected to be elected mayor this year or next. Thomas Hill is a fellow grocer and, over there by the column, that's Richard Lee who's been lord mayor twice. And the tall fellow with the grizzled beard, leaning on the font, is Ralph Josselyn, another ex-mayor.'

'You're well informed, my friend. You know them all, personally?'

I shook my head.

'Not so as they would greet me, that's for sure,' I said, aware that, though none could fail to recognise "the cripple", they would not acknowledge me if it might be avoided.

'Any news of your brother?' Sir Rob asked quietly. The service was done and we crossed ourselves as the crowd moved away, making for the door of the cathedral. I told him I'd heard nothing further, which was true enough. That Jude was hidden beneath our feet at that moment was beside the point. I worried that if he knew, Sir Rob might feel the authorities should be informed, even the duke. The first would endanger Jude and the second might imperil the commission – I dared not risk either.

• •

Outside, in the gathering gloom of late dusk, William Philpot was inviting certain folk of suitable social standing back to his home, to take supper there, but most were simply waiting about, hoping to be recognised as having come to pay their respects to a departed son of the Philpot family. I was quite ignored, as expected, but Widow Bowen was invited to sup, as was Gilbert Eastleigh, who had escaped my sharp eyes 'til he came to offer the widow his arm to escort her – again.

There was also a little knot of merchants, deep in ardent discussion, and I realised Gilbert had been part of that group. What was more, every man among them that I knew by sight was named upon that discarded list, the one I'd found in the litter of Bowen's courtyard. Alan Dale, old Harry Morton and his nephew Edmund Lacy from Cheapside, Widow Bess Chambers, Nicholas and Hugh Kent, and Master Rowley. Seeing them now I understood what most of them, perhaps all of them, had in common: they sold, amongst other stuff, artists' equipment, glues, glazes, binders and pigments in particular. Was that what Bowen's list was? Just the names of men from whom he bought his materials? Nothing suspicious there – what a disappointment. But I wasn't inclined to tear up the list, not yet. I knew Bowen had usually purchased all his materials from Gilbert Eastleigh, unless the apothecary had run out of something. In which case he would go to Morton or Lacy. So why the exhaustive list?

Only one reason suggested itself, that Bowen had planned to buy up all the stocks. That would explain all the pigments in Bowen's storage chest and why Jude had not been able to obtain a full selection for ourselves. Had that been the point? To prevent us from completing Lord Richard's commission? Even if that was the case, it still left one singularly important question unanswered. How had the penniless Bowen managed to pay for most of London's supplies of expensive colours? Unless he hadn't been the pauper he made out.

Sir Rob was talking to Sheriff Thomas Hill. I wondered if my friend was actually carrying out his earlier threat to report the watchman, but they were laughing, so it seemed Stockman's ill-manners were unlikely to be the topic of conversation.

• •

'You bitch!' A sudden screech shattered the peaceful evening as a scuffle ensued in the churchyard. 'You thieving cow! Give me back my pendant!'

Meg Bowen had pulled Widow Chambers' cap from her head and was dragging her by the hair towards Sir Robert and the sheriff. Bess Chambers was squealing, protesting at such treatment in public, lashing out at Meg in return.

'Now, now, softly good women!' the sheriff intervened, placing his stocky body firmly between them and gripping Meg's hand, forcing her to release the other woman's hair. 'Calm yourselves, Widow Bowen, Widow Chambers, and tell me what's amiss,' he ordered.

The crowd had re-gathered instantly – cat-fights were always of great interest and entertainment – and I was caught in their midst. I overheard Alderman Collins laying a wager with Hugh Kent as to the likely outcome.

'She's stolen my pendant!' Meg yelled, lunging for Bess's throat to relieve her of said jewel.

'I never did! This pendant is mine, come by lawful means! An' you can keep your greedy eyes and thieving hands off it, Meg Bowen!' Bess gave Meg such a shove she tumbled backwards, ending up sitting in the dirt in all her finery. Meg burst into tears, though whether they were genuine or an artful ruse I had my doubts. She looked more angry than hurt.

'That's *my* pendant,' she sobbed loudly. 'Bequeathed to me by my father as part of my dowry. 'Tis a reliquary. Open it. It contains a lock of Our Lady's hair.'

Sheriff Hill asked Bess Chambers politely if he might see the pendant. It looked valuable. A large cabochon-cut ruby, dark as blood, edged with pearls. He opened it with care and, just as Meg had described, it contained a lock of silken hair.

'It certainly seems to be the jewel in question,' he observed. 'Widow Chambers, perhaps you would tell us how you came by it. I'm certain there are unlikely to be two the same.'

'Fair enough.' Bess Chambers pulled herself up to her full height – she was tall indeed for a woman – straightening her cap as best she could and folding her arms defiantly. 'I dare say this was her pendant, once. But her husband used it last week, giving it to me in payment for my entire stock of pigments. I think that makes it mine in the eyes of the law.'

'Not in my eyes it bloody doesn't!' Meg cried, flying at Bess yet again, clawing her face so the poor woman screamed. Sir Rob and the sheriff pulled victim and assailant apart but blood ran down the tall woman's cheeks in three parallel scratches beneath each eye.

'You wicked animal!' Bess wept. 'Look what you've done to me! Take your accursed jewel,' she gasped, ripping the fine chain from her neck, breaking it and flinging it at Meg's feet. 'It's not worth the pain and trouble.' She shrugged herself free of Sir Rob's grip and strode off, holding her hands to her bleeding cheeks. Some of the other women scuttled after her to offer support, consolation and medical care.

• •

'Well now, that was quite a little scene, wasn't it?' the knight observed ruefully, rubbing a bruised shoulder he had come by in attempting to separate the combatants. 'I wonder King Edward doesn't sign up a contingent of London widows for his forthcoming campaign against the French. The Lord knows, they're more feisty and vicious than any soldiers I've seen. They'd have the French in full retreat on the first day. They certainly scare the bloody life out of me,' he added, laughing, still trying to ease his shoulder beneath his fine woollen doublet.

'Are you able to get home alright, young Seb?' he asked, changing the subject, straightening his clothes. 'I'm supposed to be meeting Lord Lovell for supper at the Hart's Horn, but I could see you home first, if you need me?'

I declined the offer courteously, not wishing to inconvenience him though, truthfully, I would have welcomed his pleasant company and had hoped to talk a few things over with him.

The Foxley brothers' rooms

BACK HOME I wanted to rest, drink a cup of Dame Ellen's good ale and go to bed, but as soon as Emily and I came through the door and I was sat upon a stool, Jack arrived, out of breath and filthy.

'What's happened to you?' Emily demanded. The new clothes she had sewn for him were in such a state.

'Nuffin, nuffin at all. Nuffin, I tells yer!'

She glared at him.

'You've been up to no good, I know that much for sure, you little wretch.'

'I ain't done nuffin!' Jack insisted, bristling like an angry dog.

'Don't you dare lie to me, Jack Tabor.'

'I ain't!'

'Let it lie, Em, leave him to me,' I said, wanting to avoid any arguments – I'd seen enough for one evening.

'Very well, Seb,' Emily consented grudgingly, certain the lad was in need of a sound beating at least, the way she was eyeing him. 'You dare cause Master Seb any trouble and you'll answer to me!' she warned him with a wagging finger and a dire look that threatened who knew what.

Jack nodded obediently, staring at his feet as if he'd never seen them before.

• •

'Well?' I asked as soon as Emily left. 'What's amiss now? I know you have some matter of great import with which to belabour me.'

Jack frowned.

'It's Master Jude!' he blurted out. 'He ain't in Paul's crypt no more. 'E's gone!'

'Gone? Gone where? Tell me!' I was off the stool, grabbing his arm.

'I dunno. Me an' Mark looked all over fer 'im all day, but we ain't found 'im nowhere. Let go, yer 'urtin' me.'

I loosed his arm and slumped back on my seat.

'Oh, dear God, why is my brother such an imbecile of the first water!'

'A wot?'

'A damned silly fool!' I shouted, thumping my fist on the board. 'Tell me what you know. Everything that might be significant, important.'

'Ain't much to know, master. Me and Mark went to the crypt wiv 'is breakfast and 'e weren't there! A gang o' men was moving all the timber and scaffolding what's been there fer years, but they was shifting it all, so Master Jude couldn't 'ave stayed there, else they'd've found 'im.'

'Were they searching purposefully for him, do you think?'

Jack shrugged.

'Might've been, or else they was tidying up the crypt at long last, but what a time to choose, eh?'

'Aye. They couldn't have chosen a worse. And you've looked everywhere, you say, you and Mark?'

'Everywhere I could think but ain't found no sign.'

I shook my head in despair.

'Thank you, Jack. I know you've done your best. It's too dark to search any more now. Dame Ellen has left supper for us. Eat as much as you want. I'm not hungry.' Jack hardly needed telling twice but set about devouring an entire crock of pottage. It seemed not to bother him that it was almost cold by this time. He scoffed it like a ravenous beast.

I felt tears pricking my eyes. I couldn't help it.

• •

Later, when Jack wanted to sleep, curled in a blanket beside the warm hearth, I went to my bed, closing the curtain between. Alone in my bed I succumbed to misery. I wept for Jude. Fearing Jack might be kept awake by my sobbing, I pulled the blanket over my head and stuffed my fist in my mouth to muffle the desolate sounds that escaped me.

It was some time later that I heard Jack calling out softly to me.

'Master Seb? Master Seb?'

I didn't answer, only buried my face deeper in the pillow. But the curtain was pulled back and bare feet padded to my bedside.

'It'll be alright, master, I knows we'll find 'im safe 'n sound tomorrow.'

'Aye, tomorrow we'll go to St Michael's.' I gulped back tears, sniffed hard.

'Yer think Master Jude's there?'

'No but we'll pray for him, pray hard.'

Jack wasn't much of a one for praying, I knew, but what else could we do?

'Alright, master, if yer want.'

'Come on, lad, get under the blankets before you freeze out there,' I said, making room in the narrow bed beside me. ''Tis kind of you to be concerned for me. Now go to sleep, we have a busy day tomorrow.'

· ·

At last I began to feel I might sleep myself. I was always cold in bed but Jack's young body gave off heat like a baker's oven, enough to warm us both. My aching bones and ravaged muscles were gradually easing towards slumber when there was a brief commotion outside. I heard the front door burst open, flying wide on its old leather hinges and slamming back against the wall, bringing down a shower of wood dust on the bed. The curtain was flung aside.

'For God's sake, hide me!' The voice was familiar but frantic.

Jack leapt from the bed like a cat with its tail afire, fully awake in an instant.

'In the coffer, Master Jude!' It was a tight fit, the lid could barely be closed properly, but we piled the blankets upon it and I sat atop the heap.

· ·

By the time the watch arrived in force – five stout fellows this time, armed with cudgels, led by Master Stockman, by the sound of the voice – Jude was hidden. Jack, dragging his blanket behind him, opened the front door, yawning, rubbing his eyes.

'What d'yer want? It's late!' he said rudely.

'Where's that bloody felon, Foxley? I know he's here!'

'My master's in 'is chamber but 'e ain't no felon. 'E's sick, can't sleep, but that ain't no crime.'

'Sick, eh? I don't believe yer! Get outta my way!' Stockman and his bullies barged passed Jack, a hefty boot catching the lad's bare foot, though whether on purpose or not was hard to say. By the flickering light of his torch, Stockman gazed uncertainly at me seated upon the coffer. I knew I must look poorly, my eyes red and swollen with weeping, the bruises and gashes, and I was shivering violently. Stockman saw it and I could see him wondering, was it from cold? Or perhaps it was fear that made me quiver and quake so badly.

'What's up with him?' he demanded of Jack, as though I wasn't capable of replying. It was a common enough mistake, thinking a cripple must be too stupid to answer for himself. It suited my purpose to let it pass.

'Don't ask me,' Jack said, 'I ain't no 'pothecary, but 'e's been throwin' up sumfink terrible, guts ache and bloody flux. I won't touch 'im, that's fer sure! I just has to clean up the mess after, pity me.'

Stockman shrugged.

'Pull this midden apart! Find that murdering bastard!' He cast a doubtful look at me, sitting silent, shaking like a man with the ague on top of the coffer.

• •

The men obeyed, turning the two beds upside down – literally, raking through the blankets and peering into the piss pot – obviously, their quarry was not there. In the other room, they overturned the table, swept the platters and cups off the shelf – as though a man might hide within them – threw stuff to the floor. They even rummaged through the neatly stacked kindling and logs by the hearth, emptied the ale jug by tipping the contents all over, checked the window shutters and behind each door but, unless a man could become the size of a spider, they were not likely to find him there either.

One fellow with the beady eyes, long nose and stained, prominent teeth of a rat lingered before me, weighing up the possibilities for disturbing the wretched cripple and possibly catching some filthy contagion in the process. He was about to grab my arm and up-end me off my perch when one of the others called to him, saying they were done here and he decided it was hardly worth the risk after all.

Master Stockman and his crew strode off in vile humour, back to their den to bide their time 'til the watch ended at cockcrow.

• •

Left in peace, Jack whistled through his teeth.

'Christ, master, I thought "Rat-face" would chuck yer off and search the coffer.' He helped me to my feet before sweeping the blankets aside and throwing back the coffer lid.

Jude had trouble unbending himself and getting out of the cramped space.

'You're bloody heavy, Seb,' were his words of greeting as he flexed his limbs and breathed deeply, 'Fetch me some ale, Jack, for pity's sake.'

'Ain't none. Them bastards tipped it away.'

'Well, go and buy me some more!'

'It's the middle o' the night, master.'

Jude swore profanely, realising he would not get any ale 'til morning.

'Food, then! There must be some bloody food in this place. I haven't eaten all day.'

Jack, still naked from bed, burrowed under the overturned board to find the remains of the loaf on the floor, his bare backside gleaming pale in the fading firelight. 'And put some damned clothes on, you disgusting little bugger!'

'Don't nag him Jude, please. The lad's quick thinking just saved our necks. We're all tired.'

'Tired! Is that the worst you've suffered, Seb? And there am I, fleeing for my life, whilst you lay abed.'

● ●

Jack got dressed, knowing there would be little chance of sleep now, but I told him to lie down on my bed, to rest 'til daylight. Jude and I righted the furniture – I did what I could to help him – then he sat on a stool at the board to eat the bread, swallowing it almost without chewing it first, but dry bread without ale to wash it down soon parched his mouth so he could eat no more.

I sat in silence, shocked by events and perturbed by Jude's appearance. It was to be expected that, as an escaped prisoner, he should be unwashed and unkempt. But it was more than that. His whole person, his demeanour, seemed soured and sullied by his experiences. He did not seem to notice that the stools were borrowed, the board mended. Then he looked at me for the first time since his untimely arrival.

'You're quiet. What are you staring at? What's amiss with you? Is this any sort of "welcome home" for your loving brother, eh?'

I was considering his attire. It was hard to be certain, seeing them by firelight, but those stains did not appear mud-coloured to me.

'You can't stay here, Jude. The watch will be back tomorrow. And I'm wondering how you came by the blood-stains on your clothes. It's not yours, is it? Are you injured?'

Jude pulled at his jerkin and shirt. The stains were stiffening and drying now. His expression was agonised of a sudden.

'No, 'tis not mine,' he replied, his voice sounding hollow somehow, as though echoing in an empty chamber. He put his head in his hands. 'Not mine,' he repeated, his whole frame shuddering. 'It is Meg's.'

'Meg's? Meg Bowen?' I was appalled at the possibilities.

'How many damned Megs do you know?' he cried, raising his head and flinging his arms wide. 'Yes, you stupid fool, it's *her* blood!'

'What have you done?'

'Me? I've done nothing! You think I killed her? You... my own brother. You accuse me...' Jude was spluttering, hardly able to speak as his temper and indignation overwhelmed him. 'You stupid fool! How can you think that? I- I love her, you idiot! I wouldn't hurt her, for God's sake!'

'I'm sorry. Forgive me, Jude. I never meant to accuse you of anything, you know that.' I put a steadying hand on his arm but was brushed aside.

'Leave me alone! The woman I love is dead and you think I killed her,' he wailed in his misery. 'I didn't. She killed herself and I saw her die. Oh, God, Seb, help me.'

This time, when I touched him, he turned towards me to be comforted. I stroked his head, soothed him like a babe.

'Jude, Jude, hush now, my brother.'

'She's dead, Seb... died in my arms...' he sobbed, 'What'll I do without her?'

CHAPTER THIRTEEN

Friday the fifth day of May
The Foxley brothers' rooms

BY MORNING I'd heard the whole forlorn tale from Jude. Apparently, the local gossips had been correct: Meg Bowen was with child, but not by her late husband. Nor was the child necessarily Jude's either, so she had told him, which was why she wanted to be rid of the damned thing – all this must have come as a great shock to my brother. Gilbert Eastleigh had refused to oblige her with a potion for the purpose, so she had gone elsewhere and acquired a sliver of slippery elm bark, which never failed, so she had been promised, though by whom, she refused to say.

'Meg didn't want to share her awful secret with any other,' Jude said. 'So she did the dreadful deed herself last evening, after that wretch's funeral, alone in her chamber with the door barred. But things went terribly wrong in her unskilled hands, not helped by the fact that she had drunk a good deal of wine to steel herself for the moment.' Jude turned pale, had to brace himself to continue. 'You can't believe what I saw, Seb, when all unaware, I climbed through her window, thinking to surprise her and found her life blood ebbing away, flowing across the floor as she lay by the bed. It was horrible. My poor Meg... and all I could do was to listen to her sorry words, holding her close. 'Til it was over. Then I unbarred the door so that she might be found this morning and decently attended to, before I left the way I'd come, by the window and away through the alley.

'It was a waking nightmare, Seb.' My brother was shuddering anew at the remembered horrors of last eve. 'My poor, poor Meg. She didn't deserve such a grisly end... no woman does. I wonder if she's been found yet. I hope she doesn't have to wait too long, but that Nessie is such a dolt, she may leave it a week before she thinks to enter the chamber unbidden. Perhaps I should go?'

'No, Jude! I'll not have you discovered close by Bowen's place, not after all that's happened there of late. You're in serious trouble as it is, without making it any worse. Suppose they think to accuse you of her death? Or even Kit Philpot's.'

'What are they saying of that? Philpot's death, I mean?' Jude sounded wary, as perhaps he should be. 'They haven't mentioned me, have they?'

'Not exactly, not in so many words. The problem is, Jude,' I hesitated briefly, but realised it made no difference if my brother knew, not now. 'I believe it was Kit who stabbed Matthew Bowen with your knife, after he was already dead of orpiment poisoning. So, whether you knew it or not, you had a reason to kill him. On the other hand, you also had good reason *not* to kill him, since he could have proved your innocence, if he had been persuaded to confess to his action.'

Jude scowled, the expression darkening his fair features, like storm clouds on a spring day. Anger flashed in his pale eyes.

'Why didn't you tell me this, Seb, you stupid fool?'

'I didn't know until yesterday, but what difference would it have made? You couldn't have stopped his killer, could you? Kit would still have died.'

Jude closed his eyes, shook his head, unclenched his fist to gnaw at his thumb.

'Oh well,' he muttered. 'What's done is done. There's no changing it now. The bastard deserved it anyway.' I decided it wiser to speak of other, more important matters.

'We've got to find some place for you to hide, Jude. You can't stay here. I know Stockman and his barbarians will be back from time to time, making certain you haven't returned.' I looked to Jack. 'Have you any suggestions to make, lad, seeing you must know every nook and cranny of darkest London better than most?'

Jack thought it over for a while, drumming his fingers on the board – a habit of his – until I grasped his hand to stop the irritating noise. 'Well?'

'There's the half-burnt house at the back end o' Bladder Street, by the slaughterer's place. It's on'y got a bit of a roof but no bugger's rebuilt it 'cos it stinks so bad there, that's where the butchers throw what they can't sell, what's left after the stalls pack up fer the day. If'n you can stand the stink, the watch don't never go there.'

Jude looked at me, screwing up his nose at the thought.

'I don't fancy living with putrid chitterlings and reeking guts, having liver and lights flung in upon me at day's end,' he said, pulling a face. 'I'd rather take my chances hiding in our privy out back – and it would smell a good deal sweeter.'

• •

Just then there came a dainty tapping upon the door, not the peremptory thump of the watch, thank goodness, but Jude hastened into the bedchamber, out of sight, all the same. It was most likely Emily, come to see that I'd survived the night, since she had made it clear she did not trust young Jack to tend to my needs. Jude left the bed chamber curtain open, seeing it was always so, if he closed it it would seem suspicious. This meant his own bed was fully in sight from the main room, so he crouched on my rumpled heap of blankets behind the door, keeping still so the bed should not creak.

It was Emily, bringing with her a hearty breakfast of fried bacon and oatcakes, fresh from the griddle. She set the food on the board, then noted a stool leg was missing a large splinter of wood.

'What happened, Seb? How did this get broken?' she asked. After all, much of the borrowed furniture belonged to Dame Ellen.

'Oh, that. I fear we suffered a visit from the watch last night, for obvious reasons.'

'Searching for your missing brother, I suppose?'

'Aye and they have no concern for other folks' property. 'Tis fortunate that's all they broke. They near had the door off its hinges. I'm surprised you didn't hear the racket next door. They weren't quiet about it. They tipped the ale away, as well, the miserable devils.'

'I'll fetch you some more, Seb, you must be parched.' Emily hurried off, as I hoped she would.

Whilst she was gone, Jude reappeared and piled a platter with bacon and oatcakes before returning to the bed chamber. Jack looked most concerned, seeing the better part of breakfast disappearing before his eyes. Observing the lad's dismal expression, I pushed the remaining food towards him. The lad required no urging and the platter was cleared before Emily returned.

'You two must have been ravenous,' she declared, shocked to see the food devoured, gone so swiftly, but she gave me a suspicious look.

'The food was excellent as always, Em,' I said, but she quirked an eyebrow at me and the dour expression she cast in Jack's direction made clear her opinions on the matter. She poured out a rather mean trickle of ale into the cup beside the lad's empty platter.

'There you are, you greedy little wretch. Make do with that!' She turned to pour a far more generous measure for me. 'Watch him, Seb – he'll have you die of starvation, if you're not careful.'

'Thank you, Em. I'll take care he doesn't.' I forced a smile despite growing more fearful by the moment that, if she stayed any longer, she might hear a sound or see something that would give Jude away. So I was relieved when she turned to go.

But Emily didn't leave. There, as she opened the door to depart, stood a most pathetic sight.

'Great Heavens! What are you doing here?' Emily demanded.

I went to the threshold.

'For God's sake, Nessie! Come in! Come in, off the street,' I said, pulling her inside and shutting the door hurriedly. 'Why on earth are you here?' I realised I probably knew well enough why Meg Bowen's silly little maid had come, but had to pretend ignorance. 'Sit you down, lass. Here, have my ale. Now tell us what's amiss.' I stood back, leaning against the closed door and shut my eyes – as if there wasn't enough trouble already.

'It's mistress,' Nessie sobbed, huddling into her cloak as she sat on a stool beside the fire. 'Mistress Meg, she's ever so sick.'

'Sick?' Emily asked. 'Should we fetch the apothecary?' She put an arm around the weeping girl's narrow shoulders.

'I don't know. There's blood everywhere. I don't know what else to do. Help me, Master Seb. Where's Master Jude? He'll know what's to be done, 'cos he loves my mistress.' Nessie broke down, shuddering with the force of her sobs.

'Master Jude can't help you, Nessie, he's not here,' I said quickly. Dear God, what a fix we were in. I was floundering like a drowning man, utterly out of my depth. 'Now be calm and we'll think what's best, er, Emily? What do you suppose we should...'

Before Emily could answer, Nessie said:

'And I found this poor little thing.' She pushed back her cloak, revealing blood-soaked clothes beneath, and drew out what had once been a fine silken kerchief but was now a gory rag. She put it on the board, amongst the breakfast platters, and unwrapped it. There before us lay a tiny foetus, no bigger than a woman's hand, its head large in proportion, its bloody umbilical cord still attached.

'Shit!' Jack shrieked in horror, and leapt off his seat by the board, sending his empty ale cup flying. 'It's the Devil hisself!' he cried, retreating into the farthest corner. I felt my insides heaving and struggled for control. Only Emily seemed unfazed.

'Come along, Nessie. We'll go and tell Dame Ellen everything. Then we'll clean you up and see what needs to be done. Don't worry, you're safe with us now.' She went to lead the maid away but Nessie was still concerned for what lay upon the table.

'It needs caring for,' she insisted, reluctant to leave it behind. 'It's a boy. Has it got a name, do you think?'

'I shouldn't think so, Nessie. Now, come along,' Emily insisted, all practical and efficient. As they departed, she looked back at me, mouthing: 'Get rid of it!'

When they were gone, taking my cue from Emily, I told Jack to remove the offending object.

'Not bloody likely! I ain't touching it!' He looked appalled.

'Well, it can't stay there.'

'You get rid of it, then, 'cos I ain't picking it up!'

So, it was down to me, then. Hardly daring to think what I was doing, I gathered up the four corners of the rag, opened the door and went out. The street was not too busy for the moment, a sudden squall keeping less hardy souls indoors and those who were out and about had their heads down, hooded against the rain. I hobbled up the street a little way and turned into an alley where the nearest midden was a refuge and feeding ground for rats and stray dogs. As I hoped, a couple of mangy curs were nosing through the stinking mess and I threw the rag and its unholy contents towards them. They drew back, tails between their legs, but one quickly overcame its instinctive cowardice and advanced to investigate. The filthy beast wolfed down the offering in a single mouthful. I heard the tiny bones crack in the dog's jaws and instantly lost the battle with my weak stomach and vomited there in the alley.

Shivering and unsteady, only now did I realise I'd come out without my cloak and, worse still, without my staff. Quite how I got so far without falling down, I couldn't say. Leaning against the crumbling wattle-and-daub walls of the house facing the alley, I stumbled along, stopping twice more as nausea gained the upper hand, before reaching home.

• •

Throughout all this, Jude, well fed and exhausted, had been asleep in my bed. Though he mumbled and tossed about – maybe suffering nightmares of his recent ghastly experiences – it seemed a pity to have to wake him, but every passing hour made the arrival of the watch more likely, especially now Meg Bowen's death must be common knowledge. Though Jude was in no way to blame for yet another unexpected demise in the Bowen household, it was bound to recall his escape to mind once again.

'Jude, Jude, come on, wake up! It's time you were gone.'

'Go away,' he muttered, turning over and pulling the blanket close.

'Jude! You can't stay here any longer!' I dragged at the covers, revealing my brother still fully clothed. 'Get up, for God's sake! The watch is on the prowl.'

'I don't care. Leave me be!'

'You *will* care when they cart you back to Newgate!' With that, I nodded to Jack who emptied a jug of water over Jude's head.

Jude shot out of bed, spluttering, catching hold of Jack by his skinny arm and delivering a hefty clout that must have left the lad's ear ringing.

'You little bastard, I'll skin you alive!' Jude yelled, pushing his wet hair back from his face with an angry gesture.

'It weren't me. Yer bruvver told me to!' Jack protested. Jude released the boy and glared at me.

'I'm so sorry, Jude, but you have to go, now,' I said, my tone leaving no room for argument. 'Sir Robert is coming for dinner, he'll be here soon.'

'What time is it then?'

'Almost ten of the clock.'

Jude relented, knowing I was right. He took up a cloak – his own, that he had been forced to manage without so far, and another of our depleted supply of blankets.

'Come on then, urchin, you'd best show me how to reach my new stink-ridden hiding place through the back alleyways, without being seen.' Jude almost sounded cheerful and obviously expected Jack to bear him no grudge for the punishment he had administered. But before he left, having had nothing to drink for a day or more, Jude drained the ale jug to the dregs, wiping his mouth on his sleeve and sighing with satisfaction.

• •

I felt no guilt for the lie I had told. Sir Rob was not expected for dinner, and just as well, since there was no ale left, yet again. Jude may have been thirsty, but my last cup had been drunk by Nessie and I'd had no breakfast, not that that would have made any difference after what happened in the alley. Just thinking about it made me feel queasy again. It was a relief to be alone. So tired, I closed my eyes but the recent horrors instantly crowded my mind and rest of any kind proved impossible. Pain gnawed at my left shoulder, as it did sometimes, so my arm was a dead weight, like so much raw meat hanging on an aching joint. When it was like this, even drawing was out of the question to take my mind off things. So I sat, brooding and despondent, until Emily rushed in, interrupting dark, sour thoughts.

'Have you heard, Seb? They're saying Meg Bowen was raped!' she cried breathlessly, 'I just heard of it at the conduit. Mistress Collins' maid knows all about it. So horrible, it was. She was raped with a dagger, she said, left bleeding and may die of her injuries.' My blood turned to icy Thames water in my veins.

'But it wasn't like that, was it? We know the truth, don't we?'

'Do we? I only know what Nessie said and she's got less sense than a day old chick.'

'But Meg miscarried a babe. That was the cause. Wasn't it?' My voice carried little conviction. I was too weary for that.

'Aye, we know she lost the babe but we don't know why. I never thought about it before but perhaps some devil *did* rape her and use his dagger on her. That would surely account for it.'

'Oh, Em, believe me, it wasn't like that.'

'How do you know, Sebastian Foxley?' Emily stood before me, hands on hips. I noticed her eyes flashed darkest cobalt in anger. 'Were you there? Did you see what happened?'

'Of course I didn't. How could I?'

'Then how do you know better than anyone else?'

'I just do. Believe me.' But I could not look at her straightly.

'You fear that Jude will be accused, don't you?' she said, knowing precisely what I was thinking.

'Aye, but he didn't do it, I tell you.'

'But he is at large, so how can you be so certain?'

'For pity's sake, Em, because he's my brother!'

She considered for a moment, her head on one side, like a bird listening for worms underground.

'You've seen him, haven't you? Jude's been here, hasn't he?'

I nodded, lacking the strength and the will to deny it.

'Aye.'

'Oh, Seb, why didn't you tell me? Surely you know you can trust me?' She put her arms around me, pulling me close for an instant of precious embrace.

'Aye, but do you trust Jude's word, Emily? You don't know him as I do.'

'No, but if you're certain he's innocent, that's good enough for me, Seb. We are together in this. It isn't so much a matter of proving Jude's innocence any longer. We must find the real culprit for all these deaths.'

I agreed. Could she see the pain in my eyes, in my very soul, I wondered? Not for myself, but for my brother.

'Tell me what Jude said.' Emily pulled a stool up close and sat facing me, our knees touching. It was as though her strength passed into me, warm and steadfast. I rallied and squared my shoulders:

'Jude told me Meg brought it upon herself, it was a mishap. She was attempting to rid herself of the babe but it all went wrong. That's what she said to him when he found her there. He thought she was dying, that it was too late to save her.'

'So Jude was with her?'

'Aye, he admitted to that.'

'Then I pray God no one saw him arrive or leave. That would be too much to explain away.'

I sat silent, my eyes unfocused even as my thoughts fought themselves into some kind of order.

'Em, you said *we* must find the culprit. Did you mean that? Will you help me?'

She put her hands either side of my face and tilted it, so I had to look at her. She was smiling.

'For you, Seb, I shall do all I can to aid you, even if it means helping that rogue you call "brother".'

'You have little liking for Jude. Why is that?'

'Far too full of his own importance, thinks every woman should throw herself at his feet.'

'Jude thinks that? Is that how he seems to you, Em?'

'I would rather talk about you, Seb. Are your ribs still paining you? I have a good salve I could apply for you, if you want?' She kissed me lightly on the forehead. Her lips burned like a brand. I put my hand to the spot, half expecting to feel it blistered.

'Later maybe, thank you. For now, I need to puzzle this out, if there is a puzzle, now we suspect Kit stabbed Matthew Bowen, but who strangled Kit? And why? Are these two deeds connected? I'm certain they must be. I don't know, Em, I can't understand it.'

* *

Just then, the great bell of St Martin's began to strike the hour of ten.

'Dinner!' Emily cried, 'Dame Ellen's dinner will be spoiled and she will take her broom to me and rightly so!'

'Tell her I detained you, needed your assistance, which is true enough.' Yet another suffers for my cause, I thought, as she fled next door. I let fly a curse at my predicament, flinging an empty wooden trencher across the chamber to crash against the wall. 'It goes from bad to worse. The blasted Devil farts in my face at every chance he gets because I can't fight back. Yet, if the Devil *is* against me, then surely God must be on my side,' I reasoned aloud. 'Somebody somewhere must be on my side.'

'I'm not God, but I am on your side!' Sir Rob pushed the door open. 'If that helps in the least,' he added with a grin that showed his strong white teeth. 'I take it matters are not progressing as they should?'

'No. In truth, they're worse.'

'That's unfortunate, indeed. What's happened now?' The knight eased his lengthy, velvet-clad frame onto a stool by the unlit hearth. So I repeated the gruesome tale about Meg Bowen's miscarriage, the possibility she still might die, but Jude's name did not pass my lips. Sir Rob listened without interrupting. His face was grave by the time I'd finished.

'I heard news of that by the conduit, as I was stabling my horse, but the gossips speak of rape, not miscarriage. Hopefully, Mistress Meg will live, in which case she can speak the truth as to what occurred last eve.'

'I pray she does, else my brother could stand accused of raping and killing her.'

'Ah! So your brother is still at large? This could look very bad for him, two deaths and a possible rape, all in the household of the man who dismissed him.' Sir Rob thought it through. 'If you didn't convince me otherwise, I might well suspect your brother of all three crimes myself. No doubt, others *will* see it that way.'

I nodded. Matters were becoming worse for Jude with each passing hour.

'But, for the present,' Sir Rob was saying, 'since we cannot prove your brother's innocence, we must find the felon ourselves. I admit, in the beginning, I thought the apprentice the most likely culprit but, with him being the second victim, I have to revise that.' He pushed his long powerful fingers through his fiery locks as he seriously considered the problems.

'So who would you now think to be guilty?' I asked him, feeling weary of it all. 'I could not say I know any man capable of committing such horrors. No one of my acquaintance could do such vile things, could they?'

Sir Rob shook his head.

'I'm afraid men are capable of the most hideous deeds, Seb. Some of the horrors I have seen.'

'But you are a warrior. Men must do things in battle they would never do otherwise.'

'Sadly, my friend, 'tis not always so.' He looked deeply pensive, but I was wise enough to enquire no further. Perhaps it was better thus.

'So, what should we do next do you suppose?' I asked, wishing there was some ale to offer Sir Rob. Certainly I felt much in need.

'Keep asking questions. Eventually the right one will fall into the right ear and the answer will be given.'

To me that didn't seem like a very productive course to pursue.

'Supposing the murderer learns of our enquiries: we may warn him off. What if he kills again before we can stop him? What if...' I swallowed hard, gulping down the fear that arose at such an awful prospect. 'What if he kills one of us, Emily for instance? I should not know how to live with myself if anything happened to her.'

Sir Rob gave me a searching look and I grew hot under such a knowing examination.

'You love Mistress Emily,' he said, though whether it was meant as a question or a statement, I couldn't tell.

'Of course not. That would be absurd, impossible.' Flustered, flinging my arm aloft, I almost knocked the knight on the jaw.

'She is only an apprentice-cum-servant, after all,' he added in the same unfathomable tone of voice.

'No. I-I... it matters not to me what Em may be, a serving maid or a duchess.'

'So, she is irrelevant?'

'Not at all. Em is a young woman, respectable as any fine lady. I cannot speak too highly...'

Sir Rob laughed.

'Oh, indeed, there are a few fine ladies I could not speak too highly of either.'

I was becoming angry now. Sir Rob was twisting my words, making me say things I certainly did not mean.

'Stop it! I beg you. Please.'

The knight held up his hands in a gesture of appeal.

'Forgive me, my young friend. It is unforgivable that I should mock you when I am a guest in your home. It is not so long ago since I was in love that I should forget the confusion Cupid can cause with his nasty little arrows. Forgive me?'

'But I do not feel that way about Em.'

'No, of course not. I was foolish to think it.'

'Besides, no woman could ever love a cripple like me. Now, if I had Jude's fine body and good looks, it might be otherwise, but it is not. So, please do not put such foolish thoughts in my head.'

'I am sorry, Master Sebastian. I spoke out of turn.' Sir Rob looked at me from beneath close-drawn brows. 'How did you come to be as you are?'

I shook my head.

'I have no right to ask. Forgive my ill-manners.'

'No. No, 'tis not that. Just, well, no one ever asks. I-I have nothing to be ashamed of. I'm told it happened when I was born – born awkward, my father said – my left shoulder and hip were dislocated. I killed my mother in the process...'

'You can't be blamed for that.'

'No, I suppose not. My father paid any number of surgeons to try to put me to rights but they could do naught, although one fellow suggested I be taken to the Tower and stretched on the rack to set me straight.' I near-laughed. 'Fortunately, my father didn't take that advice seriously.'

'Thank you, Seb. Thank you for trusting me with your secret. It shall go no further.' He pushed himself upright and moved towards the door. 'Now, I am hungry and I think we should visit the Hart's Horn, in search of both information and nourishment. Am I sufficiently forgiven that you will permit me to buy you dinner?'

The Hart's Horn Tavern

I WELCOMED THE ale at the Hart's Horn, but had little interest in food, even though I'd eaten nothing all morn. That was until a platter of Goodwife Fletcher's white bait in a saffron sauce was set before me. I had tasted none better and quickly cleared the plate, wiping up the last trace of the delicious sauce with my bread, and there were apple pasties to follow. The day now seemed to wear a kinder expression, looking more hopeful. Then Tom, Gilbert Eastleigh's apprentice, came in. He saw us and acknowledged us with a little bow before asking for the goodwife. The woman came out from her busy kitchen, all smiles, as usual, to take the lad's order for his master's dinner.

• •

While he waited, Tom looked about the crowded place. Sir Robert caught his eye and beckoned him over.

'Does Master Eastleigh's order include dinner for you, lad?' the knight asked. Tom shook his head.

'No, sir, there be bread an' cheese fer me, as usual, when I get back.'

Sir Rob pushed an apple pasty towards the apprentice.

'That should keep the worms at bay,' he said, grinning.

Tom returned the grin and, seating himself on the bench opposite me, made short work of the pasty. I noted how skinny were the apprentice's arms, the dark shadows under red-rimmed eyes.

'Your master works you hard,' I said, passing my ale cup to him. He gave me a strange look, wary, frowning as if he suspected my offer of drink to have some darker meaning. I knew not why he might have cause to doubt me.

'Sometimes.' No doubt he was fearful of speaking against his master.

'Master Eastleigh keeps you too long in that still-room of his, brewing those noisome potions, I don't doubt?'

''Tis not so bad, just the stuff makes my eyes water a bit, an' I hate the smell o' some o' the things I have t' stir and bottle up, but Master Eastleigh is a-a fair master, I suppose.'

Just then, Goodwife Fletcher bustled over, bearing a crock pot wrapped in a snowy linen napkin.

'Come now, Tom, your master will be taking a stick to you if you fail to get his dinner home on time.' She scolded the lad good-naturedly.

Tom took the pot, thanked the goodwife, bowed to Sir Robert and me and hurried off.

'Now, sirs, what more may I serve you?' the goodwife enquired, wiping her hands on her apron.

'Is that likely?' I asked her, nodding towards young Tom's departing back. 'Is he beaten often?'

Goodwife Fletcher shook her head.

''Tis none of my business, Master Seb, but since you ask me, either the boy is fearfully clumsy or, shall I just say he bears more than his fair share of bumps and bruises. More than once it has fallen to me to tend his hurts, even though his master is an apothecary of good reputation, but that is a matter betwixt them. But privily, sirs, I think Master Eastleigh has little liking for his apprentice and cares even less. Now, what can I get you?' Clearly, the subject was closed.

'More ale, goodwife,' we replied together.

● ●

'So, Eastleigh is not quite the pleasant fellow he appears,' Sir Rob observed, staring into his ale pot, hoping to find inspiration in its golden liquid depths.

'No, maybe not. Perhaps his father's death changed him.'

'When was this?'

I thought a while, rubbing at my healing ribs without realising 'til I made myself wince.

'Must be five years or so since, come Michaelmas. I cannot recall exactly. A pleasant old man he was too. In good fettle one day, gone the next. Though he was well beyond his allotted three-score-years-and-ten, so I suppose it was not to be wondered at over much.'

'Mm, like Matthew Bowen? It might be worth our while to make a few enquiries. But, in the meantime, I think you should go home and rest those ribs, whilst I ask the questions. Can you manage the walk alone, or shall I escort you first or find that scallywag Jack to aid you?'

'No, no, I can manage, thank you.' The last thing I wanted was for Sir Rob to go searching for Jack, fearing he might find Jude as well. Also, the knight's intention to make enquiries concerning Eastleigh's dear departed just might bear fruit and the sooner the better. 'But I will finish my ale first and then take my time walking home.'

'Very well, if you are certain?'

'Aye, I am.'

Accepting my assurances, Sir Rob rose, took some coins from his purse and lay them on the board to pay for their meal.

●　●

When he was gone, I settled back to dawdle over the ale. Sir Rob was right to be concerned for my ribs. They were very sore and I prayed the pain would ease if I rested a while longer before the walk home.

Goodwife Fletcher came over to collect the money. The dinnertime crowd was mostly off now, returning to work, and she lingered by the board, wiping up a few drips of gravy with a wet cloth.

'You seem weary, Master Seb,' she said. 'Shall I get you more ale? Or mayhap my salve will do your bruises more good?'

'If you can spare the time, goodwife, I'd appreciate your salve on my ribs.'

'I thought as much. Go upstairs. I shall be with you shortly.'

'Is that wise? What of your good reputation?' I was alarmed but she laughed.

'I treat 'em all as needs be, master, and am known for it. Besides, how much can my reputation suffer in less time than it takes to say an Ave and a Paternoster? You think you could ruin my good name in so short a space? Go on with you!' She was still laughing as I climbed the stair, needing now to hold my ribs at every step.

I believe Goodwife Fletcher was more deeply concerned when I pulled up my shirt for she seemed to hesitate to apply the salve. My chest was a mess of bruises, darker and more ominous-looking than when she had first treated them. Such changes were to be expected but the bruising had spread up to my shoulder. Though I tried not to, I winced at her touch and, by the time she was done, I felt shaken and sweaty.

'I'll fetch you something stronger for the pain,' she said, ignoring my admittedly feeble declaration that I had no need. I lay on the bed, telling myself there was no time for such luxuries – I should be working on Lord Richard's triptych and finding evidence of Jude's innocence, not lazing here. But the pillow was soft and the salve was cooling on my heated flesh. Perhaps a few moments more would not matter...

CHAPTER FOURTEEN

Friday evening

HAVING PERSUADED Goodwife Fletcher that her salve and potions had improved my case sufficiently, I insisted I was well enough to make my way home, so long as I took things slow and steady. The trouble was it was growing dark, the gloom of evening hastened by gathering clouds that threatened rain, and the wind was rising, giving an unseasonal nip to the air.

As I left the Hart's Horn, I noticed someone waiting in the doorway of the house across the way. Squinting, I thought it looked like young Tom Bowen, come to collect his master's supper, no doubt. He shouldn't stand out here, it was a chill evening, the lad would catch his death. I raised a hand in greeting but the lad turned away, hurrying off. I must have been mistaken. It wasn't Tom after all.

• •

I shivered as I limped along, favouring the ache in my left side. The same dilemma still taunted me – the more so now I was hurting – believing Gilbert Eastleigh could be the murderer in whose stead Jude was accused, yet knowing the apothecary might have the means to restore my body. For that to happen, Eastleigh had to remain a free man, at liberty to pursue his alchemical work. But then, to get Jude exonerated, the guilty man must be exposed and brought to justice. A few prayers wouldn't go amiss, I thought. They might even aid me in my decision.

• •

Since I was going to pass by St Michael's, I decided to make the effort to attend vespers. I hadn't been to church for days and fully intended to pay our overdue tithes before Father Thomas was required to remind me, yet again.

St Michael le Querne Church

I HAD REACHED St Michael's when the heavens opened but the west door gave no shelter as the wind blew hailstones hard against the timbers even within the shallow porch. So I pushed open the heavy oak door, wincing as my ribs protested at the effort, and entered into the deep shadows, the incense-laden gloom of the familiar nave, almost falling down the step I knew was there but did not see. A few candles lit the stillness.

• •

It would soon be time for vespers. Other folk would be arriving, including Emily. Then I could walk home with her. For now, the little church was silent, only the drumming of hailstones on the roof a distant rhythm that was slowing now, but at least the quiet was calming, a balm to my soul. Approaching the rood screen that divided the chancel from the nave, I took Eastleigh's precious papers from the pouch at my belt. I dared not leave them at home again. These were the cause of my troubles, the key to a new life for myself or my brother's death warrant. To be straight-backed, whole in body and fair of limb, kissed kindly by Fate who thus far had treated me with contempt. Who in this position would not be tempted? Every Christian sentiment dictated that Jude's life had to be more important than a miracle for me, and it was, wasn't it? Oh, Jude! My brother! Why? Why do I have to choose?

• •

Sobbing, I eased down slowly to my knees, using the finely carved wood of the rood screen to assist. I found I was looking into the stern face of St Michael: archangel, demon-slayer, judge of souls. I shuddered, chilled, understanding the saint's reprimand, the warning. But I couldn't decide, not now, not yet.

Below St Michael's feet was a small earthenware pot, as old as the church itself, half-buried in the floor by the rood screen. It was an acoustic pot, full of cobwebs, put there to magnify the voice of the priest or the music of the choir so the congregation could hear better. Many old churches had them.

I looked about. No sign of Father Thomas or anyone else. I folded the papers small and pushed them into the pot, rearranging the cobwebs to conceal them: safer here than at home. Who would think to look in such a place? I felt some small measure of relief at being rid of them, though I was but delaying the decision. With eyes closed, I begged St Michael to help me when the time came and, meanwhile, to guard the papers well. Making the sign of the cross, I levered myself up with the aid of the rood screen carvings and my staff.

• •

The candle flames leapt, startled by a sudden draught. Newborn black shadows began stretching themselves, gathering around the font at the west end of the nave.

I felt I wasn't alone.

'Who's there?' A candle flame staggered, flared and died. 'Who is it?'

With trepidation, I moved towards the font, into the darkness. The font was hidden beneath its beautifully carved and painted cover – a thing of wonder I often admired, but not today. The lone bell in the belfry began ringing for vespers. That explained it. Master Marlow, as churchwarden, had gone to summon the parishioners.

A tapestry hanging twitched.

'I know someone is here, show yourself.' I waited but no answer came. The remaining candles had steadied. It was nothing but an overwrought imagination. No one there. Exhausted, I eased down to sit on the steps at the base of the font, barely stifling a cry as my ribs seemed to pierce my flesh. With eyes screwed tight shut and fists clenched hard, I willed the pain away.

There was just the bell, the candles and the hurt. Yet there was another sound: the squeak of wet leather soles on the ceramic tiles. Some other sense caused me to turn slightly – a movement just barely enough to save my life.

• •

Parishioners were pushing through the door, as eager to get out of the rain as to attend the office. But Emily was to the fore and, thinking she heard a cry, was the first to see the body lying face down by the font. She hastened over but had no need to see the victim's face to know who it was, the misshapen shoulder clothed in a blood-soaked jerkin told its own tale.

'Seb! Seb! Speak to me!' she sobbed, kneeling beside him, uncaring of the blood that soiled her skirts. 'Seb!'

She touched his out-flung arm, his hand, found them still warm. Others came to her. Dame Ellen placed a comforting arm around her apprentice to draw her aside a little, leaning down to put her fingers to the man's neck, to feel his pulse.

'Fear not, Emily, he lives still, God be thanked.' Dame Ellen turned to the rest of the folk crowding through the door behind her and saw Gilbert Eastleigh and Tom Bowen standing to one side. 'Master Eastleigh!' she called, 'Attend here, if you please! My tenant is in need of your services.'

Somewhat reluctantly, the apothecary-surgeon did as she bade him, sweeping aside his fine blue gown to avoid the blood.

● ●

By this time, Father Thomas had come out of his vestry to see what unheralded commotion was delaying his parishioners from taking their proper places so he could begin the divine office. Robert Marlow had left off his bell-ringing to join the noisy crowd. Gilbert Eastleigh turned Seb's limp body over onto his back without, as Emily viewed it, paying any attention to the hurt this would cause. She gasped in protest but Dame Ellen held her back from dragging Eastleigh away from Seb.

'Bring a light here!' Eastleigh ordered. Someone brought a torchlight, another a candle. He put his ear against Seb's chest to listen to his breathing. Surprisingly, though the breathing was slow and shallow, it sounded quite unhindered, no bubbles of air gurgling through blood-filled lungs. He rolled the body over again. 'Anyone have some clean linen to hand?' he demanded.

Emily, without hesitation, ripped the hem off her linen underskirt and handed it to the apothecary. He tore it into two lengths, made a pad of one half which he tucked inside Seb's bloody shirt, pressing it firmly against the wound. The other half he passed under the unresponsive body and tied the ends together, holding the pad tightly in place.

Eastleigh stood up, looked with distaste at his blood-stained hands.

'Take him home. He needs to rest,' he ordered curtly before walking away, pushing through the crowd and leaving the church with his apprentice, back out into the rain-drenched street.

Eastleigh's apothecary's shop, Ivy Lane

'DID YOU get the notes?' Lord Lovell gave Gilbert Eastleigh's apprentice a good shaking, though he already knew the answer from the apothecary himself. The little still-room was stifling, both were sweating.

'N-no, my lord, there wasn't time. Folk came for vespers.' Tom Bowen felt like a cat caught by a skinner, so scared he could barely control his limbs. His legs seemed to fold beneath him, knees jerking as one suffering a fit. In this light, the ferocious baron looked more wolf than man, teeth bared in a snarl. The lad doubted he would see another dawn.

'So you never asked him?' Tom shook his head. 'Did you search him?'

'I tried. I meant to, but...'

'But what?' Lord Lovell stood so close, Tom was sprayed with spittle every time the man spoke. 'Don't tell me the feeble cripple beat you off.'

'No, but...'

'But, but, but! Is that all you can say?' Lord Lovell shook him 'til his bones rattled in their sockets.

'I-I think...' Tom swallowed convulsively three or four times before he could get the words out. 'The knife you gave m-me. I m-might have k-killed him with it, my lord.'

'What! I told you to threaten him with it, not to...' The man took a pace back, standing hands on hips, like a school master. 'Oh, that was very well done, wasn't it? And how will we retrieve the notes now, you stupid little fool? How can we ask him, if he's dead? Tell me that.'

'I don't know, sir. I'm so sorry. I never meant to kill him. The knife slipped. I meant to threaten him with it, make him tell me but my hand just...'

'And now he's dead!'

'I don't know. My master says he may live, my lord.'

'Then you'd best start praying that he does!' Lord Lovell picked up his cloak from the stool, seemed about to leave. 'Eastleigh!'

The apothecary came hurrying in, looking panicky.

'You send a whimpering pup to do a man's job, what do you expect? I told you to do it yourself, damn you. How dare you disobey me?'

The apothecary quivered visibly, wanting to say that was what an apprentice was for: to do the tasks he didn't want to do himself. Besides, it was the apprentice's fault the notes were lost in the first place, but he held his peace.

'You have a birch rod?'

Eastleigh nodded, fearing it would be applied to his own ageing body. God knows, Lovell looked capable of it, if he would soil his hands on so menial a task.

'Use it.' The lord indicated Tom with an imperious gesture as the lad tried to shrink to invisibility in the corner.

Eastleigh sighed with relief.

'Then do what you can to ensure the damned cripple survives long enough to tell us where he's hidden the notes. See to it!'

• •

With Lord Lovell's departure, Tom had to face the physical consequences of his fearful mistake. It was a long painful process, one he could never forget.

The Foxley brothers' rooms

BACK HOME, though it was well after curfew, close to midnight, Emily sat at the bedside, wringing her hands, barely able to look as Master William Hobbs stitched Seb's wound. Hobbs was Lord Richard's own physician and surgeon, and came with recommendations from the king himself. Sir Rob had fetched him directly he learned of Seb's near-fatal encounter.

'Any other man would have died of this injury,' Hobbs told them as he cut the silk of the last of fifteen tiny sutures, neat as any embroidery. 'I doubt the young man will relish the fact that his misshapen back saved his life. The blade could have pierced the heart or lung of a normal man but, in this case, mercifully, the misplaced bones sent the blade glancing awry. Barring the onset of wound sickness and inflammation, God willing, he will live.'

Emily was weeping silently with relief as Master Hobbs' apprentice packed away the surgical tools.

'We are grateful for your services, Master Hobbs, and to the duke for sending you,' Dame Ellen said formally.

'Widow Langton,' Master Hobbs acknowledged, bowing, preparing to take his leave.

'Your fee, sir?' Dame Ellen enquired doubtfully, but the physician shook his head.

'Lord Richard has dealt with that, good dame, you owe me nothing. Though a cup of ale would be much appreciated before we brave the rain once more.'

'Of course, of course.' Dame Ellen sent Emily off to fetch ale for everyone, including Sir Robert, young Jack, John Appleyard and the physician's apprentice, even the Marlows and Stephen Appleyard who waited in the next room, having helped to bring Seb home.

Meanwhile, Hobbs took out a small bottle.

'Two drops in a little wine will ease the patient's pain,' he instructed. 'Red wine and red meat will aid his body in making up the deficiency of blood.'

Dame Ellen, biting back the retort that she could not afford to waste such luxuries on a mere tenant, nodded agreement. Sebastian could pay her back out of his commission money from the duke. Whenever, if ever, he finally got around to finishing that triptych.

Saturday, the sixth day of May

'BUT WHO could have done this to you, Seb?' Emily was distraught at my bedside, wringing her hands. Her eyes were red and swollen this morning – more than just a lack of sleep. She'd been weeping. For me?

I did my best with honeyed oatcakes, bacon collops and a cup of watered wine. I'd told her I wasn't hungry but Dame Ellen insisted, as per Master Hobbs' instructions, and Emily was ordered to watch that I did as I was told and to make certain young Jack had no share in clearing the platter.

Instead Jack watched enviously as I pushed the bacon around with my knife, having long since devoured his own less-interesting breakfast of plain oatcakes and ale. I bit off a morsel of bacon, chewed it for an age but still had trouble forcing it down. The watered wine helped but the effort left me weary.

'I have no idea, Em,' I said after much thought, answering a question she'd posed earlier. 'It was dark in the church, he came from behind. I never saw his face.'

'There must have been something you saw,' she insisted, her agitation evident as she screwed the corner of her apron into ball. 'Anything at all? Was he tall or short? Broad or skinny? Something?'

But I could only repeat that it had been too dark to see. I leaned back on the pillows, shifting carefully in an effort to find a position whereby my latest wound was not rubbing against them but this proved impossible. I gave up and leaned forward, bending my knees up so I could rest my head upon them.

'You don't look comfortable in the least,' Em said, re-arranging the pillows behind me, but I remained as I was – my back actually hurt less in that hunched position – and I was busy, thinking. Jack added the pillow from Jude's bed to the heap but it didn't help.

'But my attacker, whoever he was, must have pushed passed you, Em. You say you heard my cry, so the deed must have been done but a moment since. How else did he escape from the church except by pushing you aside? You must have seen him leave.'

She thought it over but concluded that no one had left the church through the west door by which she and the other parishioners had entered – there had been neither space nor opportunity.

'Then either he left by another door, or... he was still in the church.'

'Aye, 'e could've 'idden in the belfry tower,' Jack suggested eagerly.

'No, he would have been seen by Master Marlow. He was in there, ringing the bell,' Emily said.

'In the vestry p'raps?'

'No, Jack. Father Thomas was in there, preparing for vespers.'

'Be'ind the rood screen, then? There's loads o' places.'

'Father Thomas would have seen him when he came out from the vestry,' Em pointed out. 'No, he must have left by another way.'

'Well, the east door is in the vestry; the south door is in the belfry tower and the north door, being the Devil's door, is only unlocked when there is going to be a baptism. 'Tis unusual for a babe to be baptised at vespers, unless it be unlikely to live 'til morning, so was there to be a baptism?' I asked Emily.

'I did not notice anyone bringing a babe,' she replied. 'But, in truth, I was more concerned for you... I was hardly going to see what other folk were doing.'

I saw the glint of moisture poised on her lashes and looked away.

'Mm, perhaps that is what my assailant was hoping, that no one would notice him.'

'So where did he go, if none of us saw him?'

I eased into a more upright position and massaged my neck. I was becoming stiff.

'Perhaps he never went anywhere, Em. After all, what better place for a man to hide but in a crowd? I think he remained there, in the church, with all of you.'

Emily looked horrified:

'But we should have seen him. He would have been covered in blood!' She shuddered. 'Your blood! Oh, Seb, I was so afraid for you.'

'But everyone was soaked from the rain, blood stains on dark cloth would have looked little different. So tell me, Em. Who was there with you in that crowd of parishioners hastening in, out of the weather?'

She looked worried. It was an unhappy thought that someone we knew well, who lived close by, could have done the deed. It was quite unbelievable and frightening. I didn't want it to be true, either.

Her apron was being wrung into a rag as she twisted it in her hands.

'I don't know. I cannot recall.' She managed to find room to pace between the beds.

'Yes you can, Em. Think carefully, take your time,' I insisted, my pain all but forgotten for the present.

'Dame Ellen and my brother John were with me, my father and the Marlows from across the way, of course. They helped us bring you home, after...'

'All the Marlows?'

'Well, Robert was there already, to ring the church bell, but Goodwife Marlow, her daughters and Robin came along with us.'

I nodded.

'Who else?'

Slowly, Emily rehearsed a short list of friends and neighbours – not so many as might have attended vespers had the weather not discouraged them.

'And Farver Thomas, o' course,' Jack added for good measure, eyeing a bacon collop left on my platter.

I handed it to him. Em didn't nag me for not eating it.

'That's all I can remember,' she said. 'Except for Master Eastleigh and Tom Bowen. It was Eastleigh who tended to your wound, probably saved you from bleeding to death, if truth be told. I ripped up my shift for him to use to bind you up.' She sniffed hard, holding her wrinkled apron to her face, struggling to hold back the tears.

'Did you, Em?' I touched her hand. 'Thank you for that. I'll buy you linen enough for two new shifts when I've finished Lord Richard's commission, I promise.'

• •

For a while we sat quietly, thinking. About what had happened. But mostly I thought about Em, how afraid she'd been for me.

'So who was it, eh? Who stabbed you, d'you reckon?' Jack piped up, no doubt growing bored with the lengthening silence.

'What of Gilbert Eastleigh?' I suggested tentatively, meanwhile working my fingers into the frozen muscles of my shoulder, trying to ease them. 'Did he come to church with you?'

'I did not notice him. I only noticed you until Dame Ellen called Master Eastleigh over to assist you. I was not watching other folk, only you.'

I squeezed Emily's hand as it lay upon my blanket, a gesture of reassurance, and let my fingers rest there, on her reddened, work-worn skin.

'So you never saw him arrive?'

She shook her head.

'So, Em, might he have been in the church already, before the rest of you got there?'

Her eyebrows raised high at the possibility.

'I suppose he may have been, him and his apprentice,' she admitted guardedly.

'Bastard! I never liked that 'pothecary!' Jack cried, ready to condemn the man on so little evidence. 'He should bloody well 'ang fer it.'

'Hold off, lad,' I warned him. 'We must consider the possibilities judiciously; not leap to unfounded conclusions. There is nought to incriminate Master Eastleigh, particularly in this instance.'

Jack snorted.

'What's it mean then? Judously, criminate? All I know is, 'e tried t' kill yer.'

As for me, this unwelcome possibility only complicated matters still further.

• ●

Later, when Sir Rob arrived, I went over it all again, thinking the knight would have a clearer insight on the matter and be less likely to leap to conclusions.

'Well, now, it is a fact,' Sir Rob said, considering, running his hand through his fiery hair as was his habit, 'that Gilbert Eastleigh's name keeps cropping up, time and again, in our investigations. I think I should look closer into his affairs. My friend, Lord Lovell, may be of use, seeing he is Eastleigh's neighbour. I'll ask him what he knows of our apothecary-surgeon. I can arrange to meet with him at the Hart's Horn, buy him dinner, pick his brains.'

I gave him a doubtful look, which my friend misread.

'You believe Lord Lovell takes no interest in his neighbours?'

'Maybe he does but rumour has it that Lord Lovell is rich as Midas. Should he not buy dinner for you?'

The knight laughed loudly.

'Aye, you are right, young Seb. Francis can pay for my dinner for the privilege of assisting our investigation.'

With that, he left, still laughing, to ride over to Ivy Lane.

The burned out house in Bladder Street

THAT AFTERNOON, whilst Seb slept the sleep of recovery, watched over by Emily, Jack was visiting the ruined house off Bladder Street. All the way there he had been trying to decide whether he should tell Master Jude about his brother's brush with death, but he feared Jude would go straight to the house to see Master Seb if he did. No, it might be safest to say nothing of it. Master Jude was that reckless, there was no knowing what he might do to avenge his brother's hurt. After all, he'd been maddened enough when he'd heard what Kit Philpot had done.

Jack found his master huddled behind a pile of rubble from a partially-collapsed wall, away from the worst of the stinking butchers' waste.

'I brung yer dinner,' he announced, taking a loaf and a cold chicken leg from inside his shirt.

'It stinks of your sweat,' Jude complained, sniffing the bread.

'Don't bloody eat it, then. I will.' Jack went to snatch back the loaf, but Jude had already taken a large bite.

'What about ale?' he demanded. 'I need something to drink.'

Jack shrugged.

'I can't manage boff at once. Yer'll 'ave to wait fer it!'

Jude grabbed him by the arm.

'You'll damn well fetch it now or you're dismissed from my service!'

'And yer'll starve and I shan't bloody care! Master Seb can't bring yer stuff.'

Jude reconsidered his empty threat. Jack was right, of course. He changed the subject.

'How's Seb managing without me?'

'Fine,' Jack lied easily.

'Is he well?'

'Aye, well as ever.'

'And how is that triptych coming along, seeing our livelihoods depend on it?'

This time the lad's answer was honest as he kicked out at a rat that was bold enough to take a look at the men who trespassed in its domain.

'I ain't seed 'im do nuffin to it lately.'

Jude swore as he threw the stripped chicken bone to join a reeking pile of offal.

'Well, tell him I said he's to get on with it. Christ Jesus, but he's a lazy bugger when I'm not there to turf him out of bed of a morn. What's his bloody excuse now, eh?'

Jack shook his head, pulled a face.

'Don't know, master, p'raps 'e runned out o' paper? Or 'is pen broked? Don't ask me. 'Ow should I know?'

The Hart's Horn Tavern

MEANWHILE, SIR Robert and his friend, Lord Lovell, were enjoying Goodwife Fletcher's eel and oyster pasties in the Hart's Horn, but the conversation was no more productive than that going on in Bladder Street.

'But, Francis, the apothecary is your neighbour. You must know something about him,' Rob insisted, swirling the liquid in his ale cup before savouring a generous mouthful. Francis sipped his wine – his drink of choice.

'Why? What do I care for the likes of a common tradesman such as he?' he retorted, dabbing his fingers on his napkin. 'So long as he stays out of my way, I stay out of his. Of what interest would he be to me, Rob?' Francis looked his companion straight in the eye, dark eyes versus blue. 'You spend too much time with common tawdry folk, that's the trouble. I cannot think why you, or Dickon come to that, waste your time and efforts on miserable bloody peasants. The world would be a far better place if the Almighty hadn't made the disastrous mistake of creating their kind in the first place.'

Rob burst out laughing, near spilling his ale as he rocked on his bench.

'I might almost wish He hadn't, Francis, just for the sheer pleasure of seeing you mucking out your own stables, fetching water, reaping corn and thatching the roof. Who else would do those tasks for you, if not peasants?'

Francis made no answer, simply frowned malevolently and returned his attention to his pasty, long black curls of hair falling to conceal both his face and his thoughts – he did not like being laughed at, even by his good-natured friend, who meant no insult whatsoever.

'Shut your mouth, Percy!' he told him angrily when Rob took too long to control his mirth.

'Your pardon, Francis, you know I mean no harm, my friend.' Rob breathed deeply to steady himself, still biting his lip to keep from grinning at the vision of the impeccably attired lord shovelling dung from his stables. He cleared his throat to stifle the last vestige of amusement before asking mildly: 'So you know nothing of the recent comings and goings in and around Paternoster Row and Ivy Lane?'

'The murders, you mean?'

Rob nodded. Francis made some noncommittal grunt. 'Who knows? If the bastards want to kill each other off, let them. What do I care?'

'You haven't seen anything untoward then?'

'I have more important matters to attend to and Dickon should know better than to have dealings with murderers.'

'So you have heard the rumours.'

'Rumours?' Francis scoffed in a most unlordly fashion. 'The scrivener Foxley was arrested, was he not? Does that not tell you he's as guilty as Satan?'

'Not necessarily, no.'

'Well, I say it does! Particularly as I saw the devil in question on the morning after the very night of the stationer's murder, sneaking out of the alley that runs betwixt Paternoster Row and Ivy Lane.'

'Ah! Then you do know something!' Rob concluded triumphantly. 'Have some more wine and tell me all about it.' He filled his friend's cup with a generous measure.

'What has this to do with the apothecary you were enquiring about?' Francis asked, taking his ease, leaning nonchalantly against the wall behind his bench whilst his fingers twitched at his napkin.

'Maybe nothing. 'Tis just that his name crops up again and again in our investigations?'

'Our investigations? Who is investigating what and why?'

'Well, it would seem I am now investigating this business alone, since my fellow investigator is no longer able. As for why, our Dickon wants his triptych finished and that's unlikely to happen when one Foxley brother stands accused of murder and the other has near-fallen another victim.'

'Another victim? Does that not make four in all, including the woman who was raped?'

'Francis, for a man with no interest whatsoever in his neighbours, you seem well informed. But no, Widow Bowen miscarried. She wasn't raped. I have it on good authority,' Rob explained.

His companion pulled a face, disgusted by the thought.

'So what happened to the other Foxley brother? Simon, is it?'

'Sebastian. He was attacked last eve in St Michael's church, before vespers. Could have died, though mercifully God spared him.'

'And I suppose, yet again, you have no clue whatever as to his attacker?' Francis asked, feigning weariness with the whole affair.

'Nothing definite, no,' Rob admitted, sighing over the last of his ale. 'But, as I said, the apothecary's name keeps cropping up. He attended poor Sebastian in the church after the lad was stabbed but no one else saw him enter the place, so it is possible he was already there.'

'That would make your Good Samaritan a likely witness then?'

Rob nodded, rubbing his chin thoughtfully.

'Aye, or else he was the perpetrator.'

'Ah, now we're getting to the real point of this discussion, aren't we. You want to prove that the apothecary is a murderer. Is that not so? And you want my assistance, presumably.'

'Only so long as it doesn't interfere with your other commitments and duty to our Dickon. I should hate to impose otherwise on your precious time.'

Francis gave Rob a hard look, uncertain whether he was being mocked or not, but decided he was not. It was difficult to tell sometimes with Rob.

'I am certain Dickon will have no objection to me helping with your investigations since it will be all in the good cause of getting his damned triptych finished.'

'You'd best not let him hear you speak of it so. This damned triptych, as you call it, means so much to him, to the blessed memory of his father and brother.'

'Can't think why he sets such store by the notion of family! Look at me. Do I not manage right well without one? No parents, no siblings worthy of note, no children, no cousins. Just a wife I never see and do not miss, just as she prefers her horses, hounds and hawks to my company. Ah! Life is more simple without family hindrances, that's what I say.'

Rob only smiled at his companion's outburst, knowing full well Francis would have been a lonely soul if it were not for his friends, Dickon and himself in particular. The whores he took to his bed filled a need but were no substitute for a loving wife.

'Perhaps I should speak with your *friend*, this Sebastian,' Francis said, bringing Rob's thoughts back to the present.

'Why? He's very poorly. How would that help?'

Francis shrugged.

'You never know. A new face, a new way of questioning, he may remember something after all. What's he like? I know he's the wretched cripple, but...'

'Contrary to gossip, the lad is a good soul and human as the next man, to the extent that I suspect he's even fallen in love with a pretty lass.'

'Hah! How ridiculous is that? He'll be sadly disillusioned there, then.'

'I'm not so sure, but if you would speak with him, he lives in West Cheap.'

'I know where he lives.'

Rob raised his brows in surprise.

The Foxley brothers' rooms

I'D BEEN dozing when Emily returned, bringing me a fine dinner of boiled beef with pease pudding and suet dumplings. She put an extra pillow behind me to prop me up to eat. I couldn't be comfortable though, for all her care. Just then, Dame Ellen bustled in.

'And how is the patient?' she asked, seating her ample backside on the end of the other bed so the wooden frame squeaked alarmingly. 'Master Eastleigh called by to ask after your progress.'

We exchanged anxious looks but Dame Ellen didn't notice.

'Was that not thoughtful of him?' she continued. 'And more than that, such a kindness. He has left you a bottle of medication, for no cost at all. Says it is the very best restorative. Shall I pour some for you?'

'No!' Unthinking, I grabbed her arm. She gave me such a look. Realising my rudeness, I released her with an abject apology. 'Forgive me. I had no right.'

'Master Seb has only just swallowed down a fair dose of the medication Master Hobbs ordered him take, mistress. He should not take more as yet.' Emily was more astute than I, but she kept her voice low, hoping to conceal the lie. I hadn't yet had my medication.

'Oh, well, take it later. Master Eastleigh said it would improve your case considerably,' Dame Ellen told me. The expression on her face said what an ungrateful tenant she was cursed with.

'Aye, I'm certain it will. Thank you, Dame Ellen.' I was dubious indeed.

'Don't forget it!' she ordered as she went out, leaving the little bottle on the board.

Emily eyed it suspiciously.

'You're not going to take it.'

I was unsure whether it was a question or an order but I shook my head.

'Certainly not. God alone knows what venomous potions are in it. If he does not manage to slay me with a knife, what better way than with a so-called medication.'

Emily picked up the bottle, holding it at arm's length as though fearing it might bite her.

'I'll tip it away in the gutter outside.'

'No, Em. We must keep it. If it is poison then it will prove Eastleigh is the murderer.'

'And how shall we find out? I'm not going to taste it and neither are you.'

'I'll think of some way to find out without risking anyone's life. Smell it. What does it smell of?'

'Are you mad?' Emily was so horrified by my suggestion, she almost dropped the bottle. 'I'm not sniffing poison.' She set it back on the board and moved away from it.

'Give it to me then. I may recognise the odour. That would help identify it.'

'And you may well die of it, even if you do. I shall throw it away, no matter what you say.'

'But that will destroy our proof.' I made a move to get out of bed to rescue the potion. She pushed me back, gently. I didn't put up much resistance, I wanted her to touch me, even if it was to put me in my place.

'I don't care, Seb. It's safer this way.' Emily again took up the bottle and went out the door, into the street.

'Em! No,' I called after her but it was useless. I didn't see her again 'til supper time.

The apothecary's shop

S IR ROBERT decided it was time he had something for indigestion. Not that he suffered from such an indisposition. The food at the Hart's Horn was well prepared and superbly cooked. Neither had he over-indulged, but he required an excuse to visit the apothecary-surgeon.

He tethered his horse to a ring set in the wall beside Gilbert Eastleigh's place in Ivy Lane. Even before he entered, the reek issuing from the open door was enough to give him second thoughts about going inside.

'Master Apothecary! Service here, if you please,' the knight called out, rapping his knuckles on the counter. The skinny, pasty-faced apprentice appeared from the back of the shop, his eyes great with fear. Who was he expecting, Sir Rob wondered, Old Scratch himself, by the look of him. 'I would speak with your master, lad,' he said, trying to sound kindly.

'H-he's not here, begging your pardon, sir, my lord,' Tom added, seeing the man so finely dressed.

'When do you expect him back?'

'I couldn't say, sir, seeing he went to attend a wounded man in West Cheap. He may be some time, I fear.'

Sir Rob frowned. In West Cheap, eh? How many wounded men could there be in West Cheap of a sudden?

'And the name of this wounded man?'

'I-I d-don't know, sir, honest.' The frightened eyes slid away to stare at the floor.

'Don't lie to me. Tell me the name.' The knight grabbed the lad's shoulder. Tom winced with fear rather than pain.

'Tell me!'

'F-Foxley. I think it might have been Foxley.'

But the man was gone already, his horse could be heard galloping away, up the lane. Tom sat on the floor behind the counter and sobbed. Whatever he did, matters just went from bad to worse. A great deal worse.

The Foxley brothers' rooms

ROBERT REINED-IN fiercely, hauling his horse to a stop before the Foxleys' door, sending a rootling pig squealing in a shower of mud and grit. He flung the reins at a small wench who came from the house opposite – the youngest Marlow.

'Penny for you, if you hold him!' the knight shouted before shouldering his way through the door.

Emily was pouring hot water into a basin on the hearth and jumped back as the door crashed open.

'Eastleigh. Is he here?'

'No, sir,' she said, voice a-quiver. 'Though he called by a little while since.'

'What did he do when he was here?'

'Nothing, sir, but he left a vial of medicament for Master Seb.'

'Did Seb take it?'

'No, sir. I have it here.' Emily took the vial from the pocket of her apron.

'Christ be thanked for that! I thought the worst.'

'So did we, sir. Which is why Master Seb didn't touch it, though he wanted to smell it. I wouldn't allow him, sir; took it away from him.'

'How is he?'

'Sleeping. And he ate a good dinner beforehand.'

Sir Rob saw her smile, just thinking of Seb, and was convinced the lad had won a heart there in the archer's daughter, whether he was too blind to see it or not.

'May I fetch you something, sir? Ale or wine?'

'Ale, yes.' He picked up the vial Emily had put on the board, examined it closely. 'Do you have rats hereabouts?'

Emily's brows went up.

'No doubt there are some, but John's terrier makes a good job of keeping their numbers down. We see them in the garden sometimes, but not often during the day.'

'You haven't got a live one in a trap?'

'No, sir. As I said, the dog does for them mostly, though I'm sure there's a wily old devil living behind the woodpile by the privy. I hear him sometimes, squeaking and scuttling about when I'm sitting quiet...' Her explanation trailed off and she blushed, telling Sir Robert such things, but he seemed not to notice.

221

'Is the dog around?'

'Probably in the workshop with John, as usual, sir.'

'Fetch it, will you, when you get my ale?'

Emily bobbed a courtesy and hurried out, worrying that the water was cooling and she hadn't yet added the herbs for a poultice for Seb's injuries.

• •

She soon returned with an ale jug in one hand and a loop of rope in the other. At the end of the leash trotted a small white dog with black ears. It came in reluctantly, head on one side, sniffing at unfamiliar odours. Sir Rob leaned forward slowly, putting his gloved hand near the floor, allowing the dog to come close and scent him. He made no move as the little animal sniffed him and then licked his glove with a tentative pink tongue.

'What's his name?'

'John calls him Needle.'

'Because he's a tailor's dog?'

'No, because he has mouth full of them, sir.'

Sir Rob laughed.

'I'll watch out for them, then. I'll need a tall bucket or a deep pot of some sort: something in which to keep a live rat.' He saw Emily looking doubtful. 'I'm going to give it a dose of this medicament, see if it kills it. Understand?'

'Aye, sir. Of course. I'll get you something.'

• •

It took an hour or more, by which time the ale jug was empty and man and dog were covered in mud, but Sir Robert had his rat. He also had splinters from the wood pile, scratches a-plenty and a nipped thumb – from the dog by mistake, not the rat. He was exhausted and filthy but the rat looked sleek and healthy and sat in the bottom of a cracked pitcher, washing its whiskers, unconcerned that it had been chased by a dog, cornered in the privy and caught by the tail before being imprisoned.

Sir Rob tore a morsel of bread from Seb's waiting supper tray and carefully eased the greased stopper from the vial Eastleigh had left earlier. He allowed a few dark green drops to soak into the bread. It seemed not to smell of anything very much, just a slight herb scent, of sage perhaps. Emily watched, holding her breath, as he dropped the morsel into the pitcher. The rat sniffed at it and retreated, then came at it again from the other side. Perhaps the creature was too wise to eat poison. But then it picked up the bread in its front paws and sat back on its haunches to eat its snack, its tail curled neatly in a perfect half circle.

It finished the bread and looked up for more. Emily had never watched a rat so closely. Its bright black eyes gleamed like beads, its whiskers never ceased twitching. She almost felt sorry that it would soon die horribly.

● ●

I came from the bedchamber in time to see Sir Rob crouching on the floor.

'You should be resting,' Emily scolded me immediately.

'I heard voices. Sir Robert, what are you doing?'

'You're just in time to witness the results of my little test.'

'But that's the vial... dear God, you haven't swallowed it?'

'No. But our little friend here has.'

I peered at the creature in the pitcher.

'It looks well enough to me.'

'Mm, but give it time.'

● ●

And so we did. Sir Robert rode back to Crosby Place, Emily went to wait on Dame Ellen and I had my supper. The rat was bright-eyed as ever and more than content to share the fat off my bacon. When Emily returned to settle me for the night, putting a fresh poultice on my wound and giving me a dose of Master Hobbs' potion, the rat was still in good health.

CHAPTER FIFTEEN

Sunday the seventh day of May
The Foxley brothers' rooms

EMILY CAME at dawn to see how I fared. She opened the shutters to let in the light.

'Your colour looks better. Is your breathing easier this morn?'

I stirred and opened my eyes, smiling the moment I saw her.

'Good day to you, Mistress Emily.' I did feel much stronger. My smile widened as I realised my wound hardly hurt at all, neither did my ribs. But Em was staring at me in silence. 'Emily? Is something amiss, lass? With me? Have I grown another nose? Has the rat died?'

She seemed to give herself a mental shake and returned my smile.

'No, no. Good day to you, Master Seb.'

'Only the one nose still, then? 'Tis just as well. And the rat?'

'Mistress Whiskers is as well as we might expect, all things considered. I'll show you.' Emily fetched the pitcher from the other room and set it beside the bed so I could see.

'Mistress Whiskers?' I queried.

'Well, Master would be quite the wrong form of address for this rat.'

'And how can you tell the rat is a she?'

'Oh, we women just know these things,' she said with a mischievous grin.

I peered into the pitcher. It was dark in there but there was movement. The rat was still alive. As my eyes adjusted, I made out the shape of the creature but there was something else. Among the dark droppings in the bottom was a pile of white things, each about the size of a man's thumbnail. There was not the least doubt that they were newly born rats.

'Sweet Saint Michael!' I felt the blood drain from my face. 'If I had swallowed Eastleigh's potion...'

Emily stared at me then burst out laughing.

'Oh, my poor Seb. You think Eastleigh's potion did that?'

'Well, it didn't kill it, did it? Something made the rat give birth to... how many?'

Emily was still laughing.

'You wouldn't be laughing if I'd taken the potion and given birth in the night to a half dozen babes, would you?'

But she was now laughing so hard she was on her knees, unable to stand, doubled up with mirth at my expense.

'Stop it! Stop it now!'

'Oh, Seb...' Emily wiped her eyes on her apron and swallowed down her laughter but too late. She had insulted me. 'I dare say the rat was already about to birth her litter. Nothing to do with Master Eastleigh's potion but at least we know now it wasn't poison.'

'Do we? Can we be so certain? It may be some devilish stuff that works slowly, rotting the body from the inside out.'

Of course the damned rat must have been pregnant already. My mind was playing tricks with me. Too much medication, that's what it was.

Em shrugged.

'Time will tell, won't it? Now, may I change your poultice before you have breakfast?, or...'

'Later! And get rid of this wretched rat.'

She nodded and left, tip-toeing out – which showed a degree of wisdom, at any rate – taking the hateful creature and its abominable offspring with her. She had made me feel foolish. I hoped she was regretting it.

Crosby Place

LORD RICHARD came from mass in St Helen's church, returning to Crosby Place on foot, by way of a gate betwixt the churchyard and the private garden of his home. The quickthorn hedge was awash with snowy blossom and birdsong. He paused to listen to a redbreast trilling his heartfelt carol from the trellis of the arbour.

'Your namesake is in fine voice this morning,' he said, turning to Sir Robert.

'Better him than me.'

'How right you are,' Francis Lovell chimed in. 'Your singing voice is an insult to the ear. Come to that, I thought the choristers in the church were off-key more than once. Sounded like tom-cats yowling, if you want my opinion.'

'It sounded well enough to me,' Rob said.

'Well, there you have it then, since you're tone-deaf, what further evidence is required?' Lovell said.

'Then why don't we listen to the birds for a moment.' Dickon held up his hand for quiet. 'None can fault their music.' He stood still, eyes closed, smiling as he heard a linnet joining the chorus.

Rob was content to wait, sniffing at a tall golden flower he couldn't name. He stifled a sneeze as the pollen went up his nose, but at least there was nought amiss with his sense of smell.

Lovell, though, always quickly bored, was scraping his boot noisily along the gravel of the path, scuffing the stones. Rob nudged him, putting a finger to his lips to silence him.

'No matter,' Dickon said, sighing as a crowd of sparrows spilled from the ivy, quarrelling, frightening away the more melodious songsters. 'The moment has past, Francis. I'm sorry you cannot spare the time for such innocent pleasures.'

'Pleasures be damned. I can think of better things to do of a Sunday than stand about, listening to birds chirping and making a din,' he said, scowling at his now-dusty boots.

'Of course. You wish to be about your prayers. I quite understand.' Dickon spoke so solemnly, Rob might have thought his friend was serious, if it wasn't for the glint in his grey eyes.

• •

In the solar with its fine tapestries, Francis made a start on the Burgundy wine rather than the Book of Hours that lay to hand on the prayer desk in the alcove. He ordered Dickon's servant to pour wine for them all before going to stand at the oriel window. From there, through the fine tracery and expensive glass, the gardens could be seen in all their late spring beauty, cowslips carpeting the verdant sward.

'Tell me, Rob, how is our young friend, Sebastian Foxley, after the brutal assault he suffered?' Dickon asked, leafing through the pages of the holy book, ignoring his wine. 'Have you seen him since?'

Rob had made himself comfortable on the cushioned banquette, fondling the ears of Dickon's great shaggy wolfhound which lay sprawled by his feet.

'Aye, Master Hobbs reckons he'll live, God willing. Apparently, he was fortunate the blade pierced the deformity on his back so never reached anything vital, the blade being too short.'

Francis turned from the window, laughing out loud.

'Well! He must be the first fellow ever to be thankful of having a hunched back,' he said. 'I've been praying for his recovery since I heard.'

'You have?' Rob's surprise sounded in his voice but Dickon only smiled.

'My thanks for that, my friend. What a good-hearted soul you are. You know how important his recovery is, not only to me but more so to his poor brother, languishing in the Whit even as we speak. Such an act of kindness.'

Rob was not so sure he believed in Francis's sudden generosity of spirit, especially when the dark-haired lord drained his fine wine in one gulp and rushed off, claiming an urgent appointment elsewhere suddenly remembered.

'Of a Sunday? How odd,' Dickon remarked, stroking his chin thoughtfully. He had joined Rob on the banquette, his book open on his knees.

Rob shook his head at the duke's naivety where Francis was concerned. Was he truly convinced by this sudden concern for young Foxley when their friend had made no bones about the contempt he felt for craftsmen and tradesmen of any kind?

Dickon closed the Book of Hours carefully, clearly unable to concentrate on it.

'What's Francis up to, eh, Rob?' he asked. The wolfhound stirred and scratched at its ear with a long hind leg. 'Cease that, Fergus, you old flea-pot.' Dickon nudged the animal with his boot. The dog sat up and shoved its head into its master's hand, demanding attention. Dickon stroked its rough coat. 'You'll be the death of my best hose, look at the hairs all over me.'

'I wish I knew.' Rob went to the sideboard to help himself to more wine. 'Shall I pour for you?'

'Thank you, but no. I haven't drunk this as yet.' The duke held up his still brimming cup. 'I would rather this was watered well. 'Tis too early to be the worse for wear.' Rob took the cup, poured half its contents into Francis's discarded cup and refilled the duke's with water. Dickon accepted it and took a sip. 'Francis is behaving a little strangely of late, isn't he? Tell me I'm not imagining it. These audiences with my brother, sudden absences, like now. This benevolence felt for folk normally beneath his contempt. I'm beginning to feel uneasy in his company too. Do you sense it also or is it just me?'

'No, I feel it as well but I can't explain it.'

'Keep an eye on our friend, will you Rob? I wouldn't want him coming to harm, whatever he's about.'

Dame Ellen's house next door to the Foxleys

DAME ELLEN and Emily had prepared a fine dinner and, as usual on a Sunday, I dined with them and Emily's brother John, and Jack as well – we had missed the repast last week. Out of kindness Dame Ellen provided me with an old cushion. But it wasn't the normal cheerful gathering, with Jude complimenting Dame Ellen, joshing John, jesting with Emily, making her blush, having us all in fits of laughter with his jests and silly stories. It was more like a month-mind feast without him – everyone sombre and downcast. Even Jack's infectious liveliness seemed subdued, despite the good food and ale and a pile of sweetmeats set before him.

Dame Ellen sat in regal splendour at the head of the board, wearing her spotless wimple and veil as a queen would her crown.

'By the by, Sebastian,' she said to me, handing around extra helpings of mutton – particularly to John. 'That cloth you found, after your rooms were ransacked. You recall it?'

'Aye, fine stuff, Emily said.'

'Well, I can tell you, the garment was made up by a tailor in Budge Row by the name of Clements, has his shop by St Andrew's church.' The old woman chewed thoughtfully for a moment, waving her dinner knife. 'Used to be a friend of my goodman, going back years. I'd know his stitchery anywhere. You could enquire of him who had him make up the garment – such good cloth, I'm certain he will remember so important a customer.

'Now, who will have more gravy? John?'

• •

Clements, eh? It would be as well to ask him, I suppose. I could probably make the walk tomorrow, as I was feeling much improved. But then Emily, thinking to brighten the conversation, no doubt, began telling Dame Ellen about Gilbert Eastleigh's potion and the rat. I sat stiff on my cushion. Was she about to humiliate me by telling everyone of my silly mistake?

'Yet the rat remained in fine health, did it not, Master Seb?' Emily concluded her tale.

'It did, aye.'

'So it wasn't poison, after all.'

'Whatever made you suppose it was, you foolish girl?' Dame Ellen said. 'Would I have told you to dose Sebastian with it if I suspected anything untoward of Gilbert? I've known him for years.'

'No, Dame Ellen, of course not.' Emily looked suitably chastened.

'Then let's hear no more of such nonsense.' The widow cut a coney pie into generous portions and dished it out with the latest gossip. 'Now, did you know that Widow Bowen's case is the talk of Cheapside? Folk are wondering how, after five years of barrenness, her late husband, God rest his soul, had finally managed to get her with child.'

She gave Emily a significant look.

'Always supposing he was the father, of course,' John put in, skilfully transferring a piece of juicy rabbit from knife to mouth. I almost choked on the morsel I was chewing – dear God! What if Jude had been the father?

Emily passed me my ale.

'Seb? Are you quite well?'

I nodded and the conversation moved on to John's efforts at carpentry and a new gown Mistress Collins had ordered for her eldest daughter's wedding next month. Emily had worked on little else since Eastertide. With the talk having turned to the subject, it proved hard to get the women to speak of anything other than marriages.

● ●

After dinner, Emily walked back with me to next door, since Dame Ellen insisted I should rest after the good meal.

Having commented on the possibility of rain later and the glorious colour of the early marigolds, Emily mentioned that her term of apprenticeship with Dame Ellen would be coming to an end in a month or so. I hadn't known and, after that, was oblivious to anything else she had to say, my thoughts reeling. Dear God, what shall I do? With Jude not here and Jack's presence not to be relied upon, I shall be helpless. Then I chided myself for such blatant selfishness. It was Emily's life. She wasn't obliged to nursemaid me.

'What will you do, afterward?' I asked, struggling to keep my voice steady as we shared a cup of ale back in my rooms.

She waved a hand vaguely.

'I dare say I shall continue working for Dame Ellen for a while. Then, when I'm ready, she has promised to help me set up my own business, as a silkwoman, and my father says I will have a good dowry when...'

And suddenly, we were back to that dread subject again.

'W-when you marry.' The words fell heavy as lead as I said them, like ice in my belly.

'Aye, I hope so.'

'Do you h-have anyone in mind?'

'May be. There is a young man but I shan't bore you with the details. Do you need anything else, Seb, or Dame Ellen will take her broom to me if I don't finish scouring the dishes.'

'No.' I swallowed hard. 'There's nothing, thank you.'

'I'll be back later to change your dressings. In the meantime, I'll leave you to rest. Best to let your wound heal. Sleep well.' She kissed my forehead lightly and skipped out the door. She seemed so happy at the prospect that thrust like a cold dagger into my vitals. I couldn't bear it.

'Damn them all to Hell!' I cried, tears scalding my eyes. In a futile gesture, I swept my arm across the board, sending the cups and the empty ale jug flying at the wall. 'God! Why do you make me live like this, in this wretched, miserable body? For pity's sake, let me die. Now!' Falling to my knees, I ripped my shirt open, as if expecting some avenging angel to oblige with a sword to my throat.

None came.

'Master Seb? Who 'urt yer, eh? Who was it? Wot 'appened, master?'

'Emily,' I cried into my hands, covering my face.

'Em? But she wouldn't hurt yer, master, I knows it.'

'What?'

'It's me, Master Seb.'

'Oh, Jack, aye, I was preoccupied.' I struggled to pull myself up by the stool but my wound was an agony of fire.

'Yer surely was, master, whatever it means. Was yer praying? Wot's amiss wiv yer shirt. The points is all tored?'

'Mm. Help me up, please.'

'Was we broked into again? On'y I 'eard such a shrieking and smashing. Then it went quiet. I never seed no thief go out the front door. Did 'e go out the back way and over the wall, into the Saddlers' Hall yard?'

'No matter, there was nobody.' I couldn't explain to him. 'How was my brother?'

'Well enough, I s'pose. 'E says it gets a bit lonely, 'iding by 'isself.'

By talking of Jude, I steered Jack's questions away from things I didn't want to discuss. I couldn't have given a sensible explanation for what the lad had seen, anyway. Best to forget it. The trouble was the ripped shirt, showing the bindings that covered my wound. What could I do about that? Emily usually repaired the odd tear, or mended my hose, but I'd have a deal of explaining to do in this case, with all eight lace holes torn through. And she was the last person to whom I could speak of things I didn't understand myself.

'I need to rest, Jack. Leave me be, please.'

'Yer sure?'

'I'm better alone, for a while. Here,' I took a half penny from my purse, 'Go, join warden-archer Appleyard's target practice at Smithfield. Buy some ale for Mark and yourself.' Jack grinned hugely and didn't require telling twice. He dashed off, my earlier predicament quite forgotten.

• •

I tried to sleep but couldn't settle, my mind far too busy. Instead, I thought I'd work on the drawings for Lord Richard's triptych while the light was good, even though it was the Sabbath, but that also proved hopeless. The silver point seemed to have a mind of its own, making marks on the paper anyhow, like an infant's doodles in the sand. I threw them on the fire. Having despaired of producing anything worthwhile, I gave up and sat there, brooding. With Jude in hiding, suffering his own torments, I felt guilty that my private tortures weighed more heavily, such that I'd hardly given poor Jude a thought all afternoon.

No, all I could picture in my head was Em. Em and her prospective husband, curse him, whoever he was. The miserable Green Man, perhaps. What was his name? If Em wed him and he wasn't kind and loving to her... God rot his soul, I'd slay him, somehow. I thumped the board. Slay him? How? I couldn't kill a day-old kitten, unless I fell on it by accident and squashed it to death. I was pathetic. Yet not so incapable I couldn't hate. Aye, I hated the nameless young man who would marry Em - handsome, strong, straightly made, no doubt. I could envisage the happy couple: Em all smiles and laughter; and *him*, faceless as yet, but the image made me weep with resentment and jealousy – an evil brew that curdled my humours 'til I felt ill with it. What *was* the matter with me? Why did I feel this way? Love? Hah! That was too absurd to contemplate.

● ●

When Emily came to change my bindings, she found me surly and unhelpful, to say the least.

'What is it, Seb? Does your wound pain you? I can put more salve...'

'Leave it! It does well enough, I tell you.'

'Let me fetch you a... Lord alive! Whatever befell your shirt? Look at it!'

I wrenched the garment away from her.

'Nothing! It tore. What of it? Leave it alone, can't you.'

'I'll mend it.'

'Don't bother.'

'It's no trouble.'

'I said: leave it.'

'Very well, Sebastian Foxley, have it your way!' Emily tossed her head and flounced out, like a petulant child. 'And sweet dreams!' she yelled back at me.

I sat there, sulking, hating myself for upsetting her. Would she ever forgive me for being so stubborn, so needlessly unpleasant? I couldn't blame her if she never came near me again. I suppose it would serve me right.

● ●

Feeling wretched, I went to my bed, kicking off my shoes but otherwise prepared to sleep in my hose and drawers and the rag of a shirt. Sleep! That was unlikely and as for Em's "sweet dreams", nightmares were more probable.

Dame Ellen's workshop behind the house

EMILY WENT straight to the workshop. It was closed and shuttered, seeing it was Sunday night. She knew her way around well enough without a light. Falling onto her workbench she shoved aside the fine silk chemise she had been stitching yesterday, left out ready for tomorrow, rested her head on her arms and wept.

'Emily! What are you doing, girl? I've been calling and calling.' Dame Ellen bustled in, candle in hand. 'What are you doing in here of a Sunday?' The old woman put a gnarled hand on Emily's bowed head.

'Oh, Dame Ellen, he shouted at me, told me to leave it, but I know he meant me to leave. He hates me, Dame Ellen.'

The old woman seated herself next to her apprentice and set down the candle, so they sat in a pool of light.

'Don't talk nonsense. Nobody hates you, girl, why would they? And who was it shouted at you? I'll give him a piece of my mind, directly.'

'M-master Seb.' Emily sobbed out his name.

'Sebastian? But he's all milk and water, that one. Why would he shout at you?'

'Because I made him angry.'

'What did you do?'

'I don't know, Nothing, nothing at all. Oh, why does he hate me? I want him to like me so much.' Dame Ellen took the younger woman's hand, chafing it as if she were chilled.

'Do you, girl? Why? You know half the young bucks of London would throw themselves at your feet, given the chance – a pretty lass with a good dowry. Don't fret over the likes of Sebastian Foxley. He's nothing, nobody.'

'But he's somebody to me, Dame Ellen. I love him!' Emily went pale, stunned by her own admission. And in that moment she knew it was true.

The Bowen house

MEG BOWEN was recovering better than any might have hoped or foreseen. With Gilbert Eastleigh frequently in close attendance upon her, despite young Nessie's blundering efforts that seemed to be all to the contrary, the widow was reclining in royal splendour on a day bed, consuming prodigious amounts of good red wine and red meat, to restore the loss of blood. A costly new hood of green velvet, lined with marten fur – Gilbert's most recent gift – also aided a swift recovery, since Meg was eager to wear it to church to impress her neighbours at the earliest opportunity.

'I could wear it to vespers this evening,' she insisted, pouting.

'No, you most certainly cannot, Meg,' Gilbert told her, though his tone was patronising, rather than stern. 'You're not yet strong enough. I forbid it.'

'You are *not* my husband, Gilbert. You cannot order me about.'

'No, not yet, my pigeon, but one day soon.' He smiled, taking her hand in his talons on the pretext of counting her pulse beats.

She allowed him that much. Now was not the time to explode his dreams.

'In the meantime, I am your medical advisor and you would do well to heed my words. As should have been the case before. I told you not to.'

'You're such a bully. *You* wouldn't do anything about it and if I had borne a child by Matthew, I couldn't be saddled with it.' Of course, she knew it wasn't Matthew's, any more than it was Gilbert's. No chance of that. 'You should have given me a potion, as I asked.'

'Such things are too dangerous.'

'For you, you mean, too afraid to risk losing your apothecary's licence.'

'You could have had the child. The Thames swallows up the unwanted willingly enough.'

'Birthing a babe is just as dangerous for a woman, you know that.'

Gilbert frowned. Clearly, the subject was not one he wished to discuss.

'Your husband suspected he was being cuckolded. Did you know? He told me so, that last evening, swore he would prove it, one day soon. Said he'd found that pearl collar I gave you. You should have hidden it more carefully.'

'Mm, yet another reason why he had to go, the old miser.' Meg laughed. 'Gone and forgotten, now. You can't imagine what a relief it is, Gilbert. We should have done it long ago.'

'The old fool told me he thought it was Foxley who was your lover. How wrong could he be?' Gilbert laughed aloud. 'A penniless journeyman scrivener! How would he ever afford such a jewel? What could a woman want with the likes of him, my pigeon?'

'What indeed?' Meg smiled over her wine cup, remembering how pleasurable it had been. She almost regretted her use of Jude as the scapegoat. Poor Jude. So handsome; so foolish. Still, London was full of such likely young men. There would be others, when she was ready.

'The use of Foxley's knife was an inspiration. What made you think of it?' Gilbert asked. 'I was impressed by your ingenuity, your resourcefulness'.

'Kit had been toying with it. I think he had ideas of his own as to where he'd like to stick it. Not that he had the nerve. Gilbert, answer me honestly, did you kill Kit? I know he was snooping around, into everything, but...'

'No. I never laid a finger on him. How dare you suggest such a thing? I heard tell, he was robbed, his purse emptied. Though others say it was Foxley.' Gilbert shrugged. 'Let them say what they will. Why should we care? With him out of the way...'

'Forgive me. I had to ask, though I never truly thought you could have.' Meg sought to soothe his indignation. She shouldn't have troubled to ask. Men were such spineless creatures.

'Soon we'll both have our rewards, my pigeon. Just be patient a little longer.' Gilbert leaned forward and kissed her bed cap. More of a chicken peck, really. It was difficult to imagine sharing her bed with him, ever. Meg sighed. Patience was not one of her virtues. But, for the time being, she would permit Gilbert to woo her with expensive presents and the promise of more, much more, in the near future. She wondered what he was up to that he could be so certain great riches were about to come his way, as he never tired of reminding her.

The Foxley brothers' rooms

I HEARD ST Martin's bell chime for the midnight office, then matins, then lauds. It would be daylight soon. I lay there, on rumpled blankets, staring blindly into the darkness of the rafters and cobwebs above, agonising over how I might make amends, if that was at all possible. And still the thought of Em in the arms of another tormented me far more than my wounds. Not that I wanted her for myself, that was a ludicrous notion, wasn't it? What woman in her right mind would want to burden herself with a cripple?

So what did I want? To see Em in a nunnery? No. There was only one possibility. I must get my hands on the Philosopher's Stone, persuade Eastleigh to distil the elixir of life for me, to make my body whole and acceptable. What I would not give for that? I'd sell my miserable soul to the Devil, if needs be. Only then could I contemplate wooing Emily Appleyard.

CHAPTER SIXTEEN

Monday, the eighth day of May
The Foxley brothers' rooms

THAT MONDAY, when Emily brought my dinner, she found me at my lowest ebb, hunched over, rocking like a man in agony. I did not so much as look up at her when she set the pottage on the board, where my breakfast still sat, untouched.

'Seb? Are you sick?' She touched me gently but I started so violently, she jumped back.

'Dear Christ, no!' I cried, whimpering like a wounded animal, trembling. 'They took him, Em. Took him! I'm next. I thought you were...'

'Seb, Seb, what are you rambling about? Calm yourself, else you'll have a seizure.' She tried to settle me but I was beyond such aid, my thoughts whirling in a tempest.

'They took him, took Jude from Bladder Street. Jack's gone. Took Jude. And a fellow, Bartholomew of Amen Lane, I think. I don't know any more.'

'Do you mean they've recaptured Jude? How do you know this?' Emily spoke slowly, as though to an imbecile. Probably, I seemed more than half-mad, twisting my fingers in my hair, tying it in knots, pulling at my clothes.

'A lad, Jack's friend, Mark, I think he said. He came a while ago, told me Jude... they took him back to the Whit, Em, that fearful hell-hole, and they're coming for me, Mark said.'

'Then you must hide. We must find somewhere safe for you.'

'I can't run – look at me! I can't hide – how will I ever pass unnoticed?'

'Well, we must think of something. We can't let them arrest you. Jude's depending on you. Lord Richard is depending on you.'

My hands ceased their agitation. I became still for a moment. Emily looked relieved.

'That's it! Lord Richard. Now what did I do with it? I can't remember where...' I was stumbling about, searching, tossing things aside, rummaging in the coffer.

'What are you looking for? Tell me and I'll help you find it.'

'The parchment... the duke's... Lord Richard... his contract.' I managed to spit the words out at last. 'The contract for the triptych.'

'That's not important now.'

'Yes. I must have it!'

'Well, then, take your time. Think what you did with it. You put it somewhere safe, didn't you?'

'Of course, but this house isn't safe, it's been ransacked once. I didn't dare leave anything. My purse! I put it in my purse, kept it with me. Now where did I put my purse?'

'It's on your belt, Seb, you're wearing it.'

'Oh, praise God!' I hugged her briefly, without thinking, then opened my purse, taking out the contract. 'I hope this will do.' I laid it on the board, unrolled the little parchment, smoothing it out. The Duke of Gloucester's seal hung at the bottom: an elaborate disc of red wax on a green ribbon. It bore the image of the duke's cognisance – a fearsome boar, its tusks prominent, its tail curled. Everyone in London knew his badge by now, after the brave showing at the May Day revels.

• •

Not long after, we heard the stomp of booted feet outside. Rather than wait until they smashed it down, now quite in command of myself, I opened the door to them. I recognised William Stockman and the rat-faced fellow from before. They didn't say anything; just made a grab for me, but I was prepared for that, barring their entry with my staff across the doorway.

'Wait! By what authority do you come barging in here?' I tried to sound as Sir Robert had done, on that occasion when Stockman had come before. I fear I sounded far too timid and afraid.

'The sheriff's.'

'Show me your warrant.' Stockman stared back at me. 'Well? Where is it?' The watchman obviously hadn't expected a cripple to be any trouble to arrest.

'Yer under arrest fer aiding an' abetting a 'scaped felon.'

'You don't have one, do you?'

'I c'n get one.'

'Aye, I dare say you could, but it might be inappropriate to trouble the sheriff when I have this.' I held out my contract for the triptych so that Stockman had a good view of the pendant seal. 'Do you know what this is?' Stockman looked doubtful, frowning at the seal. 'Do you wish to read it?' The man shook his head. I felt a surge of relief. As I'd hoped, the devil couldn't read. 'I'll read it to you, shall I?' I unrolled the parchment and read aloud:

Written at our residence of Crosby Place this twenty-ninth day of April in the fifteenth year of the reign of King Edward the fourth.

To Whom it may concern, Greetings.

Let it be known that the bearer of this warrant, namely Master Sebastian Foxley of Cheapside in the parish of St Michael le Querne in the city of London, is in our formal employ and has been granted immunity from arrest, harassment and like purposes of nuisance whilst in pursuance of his employment aforesaid. Any actions taken in contravention of this warrant will be adjudged to have offended against our jurisdiction as Lord High Constable of England, Ireland, Aquitaine etc.

Signed and given under our signet the day and date abovesaid

Richard, Duke of Gloucester, Earl of Cambridge, etc. etc.

I saw Emily standing there, mouth agape. As did Stockman and his ruffians. The watchman glared at the contract. He seemed to recall that Gloucester was indeed High Constable so, with a few parting profanities, he and his men left, in the direst of humours. God help anyone unfortunate enough to cross their path before they had a cooling ale or two under their belts.

Uninvited, Emily sank onto a stool and poured two cups of ale. It seemed we both were in need as much as Stockman.

'I didn't know your contract said all that,' she said. 'All those long words and no mention of the triptych at all.'

'It doesn't. Apart from the place, day, date and signature, I made it all up, hoping the illiterate Stockman wouldn't have the least idea what was written there.'

Emily stared at me and then burst out laughing.

'Oh, Seb. You're so clever. Who needs brawn with wits like yours?'

I looked at her shyly, smiling. It was rare that a woman complimented me for any reason, certainly not for fraud, taking Lord Richard's name in vain, and using his seal for nefarious purposes.

• •

I felt guilt-ridden. I'd run out of clues long ago as to how to help Jude any more. Nothing so far had helped in the least and now my poor brother was back in custody. Time must be short until he came to trial, a day or two at most. And the outcome was inevitable. I swallowed hard, finding my throat constricted, just the thought of that fearful rope, tightening inexorably, choked me. Tears threatened anew, but they wouldn't help. Nothing would. I was seated at the board, staring blindly at my drawings for the triptych, though I'd added not a single line to any all day.

The door opened and Dame Ellen bustled in, flapping a paper in her hand.

'Not interrupting your work, am I, young Sebastian?'

'No, Dame Ellen, I was just...' I hurriedly scrubbed my sleeve across my eyes for fear she might notice they were damp.

'Good, because I need you to pen a letter for me to my son, Dick. I received this from him this morn, from Deptford. He has a good clear hand, don't you think? Fine penmanship when you know he was never trained for it.'

'Aye, 'tis very neat.' I smoothed out the letter on the board with no enthusiasm for writing a reply. I didn't care what her precious son had to say, nor what she would say to him. It was all too much effort.

'Now, see what he says? Bella is with child! Is that not heartening news? I shall have to send her some suitable lengths of fine quality linen for swaddling the babe. Can't have a Langton grandchild clothed in anything but the best, can we? You tell him that. Tell him I shall be praying for her safe confinement, though it won't be for a few months yet. Come along, young Sebastian, why are you not writing this down? Where are your pens and ink? How disorganised you are.'

Reluctantly, I fetched my writing materials and Dame Ellen, tapping her foot, began over again.

'More slowly, I beg you. I cannot write legibly at such a pace, good dame.'

'Did you write what I said about praying for Bella?'

'Aye, I did.'

'Because her family, those Bowens, do not have such a strong constitution as we Langtons, apparently. See here? Dick says how Matthew, her father, was ailing for weeks before he died. I never knew that, did you? Most assuredly, you must have noticed, since you worked for him. Meg Bowen wrote to tell Bella of her father's illness, how he was like to die at any time, and then, pouf! He's gone, killed somehow else. Saved him a lingering death, I suppose. But you're not writing this down!'

'Mistress Bowen told them this? Are you certain, Dame Ellen? It could be important.' I was frowning up at her; pen poised.

'Not so important as my reply to Dick. Now, will you get on and write as I dictate before I forget what I wish to tell him. And then I'll tell you of my visit to Clements.'

'Who?'

'The tailor in Budge Row that I spoke of, I mentioned the violet cloth to him, the scrap you found.'

'Aye. I recall. Did he recognise it?'

'He did indeed. He made up two garments from that bolt of cloth: a gown for the Duchess of Clarence, no less. Now I hardly think it likely she turned your rooms upside down and inside out, do you?'

'Of course not, Dame Ellen. And the other?'

'Other what? Come now, I need this letter written.'

'The other garment this Clements made, who was it for?'

'Oh, aye, Lord Somebody, he couldn't recall the name but said he would look it up in his order book and let me know. Now. My letter, if you will, Sebastian?'

Monday afternoon
The Bowen house

FEELING MUCH restored I had gone to Paternoster Row with Emily, hoping to interrogate Meg Bowen. We found the workshop locked. There was no one to work there now. I tried the house door instead.

'Ooh, Master Seb, Mistress Em,' Nessie welcomed us in with her usual exuberance. 'Is Master Jude or Sir Percy coming too?'

'No, Nessie, not today.'

The little maid's face fell.

'But it's sooo lonely here, just me and mistress and Master Eastleigh. And I don't like him, neither.'

'Why is that, Nessie? Does he hurt you?' I led her into the kitchen. Nessie shook her head.

'Mistress says I mustn't say anything about anything, but I know what I seen. Them potions and powders what he brung.'

'Well, your mistress has been unwell. She needs them.'

'Not for mistress. They was for Master Bowen and Master Jude. Master Eastleigh telled mistress what to do, I heard them talking. They thought I was sleeping 'cos I snored, but I wasn't. I listened and watched. I saw what they did, but I mustn't tell. Mistress might beat me if I do.'

• •

The hairs on my neck stood on end but I had to keep calm. I glanced at Emily, saw that she also realised how important this could be.

'Shall I tell mistress you're here?'

'No, not yet.' I sat on a stool by the board, which was piled with chopped onions and cabbage in preparation for supper. Nessie took up a knife to continue her work. 'Leave it, Nessie. Come here.'

She looked like a scared rabbit, her large eyes and prominent front teeth enhancing the illusion as she came around the table to me. I wanted to touch her rough hands to reassure her, but feared it would only serve to alarm.

'Nessie, you like Master Jude very much, don't you?'

She nodded.

'Oh, I dooo. He's so handsome.'

'Aye, indeed. Then tell me about the powders. You said they were for Master Jude.'

'Only the white one was for him. The pretty yellow one was for Master Bowen. Master Eastleigh said so.'

'Eastleigh? When was this? Do you remember?'

'I don't know, master. It was a long time ago.'

'When? Last week? Last month? Think, Nessie! This is so important.' I was getting nowhere with the silly wench.

'I don't know,' Nessie wailed, covering her face with her soiled apron. I groaned in frustration.

'Nessie,' Emily said softly, taking the girl's hands in her own. 'If you love Master Jude, then you want to help him.'

The maid lowered her apron.

'Aye.'

'Did you know that h-he may die if we don't help him?'

'Master Jude can't die! He can't!'

'You can save him, Nessie. Think how pleased he will be, if you do that.'

'Me? Will he give me a present, if I do?'

'Of course he will. Now try to remember. When did mistress give Master Jude the white powder?'

'In his wine. They always have wine in bed 'cos sometimes it spills on the sheets. Mistress told her friend Mary – her who's in the family way – that they play games in bed, and they do. Sometimes it takes me all morning to untangle them. The sheets, I mean.'

'But when did Mistress Meg give Master Jude the powder?' Emily repeated. I admired her patience. Suddenly, I could understand why Jude had tried to throttle me on occasion. Now my fingers itched to give the witless wench a thorough shaking.

'The night Master Eastleigh comed home with Master Bowen, mistress put the white stuff in Master Jude's cup. She'd done it afore, I know, 'cos she said he wored her out, if she didn't make him sleep. But then my master comed back. They was both so cross, him and Master Eastleigh. Master Eastleigh said he wanted a book back. Master said he couldn't have it, said he was sick and tired of being, er, being cuckooed, that's it. That's what master said.'

'Do you mean cuckolded, Nessie?'

'That's what I said, what master said. And Master Eastleigh told him to be quiet and drink his ale, gave him the cup what mistress put the yellow powder in. I saw him. But I made out I was sleeping, though master made such a noise, shouting and all. Then Master Eastleigh went. And my master was taken bad after. I didn't know if I should go to him, but I thought he might beat me fer not being asleep and hearing what they said.

'In the morning he was so bad, he was dead. And mistress made it worse with that knife. I knew that I couldn't help him. And I had to clear up the mess after.'

'Thank you, Nessie. What you've told us will help Master Jude so much,' I said, feeling as though the weight of the ages had lifted from my shoulders.

'Will he be pleased with me? Give me a present?'

'If he doesn't, I certainly will, I promise you. Now you can go and announce us to Mistress Meg, if you will, please.'

'Master Sebastian? I wasn't expecting you,' Mistress Bowen said. 'Is Sir Robert with you? If you've come to offer your condolences, again?' We three stood in the parlour. Meg seated herself on the cushioned settle but did not invite either Emily or me to sit.

'No, Mistress Bowen. That is not my purpose. I've come to speak with you about my brother.'

'What of Jude? Have they recaptured him?'

'No doubt you'll be content that they have?'

'Content? What a strange thing to say. I don't know what you mean.'

'I believe you do. You enjoy my brother's company in your bed well enough but such services may be given just as readily by others. But my brother provides a more singular service to you as your scapegoat, made to seem guilty in your stead. Is that not so, mistress?'

She stood up and began pacing the fragrant rushes strewn on the floor, fretting at a jewel at her throat.

'Guilty in my stead! How dare you slander me so, you insolent rascal.'

'But it can only be slander if it isn't true. And I think it *is* true that you poisoned your husband with Gilbert Eastleigh's connivance.'

'Poisoned my... Don't be absurd. Matthew was stabbed to death with your brother's knife, as you know full well.'

'Stabbed, certainly, but not killed by the knife. Your husband was dead ere the knife was plunged into his flesh.'

'You cannot know that.'

'But indeed I can. Only dead men do not bleed and there was no blood upon his shirt, nor upon his person. I saw the body and the knife wound never bled. Your husband was dead already because you put orpiment in his ale. *You* poisoned him, Meg, and Eastleigh made certain he drank it.'

'Such a foolish tale.' She laughed unsteadily. 'I cannot think how you came by it. Why should I want to do so dreadful a thing?'

'Oh, I can name a few reasons. To rid yourself of a husband you no longer care for? To get your hands on his hidden hoard of money?'

'How did you know?' She stopped herself, turning away from me.

'I didn't, until now, but it seemed likely enough. The workshop was doing well, yet he always insisted there was no coin to spare. So, either he was drinking and dicing it all away, or he was hoarding it, as you have just confirmed.'

'You'll never prove it.'

'But I'll try, until my last breath, I'll try. My brother deserves that much.'

'Even when he's hanged?' She arched a shapely eyebrow.

'Even then, mistress, if I can clear his name. Though I cannot save his life, I may save his honour. Good evening to you, Mistress Bowen. Sleep well, if your conscience allows.'

· ·

'So, do you think Nessie told us the truth, Seb?' Emily asked as we made our way home in the dusk. It would soon be curfew.

'Aye, I do.'

'But she isn't very bright, is she? She may have it all wrong.'

'I don't think so, for that very reason. Nessie isn't clever enough to have invented all that. Besides, you heard what Meg said. Everything Nessie told us fits the facts we already knew and more beside. Though I never supposed Eastleigh was involved in Bowen's murder and I thought Kit stabbed the body after, not Meg, though he must have handled the knife to leave his thumb print upon it.'

'And now we know, what are we going to do about it?'

'Tomorrow, at Jude's trial, we must tell the court everything.'

'But why should they believe us?'

'Nessie will tell...'

'Seb, Nessie is a half-wit serving wench. No one will even listen to what she has to say.'

I didn't answer, fearing Emily was right. Could it be that we were no better off than before, no closer to getting Jude free?

'We have to get the letter Meg wrote to Dame Ellen's son and his wife, the one I told you about. It will prove that Meg was preparing the ground in advance of her husband's death; show she knew he was going to die, telling lies about his ill-health. We must get it, Em, show it to the court.'

'But Jude is in court in the morning. There's no time to get to Deptford and back and they may not have kept the letter anyway.'

'Don't say that, Em. They *have* to have it still. Sir Robert has a fast horse, he could fetch it for us. I must speak with him tonight.'

'Seb, they will ring the curfew bell soon. There's no time for you to walk all the way to Crosby Place now, not without the watch taking you. Then what?'

'I've got coin, I'll bribe them to let me pass.'

'But if it's Stockman, he'll not take a bribe. He can't wait to lay hands upon you.'

'I'll think of something. Now, let me see you home first.'

'No. I'm coming with you, else how will you walk so far?'

The Stocks Market by St Mary Abchurch

HAND IN hand we made our way across the darkened city like thieves, keeping to alleyways and shadowed corners. The moon was bright, both a help and a hindrance to our passage. However quiet we were, my staff seemed to tap out a deafening drum beat on the cobbles and packed earth streets. In Poultry, by Bucklersbury, I was tempted to cast it aside as a dog barked, hearing our step.

The sound of voices and heavy boots approached. The watch was out. We were caught with nowhere to hide on the open street of the Stocks Market. I dropped my staff and dragged Em into the doorway of St Mary Abchurch, kissing her long and hard, my arms tight about her, beneath her cloak. I felt a shudder ripple through her body as I pulled her closer. I could hear the watchmen laughing.

'Give 'er one fer me, yer lucky bastard!' one called out.

As I'd hoped, they didn't bother to arrest lovers, and who would suspect the fellow with a lass in his embrace could possibly be the infamous cripple? Who would dare kiss *him*?

The watch moved on, the sound of their plodding steps fading into the night. I released Em and she stepped back, gasping, covering her mouth with her hand, as though to wipe away the horrors of my kiss.

'Forgive me, Em, I couldn't think how else to hide our faces. I am so very sorry.'

She didn't speak and I felt a belated flush of blood burn my face. I wanted to touch her, to reassure her, but I had done too much already. I had upset her greatly and humiliated us both, but this was not the time to dwell on it.

'Come on, it's not far now,' she said at last, in a quavering voice. She turned and led the way.

Crosby Place

IRETRIEVED MY staff and we stumbled up Broad Street into Bishopsgate. I was leaning more and more heavily on Emily's arm. It was a relief to see the gatehouse of Crosby Place, ablaze with torches.

I screwed up my courage and approached the man on guard there. Unfortunately, it wasn't Hercules but some lesser fellow I hadn't seen before.

'Begging your pardon, sir...' I began.

'The duke don't want callers this time o' night. Come back t'morra.'

'It's important...'

'Aye, ain't it always. Clear off!'

'I must speak with Sir Robert Percy.'

'Oh, aye, life 'n' death, I s'pose?'

'Yes, it is. I must see Sir Robert.'

'S'pose he don't want t' see you, *hunchback*?'

• •

To my relief, Hercules appeared from the guardhouse, like an angel from Heaven.

'What's amiss, our Alf? Who wants t' see Sir Rob at this hour?'

'Some cripple, Sergeant Thwaites. Shall I send 'im off wi' a flea in 'is ear?'

'Nay. 'Tis Master Foxley and Mistress Appleyard, the famous archeress. They're always welcome at any hour, our Alf. Come on, you pair. I think you be in need o' some good ale whilst I send word to Sir Rob.'

• •

When Sir Robert appeared in the guardhouse where we were sipping hot spiced ale, he didn't come alone. Lord Lovell was with him.

'Master Seb, Mistress Emily. I pray you forgive the delay. I was beating Lord Dickon at chess, a rare occurrence indeed. I had to finish the game.' Rob shrugged his broad shoulders. 'Somehow I lost, yet again.'

'You should have moved the king's bishop, as I told you to,' Lord Lovell said.

'Why? It was moving the rook as you instructed that lost me the game. Still, what's a groat between friends?' The knight turned to us. 'Francis, may I present Mistress Appleyard, the warden-archer's daughter, and Master Sebastian Foxley, whom you've met before, briefly.'

Emily made a graceful courtesy to the lord.

'Mistress Appleyard,' he said, his mouth curving up at the corners, showing his teeth, but his eyes did not smile. They remained cold and hard as stone. 'Master Foxley.' The mouth straightened into a sneer.

I ducked my head, unable to manage more, I was so exhausted from the long walk.

'Well, Seb, the messenger said it was important. So, what is so urgent it cannot wait 'til morn?' Sir Rob asked, making himself comfortable on a guardhouse stool. Lord Lovell reclined on a bare wooden bench, looking out of place in his fine clothes and plumed hat but determined to stay, so it seemed.

I finished my ale, eager to tell my friend everything but reluctant to speak in front of Lord Lovell, who glared at me with unconcealed disdain.

'Sir Robert, Emily and I have uncovered the truth. We know who murdered Matthew Bowen and how. We even have a witness, of sorts. And there is evidence now but we need someone with a fast horse, for whom the watch will open the gates at night, to fetch it. It's at Deptford. Jude's trial is set for tomorrow. We must have it by then,' I explained without being too specific in Lord Lovell's hearing, but Sir Rob required the whole story. So, with a weary sigh and my cup refilled, I cast caution aside and told them everything, from the incriminating letter sent to Bella Langton in Deptford to Gilbert Eastleigh's unexpected involvement and Kit Philpot's innocence.

'And that witless wench is your witness?' Sir Rob said, looking dubious, as well he might.

'Yes, but Emily's father saw the yellow staining on the lips of the corpse, as well as I, and then the letter will prove, er, I cannot recall the legal term.'

'Malice aforethought, you mean?

I nodded.

'If it hasn't been thrown on the fire or used in the privy?' Lord Lovell added his pennyworth.

I said nothing. The case was hopeless anyway.

'You did your best, Seb,' Emily consoled me, speaking for the first time. 'No man could have done more.'

Sir Rob stood up, uncoiling his long limbs from the low stool and stretching his arms above his head, his finger tips catching the cobwebs on the beams.

'Sergeant Thwaites!' he called, loud enough to rouse the soldiers sleeping in the chamber above. Hercules came striding in, as fresh and alert as though it wasn't the middle of the night. 'Have my horse saddled and ready to leave by the time I've asked Lord Dickon's permission.'

'No, Rob.' Lord Lovell bestirred himself. 'I'll go. I don't need Dickon's say-so and I know Deptford well. Saddle my gelding.'

Sir Rob looked surprised, shocked even.

'You know Deptford?'

'I've been there many times. Where does this Langford fellow abide precisely?'

'Langton, Richard Langton,' I corrected him boldly. 'He's a shipwright there, lives by St George's Stairs, Dame Ellen says.'

'I'll find him,' the baron said. 'I must change my attire.'

'You'll require an escort, Francis. I'll come with you. Dickon will oblige me.'

'No, it will be quicker if I go alone. Why waste time asking his lordship when it will take but an hour or two?'

As Lord Lovell left, Sir Rob saw my doubtful look.

'Fear not, Seb. Lord Lovell has the duke's full confidence, as I do. You may trust him.'

'Does he really know Deptford so well?'

'If he says he does, then I suppose he must. Why would he lie about such a thing? He didn't have to offer to go all that way, but he did. We should be grateful to him.'

* *

The sound of hooves clattering out of the gateway signalled Lord Lovell's midnight departure as Rob was making arrangements for Emily and me to sleep the night. Emily was ushered away by a homely woman, who smiled all the while though her face was still heavy with sleep, and a cot was put up and blankets provided for me, there in the guardhouse. We had no chance to speak alone.

CHAPTER SEVENTEEN

Tuesday, the ninth day of May
Dame Ellen's house

EMILY WAS taken home at dawn, proudly riding pillion behind one of Lord Richard's servants. Her absence overnight should have earned her a thorough scolding from Dame Ellen and would have, no doubt, if the old woman's curiosity about the duke's town house hadn't won the contest with discipline.

'Was Crosby Place very fine then, Emily? What were the hangings like? What of the cushions, eh? Were they of silk or velvet? And what is the fashionable colour of late? Tell me everything.'

'Oh, Dame Ellen, it was dark and I only saw the guardhouse and the servants' quarters. But I had a good breakfast, served on pewter, even for the likes of me. And they were very kind.' Emily removed her cap, unpinned her hair and began combing through her silky tresses.

'Was their linen of a good quality? Was it Holland cloth or Rennes or Ypres?'

'I don't know. It was fair but well-worn. I couldn't tell.' She re-pinned her hair and put on her Sunday cap.

'Not homespun, at least?'

'No, I'm sure it wasn't, even for the servants.'

Dame Ellen blew out a breath, relieved the duke did not stoop so low as that. Like so many folk, she believed a conspicuous show of luxury was compulsory for those of high estate.

'And where do you think you're going in your best cap of a Tuesday, my girl?'

'To court, Dame Ellen. 'Tis Master Jude's trial.'

'Oh, no, Emily Appleyard. You're going nowhere until you catch up with your chores from yesterday and get some work done. That chemise still needs its ribbon trimmings and it's to be ready by this afternoon. Now get on with it, else you'll be feeling my broom on you, girl.'

'But, please, dame, I must.'

'No! I forbid it. What's the world coming to, when apprentices come and go as they please, eh? My son Dick will have plenty to say on that score, I'll warrant.'

• •

Dame Ellen huffed off to attend her own affairs, leaving Emily standing in the midst of an unscrubbed kitchen with dirty platters stacked in a bucket and a silk chemise demanding attention in the workshop next door. She sighed, pushed up her sleeves and went down on her knees to lay the fire to heat the water. Seb would have to manage without her.

Crosby Place

IN TRUTH, I hadn't meant to attend Jude's trial, not after what happened last time, but now I had things to tell the court. At least Sir Robert would be prepared for trouble on this occasion. And when Lord Lovell brought the letter, all would be well. Jude would be freed.

With a good deal of sweating and cursing from a groom and two stable lads, somehow I was hoisted up behind Sir Rob, onto the back his great stallion – my dignity barely intact. I had never been astride a horse before and found my thighs stretched so wide across its broad back, I feared to be split in twain, but Sir Rob assured me that wouldn't happen. To ride to the Bailey was the only way to be certain we weren't late. The duke's lawyer, Miles Metcalfe, rode with us on a dainty white palfrey – more of a lady's horse, I should have thought. Maybe he also disliked having his legs stretched too far. He was a long, dusty stick of a man, swamped by his robes of office, but I suspected his eyes, bright as elderberries, missed nothing. I could only pray his wits were as keen as his sight for my brother's sake.

There was just time to go home first to collect the yellow-stained linen as evidence. Clinging to Sir Rob, further from the ground and moving faster than I'd ever known, I hung on, rigid with terror, certain every moment I would come to grief, falling to my death. Another stop was made at St Michael's church where Father Thomas handed over

Jude's knife with due solemnity – the thumb-print still clear upon the handle – yet more evidence of Jude's innocence, I hoped.

Newgate Market was so crowded we came to a halt – a delay we could ill-afford. A butcher's stall had collapsed under the weight of shoppers pressing forward, eager for his cuts of mutton, sheeps' livers, hearts and kidneys, all fresh from the slaughter this morning. Goodwives were scuffling over meat that lay in the road and two mangy dogs fought viciously, snapping and snarling over yards of intestines which, I swear, were still steaming.

Somehow, miraculously, we arrived at the Bailey, all of a piece with no bones broken. It took me a little time to gather my wits and calm myself, deliberately breathing deep and slow before we entered.

The Bailey

THE OPEN court was just as crowded as before but this time Sir Rob strode forth, clearing a path to the front for me, then stood behind me, guarding my back. The list of cases, pinned up for all to see, if they could read, indicated that Jude's was the first case. Then some fellow who had deliberately misled the hue and cry, a serious matter, indeed. The others were mere misdemeanours: a purse snatcher, a regrator who'd sold on mouldy bread and a brewster who had served watery ale in short measure.

The bailiff thumped his staff and called the court to order as the judges processed to the bench on the dais. I was surprised to see how ordinary they looked, despite their crow-black robes, but these were the three men, wafting their nosegays before them, who held Jude's life in their hands. And one other, of course. Where was Lord Lovell with the letter? Surely he should be here by now.

● ●

Jude was brought into court with an escort of no less than four gaolers, like four square towers on a castle keep, impregnable. There would be no escape this time. He looked pale and thin, his eyes cast downwards in hopelessness, his hair matted with filth, a week's growth of stubble on his shadowed cheeks. My heart went out to him. I was desperate to tell him all was not lost. I started forward but Sir Rob pulled me back.

'Not yet, Seb. Be patient.'

'This court is now in session!' the bailiff announced in ringing tones.

'Is the jury sworn in, Master Bailiff?' the eldest judge asked in a querulous voice, muffled by the herb posy he held to his nose.

'Indeed, my lords,' the bailiff waved his staff towards a group of men seated on two benches at the front of the court. 'Twelve good men and true, as required under the law.'

I could only see the backs of their heads but one bald pate I recognised as Davy Owain, a Welsh butcher who sold suspect-looking meat in the Shambles, and another with unruly white-blond curls could only be the parchmenter from St Faith's whom I would not trust with a clipped farthing. If these were 'good men and true', may the Lord Jesus help us.

'The court calls Jude Foxley of West Cheap!' the bailiff bellowed. His guards shoved Jude up against the bar. 'Jude Foxley, on the first charge you stand accused of the murder of your employer, Matthew Bowen of Paternoster Row. How do you plead?'

'What difference does it make?' Jude answered, speaking so low, even standing close as I dared, I could hardly hear him.

'Guilty or not guilty?' the bailiff demanded. Jude shrugged wearily. He seemed too tired to stand much longer.

'I didn't do it. So, not guilty, I suppose.'

'And on the second charge of evading due process of the law. How do you plead? Guilty or not guilty?'

'Whatever you say, I don't care any more.'

I was most alarmed at his words. My brother truly looked and sounded as though he no longer cared what happened to him. What had they done to him in that diabolical place? This wasn't like Jude at all. Looking closer, I suspected that some of the dirt and shadows on my brother's unshaven face were more like bruises and when he raised his bound hands to wipe his nose, I saw a smear of blood, I was sure.

Where was Lord Lovell? Had he been waylaid? Got lost? Perhaps they couldn't find the letter.

'Guilty, then,' the bailiff concluded. 'No need to try him on the second charge, my lords.'

The court shuffled and sighed. Proceedings were always more interesting if the accused pleaded not guilty.

The bailiff unrolled a parchment, heavy with appended seals, and coughed.

'The charge reads...

252

'That on Friday night or Saturday morning, the twenty-eighth or twenty-ninth day of April last, in the year of Our Lord 1475 and the fifteenth year of the reign of King Edward, the fourth of that name since the Conquest, you did wilfully and notoriously and with malice aforethought murder your late employer, Matthew Bowen of Paternoster Row, by means of your knife which you did insert into his chest in such a grievous manner as to stop his heart and deny him the proper duration of his life.'

The bailiff stepped back.

The judge sitting at the centre of the bench, red-faced and bulbous-nosed from a lifetime of too much wine, cleared his throat in readiness to speak but then said nothing. He shook his head, looked to the elderly greybeard on his left who was already nodding off into his nosegay, changed his mind and gestured to a younger man on his right. Clearly, the case wasn't worthy of his efforts.

'What evidence supports the prosecution in this case?' the youngest judge enquired, though his sharply receding hairline advertised that his youth was relative.

A lawyer in his funereal garb stepped forward with catlike grace and approached the bench.

'We have witnesses, my lords, who heard the accused publicly threaten to kill the deceased just a day before the murder. We have a witness who saw the accused's own knife protruding from the victim's chest.'

'Do you have the aforesaid weapon?' the judge asked.

'No, my lord. It went missing when the body was taken for laying out in St Michael's church.'

I was about to raise my hand, to tell them I had the knife, but Lawyer Metcalfe held my arm in his long twig fingers, shaking his thin beard. I saw his nails were clean as a carven saint's.

'But we do have a witness who saw the accused leaving Paternoster Row, where the murder took place, acting in a furtive and suspicious manner shortly after,' the feline lawyer added.

I glanced back at Sir Rob. His brows were raised in question. This was worrying news to us. Who was this witness who could put Jude at the scene of the crime? Not Meg Bowen, surely. The fact that she would then have to admit to being an adulteress would make her a suspect, rather than a credible witness. No, it couldn't be the widow herself. So who?

I heard Sir Rob sigh with relief as his friend, Lord Lovell, strode through the court crowd, which parted like the Red Sea for Moses to allow him passage to the front. At the clerk's invitation, Lovell rested a gloved hand on the Gospels and took the oath in a loud, clear voice.

'My Lord Lovell,' the youngest judge spoke courteously. 'Would you please be so kind as to tell the court what you saw on the night in question. In your own time, if you please?'

Lovell briefly acknowledged the bench and turned to the jury. I saw them squirm under his gaze, his eyes mirrors of contempt for such lowly fellows.

'The night in question is not at issue here,' he said, waving a gloved hand dismissively, as if this whole affair was hardly worth his trouble. 'But rather the morning of the twenty-ninth, Saturday, just at dawn. As I rose from my bed at Lovell's Inn – my residence in Ivy Lane – and went to the great glass window within my chamber, to adjudge the likely weather for the day – whether my white-fox-furred attire or the marten would most suit – I did espy the accused behaving in a most furtive manner.'

'Dear God in heaven,' Sir Rob muttered behind me.

A fist of ice clenched my vitals. I felt as though the very blood in my veins had frozen.

'Are you quite certain it was the accused?' the judge ventured unwisely. Lovell scowled at the interruption.

'Are you questioning my eyesight, my memory or my integrity?'

'No, my lord. I beg your pardon.'

'There is no doubt whatsoever that the man I saw stands before this court.' Lovell spun on his heel, pointing the finger at the prisoner. 'It was the accused, Jude Foxley, and no other.'

The court murmured and shuffled. I felt the ache of tears threatening at the back of my throat. My breath came faster.

'Th-thank you, my lord, for making that clear for us,' the judge said. 'But, may I ask, what he was doing that drew your notice particularly?'

'Doing? As I said, he was behaving furtively.'

'Doing what, precisely?'

'Keeping to the darkest shadows, head down, looking about to make certain he was not watched. Behaving like a felon.'

• •

At this, Lawyer Metcalfe stood up to request permission to question the witness. Permission was granted.

'My lord, where was the accused when you claim you saw him?' The lawyer's northern voice rang clear through the court.

'Metcalfe,' Lovell sneered. 'I might have known you'd have to poke your pitchfork in the hay bale. Did the duke send you? I lay money, he did.'

'Please be so kind as to answer the question, Lord Lovell,' the judge put in.

'He was coming out of the alley that leads into Ivy Lane from the back of Paternoster Row.'

'And you saw him from the window in your chamber. I see.' Metcalfe's gaunt features were calm and unruffled as he spoke. 'For the benefit of those members of this court who are unfamiliar with your residence in Ivy Lane, could you describe the aspect from the window in question, please?'

Lovell had a face like a thunderstorm.

'I didn't come here to be interrogated by you,' he growled, but the duke's lawyer smiled into his wispy beard.

'Just tell us, my lord.'

'It looks out on Ivy Lane. The exit from the alley is in full view. Is that what you want to know?'

'Ivy Lane is narrow, is it not? And you say you saw the accused just at dawn, to be precise?' Metcalfe pulled at the furred cuff of his lawyer's gown.

'That's what I said.'

'But Ivy Lane runs north to south, doesn't it? So your residence on the eastern side of the lane would have cast a long shadow right across the street at that time of day. In addition, you say the accused was behaving furtively and I quote "keeping to the darkest shadows, head down". So, in the darkest shadows of a dark street at dawn, with his head down, I have to ask you, my lord, how you saw this man at all? How can you be so certain of his identity?'

'Do you have the temerity to doubt my word, Metcalfe, you blasted notary?'

'No, my lord. Just whether or not you have the night vision of an owl.'

There was muffled laughter from the crowd that caused the judge to bang his gavel and the bailiff his staff.

'Thank you, Lord Lovell. The court is grateful for your testimony. You may step down.' The judge dismissed the witness but it was clear Lovell felt insulted. His dark look boded ill.

• •

After that, various people were called forward as witnesses. One by one they swore on the Gospels to speak truly and give honest testimony. I recognised most of them as folk who lived in Paternoster Row, an alderman and a churchwarden among them.

'I heard the accused yelling at Matthew Bowen, saying "I'll kill you for this!"' the alderman recalled. The churchwarden added that he'd heard the accused threaten to "Choke the living breath out of him". A glover from Ivy Lane who had been passing remembered the accused down in the dirt, shaking his fist at Bowen, saying what he'd do when he got his hands on the man's scrawny neck, that he swore he would get his own back.

• •

I grew ever more concerned. Clearly, Jude's angry threats had made quite an impression. But Lawyer Metcalfe posed the question why, if the accused had threatened to strangle Bowen, had he then preferred to use a knife.

No one could answer that.

One very small victory for Jude.

The next witness was Gilbert Eastleigh. He stepped up, took the oath, then proceeded to describe how, in his capacity as an apothecary-surgeon, he had been summoned by Mistress Bowen early on Saturday morning, soon after dawn, to attend her husband who had been stabbed. The young judge then asked him about the weapon.

'It was a knife. It had been pushed deep into the victim's heart, causing death upon the instant. It had a bone handle, embellished with a fox's head and the initials JF inscribed upon it.'

'Did you recognise the knife?'

'No, but others did. Mistress Bowen and the apprentice Christopher Philpot said it belonged to Jude Foxley, the accused.'

'What happened to the knife?'

'Seeing I could do nought to assist the victim, his body already cold, I left the knife *in situ*, such that others might examine it also.'

'And which others saw it?'

'Master Stephen Appleyard saw it, when he came to collect the corpse, to measure it for a bigger coffin than the usual size. I believe the women who laid out the corpse also saw the knife, as did Father Thomas at St Michael's.'

'So who removed it?'

'I do not know, my lord. I cannot say.'

'And you do not know what happened to the knife after it was removed.'

'No.'

'That is most unsatisfactory.'

'My lord.' I could keep silent no longer, 'I have the knife here.'

The judge frowned.

'You have it? How come? Who are you? Why did you not hand the weapon in to the proper authorities?'

'I'm sorry, my lord. I didn't know what should be done with it, but I gave it into Father Thomas's keeping at St Michael's le Querne.'

'And you are?'

'Sebastian Foxley, sir.'

'A relative of the accused?'

'His brother,' I said quietly but the judge asked again, requiring me to speak up. 'I'm Jude Foxley's younger brother.'

'I see.' The judge made those two words sound so ominous, it sent a shiver of fear lancing through me. Perhaps my testimony would be ignored because I was family. 'The court will examine the knife in question. Have this fellow take the oath.'

I handed the weapon, wrapped in a cloth, to the bailiff who passed it to the bench. The bailiff summoned me to stand before the court and gave me a battered book of the Holy Gospels – it could do with a new binding, I noticed.

'Do you swear in the name of the blessed Trinity, Father, Son and Holy Ghost, that you will tell the truth, whole and entire and nought else?'

'I do so swear by the blessed Trinity.'

'Then you may proceed,' the judge said.

I breathed deeply and composed myself before facing the three men sitting in judgement upon the high bench.

'Y-you will see an inky thumb p-print on the handle, your honours,' I explained, struggling to keep my voice from quavering. 'I-I swear, it isn't my brother's. It is the print of another, the apprentice, Kit Philpot.'

'How can you know that?' the judge asked as he and his fellow lords examined the knife. I told them about the print being made by a thumb with a scar.

'My brother's thumb has no such scar, I'm sure.'

'Bailiff! Examine the prisoner's thumbs, all his fingers. Is there a scar?'

I prayed hard that Jude's fingers were unmarked but the bailiff took his time looking while I sweated.

'There's no scar, my lords,' the bailiff said finally.

I breathed again. I looked at Jude. His chin was up now; a glimmer of hope in his eye.

'So, are you telling the court that this Philpot committed the deed?' The judge was scowling again.

'It is his thumb mark on the knife, your honour.'

'And where is this Philpot fellow? Is he in court?'

I was uncertain whom the judge was asking. Me, the bailiff or the court generally, but I answered anyway.

'I fear, Kit Philpot is dead.'

'Dead? How convenient for you that he cannot gainsay your accusation, nor prove the print on the handle is not his.' I saw Jude's brows were creased mightily and he was shaking his head.

'In truth, it is inconvenient, my lord. I'm sure he could explain much but I'm not accusing him of murdering Master Bowen anyway.'

'This case is getting out of hand,' the judge said, shuffling papers and huffing. 'So you say the marks on the knife have nothing to do with this case? Why mention them, then?'

'Because the knife did not kill Matthew Bowen. He was already dead when the knife was used to stab his chest.'

The judge's eyebrows disappeared beneath his hat.

'And you know this for a fact? How? Enlighten us.'

I cleared my throat.

'I viewed the body before it was lain out in St Michael's church. The priest and the women will vouch for what I say, that despite the knife in his chest, there was no blood on the body, nor on his clothes. And Master Stephen Appleyard who transported the corpse will support my assertion that there was no blood at the scene of the crime, either.'

'I see. Are any of these persons present in court? We will hear their testimony after.' The judge consulted briefly with his associates on the bench before skewering me once more with eyes like daggers. 'Explain this. Why a stabbed man did not bleed.'

'Because dead men do not. He was already dead before the knife went in. The knife was intended only to...' But the court erupted in turmoil. "Dead before the knife went in?" Such a revelation stirred the crowd like a torch in a beehive. The judge was red-faced, the bailiff thumping his staff, shouting for order. Only the threat of clearing the court subdued the noise.

'And how do you know that the dead do not bleed?' the judge asked when calm was restored.

'Because I notice such things. I have watched pigs and sheep being slaughtered in the Shambles. At the first cut, the blood pours but, once the beast is dead and butchered for meat, there is hardly any blood. Ask the juror Davy Owain, he is a butcher. He will tell you I speak truly.' I muttered a silent prayer that the Welshman would confirm my words.

'Juror Owain,' the judge said, 'You may address the court, remembering you are under oath.' Owain got to his feet but did not look up. I did not realise he had spoken 'til the judge ordered him to speak up.

'It's true enough that dead beasts don't bleed much, but as for dead men, how would I know?'

'Thank you, Juror Owain, you may be seated. So, indeed...' The judge rubbed his chin in a thoughtful manner. 'Is there anyone in court who can testify to this in the case of men?' I heard a rustling of cloth behind me, a waft of lavender-scented robes and old fur.

'I can, my lord. Surgeon Dagville. I served with King Edward's army at Barnet and Tewkesbury, tending the battle wounded. If men were brought in and seemed like to die, the priest was summoned first, as is proper, then we'd prick them with a lancet, just on the finger. If blood came readily, we'd know their heart was still beating strong and there was a chance they'd live, so we treated them. If no blood came, we'd leave them to the ministrations of the priest. Master Foxley speaks true, my lord.'

'The court is grateful for your insight, Surgeon Dagville.' The judge turned to me and gave me a long hard look, leaning forward across the bench. He pointed an accusing finger towards me. 'I might wonder how it is that *you* would know this fact? Perhaps *you* have killed men yourself? Perhaps it was *you* who used the knife on Matthew Bowen?' Each time he said 'you', he stabbed the air with his finger.

'No-no, your hon...' My throat constricted suddenly. I closed my eyes, swaying on my feet. A terrible vision of Jude and me, swinging, side by side on the gallows tree, turned my guts to water. If it hadn't been for Sir Rob's painful grip tightening on my shoulder, I fear I should have swooned away.

'You are telling this court that the victim wasn't killed by the knife?' The judge's words barely penetrated my moments of nightmare.

'Aye. Th-tha's so, your 'onour.' My slurring voice did not sound like my own, seeming to come from afar. Sir Rob's fingers dug into me. It hurt, but brought me back again.

'So how do you say he died?'

'He was poisoned by the yellow pigment, orpiment.' The crowd was muttering loudly again. 'I have evidence, my lord.' I produced the stained linen but others were shouting me down.

'He cannot know that!' Gilbert Eastleigh yelled. 'I am the apothecary-surgeon and I say the victim was stabbed in the heart and died of it! And there's an end to it.'

The judges talked among themselves as the crowd became more and more agitated. Eventually, the youngest judge banged the gavel again.

'It is decided, by this court, that the charge to be answered is, as it was, murder by stabbing, and by no other means. As a mere layman, neither a medical practitioner nor a lawyer, your evidence is irrelevant, Master Foxley.'

• •

I stood frozen, stunned that my knowledge was to be discounted. I couldn't help Jude at all. There was nothing to be done. Sir Rob made consoling noises.

'Does the accused have anything to say before the jury pronounces its verdict?' the younger judge enquired. Jude did not move, stood staring at the floor. 'Does the accused have any oath-helpers to swear to his good repute?'

'Yes, my lord.' Seizing a last chance, I raised my hand.

'Who are they? The court requires names before we hear their declarations.'

'Me a-and Sir Robert Percy.'

The judge frowned.

'You do understand the requirements of oath-helpers?'

'No, sir, not really.'

'Master Bailiff, instruct him, if you please.' The judge waved a hand, sighing over my ignorance.

The bailiff stepped forward, pompous in his city livery.

'An accusation of murder requires at least twelve oath-helpers to swear that the accused be of such good reputation and renown as to be incapable of the crime. The oath-helpers must themselves be citizens of unblemished character, impartial and having no connection to the case, that have known the accused for at least three years, preferably longer. If you can number the lord mayor and a few aldermen among them, ten oath-helpers may stand sufficient. Family members cannot stand.'

'Thank you, Master Bailiff. I think that was perfectly clear and succinct.' The judge turned to his elder fellows on the bench to consult them. 'You have until two of the clock to comply and assemble your oath-helpers here in court. Case adjourned 'til after dinner.'

The Hart's Horn Tavern

S IR ROBERT, Lawyer Metcalfe and myself withdrew to the Hart's Horn to quench our thirst and compile the list. The knight and the lawyer were hopeful. I was considerably less so.

'Why was Lord Lovell there?' I insisted, slumped on my bench and not touching Goodwife Fletcher's excellent ale. 'I thought he was on our side. I thought he went to Deptford to get the letter.'

'I fear I don't know, Seb, but, in the meantime, we can look up these oath-helpers. Now, who's first?'

'Stephen Appleyard, the warden archer.'

'Good. Who else?'

'Father Thomas at St Michael's. Dame Ellen Langton.'

'A woman?' Lawyer Metcalfe furrowed his brow as he traced his finger through a spillage of ale upon the otherwise spotless board.

I pulled a face.

'They didn't say a woman couldn't stand and she is a citizen in her own right and sits on the parish council.'

Sir Rob still looked doubtful but counted off his fingers.

'That's three, then. Who else?' He munched on one of Goodwife Fletcher's almond wafers. 'Come, Seb. There must be more. What about that fellow Marlow, the church-warden, lives across the way?'

I shook my head, inspecting my hands.

'Done for disturbing the peace in a drunken brawl a few years back. You could stand.'

'Seb, I'm an in-comer and I've known your brother barely three hours, never mind three years.'

'But you're the duke's man. That must carry some weight.'

'Not enough, I fear. You must know an alderman or two, surely?'

'We know their names but they're nodding acquaintances at best.'

'What of your fellow scriveners and stationers?' Sir Rob finished the last wafer, wiping his mouth on a napkin. Lawyer Metcalfe brooded in silence over his ale-pot like a melancholy owl.

'Competitors. I doubt they'd want to swear on oath that Jude was of such good repute.'

'Oh. Your brother isn't very popular with his fellows then?'

'No. Most folk have insulted or abused me at some time and Jude won't allow that to pass without retribution. He's knocked them all down at some point, or ducked them in the conduit. It's my fault he has no friends.' I sighed and pulled at my hair. 'It's all my fault and there's nothing I can do.'

'Drink your ale and we'll have dinner. Things never seem so bad on a full stomach.' The knight pushed my full cup towards me and signalled to Goodwife Fletcher. 'Besides, Lord Lovell may have got that letter after all.'

• •

The goodwife set platters before us and Sir Rob took up his knife, eager to taste her chicken in a coffin, when Lord Lovell – of all people – strode in.

'Thought I should find you here, Robert,' the baron said, still cloaked. Uninvited, he joined us, ignoring me, but nodding at the lawyer before helping himself to a large portion of the pie.

'My lord,' Sir Rob acknowledged, though his mouth was full. He swallowed. 'I believe you owe us an explanation. How come you're a witness for the prosecution? You never mentioned it before.'

'Did I not? I dare say it slipped my mind. But the truth had to be told. Our Dickon himself would insist upon that, wouldn't he?' Lovell spooned up the rich gravy on the platter and savoured it.

'Aye, I suppose he would,' Sir Rob conceded. 'Francis, did you get the letter?'

'Letter?'

'From Deptford.' Sir Rob wiped his mouth on a snowy napkin.

'No. There is no letter. Went for fire-lighting.'

'Oh, that's a fearful blow to our hopes. So you brought the Langtons as witnesses, instead?'

'Who?'

'The recipients of the letter. They can testify to what it said.' Sir Rob's dinner knife was wagging dangerously as he used it to emphasise each word.

'No. They're not interested. Haven't the time to spare.'

'Did you ask them, at least?'

Lovell didn't answer the knight's question, stuffing his face with food.

'Did you ask them to come, Francis?' Sir Rob held the lord's arm to prevent the next spoonful reaching its goal. He was shrugged off angrily. 'You didn't, did you? I *knew* I should have gone instead. Did you even go to Deptford?'

Lovell stood up, overturning his stool and throwing his spoon in the dish, splashing gravy everywhere.

'I don't have to put up with this, er, this interrogation,' he snarled. 'I'm not the bloody accused here!'

• •

Lovell stormed off, leaving Sir Rob speechless with dismay and embarrassment.

I sat unmoving, silent tears on my cheeks. Jude would be found guilty by default. There was nothing I could do about anything.

Sir Rob tried to make conversation, apologising repeatedly and dreaming up possible excuses for Lord Lovell's failure. When I made no response to any word he said, the knight ordered more ale for himself and fell into a morose silence, like his companion, Metcalfe, and me.

'Coming?' Sir Rob asked, eventually. 'It must be nigh two of the clock.'

'I can't. I have nothing to say,' I said.

'Well, one of us has to go and explain to the court why there are no oath-helpers.'

Lawyer Metcalfe's bench scraped the floor as he stood up, making me wince but I made no move. He shook out his robes. I swear I heard his bones rattling like a *memento mori*.

'You're his brother, after all,' Sir Rob insisted, taking my arm. 'He'll want you there.'

'He won't, not to hear them pass judgement on him, to condemn him. I can't.'

'You can and you will!' The knight lifted me from the bench, as though I weighed nothing, and set me on my feet, passing me my staff. 'Family! Remember? That's what life is all about. Ask Lord Dickon. Come on, else we'll be held in contempt if we're late.'

The Bailey

I T WAS as bad as I feared. Worse. But it didn't take long. Sir Rob made our apologies for the absence of oath-helpers. Jude was brought in, guarded as before. The judges conferred briefly.

'Members of the jury, do you wish to retire to consider your verdict, or have you determined the outcome already?' the young judge asked Davy Owain and his fellows. They mumbled among themselves for a few moments before the white-blond parchmenter stood up. Ralph Fielding – I recalled his name.

'No need, my lord. We're all of us agreed.' He paused significantly. 'We find the accused... guilty.'

'And that is the verdict of you all?'

'It is, your honour.'

The judge turned to my brother. There seemed to be a thin veil of mist betwixt me and the court. I tried to blink it away but it remained.

'Jude Foxley of West Cheap, you have been adjudged guilty, as charged. You will be confined to Newgate Prison until sentence is duly carried out. The sentence is death.'

The folk in the open court cheered until the bailiff restored order by repeatedly thumping his staff.

'On Monday next, the fifteenth day of May, the day after Whitsunday,' the judge continued, as the court held its breath, 'You shall be taken from thence, drawn upon a hurdle at a nag's tail to Tyburn, hanged by the neck, cut down whilst still living, castrated, disembowelled and your body quartered, to the determent of others. And that is the sentence of this court.'

At which point, my world turned black.

The Foxley brothers' rooms

EMILY WAFTED through the door on the aroma of honeyed oatcakes, freshly made, into the close little room. I was bundled up in blankets, still shivering from the shock of it. Jude was condemned to die. Unshed tears, like a lump of molten iron, set in my throat, choking me, so I could hardly draw breath. It was as if that deadly noose tightened about my own neck. The room was dark but for a single candle, though it was daylight still outside. Dame Ellen had ordered the shutters closed, believing the brightness might endanger my recovery. So I sat, shrouded in gloom.

Setting the dish on the board, Emily removed the cloth, allowing tempting steam to escape. But I didn't even glance up. I had no interest in anything, my world reduced to a solitary cloud of dark misery.

'You must eat something, Seb, please?'

I made no move. She lifted my hair back from my eyes. I didn't blink. My sight was distorted, as though I watched through water, but it didn't matter. There was nothing to see any more.

'Sir Robert said you haven't touched food or drink all day. No wonder that you swooned and it will happen again if you don't eat something. Please, Seb, I beg you.' Her fingers closed around mine. She crouched before me, looking up into my downcast eyes, pleading with me. 'Starving yourself to death won't help anybody, not Jude, not you, not me. What would I do without you, Seb?'

I looked up. Emily's eyes were azure pools in the candlelight. I came over hot, just being this close to her, as though she gave off warmth, like a brazier. She smelled of honey, like the scent of wild flowers on a summer day. I reached out to touch her, my hand uncertain, but drew back, fearing this strange bubble of wonder would burst if I did. Then I remembered last eve, how she had shuddered with horror at the touch of my lips against hers.

'Are you warm enough?' she asked. 'I could put another log on the fire if...'

'No, too hot, if anything.' I fought free of my blanket shroud.

'Shall I open a shutter?'

'No, Em, don't move. Stay as you are.'

She looked at me, shaking her head, as though I was beyond her understanding. Perhaps I was.

She pulled my hands towards her, kissing each finger, holding them to her. I felt her tears, salt and wet, potent on my skin. I blinked, forcing my sight to focus upon her.

'Don't cry, Em. Please, don't.'

She put her lips to my hands again before releasing them, looking up at me, managing a smile between her tears.

'I won't, so long as you eat one of my oatcakes. I baked them specially.'

'Did you?' But I didn't take one when she offered the dish. Instead, I covered her hand with mine, taking it to my lips and kissing it, as she had done.

She didn't pull away.

I held her with my eyes, my gaze caressing her, brushing soft as flower petals on her skin. I drank in the sight of her, the shape of her lips, the curve of her cheek, committing every detail of her beloved face to eternal memory, fearing she might disappear, fading like mist in the morning. I watched her breathing. Of a sudden, the world was no longer empty.

'You're beautiful, Em. You are my angel,' I whispered. I hoped she believed me. I became aware of a smile sliding hesitantly across my face. I couldn't help it.

She touched my face. Her fingertips, gentle as sunbeams, stroked my cheek.

And then she was in my arms, her body trembling against mine and now I knew it was pleasure, not revulsion, that coursed through her veins.

Gently, I kissed her mouth, without haste or urgency this time, knowing I loved her to the end of days.

• •

Later I ate supper, to please Emily, though I couldn't say what passed my lips. My mind was a whirlpool of emotions: life; death; love; grief. All swooping and churning in my head 'til it spun dizzyingly. I didn't know whether to laugh or weep. Perhaps I ought to shout in jubilation because Em felt an affection for me, cared about me, loved me even, loved me despite my ugliness of body. Or should I lament my failure on Jude's behalf and grieve 'til my heart broke. The world was perverse indeed.

• •

'Emily! Where are you? Answer me!' Dame Ellen was angry, her voice clearly audible from next door as I finished my cold pottage supper. The old woman entered without the courtesy of knocking. It was her house.

'Have you seen that wretched girl, Sebastian?' she demanded, shoving back a strand of grey hair that had escaped her wimple. 'Never here when she should be!'

'No, good dame. She was here earlier, brought my supper, but that was some while ago now. Perhaps she's in the workshop.' I hoped Em wasn't going to be in trouble again.

'Then why does she not answer me? I'll take my broom to her. I swear, I will, for the second time this day. How dare she go off without permission, yet again.'

'I'm certain she hasn't gone far. Maybe to the conduit?'

'At this time of an evening? I'm going to have to speak to her father about this. I can't have an apprentice behaving in this manner. She's unreliable, gallivanting off at all hours. It's nigh curfew time and where is she, I'd like to know?'

'The privy?' I said, flushing hot at making the suggestion to my landlady.

'You think I haven't looked there already? She's gone off somewhere with some likely young lad, I don't doubt. Up to mischief.'

'But Emily isn't like that, Dame Ellen.'

'And what would you know about wayward young maids?'

'She wouldn't do that.'

'Then where is she?' Dame Ellen left in a flurry of woollen skirts, still yelling Emily's name.

• •

Later, Emily's brother, John, knocked and came in.

'You've found her?' I asked.

John shook his head and fell onto a stool.

'No, and I can't think where else to look, Seb. You were the last to see her, when she brought your supper. Are you sure she didn't say anything about going out? Meeting anyone?'

'I'm sorry, John. She served my supper and left.' I didn't think I ought to mention the long parting kiss we'd shared, that had sent tingles of life through every misaligned bone. 'Help yourself to ale.'

John did as I bade him, but there were lines of worry creasing his face, a look reflected in mine, no doubt.

'She could have gone to your father's house.'

'No. Our father is out looking too.'

'Have you asked that rascal of mine? I've not seen young Jack all day, but he has eyes everywhere.'

'Aye, he's already scouring the alleyways for her.'

'What of Saint Michael's?'

'I've been there. Not a sign.' John drained his cup. 'I suppose I should go there again. If she was making confession, I might not have seen her. Father Thomas may know something.'

'I'll come with you.'

John shrugged.

'Another pair of eyes can't hurt.'

So I took my cloak and staff and followed John.

• •

West Cheap was full of people. Despite the dark, it was busy as market day, every able-bodied man and quite a few women were out searching. It was after curfew, when anyone going about the streets without a light was reckoned a felon, up to no good, and likely to be detained by the watch. So torches bobbed through the night, into and out of alleyways, poking around midden heaps, peering down wells and knocking on doors.

But no one found any trace of Emily.

By the time St Martin's bell chimed for the midnight matins, I was half-demented with worry. So was everyone else. Despite Dame Ellen's words earlier, Emily was as reliable as sunrise.

Something was very wrong.

CHAPTER EIGHTEEN

Wednesday, the tenth day of May
Somewhere north of Cheapside

A S THE first fingers of chill dawn light touched me I awoke. A little wind was menacing the door and shutters of the house opposite. Fisting sleep from swollen, weary eyes, I wondered where I was, lying cold and cramped, propped against a wall. Then I saw John Appleyard beside me, sleeping with his legs drawn up, his tousled head resting on his knees and I recalled we had only sat to rest for a few moments. How long ago I couldn't tell. Dead torches lay beside us. We had been searching for Emily.

Emily!

• •

I shook John awake. The apprentice tailor stirred reluctantly, groggy with exhaustion.

'Where are we?' he mumbled, his mouth still full of sleep.

It took me a moment or two to recognise our surroundings in the faint light.

'We're in Catte Street, I think. This is the wall of St Lawrence Jewry, by the Guildhall. God knows how we came here. Do you suppose they've found her yet?'

John struggled to push himself to his feet, dancing about with the agonies of cramp in his leg, shaking his foot.

'My sister! We must go home – she's probably there before us, don't you think?'

'I pray so, else I know not where we should look next. Help me up, John, please. My feet are numb.'

• •

We stumbled back to Cheapside. I was shocked to realise how far I'd managed to walk yestereve. We found Dame Ellen's kitchen crowded, tired bodies propped in corners or drooping at the table. Most were sleeping. Only Stephen Appleyard hauled himself to his feet to greet his son and me, to enquire whether any trace of his daughter had been uncovered. The warden-archer's haggard features told their own tale, the other searchers had found nothing.

Dame Ellen bestirred herself to pour us ale. She looked to have aged a decade overnight, her wimple and dress in such disarray as I had never seen.

'I dare say she's been enticed away by some fine, handsome fellow,' she said to no one in particular. 'Promised a marriage bed, silks and velvets, who knows?'

'No, dame, not that. She couldn't have,' I assured her, 'She wouldn't.'

Dame Ellen gave me a thunderous look,

'And how would you know?'

'Because...' I avoided her eyes, swallowed hard, not wanting to tell. 'Because Em and I love each other and she wouldn't run off, I know for sure, because...' My headlong run faltered again. 'We hope to wed,' I mumbled, half-hoping no one would hear my words. The kitchen was near silent. Here and there, a body snored on, but the rest were staring at me, shocked beyond belief, bereft of speech.

Dame Ellen stood, mouth open, jug in hand, turned to stone.

'Great God! First she tells me more foolish nonsense than I've ever heard in my life, and now you have the same lack-wit notion,' she said at last. 'Emily and you? It can never be!'

After several minutes of exquisite torture during which eternity I near died of shame, Stephen Appleyard came over, gripped my arm firmly and forced a smile onto his anguished lips.

'I'm glad,' he said. 'You're a good man, Master Seb. I know you'll do the best you can for her. My daughter has chosen well. When we find her, I'll be happy to bless you two. When...'

In any other circumstances, I would have sung for the joy of his words.

• •

The search continued throughout the day. No one worked much that Wednesday. Emily was well-liked and the whole neighbourhood feared for her safety. John Appleyard and I, along with Goodman Marlow, a poulterer named North, whom I hardly knew, and Bennett Hepton, the fishmonger's son, had searched between St Paul's and the river 'til passed dinner time, finding nothing. I made enquiries of every soul we met, showing them a drawing I'd done of Emily before we set out that morning. No one had seen a hair of her beautiful head.

Complete strangers promised to let us know if they found any trace. At the Blacksmiths' Hall in Lambert's Hill, we were given free ale to help us in our quest, the priest at St Peter's on Thames Street let me catch my breath in his own house, giving me a sip of the Eucharist wine to revive me. I felt I was being given the last rites, I was so tired.

Eventually, I was persuaded to let Bennett help me back to West Cheap to rest for an hour or two, my one-time dislike of the young man – the Green Man – quite forgotten.

● ●

Dame Ellen was sitting in her kitchen, sewing, when I entered. She glanced up, hopefully, but I shook my head and she put another stitch in her seam.

'Help yourselves,' she said, vaguely indicating an assortment of bread, cheeses and cold meats, thoughtfully donated by neighbours to sustain the searchers. Bennett cut a huge slice of bacon and a stout wedge of hard cheese, but I declined the offer.

'I have to rest, Dame Ellen, just for an hour,' I said. 'Wake me if you hear anything?' The old woman nodded, saying nothing, fearing the worst by now.

● ●

I went next door to my empty rooms. No Jude. No Jack. And now no Emily. A desolation.

But there, on the floor, shoved beneath my street door, was a folded paper, sealed with a smudge of candle wax. It bore my name in a heavy, square script I did not recognise.

Wednesday evening
By the Steelyard

E ASTERLINGS' HALL Quay, by the Steelyard, was not a pleasant place to be at low tide; the river mud stinking of old fish and the outwash of the public privies in the humid evening. Miasmas arose from the slime along the bank, invisible yet assaulting my senses like tangible entities, festerings of ill-health.

I held my breath to avoid swallowing the worst of it as I hastened passed the bloated carcase of a dead dog, swarming with flies and other unholy creatures that devoured its rotting flesh, washed up on the grey ooze. An image swum into my head, unasked, of my own twisted body lying just so, before long, at the mercy of the tides and the denizens of the deep. I shuddered, chilled despite the warm airs of the dying day and the threat of storm.

• •

The message, pushed under my door some time since, had instructed me to go at the vespers' hour to the derelict warehouse on Cussyn Lane, beside the Steelyard, where the Hanseatic ships discharged their cargoes of timber and furs and iron ore, exchanging them for fine English wool. The Steelyard cranes were still, their windlasses and pulleys had ceased to creak, resting now work was done for the day. But the seagulls still cried above the leprous waters, their funeral oration of *dirige* and *placebo* echoing across the sullen sky. A crow, its dark feathers ruffled, sat on a mooring post by the jetty, observing me with an evil eye. I shooed it away but it simply flew to the next post to continue its disquieting watch from the sorry blue shadows.

• •

The vespers bell had rung from All Hallows. Now I must wait, but whom to expect, I didn't know. The message had been written in a bold hand, one I didn't recognise. As I leaned against the crumbling wall of the warehouse, a rat scurried by, rustling through a clump of dusty weeds, on his nightly quest for food amongst the filth. The oppressive light, forcing a way through thunderous clouds, turned everything the sour colour of river mud.

The hush and lap of the greasy waters of the Thames was soothing, soporific almost, such that the touch of a hand on my shoulder made me start, set my heart drumming. It was Gilbert Eastleigh, whose script I knew well. Not the writer of the note.

'I didn't know if you would be on time, Foxley, seeing how long it must have taken you to walk so far. And you have come alone, as directed.' The apothecary smiled, his serpent's unblinking eyes narrowed at me.

'The note said I should come if I wanted to see Emily Appleyard alive again.'

'Did it, indeed?' Eastleigh's expression changed, all trace of friendliness gone like snow in the sun. 'You know what I want. Where are my notes?'

'Safe. Where you'll never find them,' I said, pulling myself up as straight and tall as I was able, so I might look down upon the little man. 'Unless we come to an agreement. And I want Emily back first.'

'Agreement?' The apothecary's thin-lipped mouth twisted itself into a sly smile. I gripped my staff tighter, trying to still my trembling, lest it betray my fear.

'Where is Emily Appleyard? Unless I see her safe, you get nothing, nothing at all.'

'She has nought to do with this. Just give me my notes, you devil's spawn cripple.'

'Your notes are the receipt for making the Philosopher's Stone, I know that.' Eastleigh's brows drew down, the mouth fixed, but I went on. 'I also know it can be used to make gold from base metals, as well as an elixir that can heal the sick a-and the lame.'

The apothecary's serpent smile split to show uneven teeth. Eastleigh was no fool. I knew he could guess the rest.

'You want gold? No, not that. You want the elixir for yourself. That's the truth, isn't it? You think it will put your filthy, miserable body to rights, is that it?' He laughed at me, a cruel, empty sound.

I sighed and hung my head in shame. It was hard to admit it now, to confess an interest in such unhallowed chicanery, to ever having considered dabbling in the Black Arts.

'It wouldn't work for you, not in that way,' Eastleigh went on. 'It would prolong your life but you'd still be a cripple... for all eternity. Is that what you want? And you would have to drink the elixir daily or perish.'

I swear he was enjoying this, taunting me, though whether he told the truth, I knew not. He must have seen the depths of disappointment written clear upon my features.

'I did want that,' I admitted. 'But now I don't care about elixirs or riches. Just tell me where you've hidden Emily, please, I beg you. Tell me.'

'I told you; she has nothing to do with this. Give me the notes. I won't ask again.' Eastleigh held out a grasping hand, expectantly.

• •

'Problems, apothecary?'

I turned, shocked by the arrival of another, feeling the world lurch beneath me.

'M-my lord? I don't understand.' I staggered, somewhat off-balance, stumbling back against the warehouse wall. I might have fallen but Lord Lovell had a firm grip on my wrist, a painful one that was tightening inexorably.

'So, Dickon's favourite cripple got our message but is loath to comply with our demands, is he?' Lovell sneered, standing so close, I smelled the wine on his breath, saw the fierce lights of anger burning behind his dark eyes. I noticed his sleeve. He wore a coat of fine violet tabby cloth with a near-invisible repair.

'Listen to me, Foxley, and listen well,' Lovell loomed above me. 'Either you tell us where you've hidden those notes or the wench dies. Make your choice now. I don't have time for games.'

'But you cannot, she's an innocent!' I cried, struggling to prise myself free of the baron's grasp. But Lovell grinned nastily, his fingers digging deeper into my flesh.

'Innocent? Ha! But not for long, I'll see to that, unless you give us those notes you stole. What will you do, cripple? The choice is yours.'

I looked at Lord Lovell's face, the handsome features contorted into ugliness by the savagery of his nature. Despair diluted my blood. My legs were unravelling, had lost all power to bear me up and I sagged in Lovell's fierce grip. He let go, releasing me to fall in a crumpled heap at his feet. Then he grabbed hold of my frayed leather jerkin to drag me into the deserted warehouse.

• •

The cavernous place was lit by a couple of torches that flickered in the rising storm-wind whining through a high window. An old ladder, rungs missing, led up to a platform below the large window by which means cargo was hoisted from boats moored below, on the river. The warehouse smelled of pitch and decay, of cheap tallow candles and rotted caulking – a ships' chandlers' warehouse, though it was almost empty now. Almost.

'Bind his hands, apothecary,' Lovell ordered, throwing Eastleigh the end of a length of rope that hung from a hook by the door. The little man hesitated. 'Do as I say!'

Eastleigh obeyed, fumbling with the knots.

Lovell then secured the rope from an iron hook that hung from the roof, pulling me up by my wrists 'til my feet were no longer touching the floor. I cried out in agony as my shoulder was pulled straight as it was never meant to be, bringing tears to my eyes, a torture I could barely endure.

'I'm not sure about this, my lord,' the apothecary complained.

'Too late for scruples now.' Lovell went over to one of a half-dozen barrels that stood by the wall, removed the lid and tipped it over. Thick pitch, black as sin, oozed like treacle across the floor, its sharp odour eye-wateringly strong at close quarters. He stepped aside so it should not soil his shoes but a few stray splashes clung to the fine cloth of his coat. He cursed vilely.

'Now, my crippled friend, you have another choice to make, an easier one, in this case, I believe. Either you tell me where you've put those damned notes, or I set this place alight about your ears. This stuff burns very well, you know, and your death would not be the only one. Oh, no.' The red light of murder flared in his glance. 'With nobody left to protest his innocence, your precious brother will die as well and, as for the wench... This is your last chance, Foxley. Where are the notes?'

The final question came out as a shriek as Lovell's temper got the upper hand and he struck me viciously across the cheek, a heavy gold ring gouging the skin.

I gasped, shocked rather than pained – I was used to that. Defeat tasted bitter as bile in my mouth. What choice did I have? The lives of Emily and Jude depended upon my survival.

'The notes are in the church, St Michael le Querne,' I added quickly, breathless with hanging, seeing Lovell raise his hand to strike again. 'They're hidden under the rood screen on the south side, in an acoustic pot beneath the carved Archangel Michael.'

Lovell smiled, lowering his hand. Then changed his mind and hit me again. This time, the ring cut my lip and I tasted blood.

'That is much better, acquiescence. I prefer that to stubbornness,' Lovell said. The fitful torchlight showed a man content with his evening's work. 'Go, Eastleigh, find the bloody notes.'

'Supposing they're not there?'

'They will be. He won't risk letting his wench suffer, will you, cripple?' Lovell wrenched my hair, forcing me to look him in the eye. 'Will you?'

'N-no. I told you true, my lord, I swear. The notes are there.'

'Of course they are. Eastleigh! Go!'

The little apothecary scuttled off, obedient as a dog.

'Please, let me go, now,' I pleaded. It was becoming harder to breathe as my ribs pressed up into my lungs. 'I've told you what you asked, now tell me where Emily is, I beg you.' My face hurt. My bones screamed in protest.

'Let you go? And why would I do that? So you may tell my dear friend Dickon about me? I can't have him learning of my services to his brother, the king. He wouldn't approve at all. Employing the alchemical arts to make gold? Dear me, that surely goes against God's sacred will. My Lord holier-than-thou-Dickon wouldn't like that and I hold a most lucrative and comfortable post in his household, one I have no intention of losing.'

'I won't tell Lord Richard anything of this, I swear.'

'No, I know you won't because you'll be *dead*. I bid you good night, cripple.'

With a gesture of farewell, Lord Lovell took down a torch from its sconce and touched it to the pool of pitch. It caught, burning with a greedy flame that spread eagerly.

'God be with you, Master Foxley.' The baron broke my staff across his knee and flung it into the fire, stepping back from the blaze.

'Where's Emily?' I shrieked in panic. 'Tell me!'

'Oh, this is amusing. Cripple-baiting, such an intriguing new sport. Don't concern yourself for the wench. She's a pretty piece – too good for the likes of you – but she'll suit me well enough, until I tire of her.'

With that, he left the warehouse, barring the door after him, laughing: a sound to make the blood of any true Christian run cold.

● ●

What could I do? Em's life, aye, and Jude's depended upon my surviving. I squirmed and stretched, reaching for the floor with my good right foot. If only I could take the weight off my wrists, I might free myself of the hook. The tips of my shoes were touching the floor as the flames licked closer. The smoke came thick and black, stuffing itself down my throat, making my eyes stream with tears. Almighty God, Saint Sebastian, please help me, I prayed silently, help me now.

I pulled against the rope, peeling the skin from my hands so blood ran back up my arms. Knowing my strength was failing, I braced myself to make one last, great effort, straining every bone and fibre of my being to reach the floor.

• •

Pain shot through me, fierce and powerful as a lightning bolt that seared from my head to the soles of my feet, wrenching my shoulder and tearing my hip asunder, so it seemed. This was Death claiming me, piercing my soul. The torturer's rack could hurt no worse. And yet I took another breath, and another, coughing on the smoke. Breathing still. Somehow, if I strained, both my feet could now just touch the floor and I dared put my weight upon them. Twisting and wriggling, I managed to lift the rope from the hook and get free of Eastleigh's incompetent knotting, but where now? Frantic, I tried the doors, rattling them with all my strength, but they were barred on the outside. I yelled for aid but who could have heard my voice above the roar of fire and the clamour of the storm?

Blindly, I groped through the pall of smoke for the ladder I remembered, fixed to the warehouse wall, leading up to the platform beneath the high window. Behind me, the pitch barrels were burning, the flames leaping high, setting the roof timbers ablaze. The wattle-and-daub walls were already succumbing to the intense heat.

By touch alone, I found the wooden ladder. I'd never climbed before but somehow I climbed now, sobbing with the effort. It was a slow ascent, hampered by broken rungs and pain. Pulling myself up, inch by inch, feeling the scorching breath of the fire on my back growing hotter, closer. Death awaited me – unconfessed, unshriven. *Miserere, Miserere*, I prayed in my head and in my heart.

'God have mercy.' I had no breath to spare but the words of the Paternoster were on my lips as the Lord God gave me strength to climb to the platform high above. I struggled on to it and lay there, tortured lungs gasping, rejoicing in the fresh wind and cool rain upon my battered face.

But then I looked out.

There was nothing but the blackness of a night storm above and the watery grave of the river below. The tide was rising.

A broken hoist hung like a gibbet without a rope and a crow perched there, unmindful of the rain and darkness.

I stood upright, balanced on the ledge above the water.

From behind me came a woeful groaning, like an animal in deep pain. Then, with a great roar and rending of ancient timbers, the roof collapsed, tossing up showers of sparks into the storm-armoured skies.

Breathing deeply, I raised my arms aloft, turned my eyes to heaven and sang.

The crow took flight among the sparks.

The Thames

DOWN ON the river a boatman rowed his last passenger of the night through the rain on the incoming tide, making for the stairs at nearby Venours Wharf. Then, above the noise of the storm and wind and the splashing of his oars in the choppy waters, he heard singing – a most wondrous sound that delighted his ears.

He and his passenger looked to the northern bank, where a building was ablaze. There, somehow suspended betwixt Heaven and earth, was a figure, arms raised high, with the fires of Hell at its back, singing like an angel.

Crowds, ignoring the curfew bell, were gathering to watch and listen as the pure voice sang out:

Gloria Patri et Filio et Spiritui Sancto,
Sicut erat in principio et nunc et semper, et in saecula saeculorum. Amen.

'Glory be unto the Father, to the Son and to the Holy Spirit,
As it was in the beginning, is now and ever shall be, until the age of
ages. Amen.'

As the words soared heavenward on that final, glorious *Amen,* the figure fell.

The apothecary's shop

GILBERT EASTLEIGH was in his still room, setting out pieces of glassware, polishing them. Lord Lovell paced the floor, his cloak brushing the precious flasks at every turn. Eastleigh hastened to remove a beaker, which seemed most endangered of being knocked and broken.

'You have your damned notes now, so get on with it!'

'Patience, my lord, these matters cannot be hurried,' the apothecary said soothingly. 'I have laboured for years on this and I won't ruin everything because you urge me to make haste. Help yourself to wine, won't you?' And keep out of my way he wanted to add, but did not dare.

'How long?' Lovell sipped his wine, pulled a faced as the cheap, sour stuff.

'As long as it takes. Now, please...'

'Where is your apprentice? He could assist you.'

'He is no help. His clumsiness would hinder matters. Besides, he knows not what I am doing.' Eastleigh moved the little charcoal burner to heat a flask of oily green liquid. 'He knows nought of my stone nor its properties and 'tis better thus for all concerned.'

Lovell moved closer to watch. The liquid was beginning to give off the stink of hot vinegar and brimstone. He wrinkled his nose. It smelled as sour as the wretched wine.

'What is supposed to happen here?' The lord reached out to touch the flask but the apothecary grabbed his hand.

'No, no! Do not touch that!' he shrieked. 'Dear God. Would you send us all to oblivion? Leave well alone, I pray you, sir.'

Even Lovell could see the little man looked drained of blood, so fearful was he.

'I shall wait in your parlour, but I warn you, I won't wait much longer.'

'That would be wise, I think, my lord, safest for us all. But please be quiet. Do not waken my apprentice in the attic.

The Thames

T HE BOATMAN rowed frantically, urged on by his passenger, to retrieve the "fallen angel". At first they could see nothing but the ripples left behind, illuminated by their flickering torches at bow and stern.

But a jagged shaft of lightning ripped down the cloud-slashed sky, its blinding light revealing someone floundering in the water. As the thunder rumbled across the heavens, they caught him up with a boat-hook, dragging him over the gunwale to safety in the bottom of the little boat.

He lay there choking, coughing up water. Soaked, blackened and singed. He was no angel.

But at least he lived.

CHAPTER NINETEEN

Thursday, the eleventh day of May
The small conduit, West Cheap

THIS MORNING, Dame Ellen had to fetch her own water from the conduit and was making the most of the occasion, if with a heavy heart. Life went on.

'Still no sign of your Emily then?' Mary Jakes consoled her friend. 'But they say "no news is good news", do they not?'

'Aye, but that hardly makes up for the lack of a pair of hands, does it?' Dame Ellen complained, easing her back and sighing as she waited for her pitcher to fill at the stoop. 'But did you hear about my tenant, young Sebastian, escaping that fearful fire? Though the Lord God alone knows what he was doing in that old warehouse by the Steelyard. My household seems bedevilled by ill-luck of late. And I saw a filthy crow in my yard yesterday, no doubt it brought these misfortunes upon my house.'

'But you say Sebastian escaped. That was a good thing, surely?'

'Indeed it was, Mary. And better than you know. In truth, it was little short of miraculous, if you ask me.' Dame Ellen settled herself on the low wall, like some majestic falcon upon its perch, fluffing out her skirts and patting at her impeccable linen veil as if preening her feathers. 'I tell you this, he not only survived his ordeal by fire but, like the legendary phoenix, has been renewed by the flames. Well, almost. I saw him go out to the yard this morn, head held high and near as upright as any man and no crutch, I tell you!'

'How come, Ellen? Did he say?'

'No. He had not breath to speak much when the waterman brought him home last night, through that storm. But the waterman swore he was an angel that flew out of the flames.'

'An angel? Who? Your Sebastian?' Maudie Marlow added her pennyworth, looking doubtful as she set down her pail and made herself comfortable for a good lengthy discussion of the incident. Other women joined them to hear the news.

'That's what the waterman said, that he flew out of the burning building, into the river, singing at the top of his voice, like one of the heavenly host.'

'Singing? Can he sing?' Nell Warren asked.

'He has a fine voice when he sings in church,' Dame Ellen confirmed. 'But that doesn't explain how his shoulder has suddenly come straighter and his lameness near gone, does it now? If you want my opinion upon this matter, my dear friends, I'm telling you, and I'm sure good Father Thomas would confirm what I say.'

Not much in the way of work would be done this day.

The Foxley brothers' rooms

I SAT UPON my bed looking down at my feet, confused. My body had changed, I knew not how. But I knew when. It had happened whilst I hung from the wall hook inside the warehouse, straining with all my might to reach the floor with my feet. Bones had moved, somehow, as though an ancient, rusted lock had suddenly been released with a key. I couldn't explain it.

Maybe it was a miracle.

It certainly felt like one as I stood beside my bed, both feet set squarely on the floor as never before. My left leg was weaker than the right, after a lifetime of near uselessness, but I was certain it would grow stronger now. My staff was gone, broken, burned to ashes in the fire, but now I had no need of it – I would be a three-legged man no longer. The street urchins wouldn't be able to mock me with those words now.

I picked up the shirt that had been removed yestereve and spread to dry on the linen chest. I pulled it over my head – using both arms. I'd never been able to raise my left arm so high before. Every bone and muscle ached but, alongside such wondrous changes, I could ignore the discomfort, disdaining it as a nagging companion. A tentative exploration revealed an unevenness on my left shoulder blade but nothing like the disfiguring hump that had been there yesterday. And the tightness in my neck had lessened, making it easier to raise my head and keep my chin up.

I had a whole new body. Everything would be different now. Life would be marvellous. *Deo gratias*! And all because some devil had tried to kill me in that dreadful inferno.

• •

But then I recalled the reason why I'd gone to the warehouse in the first place and, suddenly, things were not so marvellous after all: Emily! She was still missing, even if, as was likely, she was imprisoned at Lovell's Inn. But knowing where she was was only half the story. She still had to be found and set free. The question was how?

And then there was Jude.

Westminster Palace

'THE KING will see you now, my lord,' the servant said, holding the door for Francis Lovell to enter. The young lord's nerves were strung taut as bowstrings at the thought of this audience.

'Ah, Francis, come in, come in. Break your fast with me, won't you?' The king smiled broadly, obviously anticipating good tidings.

Francis removed his elaborate hat of finest beaver fur and made his obeisance, deeper than was his habit.

'Thank you, your grace, b-but I've eaten already.' He hadn't, but right now he knew the food would probably choke him. He couldn't face a mouthful.

'Well, sit down.' Edward returned to his hearty breakfast, the platter heaped with greasy meats. 'Come, take your ease, at least, whilst you tell me all that happened last eve. I want to hear every detail of what came to pass at the apothecary's place. You sent word that you had recovered the receipt. Did it work? Has that fellow – what's his name?'

'Eastleigh, sire.'

'Aye, well – how much gold has he made for me, after all this long while?'

The sight and smell of the king's breakfast was making Francis feel queasy.

'We did indeed recover the receipt, your grace, as I informed you was the case,' Francis said, staring at his hands as though they were a thing quite new to him. 'The receipt...'

'Yes, yes, the receipt. Did it turn base metal into gold or not?' the king said, chewing bread and bacon, stabbing at the next piece of meat with his knife.

'N-not exactly.'

'And what does that mean? It did or it didn't? Come on, I don't pay you to speak in riddles, man. Did you make gold, or not?'

'No, your grace,' Francis said, his voice so low, the king did not hear, or pretended not to.

'What did you say?' The king's eyes flashed.

'No, no sire, I-I fear it did not work as the apothecary assured us it would.' Francis composed himself with an effort – Edward's temper was legendary. 'He created a stinking pot full of dark sludge; nothing more. He misled us atrociously. He should be punished.'

The king cursed like a fishwife, ripping the linen napkin in his hands.

'That he should and he owes me money,' he snarled. 'The useless bloody charlatan. Five hundred marks I lent that fool. I want it back, Francis... every penny. See to it.'

'Yes, your grace. It will be my pleasure. But what of the wretch himself? He knows too much, I fear, concerning your grace's involvement, and mine, in his nefarious practices.'

'As I said, see to it. Tidy up this bloody mess. I want all trace of the affair gone. Do I make myself clear?'

'Perfectly, sire.'

The king looked grim but nodded. He pushed aside his food and threw the ragged napkin into the remains of his breakfast.

'Be gone! You have work to do.'

• •

Down in the courtyard of Westminster Palace, Lord Lovell let out a sigh as he waited for a groom to bring his horse. Thank God the king had not seen fit to blame him for Eastleigh's failures, as might easily have been the case. At least *his* neck still held his head firmly in place, but the apothecary's hours would be few.

However, despite the king's instructions, he would have to be cautious. No blame could attach to himself or the king concerning this delicate matter. At least the Foxley brothers were out of the way now, no need for his concern in that quarter. The warehouse fire had been visible for miles but the name Lovell had not been mentioned in that connection.

The apothecary's shop

'**E**ASTLEIGH! WHERE in Hell are you?' Lovell announced himself by hammering on the counter board with the roundel on the hilt of his knife. One glance at the baron's dark visage sent a customer scurrying like a beetle.

The little apothecary came bustling from his still room, looking as though Judgement Day had come – which it had – quaking in his fine fur-topped boots.

'M-my lord, I d-didn't expect to see you again so soon.' Eastleigh's lips continued to mouth soundless words – ardent prayers to his maker, if he had any sense.

'No, I dare say you didn't,' Lovell said, keeping his voice as mild as he could. He fingered the dried flower petals in a bowl upon the counter, releasing perfumes that were meant to temper the stinks of less pleasant things on the shelves.

'D-did you see the king?' Eastleigh was wringing his hands in his apron.

'I did.' The baron watched the apothecary, enjoying the man's obvious distress.

'And? What did he say?'

'Not much. He was enjoying a hearty breakfast. At least, until I informed him of your disappointing results last eve, at which point his appetite was quite lost. He would have you return the money he lent you. All of it.'

'But I don't have it. It was spent on the finest ingredients. Dragons' blood and myrrh and oil of Mithridates and expensive glassware f-for...'

'Too bad. The king wants it back. Now.'

'He can't have it.'

Lovell leaned over the counter, his tone heavy with menace.

'Then you'd best produce the gold, hadn't you?'

'But, as you saw, the receipt is not yet complete. It still doesn't quite work as it should.'

'So get on with it, before the king's grace loses all patience with you.'

'H-he has given me another chance?'

Lovell nodded.

'Thank God. I thought...' Eastleigh mopped his brow on his sleeve.

'God has nought to do with it,' the baron growled. 'Come. I'll assist you, as you should have allowed last night.'

THE COLOUR OF POISON

• •

In the gloom of the still room, Tom Bowen kept to the shadowed corner, as far from Lord Lovell as the little space permitted. He watched his master setting up the still again, using the precious glassware it had taken him hours to clean. The stink was still in his nose and tainting his tongue.

'Fetch more charcoal,' Master Eastleigh ordered.

Tom went out to the yard, grateful for the sweet air, which he breathed in eagerly, coughing as his lungs exchanged bad air for good. He took his time over the charcoal, in no hurry to go back inside. If the still room was Hell. then Lord Lovell was Satan himself. Even master was scared of him. Handful by handful, Tom took the black charcoal from the sack in the lean-to, filling the wooden vessel, lingering over the task, until a vicious hand gripped his ear and hauled him back inside. His ear burned but his blood ran cold at the look on the lord's face.

'I draw the line at dealing with the likes of you!' Lovell roared, clouting Tom so hard round the head that he fell down. 'Now get to work!'

Whilst Master Eastleigh was busy, fussing over the still, Tom, cowering, kept his wary eye on Lord Lovell prowling around, looking at the bottles on the shelves and in the little wooden chests on the floor beneath. He was moving stuff about, reading and removing some of the labels that were tied so carefully to the bottles and jars. Swapping them over.

Why would he do that? Even Tom, as a lowly new apprentice, had been made aware, in his first week working for the apothecary, of the dangers of mislabelling. Someone could be poisoned, or the place catch afire, or worse, but he dared not speak up. Not now, in Lord Lovell's presence. Perhaps when he was gone, which couldn't be soon enough for Tom.

• •

Eastleigh worked tirelessly, heating, distilling, decanting. After much doubt and self-debate, he decided it had to be done, so he removed the precious silver stone from the bag that hung about his neck. He had never permitted anyone to set eyes on it before, the famed Philosopher's Stone was not something to be made known to the common sort, not to laymen. Only true practitioners of the art of alchemy – and few of those indeed – had even seen the like, but now was not the time for caution. King Edward demanded his gold and this was Eastleigh's last chance.

Lovell drew close, seeing the dull silvery gleam of the stone, but the apothecary dropped it into the seething retort upon the brazier. Bubbles of noxious fumes arose, setting them all choking. Eastleigh timed it by reciting ten Paternosters then covered his mouth and nose with his sleeve whilst using the tongs to recover the stone. Remarkably, it lay upon a cloth to cool, utterly unchanged in any way by its immersion in the fearful brew.

Lovell peered at it, reaching out to touch, but it blistered his fingers before he could snatch them away.

'Curse the bloody thing! What devilish connivance is it that you boil in acid and it changes not?' Lovell sucked at his fingers.

'That, my lord, is the Philosopher's Stone, the colour of the moon, as you see, yet constant in all things and unchanging, as the ever-variable moon is not. And if you tell a living soul of its existence, I warn you, the consequences shall be grave indeed.' Eastleigh did his best to sound bold, though his courage withered by the moment.

'Are you threatening me, you devious little worm?'

'Of course not, my lord, but if others were to learn of it, being of immeasurable value and antiquity...'

'But has it made gold?'

In trepidation, Eastleigh lifted the retort with gloved hands and removed it to a side table. There he had a wide-topped bowl with a square of fine white silk tied tightly across it. Slowly, he poured the hot liquid through the silk, into the bowl. But he had no interest in the greenish liquor but in what was left upon the silk. Terror rose like bile in his throat. The gritty precipitate left behind was black. Not a hint of gold. Nothing. He collapsed onto a stool and buried his head in his hands.

'Well?' Lovell snarled, stepping over to see the results for himself. 'As I thought: you know no more of how to make gold than a damned beggar at my gate. You're a bloody charlatan, swindling the king and making me look a fool. You'll pay for this, Eastleigh, and as a demonstration of your good intentions, I'll take this in recompense.' Lovell picked up the stone. It was still warm and weighed heavy for its size. Its pale silvery surface felt smoothly satisfying in his hand.

'No, no, my lord. I beg you, my life depends upon it.' Eastleigh tried to claw the stone from Lovell's grasp.

'You never spoke a truer word, apothecary. Now get out of my way!'

The Foxley brothers' rooms

I WAS PREPARING to go about the urgent business of finding Emily when who should appear at my door but young Jack. Fearing a beating no doubt, he slunk in like a dog in disgrace.

'Jack! Whatever befell you? Where have you been?' I watched him, appalled at the lad's filthy appearance. 'Have you been sleeping in the City ditch, or what? And you stink like a midden heap.'

'It ain't my fault, master, what 'appened to Master Jude, 'onest it weren't. I swear it.' Jack snivelled, wiping his nose on a grimy sleeve.

'No time now. Go, get yourself washed before Dame Ellen observes you, or has her senses assaulted by your reek. Hurry! Make haste.'

Jack grinned through the dirt on his face. He poured icy water into the basin and scrubbed his hands together vigorously. I watched him, impatient.

'Master! Yer tapping yer foot.'

'What of it? Hasten, will you, for pity's sake.'

'But yer can't do it. Tap yer foot, I mean, wi'out falling. And yer looks different somehow.'

'When did you eat last?'

Jack shrugged.

'Day or two, can't rightly recall. But what's 'appened to yer, master? Yer standing proper.'

'Get a clean shirt on. Emily patched one...' My voice failed me, thinking of her.

'I 'eard Mistress Em was gone. Is it true?'

I could only nod.

'Where is she then, master?'

'If I knew for certain, we wouldn't still be searching for her. Now take some bread to break your fast, then we must go. You will convey, that is carry my scrip, as a proper apprentice should.'

'Me? A 'prentice? D'yer mean it, master? I can be yer 'prentice?' Jack's smoke-coloured eyes widened and he danced about in delight.

'We shall see. You're a little young but for now, at least, you must play the part. Can you do that?'

'Yeah, course I can. Easy. 'Prentices are just lazy devils, swear a lot.'

I frowned at him, hard.

'Only jesting.'

'This is a serious matter. If you cannot convince the folk at Lovell's Inn that you are a real apprentice, our cause is lost ere it commences, begins.'

'Lovell's Inn? Yer means that great place in Ivy Lane? We going there?'

'Aye. Now behave yourself, if that's possible.'

• •

Jack hoisted my bag of artist's equipment onto his shoulder and followed me along Bladder Street and into the Shambles. Butchers' apprentices accosted us, trying to persuade us with the aromas of hot pigs' trotters, black puddings and stuffed hearts. I knew Jack would have dearly loved to sample them all, but I brushed passed, walking better than I'd ever done before, with hardly a limp.

'Was it a miracle, then, what mended yer leg?' Jack asked, trotting beside me. Now I realised that, with practice, I might become strong enough to walk as well as any man.

'Perhaps.'

'D'yer think as 'ow I should probably be 'iding still, master? But I got bored wiv it. D'yer think they're still after me fer 'elping Master Jude?'

'I dare say the watch has bigger, more important, fish to catch by this time.'

At the end of Ivy Lane I stopped.

'Now, Jack, listen well. As my apprentice, you should keep silent unless spoken to, but employ your ears and eyes to the best advantage. If Emily isn't imprisoned at Lovell's Inn, then I know not where else she may be, but we must be cautious, careful. Do you understand?'

'Aye, master.'

Lovell's Inn in Ivy Lane

I HAD TO brace myself to knock at the stout oak door, the tradesmen's entrance round the back of Lord Lovell's grand stone-built establishment. It was like a small castle with a turret and crenellations, more for show than defence. I prayed the man himself was not at home, for an interview with him would mean the end of hope.

The servant who unbarred the door had a vinegar face with invisible lips.

'Who are you? What business do you have here?'

'Good day to you, sir.' I removed my cap. 'I am Master Simon Freeman, an artist, an expert in portraiture.'

'We don't want any portrays, whatever they are. Go away.'

The man began to close the door but Jack nimbly darted inside.

'My master's the best artist in England, in the 'ole world, sir,' he added.

'Portraiture is the latest in high fashion at the court of Burgundy,' I said. 'Everyone of importance has had their portrait painted, including the Duchess Margaret, King Edward's own sister. And I know Lord Lovell for a man most interested in fashion. Would he not wish to have his image captured in paint for all time? I employ only the best materials, guaranteed to keep their colour for centuries to come.'

The man was hesitating as I stepped over the threshold to join my cheeky young apprentice.

'Well, I suppose my lord may have an interest but he is not at home, so you'll have to come back tomorrow.'

I felt relieved to hear Lovell was elsewhere.

'It would be a pity to waste my time. I have other patrons in mind for the rest of the month. But today, supposing I drew *your* portrait, good sir. Then you might show it to Lord Lovell and recommend my talent to him.'

'I don't have the time.'

'But you have such an interesting face, sir. I didn't catch your name.'

'Gregory. Lord Lovell's steward.'

'Well, Gregory, you have such fine features, a strong jaw. Jack, pass me my paper and silver point, if you please.'

Jack obliged. I took Gregory by the arm and led him down the screens passage, into the great hall.

'Ah! The light is better here. Would you turn to face the window, please? Lift your chin a little higher, there! Hold that pose, Gregory. 'Tis perfect!'

• •

With Gregory now staring at the sky, out of the window, I gestured to Jack to go elsewhere. Jack understood what I meant and tip-toed out of the hall, leaving the heavy scrip behind. I continued working with my silver point.

'Don't move, Gregory, or my work will be ruined. Keep utterly still. Perhaps when I have finished your portrait, there are others in the house who might wish to have their likeness preserved. I prefer interesting faces, though beauty is a joy to portray. Does Lord Lovell have any pretty wenches in his household?'

'No!' Gregory said hastily. 'Why would he?'

'Why would he not? Keep your position, please, for just a little longer. A fine man like Lord Lovell, in the prime of his life. I should be surprised if he didn't have at least a few lasses about him that are easy on the eye. Perhaps he would like their portraits to hang in his chamber?'

At that moment, Jack returned, eyebrows raised meaningfully as he picked up the scrip again.

'Here. You may judge my abilities for yourself.' I showed the man his flattering likeness, a drawing I had completed within a few minutes of entering the hall. Gregory stared at it.

'I really look like this?'

'Of course. Why would I draw you otherwise?'

'Well, I'm not such a bad sort. I must show this to the cook.'

Gregory rushed off, forgetful of all propriety or sense of duty, leaving us, his visitors, alone in the hall.

• •

'What did you discover, Jack?'

''Em ain't in any room I looked in round 'ere, but there's still upstairs and an undercroft, but the door's barred and bolted across so I couldn't look down there.'

'That could be of interest. After all, why would the door be bolted on the outside, unless it was intended to imprison someone within? Do they fear the rats might run off with their store of salted meats?' I smiled. 'Well done, Jack. I pray I am correct in my suppositions.'

'Yer what?'

'Never mind. Now we must find a way to get into that undercroft.'

• •

Gregory came back, towing a fleshy man by the sleeve. The man seemed eager enough but was too fat to hurry.

'Percival would have his portray done as well, wouldn't you, Perce?' Gregory said, pushing his friend forward.

The man nodded and wiped his sweaty forehead with a greasy apron, stained with all manner of food stuffs – the cook, no doubt. I wondered that the great lord employed such a slovenly cook. It explained his liking for Goodwife Fletcher's food at the Hart's Horn.

'I ain't got much time afore that spit roast needs basting, so be quick about it, Master Artist,' the cook said. 'Now where shall I stand to best effect?'

'Upon the dais?' I suggested.

'Aye, that'll do me well.' The man wobbled across to the upper end of the hall and stumbled up the dais steps. Before his lord's cushioned chair, he took up a stance like a Greek god, one stubby arm lofted high.

I glanced at Jack who was biting his bottom lip, mirth dancing in his eyes as he tried his best not to laugh out loud. It wasn't easy even for me to keep my face straight as I sketched this fat Bacchus in as few lines as possible.

'It's a good likeness of you, Perce, he's caught you exactly,' Gregory announced, looking over my elbow as I worked.

'I told ye afore, I ain't got time.'

'It is done,' I said, handing the drawing to the steward.

'That was swift. You took far longer over me,' Gregory said.

'Your face is more interesting,' I whispered.

The steward laughed.

'I think we all deserve some ale – the good stuff – Master er...'

'Freeman. Simon Freeman.'

• •

We made our way to the kitchen, the fat cook first. Ale was poured all round, except for the poor spit boy, blistering his knees by the hearth.

'It was him what told us 'bout th'undercroft,' Jack whispered, indicating the lad with his eyes. 'And I'm going to need the jakes, master, I reckon... soon... now.' Jack was grinning.

'My friends, my apprentice has a need more urgent than ale,' I said. 'Perhaps your spit boy could show him the way?'

While Jack was gone, I made a show of guzzling my ale, helping myself to more when the cup was empty and refilling those of the steward and the cook. By the time Jack returned – and quite a time it was, enough for the lad to have searched upstairs – all three of us were laughing together and the roast was beginning to scorch. The spit boy rushed to his post, as though expecting a thrashing, but none came.

Gregory was slurring his words, the "good stuff" getting the better of him, and Perce was sweating freely, his grubby shirt quite wet about the collar and armpits. I appeared worst affected, lolling on the greasy board beside a chopping block strewn with bits of gristle.

To avert Jack's fears, I lifted the cup to my lips then, out of sight, trickled the contents onto the floor beneath the board where it puddled in the straw amongst the vegetable waste. I caught Jack's eye and winked as I replenished all the cups from the flagon.

'Can I have some ale, master?' Jack asked.

'Not the good stuff, too, too strong for a lad s'young as you,' I said in a sing-song sort of voice I hoped made me sound tipsy.

Gregory got up to fetch a jug of the weak, third brewing that was meant for servants and children. He barely made it there and back, having to lean against the wall, I was pleased to see. The cook looked half asleep on his stool.

'I fear I've, er, the same need as my 'prentice,' I mumbled into my cup. Gregory nodded.

'Find it y'self,' he said, probably not meaning to be rude but too unsteady to show me the way. I pushed myself to my feet uncertainly – I'd had much practice in the past.

'Show me where, Jack.'

Jack took my arm.

'Yer leg's not gone bad again, 'as it, master?' he asked, looking concerned as he guided me out of the kitchen, into the screens passage.

I grinned at him, straightening my shirt.

'How was I? Good enough to convince them?'

'Aye, master, yer 'ad me worried proper. Em's nowheres else I searched upstairs. The undercroft door is this way.'

• •

Silently I unbarred the door and drew back the bolt, praying it would not squeak, but it was well greased. A flight of wooden stairs went down into the gloom, reminding me all too much of Newgate gaol, but there was a glimmer of light below and the air, though chill and stale-smelling, was not rank. We crept down the stairs – something I could not have managed before without assistance.

At the foot, the undercroft ran the length of the house above, its vaulted alcoves stacked with smoked and dried meats and cheeses, a rusting assortment of old-fashioned chain mail and bits of plate armour, a stack of pikes and halberds, some broken bow staves, their ends snapped off, and a pile of yellowing linen and napery.

Other alcoves held horse harness, a jousting helm and shield, its colours invisible beneath the dust of decades. The only light came from a flickering torch set in an alcove at the far end.

And there was Emily. She lay on a straw palliasse on the cold stone floor, huddled up for warmth.

'Emily. Em,' I called softly, so as not to startle her, my heart in my throat, fearing she might not be breathing. She was chill to my finger-tip touch but stirred a little. 'Em! Em, thank God we've found you.'

She turned and sat up, brushing her tangled hair aside.

I lifted a strand back from her face, saw the light of hope spark in her eyes. Then it was gone.

'Seb,' she said. 'What are you doing here?'

I was puzzled. I'd expected she would be overjoyed to see me, eager to be rescued. But she didn't sound it.

'You shouldn't be here. Lord Lovell will be back any moment.'

'I've come to rescue you, Em.' Surely, I didn't have to explain that, did I? Had Lovell dosed her with some potion or other, to keep her quiet?

'I don't need rescuing. There's nought amiss with me.'

I crouched beside her, tried to take her hand, but she snatched it away.

'But you're not here from choice, are you? And he's shut you in down here with...' I looked around, noticing a cup of ale, half full, a platter strewn with crumbs and a necessary bucket, 'without even a blanket to keep you warm.' I gestured, palms up, having no understanding of the circumstances here.

'Just go, will you?' She sounded angry as she turned her back to face the wall. 'I'm safe enough, you're not. Go, for pity's sake!'

I heard the quaver of desperation in her voice as I stood up, but I wasn't leaving without her. Now I'd found her, I wasn't taking my eyes off her.

'Come, Em, we don't have time to discuss this.' I reached down and pulled her to her feet. Her gown fell open, revealing bruised flesh as she tried frantically to cover herself. I looked away. 'What did that filthy devil do to you?'

'Nothing, compared to what he'll do to you,' she sobbed. 'He said he'll kill you, if I don't do as he says. And I know he will, if he finds you here. Go, now, please, I beg you.'

'He has already tried to kill me and failed. I'm not leaving you, Em. You stay, I stay. Simple as that.'

I sat down on the floor beside her palliasse – something else I couldn't have done yesterday – refusing to watch her, standing there, twisting her hands in the torn cloth of her skirt.

• •

'Master, we've got t' go. I can 'ear folks upstairs. Maybe 'is lordship's come 'ome.' Jack hopped about in his anxiety. 'We *must* go!'

Emily didn't even register the small miracle when I got to my feet, unaided. I grabbed her arm and headed towards the stairway, pulling her with me, despite her attempts to free herself.

'He'll come after you, Seb, if I'm not here when he returns. You must leave without me!'

'Never!' With that, I hoisted her over my shoulder and climbed the stairs to freedom. Em did not resist. The wooden steps creaked beneath our combined weight. At the top, I set her on her feet and pulled her gown across to cover her, but it wouldn't hold together, so I took off my jerkin and put it round her. For a moment, she watched me.

'Seb? How did you do that? The stairs? You carried me. How?'

'I'll explain later. Come, the door is this way. Hurry.'

• •

But the tradesmen's door was closed. Lord Lovell was leaning against it, cleaning his nails with the long, gleaming blade of his roundel knife whilst he waited.

Emily gasped. I felt a shudder of terror tremble through her body as I pulled her behind me, so I stood as her shield, keeping hold of her icy hand.

'So, cripple, what bastard demon saved your skinny neck then? I hoped I'd heard the last of you. And you need not think you're going to run off with my prize, either. I've won nothing else from this bloody shambles. At least I get the wench.'

'You will keep your filthy paws off her!'

'Or what? There's always an "or else". What will you do, cripple? Curse me? Hit me with your crutch? Oooh, I'm so afraid.' If wolves ever laughed, that was the sound Lovell made now.

Emily shook herself free of my grasp and ran to the baron.

'I'll do whatever you want, my lord, just let them go, please.'

'No, Em, you mustn't sacrifice yourself.'

'I believe she just has,' Lovell said, roughly pulling her against him. 'How touching it is... two lovebirds. Or perhaps not. Perhaps she has made her choice, preferring me to the likes of you, and who could blame her, eh? What right-minded woman would choose a bloody cripple?' He forced his lips hard against Emily's and then shoved her aside, freeing his arm. The long-bladed knife was still in his hand and it was clear that he meant to use it. He could have summoned his servants to assist, but maybe this was too personal.

• •

I would never be a fighting man but, for Emily, I couldn't stand by and do nothing to save her. I had no weapon but my penknife at my belt, used for cutting quills. The worst harm it might do was a bad scratch, though men had been known to die of less, eventually.

Lovell was watching me, waiting, letting me make the first move... if I could think what move to make. Paint him to death?

Without warning, I grabbed the heavy scrip from Jack and swung it by the long strap, catching Lovell across the face, knocking him backwards, against the door. He lashed out at the bag with his knife, cutting it open.

The art materials: pens and pots of pigment, paper and brushes, flew everywhere. A pot lost its stopper, showering Lovell's face with yellow powder that glittered reddish as it clung to his skin and clothes.

'Don't touch it!' I yelled as I steadied myself against the wall. 'It's deadly poison!' Lovell was coughing, trying to brush the yellow stuff off.

'You're lying!' he spluttered. But the knife was wavering.

I leapt forward and grabbed the blade, feeling it slice along my fingers, wrenching it away.

The baron was on his knees, tearing off his coat, scrubbing at his face in panic, until I held the knife cold against his cheek.

'We're leaving now,' I said. 'Don't try to prevent us, or Lord Richard will hear your whole sorry tale. Come near us again, and I'll tell the duke everything.'

'But you've poisoned me, you bastard! It's the same stuff they used to kill Bowen, isn't it? You'll pay for this. Somehow.'

Now it was my turn to laugh.

'I've never heard of anyone dying of saffron poisoning, but I'm grateful for the information. Incidentally, your face and hands will be stained for weeks, your clothes ruined. Sorry about that. Good day, my lord. Jack, pick up my stuff, will you, please?'

I had never been less sorry about anything in my life. Jack scrabbled about, collecting up my precious materials, folding them inside what remained of my scrip.

Once outside, I threw Lovell's knife down the well in the front yard. Then Emily clung to me and kissed me on the lips, not caring that Jack could see. He gave a rowdy cheer as I felt the hot blood racing to my cheeks, but Emily stepped back, laughing.

Ivy Lane

O UT IN Ivy Lane Emily paused, insisting on binding my cut hand with cloth from her torn shift and I was more than content to allow it, smiling all the while, immune to any hurt with her at my side, even singing snatches of my favourite motet *Mater ora filium* – Mother worship thy Son – as we went along. It always made me wonder what my mother would have said to me, had she lived long enough to know me. What would she think to see me now, rescuing my love?

We had reached the top of Ivy Lane and were about to turn along the Shambles, me with my arm tight around Emily and Jack trailing behind, when there came such a thunderous explosion, as though Hell had erupted behind us.

Looking back, the lane was filled with billows of greasy black smoke, debris raining down on the cobbles. Shouts and cries echoed from house to house, a horse whinnying in terror, dogs yapping. As I ran back, the smoke thinned a little.

'It's Gilbert Eastleigh's place!' I cried, plunging into the smoke-filled building, only to be driven back by flames. 'Master Gilbert! Tom Bowen! Are you there? Anybody?' I thought I heard a voice; a whimper above the roar of fire, the tinkle of breaking glass, the hiss of steam. The smoke was greenish now, choking, brimstone burning my eyes and throat. I had had enough of fire two days before. 'Gilbert! Tom!' A coughing fit stopped my voice.

I grabbed up the remains of a once-fine cloak, dropped on the floor. Wrapping it round my head, I advanced further into the shop, vaguely aware that others were calling out behind me.

I found a body sprawled behind the counter, took it by the arms and dragged it out into the street before collapsing beside it in the gutter, heaving for breath, coughing fit to tear my lungs.

• •

Tom Bowen lay very still, smoke-blackened, limp as wet paper. Folk gathered round us both until Emily shoved her way through the crowd.

'Seb! Seb! You foolish, stupid, brave idiot! Look at you. You could have killed yourself. I'm so proud.' Tears were pouring down her face, dripping on my head as I knelt in the filth of the gutter, still coughing.

'The lad... how...' I choked again, my throat raw, burning.

'Who knows? You're my only concern now,' she told me, hugging me close until I was seized by another coughing fit and she released me, rubbing my back, which helped. Even if it didn't, I was content to know she was so close, touching me, caring.

Dame Ellen's house

A T HOME, in West Cheap, Emily was welcomed back with joy, Dame Ellen praising God for His great mercies, Stephen Appleyard, the solid, dependable warden archer, weeping like a little maid in his relief at his daughter's return. And all the neighbours cheering and congratulating each other that the search was ended in success. Only her brother, John, came over to thank me and Jack, wrinkling his nose at the stink of smoke and singed hair, though he made no comment before returning to the impromptu celebrations as a keg of cider materialised, seemingly by magic, in Dame Ellen's kitchen.

Emily was led away to be washed and decently clothed by the women, leaving me and Jack standing by the door, of interest to no one as the keg was tapped and the cider flowed.

Jack would have joined in but I required his assistance back to our rooms. I was limping quite badly now, my left leg ached beyond telling but I knew my recovery was assured. Before, my leg had always felt like so much dead wood, dragging behind me, with no sense of pain at all. To feel pain in that limb was an improvement.

'Come, lad, let's leave them to their carousing. I haven't strength left for this.' I meant to question Jack closely, concerning his activities since Jude's re-arrest but, once seated at the board in my room, exhaustion gained the upper hand and I sat in silence, weariness weighing heavy upon me.

'Master? Yer going to tell me what 'appened to yer? 'Ow yer leg got mended?' Jack put my scrip and materials on the table. ''Ow come yer can walk now, wi'out the crutch? Was it a miracle or the like?' He was kneeling on the stool beside me, his face close, eyes bright with expectation, as if I might walk on water next.

'I don't know, lad. Just now I'm too tired to understand. I'm thankful, that's all.' I sorted out my silver points from the bits and pieces, taking a linen cloth to wipe them clean of saffron powder.

'We saved Em though, didn't we? Got 'er away from that wicked devil, Lovell. I never liked the look of 'im, I didn't.'

'No, you were correct not to.' I shook out another piece of linen and something rattled onto the board. A gleam caught my eye, a silver pebble of some kind. I picked it up, polished it on my sleeve. 'Where did this come from?'

'An' yer saved Tom Bowen, I reckon. What's that, master?'

'I've no idea. It was with this stuff. Did you pick it up at Lovell's Inn?' Jack shrugged.

'Might 'ave. Pretty though, ain't it?' He held it to the light betwixt finger and thumb, examining it. 'D'yer reckon Tom'll mend?'

'I'm not certain. He was in a bad way.' I unfastened my purse to make myself more at ease, removed my scorched, smoky hat and kicked off my shoes. 'Sorry, Jack, I have to rest. I'm so tired.'

'Yer could give this stone to Mistress Em, a sort of coming-home gift. She'll like it, I know.'

CHAPTER TWENTY

Friday the twelfth day of May
The small conduit in West Cheap

'THEY'RE SAYING it was a terrible accident,' Nell Warren was telling her friends as they chatted by the conduit. 'Poor Master Eastleigh mixed his potions all wrong and bang!'

Mary Jakes jumped, spilling water from her pitcher.

'The shop goes up in flames,' Nell continued, revelling in being the centre of attention. She lived on the corner of Ivy Lane and the Shambles and had witnessed much of the previous day's excitement in person. 'They found nought of the apothecary and Surgeon Dagville's not sure young Tom Bowen will come through, either. His life hangs by a thread, so I heard tell, and it's all thanks to your Sebastian, Ellen, that the lad breathes at all.'

'Sebastian? What did he have to do with it?' Dame Ellen asked. 'He was still out searching for Emily, yesterday. What would he be doing at the apothecary's place?'

She had been about to go home, but the conversation had taken such a curious turn, she decided to stay. Business could wait another hour.

'Your Seb went into the place, through the smoke and flames, and pulled the lad to safety. I saw him drag the apprentice out myself. He was coughing in the street, not far from my door, so I gave him a cup of water.'

'Who? Tom Bowen?'

'No, Sebastian. Your Emily and that dirty urchin were with him, took him home after.'

'I'm sure you're mistaken, Nell. How could Sebastian Foxley do such a thing? I know he's somewhat better than he was, but he's a poor cripple, remember, though he can't help that Satan cursed him, of course. I saw him come home yesterday, limping, bad as ever.'

'Well, I'm only saying what I saw,' Nell said, folding her arms across her generous bosom.

'Perhaps he recovered again,' timid little Mary Jakes offered. 'I heard about a miracle happening at old King Harry's tomb.'

'Don't be absurd, Mary,' Dame Ellen scolded. 'Miracles don't just happen to folk like us. You have to be prayerful and deserving of God's grace.'

'Maybe your Sebastian is...'

'No, he isn't. He's foolish as the next silly youth, thinks of naught but wenches, like all the rest, despite being what he is.'

'No harm in hoping,' Mary said.

'You won't believe what he said the other day,' Dame Ellen beckoned her friends closer before she revealed her outrageous news. 'He said Emily was going to marry him! Did you ever hear such impertinence? As though my Emily couldn't choose sixty young men better than him.'

'Mind you, Ellen,' Nell Warren put in, 'She can't be so particular now, can she? Not with her reputation in shreds.'

'What *do* you mean, Mistress Warren?' Dame Ellen stood up to her full height, like a ship hoisting sail. 'How dare you go casting aspersions on my apprentice. There's none can say a word against Emily Appleyard.'

'Well, they are. What about her state of undress yesterday, hair hanging loose as a strumpet's and wearing a man's jerkin? She didn't get like that picking daisies, now did she?'

'You have a malevolent tongue, mistress, and I have better things to do than suffer your ridiculous gossip.'

Dame Ellen stormed off along West Cheap, chickens and children scattering before her.

'I'm sure young Emily *was* only picking flowers,' Mary Jakes said.

Nell Warren sighed at the foolish unworldliness of her neighbours, all of them.

'Come along, Mary, I made a fine cowslip tart yesterday. We'll finish it off over some ale.'

She led the small woman away.

'Now, did you hear about Bess Ashley and that vintner from St Andrew's Undershaft? Well, I heard tell...'

Saturday, the thirteenth day of May
The Bowen house

IVY LANE still smelled of smoke as we went that way to the Bowens' house in Paternoster Row. The apothecary's shop was reduced to a pile of charred timbers, flakes of ash still floating in the air like dirty snowflakes. The glover's shop next door stood roofless and blackened and I noticed the glass was broken in the fine windows of Lovell's Inn opposite. Well and good, I thought.

• •

Young Tom Bowen lay in the bedchamber he had occupied for years, before becoming the apothecary's apprentice. Now he was back in the house in Paternoster Row that would pass to his elder sister Bella and his brother-by-marriage, Dick Langton.

Emily and I tip-toed in, trying not to disturb the poor lad, but at least his breathing was noisy enough there was no doubt he lived.

'A few minutes only. He needs to rest,' Surgeon Dagville told us.

'But he will recover?' I asked.

'Thanks to you, it seems likely, having youth on his side. But don't tire him.'

• •

The lad had been cleaned up, his cuts – mostly from flying shards of shattered glassware – had been stitched and smeared with ointment, leaving greenish circles around the healing scabs. A deeper gash on his arm had been bound with linen. But his breathing still sounded laboured, his lungs being filled with smoke.

I moved to the bedside and touched Tom's hand as it lay on the blanket.

'Tom? Tom, can you hear me?' Even my voice was still husky from the acrid smoke. I cleared my throat. 'Tom?'

The patient stirred, opened his eyes reluctantly, squinting in the daylight from the unshuttered window.

'Master Foxley?' he croaked, 'Why? What are you doing here?'

Emily poured water into a cup and held it for the lad to drink.

'Master Seb saved you from the fire,' she told him. 'He carried you out of the wreckage when the shop went up in flames. Such a brave action. Do you remember?'

I stood by the window, looking out, embarrassed by Em's recounting of my deeds.

'Maybe,' I heard Tom say. 'I can't get things sorted out in my head yet. So much smoke... couldn't breathe... thought I was dying...'

'You would have, if not for Seb.'

'If you saved me. I didn't deserve it, not after what...'

I went to sit on the bed, careful of Tom's injuries. I nudged Em to keep silent, not to make me out to be some kind of hero.

'Never mind that, Tom. How are you feeling? The surgeon reckons you'll make old bones yet.' I smiled at him in what I hoped was a reassuring manner.

'I've felt better. Don't know what'll happen now. They say my master's dead, the shop gone...' He paused to heave a shuddering breath. 'And if Lord Lovell comes back...' Tom began to sob so I patted his hand. I was never very good with folks in tears.

'Say nothing of Lord Lovell to anyone and he'll hold his peace, I'm certain.'

'But it was all his doing. I saw what he was about, changing the labels, swapping simple waters for dangerous distillations. I tried to warn master but he wouldn't listen. He went on, brewing his concoctions 'til BANG! Everything's flying about and going up in flames. It was Lovell's fault, I know.

'But how come you saved me? St Michael's was an accident, then Lovell told master you were dead and I know that was my fault too.' The lad sniffed hard, coughed. 'It was me who pushed Lovell's note under your door. He told me to. I never knew what it said, truly I didn't.'

'It doesn't matter now. As you see, I survived, despite Lord Lovell's efforts to the contrary. I'm just glad to see you recovering.'

Tom sighed and lay back on the pillows.

'Come, Em. He's delirious; needs his sleep. 'Bye, Tom.'

• •

As we were leaving, Tom's elder sister, Bella, arrived, together with her goodman, Dick Langton. We'd never met but his family likeness to Dame Ellen was unmistakeable – the same no-nonsense set of his mouth, the firm jaw and knowing eye. Nell Warren, a kindly neighbour who was nursing Tom – his step-mother having no intention – introduced us:

'Master Dick, Mistress Bella, this is Emily Appleyard and Sebastian Foxley – your mother's tenant, Dick – your Tom owes his life to him, I can tell you.'

'I'm n-not so sure,' I stuttered, but Dick Langton seized my hand in a powerful grip.

'Bella's immensely grateful to you, Master Foxley, as am I.' His voice was deep, resonant in a broad chest. 'Young Tom is all the family she has now, since her father passed away, may God assoil him.'

We all made the sign of the cross.

Bella looked at me, tears in her eyes.

'Of course, Mistress Bowen was considerate enough to warn us that my father was not a well man but said there was time enough and he wouldn't want to be fussed over. Which I know was always his way. So we didn't make haste to visit him and now we regret it. I always shall.' Bella turned to her goodman for comfort and he enfolded her in his arms. She looked like a bird embraced by a bear.

'We were told there were "unforeseen circumstances". Whatever that may mean,' Dick said.

I nodded.

'May we speak privily, Master Langton? A few moments only.'

'I owe you that much, at least, Master Foxley,' he said, smiling. 'Bella, go with Nell, won't you. Have some ale to calm you.'

'My goodwife is with child,' he explained as we went into the empty parlour of Bowen's house. 'Highly strung as an unbroken colt at present. Tears for no reason so, when there is reason, you can imagine, there's no stopping the torrent. Now what did you have to say to me?'

'I'm sorry but I don't know how to say this gently, Master Langton, but it happens that Matthew Bowen was murdered and my brother will be hanged for it come Monday morn. But he is not guilty of it. Someone else killed Bella's father.'

'Dear God in Heaven.' Dick Langton subsided onto the settle. 'We were told nought of this but that Bella's father had died. Are you certain?'

'Aye. I heard the truth from the killer in person – as good as – and there is a witness.'

'The killer admitted it? Why?'

'Because I have no evidence to prove it, as yet. But it may not be too late to save my brother.'

'Who did it?'

'Meg Bowen poisoned her husband.'

Dick's jaw sagged. He spluttered to himself, shaking his head, but I persevered.

'That's why she wrote the letter to your goodwife, saying her father was ailing. It was a lie. I worked for Matthew and he was in fine fettle but Meg was preparing the ground, sowing the seed so you would not be so shocked when his death came to pass, so you should not enquire too closely. Then she poisoned his ale with orpiment – a lethal pigment – before stabbing him with my brother's knife, in order that he took the blame.'

'Are you speaking truly, Master Foxley, for your story is not easy to credit?'

'As God and His saints bear witness.' I made the sign of the cross. 'I'll swear upon Holy Writ if...'

'I suppose I do believe you. Somehow, your tale has the ring of truth to it. I'll summon the sheriff and the coroner and whoever else...'

'You need evidence. If I'd had proof, she would have been in custody afore now.'

'Evidence? Do we have anything?'

'Do you still have the letter she sent, telling you Matthew Bowen was a sick man?'

'Maybe.'

'If you show that to the court, any number of neighbours, customers, can swear there was nought amiss with his health until the day he died. That may help prove Meg Bowen was already planning his death. That makes it a case of murder in cold blood. But we must have that letter.'

'I'll go home to Deptford. I'll find it, bring it back. I'll leave Bella here. I shall make the journey more swiftly alone. But Master Foxley, I beg another favour of you.'

'Anything. That letter will set my brother free.'

'Keep Bella and her brother safe from Mistress Bowen 'til I return.'

'We can take them both to your mother's house.'

He nodded.

'I'll be forever in your debt.'

Then he left.

And I'll be forever in yours, I thought, if my brother can be proven innocent.

Sunday, the fourteenth day of May, Whitsunday Westminster Palace

DUKE RICHARD seethed inwardly at yet more delay. After low mass that morning, he had come to beg audience with the king. The same matter, those damned benevolences were being demanded of the Londoners again and, just as before, the lord mayor had requested the king's favourite brother to plead their case.

Favourite brother? Aye, he wondered how long that would remain so, if he had to keep annoying Edward over this wretched business, but he'd thought of a way – he hoped – of persuading the king to ask no more of the Londoners.

High mass had come and gone, though he should have been attending the baptism of a servant's babe in St Helen's church. The king had not even extended him the courtesy of inviting him to dine, so he missed dinner, kicking his heels outside the privy chamber. The vespers bell had rung a while since and still he waited, his temper fraying moment by moment. He was a patient man but, curse it, he had his limits.

* *

Of course, his brother thought he knew the purpose of this visit and would put it off indefinitely, but each time a servant came or went, the duke pointedly told them to remind the king that he waited, still. The last time a servant had gone in, taking another jug of wine, he had been informed that the king had important matters to attend to, even though, through the half-open door, he could see Edward playing chess with his chamberlain and hear the merry sounds of a lute and recorder.

'The king's grace will see you now, my lord.'

After so many hours, Richard was actually not ready when the call came, felt unsettled. He breathed deeply a few times, knowing he must stay calm because, most probably, his brother would not. He braced himself to face the inevitable.

'Dickon, what an unexpected pleasant surprise,' the king greeted him with a lie so blatant and a smile just as false.

Richard bent the knee and removed his hat but his brother had turned away, back to the chess board. At a glance, the duke could see why he was summoned now. The king was losing the game. 'Pour my brother some wine, Will,' the king told the chamberlain. 'So, what's the bloody complaint this time, Dickon, eh?'

The musicians were silent now. A hawk, hooded and jessied, fluttered on its perch in the corner, jangling the little bells around its leg before settling again.

'No complaint, your grace. I brought you these.' The duke took a leather pouch from his belt, emptied it onto the chess board. Rings and precious stones, a pearl brooch, an emerald clasp fell among the pawns and knights. 'It's all I have to spare, Ned. I must provision and equip my own contingent for your French enterprise and, although you indentured me for a hundred and twenty knights, I have a hundred and fifty-three signed up thus far. There are also more men-at-arms and archers than specified. The northern shires are eager to follow you to war.'

'You have done well, little brother. I commend your diligence. Let's drink to King Louis' downfall.' Edward smiled broadly, toying with the valuables strewn on the chessboard. 'What of the ring you're wearing? Will you spare that also?'

Richard frowned, then looked down at the pigeon's blood ruby on his right middle finger.

'It was our lord father's ring. 'Tis all I have of his.' Even so, after a moment's thought, he tried to remove it. Usually, it sat quite loosely but now it was a struggle to get it off, as if the ring itself did not wish to be parted from its owner. Finally, it came free and Richard held it out in his palm.

Edward did not take it. Instead, he folded Richard's hand around it, clasping his brother's slender fingers in his own great paw.

'Keep it. I know how much it means to you, Dickon. I simply wondered if you would.'

'Thank you.'

'But I'll have the jewel from your hat.'

'Oh, aye, I'd forgotten it,' Richard said, unpinning a sapphire brooch from his hat. It had been the king's New Year gift to him, so he probably knew its worth to the last ha'penny. Edward was like that. Richard had no qualms about parting with it.

'So, let us drink to war!' Edward quaffed his wine, almost laughing.

But Richard wasn't. War was a serious business indeed.

'Promise me, Ned. No more benevolences, please. No more dabblings in alchemy.'

Newgate Gaol

T HEY LET me in to see Jude, alone. He wasn't in the usual hellish pit. He was in a room upstairs, awaiting the services of a priest, the gaoler told me, grinning, showing his black stumps of teeth. He led me up the outside stairs. I stepped carefully, the wood looked rotten.

I didn't know what to expect of my brother on this, his last eve on earth. I had little hope – if any – that Dick Langton would return in time with the letter, not now.

The upper room was bare but for a rickety board, two stools and a bed frame with a filthy mattress. Jude was standing, watching out the barred window.

'There are swallows building a nest under the eaves there,' he said without looking round. 'You'd think the silly buggers would have more sense than to choose this stinking rat hole.'

'I suppose so. How are you, Jude?'

He didn't answer me at first, craning his neck to see more sky. The riotous colours of the dying sun were cast across the western sky, vivid as flame. His last sunset.

'I still breathe, for now.' He turned so we faced each other across the empty floor. He was gaunt, filthy, but still had the outward semblance of the brother I'd known all my life. Yet the eyes were not Jude's. They were blue, like his, but they sparked with... I don't know what. Desperation? Fear? The dreadful waste of it all.

'I've brought you wine, meat and bread.' I put a sack on the board and took out cups and platters and set them out for a meal. All the while he said nothing. From the bottom of the sack I pulled a neatly rolled bundle. 'And clean clothes for...' I could not say more.

'Why?'

I didn't understand the question.

'So you may eat a decent meal.'

'You fear I might starve to death before the hour appointed?'

'I thought we could share.'

'And fresh linen that the crowd may pelt with shit and mud? Take it away. The hangman gets my clouts after. Why give him my best shirt when you can have use of it? Keep it.'

'At least drink the wine. I bought the best.' I filled a cup to the brim from the leather bottle and handed it to him, poured another for myself. I hoped we'd both be too drunk to care afore long.

'This is good,' he said, savouring the ruby-red Burgundy as he lounged on the bed, leaning back against the wall. I took a stool at the board.

'At least you have a chamber to yourself.' I helped myself to a sliver of cold chicken, no point in wasting it.

'Aye, but only because some God-botherer is coming to hear my confession. I thought you were he.'

'Me? A priest?' I stifled a giggle. I wasn't used to drinking wine. 'But you've nought to confess, being innocent.'

'Aye, innocent as a new-baptised babe, if you believe that.'

'But you didn't kill Bowen.'

'No. Did you find out who did? Not that it matters now, too late...' I gulped my wine. Jude wasn't going to approve of my answer:

'It was Meg Bowen, with the connivance of...'

'What?' He leapt off the bed, spilling his wine. 'Don't lie to me, little brother, not now. Not at this late hour. Tell me true, damn you!'

'It is true, I swear on our parents' souls.'

He knew then that I meant what I said.

'How?'

● ●

So I told him about the orpiment poisoning, about Meg drugging his own wine with a sleeping potion – supplied by Eastleigh – to be certain that he spent the night, not leaving until after Bowen was dead, but unable to interfere. I told him how she'd used his knife on the dead man, to ensure he was accused of the murder.

When I was done, he looked at me like a drowning man denied a helping hand.

'I thought she loved me.'

'I'm so sorry, Jude.'

He paced from bed to window and back again, like a caged beast. Which, I suppose he was.

'Have they arrested her?'

'We need proof and we need it now, before morning.'

'It isn't going to come, is it?'

I said nothing.

He shrugged.

'So let's drink the wine,' he said, going to the bottle. 'Let's drink to...' he raised his cup high, 'Brotherly love! Since you're the only one fool enough to care if I live or die.'

'Oh, Jude, I'm not the only one. Emily, Sir Robert, Dick Langton, even Jack, we're all doing what we can.'

'Dick Langton?'

'Dame Ellen's son.'

'The legendary?'

'The same.'

'What has he got to do with this?'

'You'll see.'

'Will I?'

'Aye, you will. I promise.'

Jude snorted.

'Faith is a wonderful thing, Seb. You keep a firm hold of it. When I'm dead you can go on praying for my soul with faith enough to know you'll save it, in the end. Spare me a single moment or two from my aeons of time in Purgatory.'

'Don't say that, Jude. I know you're innocent. God knows it.'

'Ha! You think the Almighty ever set eyes on this, this fearful place? You think He cares, in His omniscient schemes, what happens to my grubby little soul?'

'Christ died for us all!'

'Then He shouldn't have taken the trouble for me. But you're a different matter, Seb.'

'No, I'm not.'

'Look at you. That's what's different. I knew there was something. Standing on your own two feet, without your staff. And your back! Turn around, let me see. What happened to you?'

'I told you. God is there, watching over us, knowing all.'

'But what happened to you?' he repeated, holding my shoulders, feeling my bones with his fingers.

'I don't know, Jude.'

'So this is it then, proof.'

'Proof?'

'That your all-knowing God is there, taking the trouble to see that faithful servants like you can manage well enough when a sinner like me is no longer there to look out for you. He's set you to rights so you don't need my aid any longer. You'll prosper. Get that damned triptych finished, wed some pretty wench... when I'm gone.'

'No, Jude. No!' I cried, stuffing my fist in my mouth to keep from screaming out loud. 'Don't say that. I do need you, always. I can't...'

He pulled me to him, crushing me close. Our arms locked around each other. The feel of him pressing against me. I never wanted him to let go. I felt him shudder in my embrace, the wetness of his tears on my cheek mingling with mine. We were more of a height now. I stroked his dirty hair, sobbing into the matted strands.

'I love you, my brother,' I whispered. 'Always.'

'I know.'

• •

We stood, melded together, until the priest arrived and I was told to go. The man-of-God would stay with Jude 'til dawn, offering consolation in which my brother no longer believed. I left without bidding him farewell. I couldn't. Words meant nothing now. They would clang hollow in this time of emptiness.

I heard a crow, cawing his mass for the dead in the yard below, but my sight was too blurred by sorrow to see the wretched creature in the fading light of day.

CHAPTER TWENTY-ONE

Monday, the fifteenth day of May
Crosby Place

THE DUKE awoke with a cannon shot to his head. That was how it felt. Last night had been an ordeal. The king had been so merry, Richard found it wearisome. Ned was always heavy-handed, whether in anger or joy. And throughout the audience – if so polite a word could be used to describe a meaningless, riotous celebration – Will Hastings had kept his cup filled with the rich red wine the king preferred.

He hadn't realised how much he'd drunk, until the cool air in the courtyard hit him like a hammer. An abstemious man, liking pale Rhineland wines and drinking those well-watered, he should never have had so much. And then there had been those insolent devils at Ludgate, refusing to open the gate into the city because the curfew had been rung hours before, pretending they did not recognise him or the livery badges of his escort. With them, he had finally loosed the temper that had been held on a choking-tight rein all day.

Now he paid the price with a thundering headache that must surely boil out of his ears. And some unwary soul was banging on his chamber door, or on his forehead – the effect was much the same.

• •

Pulling a loose gown about him to cover his nakedness, Lord Richard wrenched the door open himself. It was Sir Robert who stood there, his hand raised to knock again.

'What? God have mercy, man. I'm not even dressed yet.'

'My lord, I apologise, but this is of the utmost urgency. I tried to speak with you last eve, but you were elsewhere.'

'With the king.'

Rob nodded.

Richard noticed the knight was booted and spurred already, even so early as this.

'The hall besieged, is it?' He quirked an eyebrow. It hurt. 'Life or death, must be.' He meant it as a jest but his friend's answer shocked him.

'Aye, it is. An acquaintance of ours dies within the hour unless you do as I ask.'

'Who?'

'Jude Foxley. He is to hang this morning and there is now evidence to prove this would be a grave miscarriage of justice. He's innocent, Dickon. I need a stay of execution. As Lord High Constable of England, you can...'

'I'm well aware of my privileges as constable, Rob. What is this new evidence?'

'A letter. But there's no time to explain. I must have the necessary documents to stop the execution. Now!'

Richard scrubbed his hands over his face, trying to dispel the cobwebs. It would take too long to summon his secretary so he sat at his writing desk, took pen and paper and wrote the document himself.

'You'll have to show me the letter later. In truth, I shouldn't be writing this without seeing it and speaking to any witnesses involved.' His usual neat, legible script looked as though a sick spider had crawled through the ink, but it would have to serve, seeing his eyes could barely focus. The heavy seal was probably all the sheriff would bother to look at anyway.

'The sentence will have been carried out, if I delay now,' Rob said.

Richard sighed as he signed his name.

'I pray you are in time, Rob. He'll have to go back to Newgate, of course, but see he's decently lodged there at my expense, until I have persuaded the king to grant him pardon, if he will.'

The ink seemed to take an hour to dry. He couldn't find the pounce box to blot it.

Rob snatched the sealed paper and was gone with no word of thanks.

The duke watched from the window, saw his friend fly down the steps and leap onto his mighty war destrier in the courtyard below before charging out the gateway of Crosby Place, showering servants with dust in his wake.

Then the duke went back to nursing his distemper, which had swelled to hideous proportions in the meantime. He did not relish the prospect of another audience with the king so soon, especially not to beg a favour for some Londoner he hardly knew. But justice had to be seen to be upheld, for the innocent as well as the guilty.

Newgate Gaol

NOW WAS the hour. The priest had finally exhausted his reserves of pointless platitudes and the glimmer of gold in the eastern sky meant time had run out for Jude. The executioner awaited him at Tyburn but his life wasn't done yet. There was one more task to accomplish. He had nothing to lose. The conundrum, the freedom of a condemned man.

The gaoler, his tormentor, his defiler, was grinning that rotten-toothed parody of a smile of his. Jude had sworn to wipe it from his leering mouth after their first encounter in the dead hours of the night. And either he did it now or never.

There were two guards, solemnly doing their duty. One tied Jude's hands, gave him a look that held a measure of sympathy, perhaps. The other seemed indifferent, just another job to be done.

'Yer steed awaits, sire,' the gaoler mocked, shoving Jude towards the open door. 'Do you a fine ride, all the way t' Tyburn tree, any road.' He laughed, scratching at his crotch.

'And you'll be in Hell before me,' Jude whispered in his ear. The fellow pulled a face and laughed loudly as he elbowed Jude aside over the threshold. The old wooden stairs, open to all weathers, were worn and worm-eaten, the treads slippery.

• •

Afterwards, the guards said they couldn't tell what had occurred in a few moments of confusion. It seemed the prisoner lost his footing and toppled against the gaoler. The guards grabbed the prisoner, fearing some vain attempt at escape. But neither guard thought to lay hold of the gaoler. The prisoner's feet seemed to become entangled with his keeper's. The man overbalanced, snatching at the handrail but it broke in his grasp. The gaoler fell from top to bottom of the stairs to lie, unmoving, in a puddle of filth on the flagstones below. His lousy head was twisted impossibly – the neck broken.

The prisoner watched, unmoved, as he was restrained by the guards. His mission was completed and they couldn't hang him twice. Besides, it was an accident. Those steps were treacherous indeed. He was smiling as they tied him on the hurdle, to be dragged to Tyburn by the sorriest nag in London.

Tyburn, by the city of London

E MILY AND I stood at the edge of the crowd at Tyburn, Jack beside us. There was still no sign of Sir Robert and the first of the hangman's customers for today was already being pushed up the ladder to meet his fate.

'Will 'e come, master?' Jack asked, yet again. 'Will Sir Rob get 'ere in time, you reckon?'

I didn't answer, having no more idea than the lad. I was carrying Emily's longbow. She had attracted notice, a woman armed with a bow on a Monday morning was an unexpected sight. Until last week, carrying a bow myself would have looked even more absurd but now, with my straighter back, it was not so odd, even though I'd never used the weapon in my life. Maybe, one day soon, I would try my hand. But now was not the time.

'What they doing, master? I can't see,' Jack complained as the crowd applauded and cheered.

'Never you mind,' I said. No way could I have described the horrors of seeing a man's body slit and quartered. I turned away from it, like Emily, staring behind us, watching over the heads of the crowd for Sir Robert's arrival, wondering how others could revel in the gruesome spectacle that turned my stomach over.

• •

'Sweet Jesu have mercy,' I said, crossing myself frantically as Jude was pushed towards the ladder, the noose already round his neck. 'Dear God in Heaven. I-I can't watch this. Sir Rob's too late...'

'I said give me the bow, Seb!' Emily gave me a sharp shake. 'Get a hold on your wits, we're not done here yet.'

Just then, I saw the sheriff move towards the ladder, pulling Jude down again.

'Look! Look, Em. The reprieve must have come already. They're getting Jude off the ladder, sending that poor lad up in his place. Oh, thank Jesu for His mercy.'

The sheriff was talking to Jude, looking at a paper in his hands. Then the name of the boy was read out. He looked not much older than Jack but at least his end was swift.

• •

I watched, my heart lurching anew, stuttering in my chest, as Jude was sent up the ladder a second time.

Emily strung her bow with deft efficiency and took up an arrow from her basket, elbowing herself some room on the edge of the crowd. One of the executioner's assistants tied the end of Jude's rope to the gibbet. Another twisted the ladder away.

Jude fell.

The instant the rope went taut, I closed my eyes but felt Emily loose the nocked shaft. I heard the thrum of the bowstring.

The crowd gasped.

The rope broke.

Emily's arrow had been but a blur, disappearing into the bushes behind the scaffold. As she quickly lowered her bow, only folk around her had any idea that the snapped rope was aught but an accident, a bungled job by the hangman and his helpers.

Now a new noose was required to finish the task. Jude was pulled to his feet, looking dazed.

'Did you get the rope, mistress?' Jack asked, but she didn't answer, still looking along the road in the direction of the city gates for a sign.

• •

Jude was at a loss. They'd cut him down too quickly. He'd prayed he would be already half-dead, unaware when they took the butcher's knife to him, but now it seemed he would feel every cut. If only the scaffold boards would open up beneath his feet, swallow him whole before...

Oh, God, why were they putting another noose around his neck? What was happening?

There were shouts, cries from the crowd.

A horse was neighing.

Shouts of 'Hold, hold!' and 'Make way there!'

A great warhorse barged a path through the crowd, snapping with its teeth and striking out with mighty hooves, vicious as the Devil as Sir Robert Percy urged it forward, forcing his way right up to the scaffold.

'There is a stay... of execution for...' The knight was as breathless as his mount, '...for Jude Foxley... by command of the Lord High... Constable of England,' he panted, thrusting a paper at the sheriff.

• •

After the final execution – a man named Bartholomew, whom he vaguely remembered from somewhere – ah, yes, the orchard at Warwick's Inn – Jude was on his way back to Newgate, under escort. He still wasn't sure why, though every extra minute of life was welcomed, especially all the while blue sky was above him and good earth beneath his feet. Every step might offer a chance of escape.

'Master Foxley.' Sir Robert reined in beside him and dismounted to lead his brutish-looking beast along. Fortunately, the animal was quieter now, a little less dangerous. 'I'm here at your brother's behest, to tell you he has evidence of your innocence. We're going to request a royal pardon for you, but that takes time, I fear. Meanwhile, you must stay at the Whit, though you'll be well lodged at Lord Richard's expense. Your brother will visit you later to explain.'

Jude nodded. It seemed the correct thing to do.

'Thank you, sir,' he said, though he wasn't sure what he was thankful for. His head was full of fog and nothing made sense any more. He touched his fingers to his neck. The lesions were sore and painful but he was still alive. That at least he understood.

Newgate Gaol

THAT AFTERNOON, Sir Rob and I arrived at the Whit to visit Jude. We were met by a different fellow, not the usual gaoler but no less obnoxious.

'We've come to visit Jude Foxley. He was reprieved.' I told him, hating those blotched stone walls as much as ever.

'Aye, so I heard. 'Nother poxy mistook they made there, lettin' him orf. Be back, he will, sure 'nough, sooner or later. I seen his sort afore. He'll be back.'

'That's enough of that talk, you,' Sir Rob said. 'The man's innocent. Now show us where he's lodged.'

• •

This time we were led not into the bowels, thank God, but to a side way and a flight of stone steps leading up. Sir Rob went first but kept looking round to be certain I was following. The knight couldn't get over the miraculous improvement in my condition, mounting the steps like anyone else, though I did keep a hand on the wooden guard rail, out of habit.

Jude was in a room leading off a passageway. It was small but had windows looking out towards the Fleet River. Light from the late afternoon sun streamed in, showing up the cobwebs in the corners and the dust motes dancing in the draught as we entered. My brother was seated on a stool at the window, the remains of a meal on a little table beside him. He might have been at home but for the bars on the window. He glanced up but did not rise to meet us. If I had expected a joyous welcome, I was to be disappointed.

'Jude? Are you well?'

'Well? I had a bloody noose round my neck this morning, but I'm still alive, if that's what you mean.' He sounded somewhat hoarse and I saw his fingers kept straying to his neck where a collar of angry red abrasions testified to his close encounter with Death. If Emily's shot had been but a few moments later. I shuddered at the thought.

'But we got you a reprieve,' I said.

'Aye, until they change their damned minds again. They did that once already today. You know about that stinking gaoler?'

'What about him? He wasn't here when we arrived.'

'Had a mishap, didn't he? A timely accident. If they try to accuse me of that...'

'They won't. Lord Richard will see to it.'

'Were you there? This morning? Came to gloat, did you?'

'Jude, that's unfair. We wouldn't. Anyhow, they won't change their minds this time. We have witnesses, evidence that Meg Bowen planned her goodman's death all along, with the connivance of Gilbert Eastleigh and Nessie told us everything.'

'Nessie? Nessie is your witness?' Jude began to laugh, though there was no hint of humour in it. 'She with the wit of an imbecile sheep, she is your witness? If you believe a word she says, little brother, you're as stupid as she is.'

'It isn't only what Nessie says. We have the letter. See? I have it here. Dick Langton brought it.' I took the paper from my purse, held it out to him.

But Jude turned away, getting up to stare out the window, fingering his sore neck.

'On a clear day, when the light is just so, I'm told you can see Tyburn tree from here.'

317

'Why don't you have the good grace to listen to what your brother has to say?' Sir Rob rounded on my brother. 'He's gone through Hell and high water, trying to prove your innocence. The least you can do is hear him out.'

Jude faced the knight with a snarl, but Sir Rob looked him in the eye. It was Jude who backed down, subsiding onto his stool, gazing at the few rushes scattered on the floor. A black beetle struggled over a dry stem. Jude crushed it with his heel, grinding it into the boards.

When I offered the letter again, he took it, holding it towards the light to read.

'So? What has this to do with me? This is a private letter betwixt Meg and her step-daughter. How come you've got a hold of it?'

'Dick Langton and Bella are in London. They've come from Deptford to see about her father's estate, and to see poor Tom,' I explained but Jude looked mystified. He knew nothing of the fire in Ivy Lane nor of a host of other things, but I tried to tell the story in short. 'Bella will inherit, of course, but Tom's too young as yet, but they wanted to be certain Meg didn't get her greedy hands on his share, as well as her own. But now, piecing things together, Meg won't be getting anything.'

Jude was scowling.

'I've been thinking over what you told me last eve and I'm not sure I believe a word of it. Meg's not like that. She's sweet-natured enough, if she's treated right. All this nonsense you spout about her planning Matthew's death. Though Eastleigh is a horse of another colour altogether. He could have done this but not my Meg.'

'Well, Eastleigh has met his end already and your precious Meg will be fortunate if they don't send her to the stake,' I spluttered, emotion getting the better of me. It was hard to credit Jude was trying to defend the woman who had used him so maliciously.

'No!' Jude cried out, jumping up. 'They can't do that to her!'

'I think they can and they will, when Lord Richard is informed,' Sir Rob said.

'Don't tell him, please, can't you just say nothing?' Jude begged.

'Then you die in her place. Is that what you want, Master Foxley?'

• •

Jude returned to his stool and sat silent, biting his thumb nail. No one spoke as the sun tracked lower in the west, beyond the barred window.

'Do what you must,' Jude said at last and went on gnawing his nail. He never looked up as we departed.

EPILOGUE

Saturday the twentieth day of May

I T WAS all over. Meg Bowen had been taken into custody last eve, by the sheriff in person, screeching her innocence as they dragged her from the house in Paternoster Row. Then she tried to persuade the sheriff with fluttering eyelashes and coy looks, but he hardened his heart and had Stockman and his cronies haul her off in the cart, weeping. Neighbours had watched, stunned, but the rumour ran that the Duke of Gloucester, as Lord High Constable, had ordered it so. Justice must be done.

• •

That morning, Lord Richard had handed me the king's pardon for Jude, following three days of questioning by King Edward's men of law before a panel of five judges in Westminster Hall. I had told them all I knew of the murder. Dick Langton and his wife Bella, Stephen Appleyard, the women who had laid out Matthew Bowen's body, even Nessie, were all summoned to tell their stories. I had worried that it would be too much for the serving wench but she surprised us all with her lucid and coherent account of her mistress's activities. Not such a lack-wit after all and she was as desperate as anyone to have Master Jude released.

• •

Now Jude was home. A free man at last. Not that you'd know it, not from the downcast look, the sombre mien. I expected we should celebrate but Jude was morose and overly quiet. It must be that he truly loved Meg, unlikely as that seemed, but I could think of no other reason for my brother's strange mood.

Hopefully, it would not prevent us from working on Lord Richard's triptych, getting it finished, as I was brim-full with new ideas for the images, could picture them vividly in my mind's eye, the colours, the gold.

• •

In the meantime, Emily, Jack and I made our way to St Paul's, leaving Jude to mope. Emily was wearing the stone we'd found in my scrip after her ordeal at Lovell's Inn. She had made a tiny silken net from some thread left over in Dame Ellen's workshop and the stone now nestled in the green silk suspended from a cord of the same. Em seemed quite taken with the pebble – whatever it was – kept holding it up to look at it. I was intrigued by the way it reflected the moon-beam glint in her eyes as she did so.

St Paul's Cross was busy with some fire-and-brimstone preacher shrieking at his audience, telling them what horrors Satan had in store for the unrepentant. I hurried the others around the crowd. I'd had enough of hellfire and brimstone recently and wanted none of it.

I led them into the nave where, as I hoped at that hour, the choristers were going through their scales, warming up for practice before vespers. We stood by the rood screen, watching through the lattice.

'Why're we 'ere, Master Seb?'

'Shh, Jack, just listen.'

The precentor was nagging someone for not paying attention, another for singing "worse than a goat with a quinsy", which brought a few giggles from the younger lads. Then he ordered the bellows boy to pump up the little organ. He played a single querulous note and the choristers took a unified breath. They hit the note perfectly. And so did I, standing tall beside the rood screen.

We sang *Jubilate Deo, omnis terra, alleluia!* "Rejoice in the Lord, all the earth, alleluia!"

And I sang as I'd never sung before.

• •

Folk in the nave had stopped their business and drawn near to listen. Emily was weeping and Jack's mouth hung open. Only as the anthem of thanksgiving ended with a glorious "Amen" still echoing to the roof, did I realise the precentor had silenced the choir and stood beneath the rood screen arch, beckoning to me.

'What do you mean by this?' The precentor looked stern in his dusty black, wagging a finger.

'Forgive me, sir, I did not mean to disturb you, I only came to thank God.'

'Come with me.'

The Foxley brothers' rooms

J UDE SAT alone, tormented by his own demons, that bloody gaoler would haunt his worst nightmares until the end of his days. As for women! Those fickle bitches, he'd never waste time on their kind again.

And then there was the spectre of Kit Philpot's shade, crying out soundlessly for vengeance upon the man who had choked the life from him in a dark alley. It was meant to be justice for a crippled younger brother upon whom God had now chosen to smile, even as He turned his face away from the elder, leaving him broken, suffering in his own private Purgatory, a legacy of guilt that none must ever know. The scars about his neck were not the only ones he would carry until the end of his days.

THE END

AUTHOR'S NOTES

HISTORY RECORDS that King Edward went to war that summer, crossing the Narrow Seas with the largest English army yet to depart these shores. But the war never happened. Not an arrow was loosed in anger, not a single sword drawn from its scabbard.

King Edward signed a treaty with King Louis, promising to withdraw his army peaceably from French soil in exchange for a very generous purse and a pension thereafter. Edward was content. As were his battle captains, each of whom was paid off with expensive gifts from the King of France.

Except for Richard of Gloucester.

He refused to put his name to the treaty, which he called 'dishonourable', 'inglorious'. He withdrew his contingent – the largest – back to England first, wanting nothing to do with the lavish feasts and celebrations the French laid on for their new-found friends.

In England, Richard was welcomed as a hero. Upon his return, King Edward sent paid 'cheer-leaders' ahead of his retinue to drown out the jeering and cat-calls.

However, King Louis, fearing such a man as Gloucester remaining an enemy, sent Richard some expensive presents, the sort a warrior would approve: Arab horses and a 'great bombard'. Richard intended to refuse the gifts but King Edward threatened him – we know not how – into writing a letter of thanks to Louis. The letter still exists. The bombard also exists. Richard took it to Scotland to besiege Edinburgh Castle, but the castle surrendered and invited him into the city. When he left, the bombard was too huge and cumbersome, so he left it in Edinburgh – the famous 'Mons Meg'.

After that Scots campaign of 1482, King Edward finally made Francis Lovell a viscount and the lord continued to serve Richard, both as duke and king.

When Richard became king, one of his first actions was to make 'benevolences' illegal.

Sir Robert Percy died at the battle of Bosworth beside King Richard, on 22 August 1485. Viscount Lovell lived to fight another day.

As for the Foxley brothers, unrecorded by the annals of the city of London, their adventures continued. Sebastian completed Duke Richard's triptych to such a high standard that he was swiftly recognised by the City Guilds as a Master of the Craft and Mystery of Stationers, Illuminators and Limners. He and Jude went into business on their own account.

Sebastian wed Emily Appleyard and took over the Bowen house and workshop, getting it at a knock-down price from Dick and Bella Langton, maybe as a favour or perhaps because nobody else wanted the place with its gruesome past.

NB: For the Philosopher's Stone, I have used the properties of the element platinum which had been discover in Ancient Egypt but was not recognised for what it was until the nineteenth century.

The post of warden-archer is my invention although, since archery practice was compulsory, as I describe, surely someone must have had to organise and train the bowmen.

ACKNOWLEDGMENTS

I have to thank the Open University students, studying A363, Literature and Creative Writing course, way back in 2010-11, who encouraged me to complete the first draft of this novel, else it would never have been written. I'm grateful to Tim Ridgway at MadeGlobal for his enthusiasm about the project and to Diane Wordsworth for her invaluable editing skills. And of course I could never have completed the book if it wasn't for the full support of my husband, Glenn, and the Mount family.

• •

Toni Mount

Toni Mount

Toni Mount earned her research Masters degree from the University of Kent in 2009 through study of a medieval medical manuscript held at the Wellcome Library in London. Recently she also completed a Diploma in Literature and Creative Writing with the Open University.

Toni has published many non-fiction books, but always wanted to write a medieval thriller, and her first novel "The Colour of Poison" is the result.

Toni regularly speaks at venues throughout the UK and is the author of several online courses available at www.medievalcourses.com.

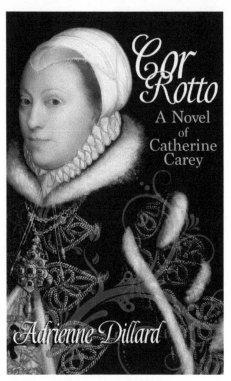

Cor Rotto

A Novel of Catherine Carey

Adrienne Dillard

978-84-937464-7-6

The dream was always the same ... the scaffold before me. I stared on in horror as the sword sliced my aunt's head from her swan-like neck. The executioner raised her severed head into the air by its long chestnut locks. The last thing I remembered before my world turned black was my own scream.

Fifteen year-old Catherine Carey has been dreaming the same dream for three years, since the bloody execution of her aunt Queen Anne Boleyn. Her only comfort is that she and her family are safe in Calais, away from the intrigues of Henry VIII's court. But now Catherine has been chosen to serve Henry VIII's new wife, Queen Anne of Cleves.

Just before she sets off for England, she learns the family secret: the true identity of her father, a man she considers to be a monster and a man she will shortly meet.

This compelling novel tells the life story of a woman who survived being close to the crown and who became one of Queen Elizabeth I's closest confidantes.

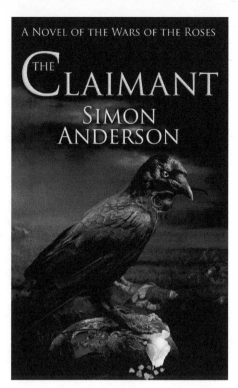

A NOVEL OF THE WARS OF THE ROSES

THE CLAIMANT

SIMON ANDERSON

978-84-937464-9-0

The harvest is gathered and the country wears its autumn livery. Four years after the first battle of The Cousins' Wars, later known as The Wars of the Roses, the simmering political tensions between the Royal Houses of Lancaster and York have once again boiled over into armed confrontation.

Nobles must decide which faction to support in the bitter struggle for power. The stakes are high and those who choose unwisely have everything to lose. Sir Geoffrey Wardlow follows the Duke of York while others rally to King Henry's cause, but one in particular company under the Royal banner is not all it seems, its leader bent on extracting a terrible revenge that will shatter the lives of the Wardlow family.

Edmund of Calais has a private score to settle and is prepared to risk everything to satisfy his thirst for revenge. Riding the mounting wave of political upheaval, he willingly throws himself time and again into the lethal mayhem of a medieval battle as he strives to achieve his aim. One man is out to stop him: his half-brother, Richard.

Born of the same father but of very different minds the two young men find themselves on opposite sides during the violence that erupts as political tensions finally reach breaking point. Each has sworn to kill the other should they meet on the field of battle. As they play their cat-and-mouse game in the hope of forcing a decisive confrontation, their loved ones are drawn inexorably into the fray, forcing the protagonists to question the true cost of victory...

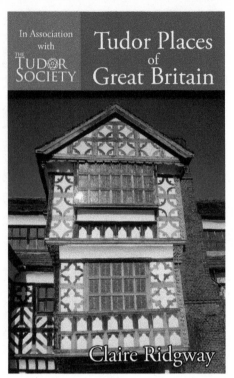

In Association with

TUDOR SOCIETY

Tudor Places of Great Britain

Claire Ridgway

978-84-944574-6-3

The Tudor dynasty ruled from 1485 to 1603 and had a huge impact on England and Wales, not only on society but also on the British landscape. Henry VIII was a keen builder, building and renovating properties to serve as pleasure palaces, but his Dissolution of the Monasteries also led to historic properties falling into ruin. Tudor favourites spent their new-found wealth building lavish mansions or converting castles into sumptuous manor houses as statements of their success and to impress the visiting monarch.

In **Tudor Places of Great Britain**, Tudor history author and founder of the Tudor Society **Claire Ridgway** guides the reader through properties linked to Tudor monarchs and prominent people of the time, from impressive palaces like Hampton Court Palace, through romantic monastic ruins and merchant houses, to unspoilt villages like Lavenham and Weobley.

With over 175 listings, which include descriptions and highlights, full address and website details, Tudor Places of Great Britain is a comprehensive guide to British Tudor places.

978-84-943721-8-6

The Truth
of The
Line

Melanie V. Taylor

In 1572, the good looking and talented Nicholas Hillyarde paints the first of many portraits of Elizabeth I, England's "Virgin Queen". His ability to capture the likeness of his patrons make him famous and his skills are much sought after by the rich and powerful members of the Elizabethan Court. His loyalty to Elizabeth even leads him to becoming part of Sir Francis Walsingham's information network.

One day he is approached by a young man with an intriguing commission. Hillyarde is to paint the man holding a lady's hand - a hand which descends from a cloud - complete with a puzzling motto: "Attici Amoris Ergo"...

There is something familiar about this young man's face, and Hillyarde is led down a dark path of investigation to discover who this young man may be.

Who is the young man? Has Hillyarde stumbled across a dark royal secret, and, if so, is there evidence hidden elsewhere?

Non Fiction History

Anne Boleyn's Letter from the Tower - **Sandra Vasoli**
Jasper Tudor - **Debra Bayani**
Tudor Places of Great Britain - **Claire Ridgway**
Illustrated Kings and Queens of England - **Claire Ridgway**
A History of the English Monarchy - **Gareth Russell**
The Fall of Anne Boleyn - **Claire Ridgway**
George Boleyn: Tudor Poet, Courtier & Diplomat - **Ridgway & Cherry**
The Anne Boleyn Collection - **Claire Ridgway**
The Anne Boleyn Collection II - **Claire Ridgway**
Two Gentleman Poets at the Court of Henry VIII - **Edmond Bapst**
A Mountain Road - **Douglas Weddell Thompson**

"History in a Nutshell Series"

Sweating Sickness in a Nutshell - **Claire Ridgway**
Mary Boleyn in a Nutshell - **Sarah Bryson**
Thomas Cranmer in a Nutshell - **Beth von Staats**
Henry VIII's Health in a Nutshell - **Kyra Kramer**
Catherine Carey in a Nutshell - **Adrienne Dillard**
The Pyramids in a Nutshell - **Charlotte Booth**

Historical Fiction

Between Two Kings: A Novel of Anne Boleyn - **Olivia Longueville**
Phoenix Rising - **Hunter S. Jones**
Cor Rotto - **Adrienne Dillard**
The Claimant - **Simon Anderson**
The Truth of the Line - **Melanie V. Taylor**

Children's Books

All about Richard III - **Amy Licence**
All about Henry VII - **Amy Licence**
All about Henry VIII - **Amy Licence**
Tudor Tales William at Hampton Court - **Alan Wybrow**

PLEASE LEAVE A REVIEW

If you enjoyed this book, *please* leave a review at the book seller where you purchased it. There is no better way to thank the author and it really does make a huge difference!
Thank you in advance.

Lightning Source UK Ltd.
Milton Keynes UK
UKHW03f1118130318
319352UK00002B/84/P